# TICK . . . TICK . . . TICK

Delores was still seated against the far wall, seemingly oblivious to the countdown at hand. With a smile, I took Delores by the hand and noticed she was no longer trembling. "In just a few seconds, we'll have you out of this, then we'll clean up the mess we made."

She sighed. "I'll never be able to thank both of you enough."

Nick very softly announced, "We're cycling down at five . . . four . . . three . . . two . . . one." The instant the timer hit one, the clock in the back of the vest began to rhythmically squeal. Delores tensed, and her eyes went wide.

"Can you make it stop?" I yelled.

He nodded, slipping the battery out with a grin that quickly faded. "What the hell?" he muttered, tugging out a tiny piece of paper that had been hidden behind the battery.

Together, Nick and I read the simple, block printing on the slip of paper:

## BOOM!

Our trance was shattered by an unmistakable sound echoing through the empty store. *Beep! Beep! Beep!* was the last thing we heard before all hell broke loose.

# RENDER SAFE

## Jackie Nida

**B**

BERKLEY BOOKS, NEW YORK

RENDER SAFE

A Berkley Book / published by arrangement with
the author

PRINTING HISTORY
Berkley edition / October 2002

Copyright © 2002 by Jodie Larsen Nida.
Cover photography by Picturequest.
Interior text design by Julie Rogers.

Visit our website at
www.penguinputnam.com

ISBN: 0-425-18720-9

BERKLEY®
Berkley Books are published by The Berkley Publishing Group,
a division of Penguin Putnam Inc.,
375 Hudson Street, New York, New York 10014.
BERKLEY and the "B" design
are trademarks belonging to Penguin Putnam Inc.

PRINTED IN THE UNITED STATES OF AMERICA

10  9  8  7  6  5  4  3  2  1

*For D. L., a man who knows
the true value of family, compassion, and life.*

# acknowledgments

Special thanks to Tracy Rafferty with the Kansas Highway Patrol and all the courageous and helpful law enforcement officers and bomb technicians who so readily answered my seemingly endless list of complicated questions. Any technical errors in this book are mine, and mine alone.

I would like to thank all of my friends, especially Mark and Judy Olender; Ben and Kathy Gorrell; Chester and Debbie Cadieux; Julie and Ken Smith; Joy and Fred Ondracek; Brent and Melanie Blackstock; Dale, Nancy, Jessica, and Natalie Nida; Gary, Vivian, Brooke, and Hunter Nida; John and Vivian Nida; David Nummy; and Rick, Miramar, and Jesse Cohn. My family, Mark, Amanda, and Jon, provide the unquestionable love all writers must have to be creative. I sincerely appreciate Joan Rhine, Jan Sharkey, and Pat Larsen for enthusiastically proofing the manuscript and offering indispensable insight from the reader's point of view.

Last, but not least, this book would not have been possible without the guidance and encouragement of my agent, John Talbot, and my wonderful editor, Kim Waltemyer.

# one

I only had a half mile left of my morning run when my beeper quivered against the sweaty flesh of my waist. Without stopping, I read the digital display.

"Damn."

My hamstrings complained as I kicked open my stride, but the push felt good. The rush of adrenaline managed to hush the part of my brain that warned me to slow down before I stumbled. I felt almost graceful as I rounded the corner to dash past the other houses on my block.

I say *almost,* because that awkward stage where coordination and agility escape most teens seemed to have lasted half my life. Even at thirty-eight, I remembered all too well tripping over my own feet as I crossed the stage to be inducted into the National Honor Society my junior year in high school. Now I love being tall, but back then I was certain that I was destined to grow old alone, using my bird's-eye view of the top of men's heads to watch their bald spots spread. If it weren't for my height and strength today, I'm sure I wouldn't have made it in my line of work.

As I ran, I wondered what today's test would be. Every bomb call is a test of some kind. Most are like pop quizzes, with a robot and my certified bomb-sniffing dog, Romeo, doing most of the work. A few are midterms, requiring one of our team to don the dreaded bomb suit. The worst are finals: short fuses, lives on the line, up close and personal to the very end. Even with years of training, the thought made me shudder. As a bomb tech, my life was constantly in jeopardy and so, as a single mother, my son Matthew's future was always on my mind. Especially today—his fourteenth birthday.

Once inside, I grabbed a towel, ran it under cold water, and started cleaning up. Dialing the number on my digital pager, I reported in. "This is Sergeant Jamie Stone. I was just paged by Officer Campbell." As I waited to be patched through, I stuck my head under the cool stream long enough to thoroughly wet my short, wavy hair. Romeo's sixth sense must have been working, since he was already alert and pacing by the back door.

Officer Campbell sounded tense. "Sergeant Stone?"

"Yes."

"Sorry to start your day this way, but we have a critical situation at Jasper's Jewelers. The manager is strapped in some sort of vest. The guys who robbed her said it would explode if she moves."

Although I'd never set foot inside, I instantly visualized the store. Matt and I had passed it on the way to his guitar lessons for years. "How did she notify you?"

"The owner of the store next to hers noticed the door standing open when he arrived at work. He called nine-one-one."

"Make sure his place and the others in the vicinity are evacuated. Do you know if my partner, Lieutenant Terrell, has answered his page?" I asked as I dropped the towel in the laundry basket and reached for a clean pair of jeans.

"No ma'am, he hasn't responded yet."

"When you hear from him, tell him I'm on the way and have him call my cell phone. We'll need fire and ambulance personnel to respond to the scene. Where is the manager?"

"Inside the store."

"Alone?"

"Yes."

"Tell her that help will be there in a few minutes, and not to worry; most of these devices are nothing more than elaborate hoaxes. Establish a perimeter at one hundred feet and stand by. I'll call you back en route for more details. Okay?"

"Got it."

By the time I hung up, I was feeling almost presentable. Makeup and I have one of those on-again, off-again relationships, mostly the latter. Luckily, in spite of a liberal application of sunblock every morning, in the summer I tan well enough to look presentable without makeup. After putting on what my son jokingly calls my Xena: Warrior Princess vest, I grabbed a Kansas State Patrol knit polo shirt and tugged it over the rather awkward molded cups of the bulletproof material.

For years, my grandmother took up the parental slack that the demands of my job created. She was always there when I left without warning, ready to fill in at PTA meetings and be an escort service to whatever destination was scribbled on the calendar by the refrigerator. Her passing last year left a gap in our lives, one that slapped me hardest whenever I was rushing off to answer a call. At fourteen, Matthew was old enough to be left alone. He knew that if he awoke and I was gone, I'd call him as soon as I had a chance. Even so, a motherly flutter of guilt usually knotted my stomach as I dashed off.

"Come on, Romeo. We've got a hot one." He barked enthusiastically in reply, practically leaping over me as I opened the door of my Suburban. Although technically I'm a trooper for the Kansas State Patrol—KSP for short—I've been assigned an unmarked car with four-wheel drive. The rear end is filled with an assortment of bomb squad equipment too bulky to fit in the trunk of a standard-issue Crown Victoria. Since our unit can be called to respond in any kind of weather, no matter how treacherous the road conditions might be, we try to have everything we might need on hand at all times.

Before I made it out of the driveway, my cell phone rang, and I knew from the digital display that it was my partner, Nick Terrell. "Good morning, Nick," I said in the most chipper voice I could muster.

"What's good about it?" he grumbled.

"Where are you?" I asked.

"Getting dressed. Wish I had time for a shower."

No one would ever describe Nick as a morning person. It's one of the few characteristics that we don't share. I believe the best part of the day is that quiet time when most of the world is still sound asleep. If given half a chance, Nick would stay up to watch the morning dew form on the grass, then happily snore as the sun lazily crawled across the sky.

"It sounds like the same guy has hit again," I said.

"Another robbery with a vest?"

"Yeah. What's your ETA?"

"With traffic, it'll probably take me at least twenty minutes."

"I'll be there in less than five," I said.

"Then you're up. Let's use secure com two. I'll monitor in transit."

"Will do."

Nick hesitated before he added, "Just because the first two vests weren't *real* bombs doesn't mean this one isn't. Be careful."

I couldn't help but smile. A few years ago, when I was a rookie in Nick's tactical operations class, he pulled me aside to tell me that he thought I should consider applying for a spot on the Hazardous Device Unit. Taking me under his wing, he had helped me qualify at the state level. He was at my side every grueling step of the way while I went through the demanding training sessions to receive accreditation from the Department of Justice. No doubt about it, without his guidance I would not be where I am, doing what I do. The only negative side effect I could see was that he felt responsible for my welfare. Since our lives depend on each other's rational decisions, I worry that he'd jeopardize his own safety to play the hero and protect me in a tight situation. Even so, it's good to know I can always depend on him.

"Our man seems to be stepping up a level with each apparatus," Nick said.

"I'm fully aware of that. I'll be careful. See you in a few minutes."

"Jamie . . ."

I recognized the intimate tone, the warning in his voice. "Nick, I know what I'm doing! I'll be careful, I promise."

"No doubts . . ." His words were half statement, half question. *No doubts* meant double- and triple-checking the device before making any decisions that could be fatal. But between Nick and me, it was also his way of asking if I was sure I was okay with the risk. Especially today, when essentially I'd be walking the tightrope without any net and with little hope of surviving a fall.

With only a hint of hesitation, I replied, "No doubts, partner."

# 2

As soon as I hung up with Nick, I called Officer Campbell again. To ensure I made every second count, I needed to know as much as I could about the situation I would be handling before I arrived at the scene.

"Is the vest made of cloth or metal?" I asked, weaving through traffic.

"Cloth."

"Any timing device evident?"

"No."

"Is the woman injured in any way?"

"She's been better, but nothing life threatening that I could see. Well, except for the fact that some jackass strapped a bomb to her chest."

I nodded, double-checking traffic before I cruised through a red light. "Has she been identified?"

"The man who found her says her name is Anne Jasper White. Her father owns all the Jasper's Jewelers stores in Kansas. We're working on tracking him down."

*Anne. Anne. Anne.* I've always had a hard time remembering people's names, so I wanted to drill hers into my memory. A crucial part of every call where a life is at risk is establishing a good working relationship with the victim. Being on a first-name basis helps, and appearing calm at all times is essential. Whipping around a slow-moving van, I said, "Good. Is the vest cinched around the groin or neck?"

"Both. In fact, a couple of wires are wrapped around her neck pretty tight."

*Shit!* I thought. The easiest way to handle most explosive vests is to just wiggle the intended victim out through the neck hole. Obviously, the easy way wasn't going to work this time.

I asked a few more questions about her location and the type of building, then saw the flashing lights of the ambulance turning in just ahead on the right. As I pulled into the parking lot of Jasper's Jewelers, I took in every detail. Officer Campbell's supervising sergeant had arrived, and they seemed to have done a good job of keeping people back. The front door had been propped open, and the store looked vacant. A small group of emergency personnel had gathered well behind the line of bright yellow crime scene tape. I backed into a space alongside the ambulance, ordered Romeo to stay, and rushed to open the rear doors of the Suburban.

Our unit covers more than half the state of Kansas and works in conjunction with Missouri, Oklahoma, and Iowa when needed, so I don't personally know many of the law enforcement officers who request our help. As I noticed an authoritative officer, probably the supervising sergeant, head my way, I grabbed my jump bag. Every tech has a small duffel bag that contains the gear that they can't always carry but that they'll need to work a scene. It's also where we put personal things like our wallets, rings, and guns when we arrive. Minimizing the presence of metal objects is imperative, since a wrong move might bring them in contact with a part of a live device and complete a circuit.

My jump bag has my communications gear, binoculars, biohazard gloves, spare sets of keys to both Nick's Suburban and mine, small towels, deodorant, a razor-sharp knife, a window punch, a laser pointer, an extra shirt, a non-metallic watch, and a Sig Sauer double-action pistol identical to the one I carry while on duty. Pulling off my ring and watch, I zipped them into a side pocket, put on my bomb tech watch, then dug out my communications equipment. Setting it to secure com two, I slid the headset on and adjusted the microphone so that it was just slightly in front of and below my lips. The hands-free, voice-activated headgear resembles those used onstage by performers who need the freedom and mobility to work a crowd.

As I collected all the tools I thought I might have to use, I took a long, deep breath. From that point on, every word said on the secure com would be recorded at headquarters to leave a permanent account of my actions, my conversations with Nick, plus any background noise. I've gotten used to saying things aloud that most people would think, because doing so leaves a thorough trail. If anything were to go wrong, the FBI would study the tape to find which step in the defusing process I blew. Literally.

Every bomb squad unit across the country must undergo rigorous, continuous training to remain certified by the Bomb Data Center, which is a branch of the Federal Bureau of Investigation. Ultimately, we all work within the domain of the U.S. Department of Justice. We learn, and follow, procedures that minimize the risk of an inherently dangerous job. It may sound cold, but mistakes provide valuable learning tools, tools that can save the lives of other techs in the future. Underlying all the complicated rules are two very simple ideas: *Property can be replaced; people can't,* and *What you don't know can kill you.*

In a job where every second could be the difference between life and death, you rarely have the time to bother with pleasantries. After stuffing a couple of blasting cap protectors in my back pocket, I grabbed the case that held the portable X-ray equipment and my hand entry kit, then brushed past the sergeant as I signaled for Romeo to come to my side. Snapping on his leash, I stated, "Have one of the ambulance paramedics get ten to twenty milligrams of Valium and a bottle of water ready. On my signal from the doorway, I'll need someone to escort my dog back to the Suburban. Just have them say, 'Truck,' then 'Stay,' and Romeo will be fine."

The sergeant ran to catch up. "You're going in there dressed like *that?*"

"This is a one-on-one situation. The bomb suit would scare the hell out of her and reduce my mobility too much to work."

Shooting me an incredulous look, he dropped back and called, "Good luck!"

I sat my equipment near the door to free my hands. Romeo is a handsome ninety-five-pound blond Labrador. His nails clicked on the hardwood floor as we cautiously entered the store. Even though I couldn't see the manager behind the semicircle of fancy glass counters, I already knew she was sitting against the far wall outside the open vault. Before we went any farther, I softly said, "Anne, I'm Sergeant Jamie Stone with the KSP Hazardous Device Unit. I want you to know that I've been trained to deal with this type of situation. From this second on, we're a team. In a few minutes, we're both going to walk out of here alive and well."

In a weak voice, Anne replied, "Please . . . hurry."

As I spoke, I scanned the store, looking for anything out of the ordinary. "I know how hard this is, Anne. But we have to be careful. I'm just making sure these guys didn't leave anything else behind." One of the nastiest parts of being an officer of the law these days is dealing with secondary devices: those designed *specifically* to injure or kill first-response emergency personnel. "The room appears to be clear," I said.

Stepping forward, my eyes met hers. I'll never forget

my first impression of Anne. I was amazed that she was conscious. Except for a pinkish purple welt along her left cheek, her skin was the whitest shade of pale I'd ever seen in someone still breathing, which seemed like a miracle, considering the way the wires had dug into the soft skin of her neck. Her entire being quivered as though she were caught between the tines of an enormous tuning fork. Terrified didn't come close to describing the intensity of her fear.

In a soothing voice, I urged, "Anne, I want you to stay calm." Moving closer, I added, "My hairy boyfriend, Romeo, is going to sniff around the store for a few seconds. Don't worry, he's very friendly and has done this hundreds of times."

Anne nodded. I gave Romeo the command, "Find it, boy! Find it!"

I was pretty sure what Romeo would do, and he didn't let me down. Leading me, he pulled the leash taut as he methodically sniffed the section where customers would normally stand, walked around the end of the open area, then made a beeline straight to Anne. Every muscle tensed as he carefully lowered his hindquarters onto the plush carpet in the space behind the glass display counters. As always, he looked at me for approval. I smiled and said, "Good boy!" Although he didn't break his position, his tail swished back and forth, mopping the floor with uninhibited pleasure.

For the benefit of Nick, who was listening via the secure com, I said, "Romeo just alerted next to the vest." To comfort Anne, I added, "Anne, there have been two other robberies like this in the last six weeks. In both cases, Romeo correctly recognized the presence of chemicals that could be evidence of an actual bomb. Neither one was. The vests were designed to *look* and *smell* real, but they were harmless."

"Is that supposed to make me feel better?"

I smiled. "Yes. It means there's a good chance you're perfectly safe right now."

Tears welled, and her lower lip quivered as she asked, "Why would they do this to me?"

"Mostly for profit, but some criminals enjoy seeing their victims . . . *sweat.*" I had almost said the first word that popped into my mind, which was *suffer,* but caught myself at the last moment. I quickly praised Romeo again, then walked him to the door and gave him a treat. At my signal, Officer Campbell ran up, took Romeo, and handed me the Valium and a bottle of water. Moving back to Anne's side, I said, "I know how stressful this is. If you're not allergic to any medication, I can give you something to help keep you calm. It's not enough to knock you out, but it might help you relax."

Anne barely nodded, then her eyes went wide. "I can't! I can't move!"

"Just tilt your head up a little, I'll drop the pill in, then give you a sip of water."

"Oh . . . okay."

After she managed to swallow, I sat the bottle on the counter and touched my headset as I said, "My partner is listening over this communications link en route, so for his benefit, I'm going to describe the device. Then we'll see what we can do to get you out of it as fast as possible."

We try not to break radio silence unless the other party is prepared, since an unexpected noise might make a tech flinch at the wrong time. To signal I was ready, I softly said, "Nick?"

"Heard every word. So far, so good. I'm still about ten minutes out, but from what I've heard, you've got everything under control."

The sound of his voice always has a calming effect on me, and I took a deep breath. "See you, soon."

A single tear rolled from the corner of Anne's eye. "Can I talk to my kids? Please? I don't want to die without telling them how much I love them."

I instantly thought of Matt, of his birthday present—a new guitar—hidden under a blanket in the back of the Suburban, then softly shook my head. "I know exactly how you feel, but right now, we have to concentrate all our effort on getting this thing off of you. This is my son's birthday, and I have no intention of missing the party tonight. How old are your children?"

"Char is fifteen, and Brandon is ten."

"Matt's fourteen today."

"Are you married?"

"No. The man in my life is living in Budapest right now, teaching the former Soviet countries how to function as democracies."

She seemed impressed. "My husband is a stockbroker." After a brief hesitation, she added, "I'm kind of surprised . . ."

I smiled. "That I'm a woman?"

A tiny nod was her reply; then she quickly added, "Not that that's a bad thing. . . . I just didn't expect a woman to . . . you know . . . handle such a dangerous assignment."

All my life I've dealt with similar comments, from teachers to prospective employers. In my younger days, I would've been irritated that gender so easily masked the qualities of the inner person. But motherhood and experience apparently mellowed me over the years. By the time I was in my midtwenties, I had started looking at the positive side of the argument. Instead of feeling that such comments were keeping women confined, I chose to feel liberated by the fact that I'd successfully broken free of society's invisible restraints. Occasionally, I still encounter a person whose obvious discrimination makes me furious, but for the most part, I've worked hard to earn the respect of my peers and the people in the community who need my help.

Knowing Nick was listening, I commented, "Anne, if you'd feel more confident with a male bomb technician at your side, my partner will be here in a few minutes. He's very qualified and has been a bomb tech since the dawn of time."

Anne quickly replied, "Heavens, no! I'm sure you're good at what you do. Please, just get me out of here!"

"Don't worry, I will. Right, Nick?"

His voice dripped with sarcasm as he slowly replied, "Right . . ."

Relieved that Anne had faith in me, I silently repeated my main objectives: *Keep Anne talking so she stays calm and provides information. Find out as much about the bomb as possible before touching anything. Describe it in detail for the benefit of Nick and the record.*

Knowing the situation demanded a fast determination of the level of risk, I continued, "Anne, I need to tell my partner about the device now." She smiled, and I continued, "I've got what appears to be an ordinary fishing vest with a few extra layers of a white, cottonlike material sewn inside using a rather sloppy whipstitch with orange thread. Although it is similar to the device Nick worked with in Saline County a few months ago, this one has Y-shaped straps that go between Anne's legs and has double wires that loop around the neck and disappear into the top front side. There are four standard phone jack connections that lead to wires hidden beneath the white inner layers. Visible wires lead down and around to the back. No sign of color-coding."

I softly sighed. It's much easier to trace wires that are color-coded, so I knew my job would be tough. Dealing with multiple identical strands of wire takes more time, since each one has to be traced from one end to the other. Shifting slightly back, I added, "From everything I've seen, I'd bet my next paycheck that this is the same guy's handiwork."

At that point, I leaned close, focusing on the connections that closed the device in the front. "Anne, do you remember what order they plugged these together?"

She softly shook her head. "They put my head in a black cloth bag. I couldn't see anything at all."

As she spoke, I stood and tried to see as much of the back of the device as I could. "Did you *feel* the pressure, *hear* anything?"

She was beginning to shake harder. I hoped the Valium kicked in soon.

"I just . . . I don't know. . . . It all happened so fast," she cried.

Making sure her eyes met mine, I smiled and said, "Take a deep breath." She did, and I could see a little of her confidence return. "Okay, let's start at the beginning. Tell me what you did first thing this morning."

After a brief hesitation, Anne shook her head and sighed. "It hasn't been my day. I was trying to leave early because today is our monthly breakfast meeting. Just as I was about to walk out the door, I ruined my hose. When I went back upstairs, I didn't have a new pair, so I changed into this pantsuit. I was in such a hurry when I rushed to my car that I didn't even turn on the burglar alarm before I left the house."

While she was talking, I was searching the vest for danger signs such as antennas and pressure switches. To encourage her to go on, I nodded and said, "You're doing great. What happened when you went outside?"

She closed her eyes. "I was about to unlock my car when he grabbed me from behind. He said that if I didn't cooperate . . ."

"Breathe, Anne. You can do this. I know you can."

Swallowing hard, she nodded. "If I didn't cooperate, he said he would go inside and kill my family. I didn't even set the burglar alarm! He could've forced the door open, or used my keys, and . . ."

"And so you did the smart thing. You did exactly what he told you to do."

A contrite nod. "Like I said, he put a black sack over my head and forced me into a van."

"Why do you think it was a van?"

"I heard the door slide closed. Then they put this horrible thing on me. . . ."

Softly cradling her face in my hands, I looked directly in her eyes and declared, "Everything is going to be *fine*. We're a team, Anne."

When she had calmed back down, I leaned to get a better look at the side of the vest that was pressed up against the wall. I could see the edge of something in the lower middle of the back, but the angle was such that I couldn't get a good look at it. Shifting to the other side, I tried to reassure her, but I still needed more information. "It's okay. You've done great. How many people did you see?"

"Two. No, I actually only *saw* one of them. But the guy who grabbed me was talking to someone else."

"What were they talking about?"

"Something about getting the sequence right or we'd all be blown to kingdom come."

"Kingdom come? Those were his *exact* words?"

She nodded. It was the same phrase reported in the two prior incidents.

"Nick, I can see a hard edge of black plastic in the lower center of the back. Because she's seated leaning against the wall, I can't tell what it is at this point." I asked Anne, "Did you walk in here on your own?"

"Yes."

"Were you still wearing the black hood?"

"No. He was behind me when he pulled it off and said not to look back. They made me come in first, turn off the security system, cover up the security cameras, and open the safe."

"And you did all of that?"

"Yes. My family . . ."

"It's okay, Anne. Money and jewels can be replaced. Human lives can't." A soft smile lit her eyes, and I could tell she felt better. Still probing, I asked, "Who came inside? Just one of the men? Did you see either of their faces? Notice how tall they were?"

She shook her head. "Only the one who first grabbed me came inside. He must be pretty tall, because I could feel his chin on my head when he dragged me toward the van. But he had on a mask, so I never got a look at his face."

"What kind of mask?"

"One of those realistic-looking Halloween masks. It was the guy from Kiss, you know, tons of black and white makeup." She scrunched her nose as she added, "And a hot-pink, pointed tongue hanging out."

I couldn't help grin. "What about his hands?"

"He had on gloves."

"What kind?"

"O. J. gloves." In response to my raised brow, she added, "You know, expensive black leather."

"Did he touch the vest in any way during that time or before he left?"

She shook her head. "He just pointed the gun at me and told me to sit against the wall. He said if I moved, I was dead, then he cleaned out the vault and ran."

I was relieved. From her description, he hadn't manually activated any switches before he left the scene. Chances were good that the plastic thing on her back wasn't a pressure-sensitive switch, or he would've been risking blowing himself up while he worked. Although I could use a small mirror to get a better look at it, I knew that we would have to get X-ray plates behind her before we could defuse the device. Either way, leaning forward was in her near future. It was my call at this point, and I decided the risk was minimal. Keeping my voice absolutely steady, I said, "Anne, I need you to shift slightly forward so I can see the back of the vest. Don't worry. Nothing will happen."

"But he said if I moved it would explode!"

"Yet you walked in here and opened the safe, right? And after that, he just kept a gun trained on you. He didn't touch a button or flip any switches. Trust me. My life is in jeopardy, too. I'm totally vulnerable, but I'm not leaving. Remember, we're a team."

Our eyes met and held. I was on trial. I couldn't blame her. After all, a total stranger was telling her to let go of the single thread she thought was keeping her alive. I either looked trustworthy, or she decided that doing what I asked was the lesser of many evils. With a deep breath, she closed her eyes and shifted her body weight forward a few inches.

I slid down in an awkward position until my face was pressed against the cold wall. The headset objected, but I held it in place with my free hand. Although I was already perspiring, the instant I saw the flashing fluorescent blue numbers of the digital timer, I felt the blood rush to my cheeks. As I leaned back, I hoped Anne didn't notice the drastic change in my attitude.

Choosing my words carefully, I did my best not to alarm her. "Nick, the back is like the others, the extra lining hangs down about six inches and is rolled along the edges. The only difference is that in the lower middle of the back there's a thin chronometer, about four inches wide and three inches long. It's descending at fourteen-twelve."

Anne stiffened. "What's that mean?"

I lied. "Nothing you should worry about. It's just technical jargon for the location of a common part found on devices like this."

Although Anne relaxed slightly, my heart was pounding, and a chill started at my scalp and crawled to my toes. The air suddenly felt thin, as though I'd just reached the summit of Mount Everest. A drop of sweat trickled into my eye, making it burn. I wiped my forehead with the back of my hand, knowing all too well that in less than fourteen minutes we would find out one way or another if this was just another hoax or if the sick bastard had finally stepped up to the real thing.

# 3

As I dashed to where I'd left the X-ray equipment and my other tools near the front door, I lowered my voice to say, "Nick, if you're not running balls to the wall, I'm gonna kick your ass." *Balls to the wall* is trooper jargon for full emergency status: lights, siren, the works. Risking one tech's life is enough, so I knew that if we strictly followed procedure, I would be the only one with Anne until the device was rendered safe, but having him nearby would boost my confidence. After all, misery loves company.

Nick's voice conveyed every ounce of his frustration. "I'm rolling through the grass on the shoulder of the interstate. Between a wreck at the loop and construction, traffic is backed up for a mile. By the way, I notified ATF." ATF stands for the federal government's Alcohol, Tobacco, and Firearms agency. Since we couldn't yet determine if a state line had been crossed in the commission of this crime, an ATF agent would be responsible for follow-up work on this case. When state lines are crossed, the FBI joins in the fun, too. "Who's responding?" I asked.

"Simon Stanley, and he's going to have your vote for man of the year, Frank Nichols, with him."

I groaned. In general, ATF agents aren't exactly people you'd put at the top of your party list. Simon was tolerable. He showed up, did his job, then left. He was frequently late, a habit that saved him hours of work, since the rest of us routinely took up his slack. Simon was a handsome specimen in his early forties: six feet tall with a broad chest, a mane of graying hair, and a smile that would make Vanna White jealous.

Simon's partner, Frank Nichols, was in a league of his own. Frank was well known by his colleagues for his brusque personality whenever he was at work. Oddly enough, at picnics and social events, he was a completely different person, the first to toss a baseball with the boys or organize a game of tag football. Frank was older, in his fifties, and was set to retire at the end of the year. In spite of all the strict policies on discrimination and sexual harassment, Frank made no secret of the fact that he believed women had no business in law enforcement, much less on special operations teams.

Whenever Frank worked a crime scene, I felt as though

I were invisible. He made a point of talking to Nick about anything important. Apparently, women were only fit to fetch and clean. Frank was one of the few people who routinely made women in the workforce feel inferior, and I was no exception. Knowing he'd be at the scene any minute actually made my head ache.

Nick asked, "What are you planning to do next?"

"A double-plate X ray to pinpoint blasting caps." X rays detect the lead azide in blasting caps, plus the wiring can be traced *if* there's time.

"Great. Listen, I have a feeling our man is getting serious."

"Me, too."

"Remember, layer by layer, just like at Redstone. Jamie, you can do this."

He was referring to our FBI/Army training sessions at the Redstone Arsenal in Huntsville, Alabama, which still rank as some of the most grueling experiences of my life. During a practice run, I choked on a vest device similar to this one. It had a decaying switch, one fueled by the declining life of a battery. When the battery dies, the switch closes. *Boom,* or in my case, *buzz.* If it had been a real bomb, I'd have been blown away along with the poor soul who had trusted me to get it off of him in time. That night in Hoppers, the bar at the Holiday Inn where the bomb techs go to blow off steam, I was ready to quit. Nick talked me into staying, convinced me that running away wasn't the solution. At that moment, I couldn't help but wonder if I had made the right decision.

With a deep breath, I signaled the sergeant. "Keep this perimeter clear, and have the ambulance crew ready to roll!" I could see the muscles along his jawbone tense as he nodded. Even though he wasn't privy to the conversation on the secure com, it was obvious from my demeanor that the stakes had just been raised. A small crowd

of officers, paramedics, and onlookers had gathered behind him, each bearing a wide-eyed look of impending
doom that did nothing for my self-confidence. As if that
weren't enough, I caught a glimpse of an off-duty trooper
and instantly felt a chill run down my spine. *What the hell
is he doing here?* I wondered, but there was only time for
the thought to sprint across my mind before it was pushed
aside by more pressing problems.

The X-ray case weighs about twenty-five pounds, but
it felt light as a feather as I grabbed it and said, "Nick,
I'm going back in."

"I started my timer on your signal. You're at eleven-
seventeen. That's plenty of time to locate and neutralize
any caps."

"Right."

If the *Guinness Book of World Records* had a category
for setting up portable X-ray equipment, there is no doubt
in my mind that my name would be listed for my performance that day. When I finished, I was relieved to see
that the Valium had wrapped Anne in its soothing em-
brace, because she had finally stopped shaking. Overlapping two twelve-by-ten panels of film against the wall
behind her, I explained, "Okay, Anne. It's time to kick
ass. First, I'll X-ray the vest to get an idea of what we're
up against. This is delicate work, so I need you to stay
very, very still. Holding your breath would help, too."

The portable X-ray machine is eighteen inches long and
looks like an overgrown box of Velveeta painted silver
and blue. As soon as Anne sucked in a deep breath, I
pushed the button on it. The timer counted down fifteen
seconds, then made a series of soft clicking noises as the
gamma rays were emitted. I immediately said, "Okay, you
can breathe again," as I snatched the panels and began
cranking them through the portable developer. Inside it
are two rolling pins that squish chemicals against the

panel to begin the reaction necessary to process the film. I set the timer on my watch for the forty-five-second developing time.

Anne grinned like a teen experiencing her first beer buzz.

Using every minute, I opened my hand entry kit, which folds out like a fancy tackle box. Each tech has his or her own preferences on the types of tools they like to use, since many items are selected based on the size of their hands. My kit has a dozen razor knives, a magnifying glass, needle-nose pliers, a roll of silver duct tape, a roll of electrical tape, a wide assortment of nonmetallic probes, and a set of miniature tools used for delicate work, similar to what a dentist or jeweler might use. I also have an assortment of tape in a rainbow of colors to use for color-coding wires like those in this vest.

With the clock ticking down, I knew there wouldn't be time for such meticulous work. Although it's a scary thought, successfully defusing such a device requires a tech to recall and implement months, sometimes years, of training in a matter of seconds. It's the technical equivalent of being an emergency room doctor, except the stakes are higher. If a bomb tech's split-second diagnosis is wrong, the tech stands as good a chance of dying as the victim.

Grabbing the rolls of duct and electrical tape, I began tearing off six-inch strips and sticking them along my jeans between my hip and knee. My watch beeped to indicate the developing time was up, so I peeled back the top layer and spent thirty seconds studying the pictures. Unlike the transparent, negative-image X rays most people are familiar with from trips to dentists and doctors, we use positive-image film because we don't usually have a reliable source of backlight to help us view them. Since we use different film, our X rays look like black-and-white photographs.

The first thing I did was check the calibration guide we keep in the top corner of the X-ray plate to confirm the machine was set properly. If it is set too low, the image will be too dark to be used; too high, and the over-exposure can wipe items completely out, washing away traces of wiring that are crucial to our job. Since all the test wires clearly showed at the top of the frame, I knew the X ray I had shot was an accurate, reliable image.

I took a deep breath. "The X rays show wires leading to two potential caps, one located under each arm. I'm going to tackle the right side first. Anne, I'll need you to hold your arms over your head so I have room to work. Okay?"

Anne shot me a wide-eyed, *you've got to be kidding* glare.

"We're a team, remember?" I reached over, took her wrists in my hands, and gently crossed them over her head. When I let go, each of her hands was holding the opposite elbow. "Now, don't move. Time?"

Anne mumbled something about there never being enough time, but Nick knew what I needed. His reassuring voice echoed in my head. "Eight-ten. Doing great. I'm four or five minutes out. No doubts, Jamie?"

Biting my lower lip, I looked at the X rays once more and softly said, "No doubts."

Since Anne thought I was talking to her, she replied, "I have lots of doubts. I worry about my kids, my husband, my job—" She snickered. "Well, not that my father would fire me or anything, but making sure the store is the best it can be. Jamie?"

Still working, I replied, "Yes."

"Why are you doing this?"

"Isn't that rather obvious?"

"No. I mean why aren't you a lawyer or an accountant, you know, something that isn't so"—another snicker—"macho."

"Well, let's see. My father was a flight mechanic for the Oklahoma Air National Guard. I grew up crawling all over jet fighters and dreaming of becoming a fighter pilot. Unfortunately, I grew a little too tall, and my vision wasn't perfect, so I had to let go of that particular dream."

She nodded, pleasantly adding, "You are a little on the lanky side. But pretty, too. If you weren't so muscular, you could've been a model."

I knew Nick was probably about to burst, so I said, "Go ahead, Nick. Give it your best shot."

The laughter in his voice was apparent when he replied, "Nothing wrong with being muscular. Or lanky, for that matter. How's the vest?"

"Coming along fine. Where were we, Anne?"

"You were telling me why you became a cop."

"Oh, yeah. Well, since I couldn't be a fighter pilot, I decided to major in political science. I got my degree but couldn't find a job. One of my friends joked that I should be a police officer, and for the first time, I gave it some thought. The more I thought about it, the more I knew I could do it. And, as they say, the rest is history."

"Cool. I always wanted to be a veterinarian."

"So why are you managing a jewelry store?"

She shrugged. "My grades weren't good enough to get into vet school, so my father told me I could run this store until I decided what I wanted to do. I met my husband, we got married and had kids. . . . I guess my priorities changed."

I had finished all the preliminary work and was about to begin the critical part of my job. Hoping to keep her mind off of what I was about to do, I smiled at Anne and suggested, "Why don't you hum your favorite song while

I work?" Even though she gave me a funny look, she began humming, softly at first, then with a little more confidence.

After taking a deep breath, I stated, "I'm making the first cut vertically an inch from the side seam." I applied pressure to my razor knife, wishing the outer layer wasn't constructed of such heavy material. Although I was being careful, I was fully aware that I had less than eight minutes to get both sides neutralized. "So far, so good. I'm ready to I-cut the top and bottom one side at a time, then tape the outer layer back."

All live blasting caps have "DANGER—HIGH EX-PLOSIVE" printed on the side, and most are traceable to a certain manufacturer. So far, the vests had always had fake caps: everyday fuses made to look real on an X ray. Grabbing a strip of duct tape, I peeled open the first layer of cloth and taped it back. Instant, almost overwhelming relief coursed through me. The doughlike substance I had revealed didn't look quite like any actual explosive material I had ever seen. The color was slightly off, and—I leaned close to inhale—it smelled a little too much like modeling clay to be real. Very slowly, I began pinching off pieces, tossing them aside as I described the color and texture for Nick.

Anne stopped humming long enough to state, "You're making a mess on my floor."

"I know. I promise to clean it up later." Finally, I could feel the slick surface of the cylindrical tube beneath my fingertip. Using my nail, I scraped until the exposed half was clean. For a moment, I froze. The letters $E$-$X$-$P$-$L$-$O$ were staring me in the face.

Those simple block letters left no question in my mind that I was dealing with a real blasting cap! All bets were off. Even though Anne appeared to be in la-la land, I couldn't risk having her panic at this point. I chose my words carefully so that Nick would still understand. "I just exposed the wired end of a cap and a few letters. Markings are Edward, X ray, Paul, Lincoln, Ocean. . . . I'm now working to uncover the rest of the cap and a little wire."

Another drop of sweat burned as it washed over my eye, but I barely noticed. Working faster, I kept upward pressure on the outer cloth by holding it with one hand while I cut with the razor knife. I wasn't being nearly as delicate now, and the floor around my knees was practically covered with brownish white clumps of the claylike substance. I exposed the words "Danger—High Explosive" on the two-inch-long cap. I've always been amazed that something so small has so much destructive power.

Inside a blasting cap is a microfilament that is thinner than a human hair. When ignited, it generates a flash of intense heat. When the flash comes in contact with the highly explosive, unstable substance that fills the last eighth inch of the cap, an explosion occurs. The blasting cap's discharge generates a shock wave capable of detonating substances like C4, a common commercial explosive. The entire chain reaction is activated by a simple pulse of electricity.

Caps that have been removed are still dangerous, so we utilize cap protectors to be certain they are safely handled. A protector is a six-inch metal tube designed to insulate and direct the blast, thus stopping the reaction and rendering the cap harmless. In a device like this, the timer built into the vest is used to send a pulse of electric current through the wire. When the pulse reaches the cap, it ignites, which provides the energy needed to detonate the high explosive. *Boom!* would be putting it mildly. In this case, I knew the cap had been manufactured for military use because the wires were brown. All commercially produced caps have brightly colored, very distinctive wires.

Now that the entire cap was exposed, I reached for my wire cutters. Holding the cap in my left hand, I cut the wires with my right, placed the cutters on the floor by my knee, then picked up a cap protector and slid the blasting cap inside. "One down, one to go." I sighed as I positioned the protector on the floor pointing away from Anne and the mess I'd made.

"The right side is neutralized. I'm moving to the left side now. Nick?"

I could hear Nick's siren in the distance as he replied, "Great work, Jamie. Keep it up."

Anne had started softly singing. I gently reminded her to stay as still as possible, then started the process again. After double-checking the X rays, I took another deep breath and made the next cut. "Nick, time?"

"Three-oh-five. I'll be with you in less than two minutes."

Pressing my face against the wall, I gently pushed Anne forward to verify we were still in synch with the vest's timer. "Three-oh-five is visually confirmed with the device. I'm starting on the left side now. And, Nick, in case you were considering otherwise, you need to hold at the perimeter."

"What? And miss all the fun?"

"There will be plenty of fun after I neutralize this cap."

"Figures. You do the exciting render safe and stick me with the paperwork. Some partner."

"Shhhh. I need to concentrate."

Anne suddenly stopped her welcome serenade, sending the room into a morguelike hush. "Anne, I wasn't talking to you. Keep singing. You have a beautiful voice."

Happy again, this time Anne appropriately chose "Yesterday," an old Beatles favorite. Working quickly, I continued to cut, fold, tape, and scrape. Just as I was making the last cut, another drop of sweat temporarily blinded me.

A second earlier and I might've nicked a different wire, one that could have been deadly. "Shit!" I muttered.

"What?" Nick's voice boomed in my ear.

"Nothing. Remind me to put a sweat band in my hand entry kit. Nick, clock me down."

Nick began a steady chant, reminiscent of a NASA countdown. "One-twelve, one-ten, one-oh-eight . . ."

I knew I could do it. I worked as I'd been trained. Methodically. Step by step. When he reached twenty-two, I sighed. "I'm cutting the second cap . . . now." After I slid it into the protector, I leaned back and announced, "Both apparent caps in the vest have been neutralized. There isn't time to get to the batteries in the clock, to be absolutely certain we're clear, but from the X rays, I'm confident the device has been rendered safe. Nick, any other ideas as we approach zero?"

Technically, to *render safe* is to address the device, to make it harmless by separating the detonators from the explosive, which prevents the bomb from functioning as designed. Although I was certain I'd done everything by the book, there's always a chance that a creative bomber has made up a few new rules.

"You strictly followed protocol, Jamie. I could come inside to double-check the X rays for shadows, but it's your call."

I gnawed on my lower lip. Anne was oblivious to the clock on her back that was slowly but surely cycling down to zero. If I had missed something, chances were good that we could both still die from the explosion. But if Nick came in and spotted another problem, our only hope would be to blindly cut the vest off of her. Either way could end in disaster. The answer was clear. Even though the risk was minimal, it was still a risk. I helped Anne slowly lower her arms as I held her hands and declared, "Anne and I are a good, solid team. Let's count it down."

Nick hesitated. I knew he was dying to come in, to see for himself, to make sure I would be okay. More importantly, I knew he was proud of my answer as he resumed counting, "Fourteen, thirteen . . ."

Ignoring his voice, I took her hand in mine as I asked, "Anne, do you sing to your kids?"

She grinned. "I used to. When they were babies, I'd sing them to sleep every single night. Now that they're older, I don't. But I should, shouldn't I?"

"Yes, you should."

"Do you sing to your son?" she asked.

I laughed. "No. He'd probably scream and run away. Matt plays the guitar and has a great voice, but he certainly didn't inherit those genes from me."

I must've blocked out the last few numbers, concentrating so hard on Anne's words. I didn't realize it was over until Nick was at my side. Jerking me to my feet, his bear hug was so fierce that I was afraid the steel-reinforced boobs of my bulletproof vest might leave permanent dents in his chest. When he finally let go, I managed to say, "Anne, this is my partner, Nick Terrell."

"Nice to meet you, Nick. I'm taking requests. What's your favorite tune?"

Nick laughed. There was a lot of work left to do, but for a few moments I relished the feeling of sheer joy left in the wake of the fading tension. When you cheat death time after time, you learn to celebrate life whenever you get a chance.

# two

## 1

Once our heart rates had a chance to drop back to normal, we slipped into the less stressful part of our job: completing the investigation. Wrapping up the fieldwork at Jasper's Jewelers took almost three hours. We shot more X rays from the side to be certain there were no other blasting caps waiting to surprise us, then Nick and I carefully cut the vest off of Anne layer by layer, observing every intricate detail.

To put it mildly, Anne was relieved to be free, only to be stunned by the horde of media people waiting outside as she was rolled toward the ambulance. Although we were all confident that Anne was fine, it's always best to have a victim checked by a doctor to be absolutely certain.

When she was safely on her way to the hospital, Nick took pity on me and gave the media a brief interview while I went back inside the store. Being on-camera unnerves me. My heart races as though the red dot of a laser sight is leveled right between my eyes. It's a different kind of rush than I feel when I'm defusing a bomb, a kind that makes my hands go ice cold and my stomach knot. I honestly, truly, hate it.

Besides, Nick had been to bullshit school. Of course, that's not the technical name, but it should be. There are actually classes that teach high-profile people how to answer questions in an intelligent way that conveys virtually no useful information. *Political sidestepping* would be a polite way to word it. Nick's a master of the game. His rugged good looks distract half the audience, while his ability to skirt the truth with technical mumbo jumbo usually satisfies the rest. There was little doubt in my mind that every local channel would cover the story that night and that the viewers would be impressed, even though they learned very little about the incident. It was actually rather amusing.

After he satisfied the media's curiosity, Nick left long enough to swap his Suburban for the bomb truck. We keep the bomb truck parked in its own covered space at the KSP Training Center on the outskirts of town. The training facility sits on twenty acres, which allows us ample room to do test blasts and store our hazardous materials. It's fenced and well-lit but much less accessible than the headquarters in town.

Although we call it a truck, in reality it's a van on mega-steroids. Our unit is lucky. We have one of the best setups in the country, thanks to the generosity of the citizens of Kansas. I've always considered it a blessing that the truck is roomy enough for me to stand tall without worrying about hitting my head. In fact, it feels more like a small, high-tech kitchen than a cramped work area. The truck holds an impressive assortment of equipment in metal drawers and shelves that line both inner walls.

Everything is painted glossy red, except the floor, which has a special kind of tan antislip vinyl covering.

Whenever we go to schools to speak about safety, the children are most impressed by two things about the bomb truck: the television monitor and controls like those on their computer games, which we use to remotely operate the robot, and the fax machine mounted on the dashboard. I find it amusing that technologically enabled kids, who've grown up with cable television, cell phones, and laptop computers, are still fascinated by the concept that a printed piece of paper can travel from one place to another completely through the air.

Simon Stanley and Frank Nichols, the ATF agents assigned to the case, arrived at the scene just moments after Nick returned. As usual, Frank seemed to go out of his way to avoid dealing with me. I found it irritating, but I'd learned long ago to ignore him, especially on a case like this. After a brief look around, Simon promptly announced that he had an errand to run and would be "right back."

Frank made a beeline to Nick, becoming his shadow as he kept working. Although I tried not to eavesdrop, I couldn't help but hear Frank's glowing remarks about the Vest Bomber's latest technical feats. I suppressed the urge to ask if he wanted to become president of the guy's fan club.

By the time Simon returned, the most tedious part of our work was done. As usual, Nick was furious, but Simon's absence hadn't bothered me; I'd just as soon work without him, or anyone else for that matter, looking over my shoulder.

To me, the cleanup phase can be just as interesting as the render safe. Dissecting a defused bomb is like reading a poem—the complicated ones must be taken line by line, making certain you understand every nuance the creator had in mind. As I peeled back the material closest to the clock, I slowly shook my head. The ends of the wires on the blasting caps were still factory shunted and taped. Since the shunts had not been wired into the timer, even if the explosives had been real, the device would not have detonated. In a strange way, I felt cheated, as though I'd been robbed of a precious reserve of adrenaline that I'd never be able to find again.

I was collecting the last of the brownish white globs off the floor when we heard a commotion outside. Even from a distance, we could tell it was Anne's father creating a scene. Apparently, he wasn't used to taking no for an answer. He wanted to go in his store, and he wanted the "sons of bitches" to "fry" for what they had done to his daughter. Nick grinned, then slowly shook his head as he declared, "Looks like a job for supernegotiator. I'll be back in a few minutes."

"Have fun," I said with a smirk. Simon was milling around near the far counter, so I asked, "Could you hand me the digital camera?"

"Sure," he replied, tossing it twelve feet as though it were a tennis ball instead of a delicate, *expensive* piece of equipment. The look on my face must have expressed the degree of my annoyance, because he shook his head and shrugged. "Sorry. I forgot how protective you two are of your precious gear."

Dismissing him, I took several close-up pictures of the shunts. When I finished, Simon was at my side, so near that I sidestepped to regain my personal space. With a sheepish grin, he declared, "Come on, Jamie, don't look at me like that. I said I was sorry."

I shrugged, making certain my facial expression remained neutral. "What do you want?"

He stepped back, pretending to be insulted. "What makes you think I *want* something?"

I turned away, unwilling to get sucked into one of his typical mind games. "I can see it in your eyes. Cut the bullshit. What is it?"

"You're good, Jamie Stone. No doubt about it. No matter what Frank thinks, you're damn good." He paused, waiting to see if I'd take his bait. When I didn't, he admitted, "I noticed the TCV is here. It's parked in an area that's got plenty of open space. I don't suppose there's any chance we could save some time and do the tests on the vest gunk now. . . ." His voice trailed off, and he tried his best to plead with his clear blue eyes.

Simon was referring to the total containment vessel, or TCV, that Nick had fought long and hard to get for our unit. A TCV is used to detonate devices at the site where they're recovered, so that they don't endanger the public during transportation to a safe facility. Our old system had merely directed a blast upward, which was better than nothing but still left anyone in the surrounding area to contend with the resulting shock wave and shrapnel. The new unit would fully contain an explosion, with no harm to its surroundings—a necessity in light of the growing threat of biological and chemical weapons of mass destruction. Bomb squad budgets are tight, and TCVs cost almost $125,000. But Nick employed his two most powerful tools: persuasion and persistence. We acquired a NABCO total containment vessel made of high-strength, high-impact steel that can be moved via a motorized pallet whenever necessary. Suspected explosives can be loaded into it through a two-foot opening, then safely detonated.

Although the TCV could be used to do the test blast in the parking lot, we normally perform them at the training facility on the outskirts of town to minimize risk to the public. Knowing Simon, I was certain he simply wanted to save himself another trip. Since he was the primary ATF agent assigned to this case, he would have to witness the test blast in order to testify in court that the evidence had been properly destroyed. That is, *if* the case ever went to trial. Plastering a sweet smile on my face, I replied, "You know how much I'd like to help, but Nick will call that shot."

Simon cocked his head and whispered, "If *you* ask him, he'll do it."

My voice dripped with sarcasm as I replied, "At least you're smart enough to correctly assume that if *you* ask, he won't."

"Come on, Jamie. Frank just bailed out on me."

I grinned, feeling instantly more cooperative. "You mean he's gone?"

"Yes. You sound relieved."

"Aren't you?"

He shrugged. "Frank is one of those guys you have to know for a while before you understand what makes them tick. At the rate I'm going, that'll be about sixty years from now. You really shouldn't let him get to you. That's his goal."

I couldn't help but smile, but it quickly faded when I saw Simon's expression soften as he leaned close. With pleading eyes, he added, "Listen, Jamie, I have a million things I need to do. My mom fell and broke her hip a few weeks ago. She called this morning to tell me her air conditioner is acting funny. And, of course, she said there was no hurry, that she had managed just fine in this kind of heat for almost seventy years, and another few days wouldn't kill her."

A memory of my grandmother washed over me. She had always been stingy with anything electrical. Lights, heating, air-conditioning, you name it. According to her, our generation took too much for granted. We didn't understand hunger or the true meaning of being poor. So every time she passed a thermostat, she nudged it one way or the other, whichever direction would lower the power bill. On a hot summer day, it wouldn't be unusual for me to come home to find all the windows open. The need to "air out" a house was just another thing Matthew and I didn't fully appreciate, just as neither of us realized how much she meant to us until she was gone.

Simon cleared his throat, reminding me that he was waiting for an answer. I certainly didn't want to be responsible for his mother having a heat stroke. Feeling like I had Sucker tattooed on my forehead, I muttered, "Okay, I'll do it."

With a genuine smile, he said, "Thanks, Jamie. I really appreciate your help."

I nodded, then cornered Nick near the vest as soon as he was back inside. "How did things go with Mr. Jasper?"

"Better than I expected. He's a nice guy. He must have said thank you thirty times."

"Good. Got a second?"

"You bet."

"It crossed my mind that Matthew's birthday dinner might be delayed if we have to wait all afternoon for Simon to show up at the range for the test blast. Might save us all some time and frustration if we did it here. Besides, I'd bet a week's salary that this is the same stuff we worked with in Salina and Hutchinson."

Nick half nodded, obviously preoccupied with the vest. "Fine by me. Factory shunted and taped. Son of a bitch. The bastard is showing us that he knew what he was doing. That he could've wired it hot if he wanted to. So why didn't he?"

I replied with a shake of my head as I added, "I'll get everything ready."

Since I had already gathered all the "explosive" mixture scraped out of the vest off the floor, I easily molded a couple of two-ounce samples to use as test material.

Simon was waiting by my truck, scratching Romeo behind the ears, when I walked outside carrying what looked like two dirty golf balls in my gloved hands. To my surprise, his newly improved attitude rubbed off on me. Seeing the blanket covering the guitar nestled against the backseat, I started getting excited about Matthew's birthday party as I gathered the supplies I would need from the drawers built into the back of my Suburban. Simon followed me across the lot to the bomb truck, which Nick had parked off to the side, well away from all the other vehicles and buildings. For our purposes, doing the test in town wouldn't be a problem, since the size of the blast would be minimal.

We routinely perform two tests to determine if a substance is actually an explosive. First, we do a test burn to see if the sample will ignite. Occasionally, a material will not only burn, it will create a small explosion, which indicates the material is unstable and must be handled using precautionary measures. I didn't expect either of those things to happen as I stooped to open one of the bottom drawers inside the bomb truck.

As a safety precaution, the explosives we carry are never stored near the caps or fuses. Each has its own insulated compartment. Since most of the materials we deal with are sensitive to humidity, we keep our supplies sealed in Tupperware. Fuse that has been exposed to moisture burns at an uneven rate, which can lead to dangerous miscalculations, so we carefully burp the lid each time one is resealed to keep the containers as airtight as possible.

To prepare for the first test, I opened two different containers that each held a twenty-five-foot coil of fuse. From each coil I cut a four-foot piece, trying to keep them as close to the same length as possible. Using different coils minimizes the possibility of duplicate failures. Fuse is a thin green cord, slightly smaller than the diameter of a pencil. If you look straight at a cut end, you can see the green sheathing encases a graphite-colored substance that resembles gunpowder. Fresh fuse burns at a rate of one foot every forty-five seconds, so we always use enough to allow plenty of time to distance ourselves from the blast—normally three to four minutes. We're trained to allow additional time, since there should never be a need to have to *run* away.

Due to Hollywood theatrics, most people envision fuses that burn with bright sparks, even some flame. In real life, as a fuse burns, it only produces a thin line of smoke. Nothing else. Stomping on a fuse won't put it out. The actual fire inside is burning beyond the line of visual smoke. The only sure way to stop a lit fuse is to cut it at least four to six inches in front of the smoke, then watch it carefully. In a critical situation, we're trained to cut the fuse as close to the bomb as possible to minimize the possibility of unexpected combustion.

Carrying the fuses to the TCV, I inserted the end of each strand into the first test ball of brownish white clay material. Positioning the ball in the center of the TCV's rack, I waved at Nick, signaling we were ready. Within seconds, he was at my side. Although we could've closed the TCV's hatch, it wasn't necessary for a test like this. From my pocket, I withdrew two waterproof igniters, or WPIs, and handed one to Nick. They're small green tubes, about the diameter of a penny. On each end is a cap. One covers the opening where the fuse is inserted, the other cap screws off to reveal a string. In a way, WPIs are like the party poppers that blow confetti at kid's birthday parties. Once the fuse is in place, the string is pulled, and the WPI generates the heat needed to light it. We use them since they aren't affected by wind and rain, although on a hot summer day, a simple match would've worked just as well.

Standing next to the TCV, Nick and I began the routine we'd used for years. Each of us held a WPI attached to a length of fuse. "Ready?" I asked.

"On three," Nick replied.

I stated, "One, two, three." We both snapped our WPIs, generating a noise similar to two small firecrackers popping. We always obeyed department procedure. Following the same steps every time makes it easy to testify in court. The moment each of us visually verified our fuse had lit, we announced, "Smoke," and started the timers on our wristwatches.

Two fuses are used to ensure that a tech doesn't have to approach the explosive material, should a fuse not function as anticipated. Misfires can cost lives, and safety is always our first priority. Stepping away, we waited four minutes, then went to check the results.

Inside the TCV, the ball had been discolored by the smoke, but it hadn't ignited. High explosives, the kind that are detonated with blasting caps, don't burn. At least, not yet. God only knows when a chemist will concoct a formula with even more destructive power, and we'll have to run both tests every time. For now, if the test burn is negative, we move on to the test blast. Nick jotted down the results while I went back inside the bomb truck to get two blasting caps and two more four-foot lengths of fuse. Simon followed like a concerned bystander, plodding along, pretending to be interested, even though I strongly suspected he wanted nothing more than to finish the task and be on his way.

Any material that explodes when a blasting cap is discharged is considered cap sensitive and extremely dangerous. We followed basically the same procedure, except this time we had inserted number eight blasting caps into the sample and closed the TCV's hatch. Glancing at Nick and Simon, I asked, "Ready?"

They both nodded and I declared, "On three. One, two, three." Again, the still summer morning was broken by the sharp snap of the WPIs. Again, we waited. This time, the muffled explosion of the blasting caps occurred exactly on schedule. After four minutes, we approached the TCV and opened it. There were brownish white bits everywhere, which meant the substance had been an imitation. "Just like Saline County," I said.

Nick nodded. With a sly grin he looked at me and added, "You're up. I took care of the mess last time. Simon, are you going to bag the vest so we can get out of here?"

Simon nodded and headed back inside Jasper's Jewelers to finish processing the evidence.

It was already getting hot, and I knew that scraping bits of gunk out of the inside of the TCV wouldn't be fun. Scrunching my nose at the glaring sun, I said, "I'll make it fast." I did, and was relieved to be finished in just ten minutes.

Sweat had soaked through half my shirt and was trickling steadily down my face as I pulled my head out of the TCV for the last time. As I sealed the last of the evidence in a bag, I caught a glimpse of a familiar figure on a motorcycle parked in the far corner of the lot. Most of the crowd had departed, but just as I was about to point him out to Nick, the engine started and the vehicle sped away. Strange that the officer hadn't acknowledged either Nick or me. Heading to my Suburban, I poured Romeo a bowl of water and drank the rest of the bottle myself.

I was certain that when the results came back from the FBI, they would show that Romeo had alerted on the vest because the bomber knew enough to make his fake plastic explosive with a dash of a substance like Aqua Velva that

contained ammonium nitrate, a chemical any bomb-
sniffing dog would detect.

Nick and I spent a few more minutes wrapping up our
work at the scene, then discussed the details of the kidnapping with Simon. Nick has never disguised his dislike
for Simon, or vice versa, so I was relieved when we
agreed to simply forward him a copy of the incident reports and go back to headquarters. Since ATF is responsible for the evidence in a case like this, it was Simon's
job to finish processing the disassembled vest. Relieved,
we headed to our office.

# 2

Every bomb squad activation requires detailed paperwork.
Although the main branch of the Kansas State Patrol is in
Topeka, we work out of a satellite headquarters in Kansas
City. Much of our time following a call is spent at our
shared office in the far back corner of the KSP building.

Nick's desk faces mine, and if I look to the right while
he looks to the left, we have a beautiful view of the parking lot. Mind you, I would never complain. With law enforcement's budget problems, having *any* office is a
privilege. Romeo's home away from home is beside my
desk. He sleeps on a hand-woven Indian blanket Matt and
I found on a ski trip to Angel Fire, New Mexico. Beside
his bed is a ceramic water bowl with his name painted in
blue on the side. The dish was a gift to him from a twelve-
year-old girl he once helped save, and every time I see it,
I smile. It's a constant motivator.

Since my typing skills greatly exceed Nick's, I com-
pleted the report for the Bomb Data Center of the FBI.
Their new computer system allows on-line filing, so once
Nick approved it, I zapped the report to them, complete

with digitized copies of the photos we had taken at the scene. I always transfer two copies of the photos onto diskettes: one for the squad's files and one for our case file. I labeled them both Jasper's Jewelers Vest along with the date, and handed them to Nick.

At a local level, the record-keeping isn't quite as high tech. We complete a Special Unit Utilization Report that details the who, what, when, where, and why of every mobilization. Once both were finished, Nick and I agreed to break and meet back at the office in two hours.

I had just pulled into my driveway when my cell phone rang. From the caller ID, I knew it was Nick. I snapped, "You promised I had time to take a shower and eat."

Nick laughed. "Since when do I keep promises?

"The way things are going this summer, I should've known better than to expect a few minutes of peace and quiet. What's up?"

"We've been summoned to Topeka by Lieutenant Colonel Jones. In fact, every available member of our squad has been called. I'm leaving Bill and Larry in town to cover any emergencies, but the rest of us are supposed to report in two hours. Jeff and Marcus are going to meet us there."

I sighed. Lieutenant Colonel Jones was the highest-ranking trooper in our area. In all my years as a trooper, I'd never met him, and I wasn't looking forward to it. Jones had more than his share of shadows darkening his reputation. Although I'd only heard rumors, I had a hunch that many of them were based in fact. "How soon will you be here?"

"I'm about five minutes out."

"Great." I hung up and unlocked the back door as Romeo took care of business near his favorite tree. Rushing into the laundry room, I whipped off my shirt and slipped out of my bulletproof vest. My neck and back muscles instantly relaxed. Stripping off the dirty jeans, I dropped them into the washing machine and slammed the lid closed. It was a relief to take a deep breath and not have my chest and back muscles protest. Equally nice was the smell of fresh air, since I'd been inhaling the peculiar fragrance of sweat mixed with chemicals for several hours.

By the time I wiggled into a freshly dry-cleaned uniform, I felt almost presentable again. Walking through the kitchen, I noticed a package on the table. On top of it was a note from Matt:

> *Mom—*
> *Went to Jesse's. Be back in time for my birthday dinner. Some guy dropped this off for you. He said he was really sorry he didn't get to deliver it to you in person.*

I instantly felt relieved that Matt wouldn't be home alone all day. Matt spends as much time at Jesse's house as he does at ours, and vice versa. They've been best friends since the third grade, swapping videos, clothes, and computer games so much that I doubt if anyone really knows (or cares) who actually owns what.

Jesse's father is Jewish, his mother Catholic. They're an amazing couple, and they've raised three fine children. As a family, they alternate celebrating Hanukkah and Christmas, and last year Matt and I were invited to Jesse's bar mitzvah. It was a wonderful experience, one neither of us will ever forget. Jesse's two older sisters are away at college most of the year, so he, too, needs a close friend. As a single parent, I've always been grateful for the loving support Matt feels from being close to the Coleman family.

Picking up the package, I noticed it was bundled in

what had been a brown paper grocery bag. A simple wrap of white twine tied in a bow held the paper in place. My name and address were written in block letters in the center, but there was no return address on the front or back. I glanced at Romeo, who seemed to have no interest whatsoever in the box. Even so, years of training were impossible to ignore. Deep down I had been nervous for weeks. That nagging sense that someone was watching me had repeatedly made my skin crawl. What bothered me most was that there wasn't a single concrete piece of evidence to justify my feelings. In a profession based on scientific knowledge and reason, there was little room for what most people wrote off as women's intuition. Even though I felt certain I was letting paranoia slither way too far into my life, I decided it was better to be safe than sorry.

Knowing Nick would be there any minute, I ran back to the Suburban and grabbed the X-ray equipment. Working fast, I shot one panel and cranked it through the developer. While I waited for it to process, I jotted a note to Matt wishing him a happy birthday and promising to be back in time for dinner. He was far too old to have a party, but he had wanted Jesse and Nick to join us at his favorite restaurant. In many ways, Nick was the only father figure Matt had ever known, and Jesse was like a brother.

The developing time was up just as I heard Nick pull into the drive. One brief look at the X ray was all it took to know I'd been wrong. There was nothing even slightly threatening inside the box. I stashed the equipment in the laundry room, grabbed one of the sandwich bags full of dog food I keep in the pantry, and reluctantly snatched my bulletproof vest and campaign hat. After tucking the mysterious box under my arm, I locked the door and left.

Romeo settled in the middle of the front seat next to Nick, who greeted him with his usual rough half hug.

Most bomb dogs are kept in cages when they're transported, but Romeo had always had such an easy disposition that I had never found caging him a necessity. I climbed in, tossed my vest into the backseat, the box onto the floorboard, and buckled up.

Nick snidely quipped, "You certainly look more comfortable."

"What woman wouldn't love being able to shed a few pounds in a matter of seconds?"

He raised one eyebrow. "You know, technically you're supposed to don the warrior princess vest all the time."

"I know. But it needs to air out. Trust me. After this morning, you wouldn't want to ride in the same car with me if I had it on. I'll put it on when we get there."

In his macho-sergeant voice he snapped, "Bulletproof vests save lives. All KSP personnel will wear them whenever they are in uniform. Personal hygiene is not as important as being protected at all times. Do you understand?"

"Yes, sir!" I poked his ribs and felt the lean muscles there. "Look who's talking. You took yours off, too."

He grinned. "Good point." After he merged onto the interstate, Nick abruptly stated, "Factory shunted and taped."

I knew he was talking about the Jasper's Jewelers vest, so I replied, "To show he's capable of manipulating us? Establishing that he could have easily gone all the way if he wanted to?"

"Yes and no. Now that he's proven that he knew how to wire it, we have to assume that his next bomb will put that knowledge to use. I think he's practicing. Building a better device each time, waiting until he's perfected his method before he risks his own life with real explosives. It's like he's working up to some critical event."

"Can't wait to see who he invites to *that* show. By the

way, I think we can count on the fact that he's right-handed."

"The stitching again?" Nick asked.

"No, the way he hit Anne. It's her left cheek that's bruised."

He nodded, apparently impressed.

Looking at Nick's profile as he drove, I said, "I still think he's toying with us. If he just wanted to scare the hell out of Anne, he would've put the clock on the front of the vest where she could see it. He left the vault and the front door wide open, knowing full well that someone would pass by and give us a call within a few minutes. Otherwise, installing the clock was just a waste of time. She could've sat there for hours before anyone found her."

"True. I've got a bad feeling about this guy. Like I said after the last one, I think the take from the robbery is secondary. It's building the vests and terrorizing people that's getting his rocks off."

I groaned. "I know the media has dubbed him the Vest Bomber because we've never leaked information about the existence of a second suspect, but have you noticed we always talk as if it's just one person, too? All three witnesses say they've heard him speaking to someone else, but to me, it still *feels* like we're up against one person."

That made him pause. "I don't think the driver is our problem. The bomber has consistently given the orders and always entered the stores alone."

"It's still odd. Something just doesn't sit right." I made a mental note to call the victims again and run through exactly what they heard one more time.

Nick nodded. "You're remembering your training at Redstone. FBI profilers would predict that we're up against a loner. They point at people like Ted Kaczynski, the Unabomber, and claim that all serial bombers are creatures of habit who build the exact same device over and over. *Insane* creatures of habit, mind you."

"Our guy definitely doesn't fit that mold. Every vest has been different."

"More complex."

I sighed. "More dangerous. And his robbery techniques certainly aren't sloppy. Not a scrap of trace evidence. He's smart enough to use the right precautions." Glancing down at the package I'd tossed onto the floor, I asked, "Do you suppose it's a coincidence that all three vests have been on our shift?"

Again, Nick was quiet for a while, "Technically, we're on call twenty-four-seven, unless we're out of our coverage area."

"True, but we rotate duty with the two other KSP teams. Neither has responded to a hand entry vest call yet. And I contacted the bomb squads in Iowa, Nebraska, Missouri, and Oklahoma yesterday. We're the only one dealing with this problem . . . so far."

"You think *we're* being targeted? How could any crook possibly know which team is going to be called to respond to a nine-one-one?"

I rolled my eyes. "Paranoid, huh?"

"Not necessarily . . ."

There was a hesitation in his voice, something only I would have noticed. Being a woman in an all-male profession tends to make one slightly defensive. The logic behind his reluctance suddenly struck me like a sharp slap. Wide-eyed, I turned to him and said, "You think he's focusing on our team because I'm a *woman!* The sick, psycho bastard thinks I'll crack under pressure when my testosterone-saturated male counterparts would have kept their cool."

Nick shook his head. "Jamie, I hate it when you jump to conclusions. That thought never crossed my mind." He winked, then added, "But now that you mention it . . ."

I punched his arm hard enough to make my knuckles ache. Romeo instantly sat up and whined, certain our argument was an invitation to play. After I finally settled him back down, I reached for the box near my feet. "Someone dropped this by my house this morning."

"That's odd. Who left it?"

"Don't know." I was glad that I had waited until we were well on our way. I wanted to see Nick's honest reaction, plus I needed to find out if the stress of the last few weeks was really getting to me or not.

He took it and gave it a quick inspection as he drove. "Awfully light. No postmark. No return address. Common wrapping paper. Were you expecting a delivery?"

I shook my head and snatched it back from him. Just as I started to rip the outer paper, he braked and whipped onto the shoulder.

"Something wrong?" I asked innocently.

He angrily declared, "We've got a serial bomber working our butts off, who may or may not have us in his sights. I think we'd better make sure he hasn't taken his message a step closer to home."

I grinned. "I already X-rayed it, if that's what you had in mind."

Fuming, Nick seethed, "Why the hell didn't you say so?"

"Just wanted to see if we shared the same professional opinion."

He glared at me for a moment, then sped back onto the highway. While he sulked, I opened the box. I actually gasped when I peeled open the white tissue paper. Inside was a long, brightly colored cloth, obviously hand woven in an intricate series of patterns. As I tugged it slowly out of the box, a cream-colored parchment envelope with my name on it was revealed. I instantly recognized David's handwriting.

"Well?" Nick asked.

"It's from David."

"At last, the fairy princess hears from the gallant knight, off on a quest to expand the boundaries of the free world."

I ignored him. Nick and David were like oil and water. If you put them together and shook long enough, they might bond for a few seconds, but each would be silently kicking and screaming to get away from the other. Picking up the elegant cloth, I said, "Isn't this gorgeous?"

"Very impressive. Then again, even I could impress a woman if I only had to do it once every six months."

"Hah! You don't have a romantic bone in your body."

"I used to send Lori flowers!"

"Only when you had a fight," I snapped. "Women don't want guys who try to buy back bitter words. We want someone who catches us off guard, who shows us they care by doing something special for no particular reason. Something out of the blue, completely unexpected."

"Right. Just let him forget your birthday or anniversary, and we'll see how far that theory flies."

Again, I decided it was best to ignore him. His divorce from Lori would be final in a couple of weeks, and the last thing I wanted was to open another discussion of what had gone wrong. Carefully breaking the seal, I tugged the letter out of the envelope. As I unfolded it, a small silk pouch fell onto my lap. Totally enthralled, I pulled open the tiny string that held the scarlet fabric snug at the top. Tilting it, I gasped when an emerald-cut loose diamond tumbled onto my palm.

"Damn, that's one helluva rock!" Nick remarked.

Stunned to silence, I nodded my agreement.

After watching the gem gleam in the sunlight for a few

moments, I slipped it back into its silk bag and opened David's letter. Silently, I read:

*Dear Jamie:*

*I'm sorry I haven't been able to contact you lately. I've been in Armenia and Ghana, and couldn't find the part to repair the modem on my laptop. When I heard Garrett Blake, a fellow U.S. advisor on economic development, was making a stop in Kansas City, I seized the opportunity to get this message to you.*

*I've enclosed a cloth from Ghana. It's a hand-woven native scarf, typically used in wedding ceremonies. Each bright pattern has historic significance based on tales passed from mother to daughter. I had a fascinating discussion with several of the local shopkeepers about each design, but I'm afraid the spirit of the symbols would suffer in translation. The diamond is from Armenia, where they have a long tradition of trading gemstones at an informal market in an open field on the outskirts of town. When I saw this diamond, I thought of you.*

*I hope that both you and Matt are having a wonderful summer. I am well, although I miss you and worry about you. Have you been giving thought to our discussion about finding a desk job? Knowing you were safe would certainly make me sleep better at night.*

*I have it on good authority that I could be stationed on the East Coast within a year if I play my cards right. I would still travel to Europe regularly, but my home could be with you and Matt. Maybe you could work at the FBI training facility in Quantico, and we could start a new life to-*

*gether. It's an intriguing idea, isn't it?*
  *Remember, when one door closes, another opens. . . .*

  *Take care,*
  *David*

I let the letter fall to my lap as my emotions clashed. Half of me was thrilled and excited to hear from David; the other was irritated that he was still pushing me to quit the job I loved. I was brought back to reality when Nick unexpectedly plucked the letter from my hand. "Nick! That's personal."

"Then you should've left it at home."

I growled, Romeo bristled, but Nick kept the letter and read it as he drove. When he was finished, he tossed it back to me and flatly said, "He wants you to quit the squad and move to the East Coast."

"What he wants and what I'm willing to do are two different things," I replied, tucking both the diamond's pouch and the letter into the parchment envelope.

Nick snapped, "He shouldn't ask."

"Why shouldn't he? I haven't exactly been silent about him exposing himself to terrorism on a daily basis."

Nick glared at me. "There's a big difference. He is physically putting himself in countries where Americans, especially American diplomats, are targets."

"He would argue that my job makes me a target twenty-four hours a day."

"Then he doesn't understand how we work."

"Think about it, Nick. No one who hasn't done this for a living really understands. They don't get it, because they can't. They haven't been there to see the terror on Anne White's face, or to feel her gratitude when it's over. Only a handful of people in the world know what it's like.

David is just doing what comes naturally. He's trying to protect someone he cares about."

Nick was quiet for a few moments, then said, "I'd think long and hard about what you're getting into before you go much farther. I should have known from the beginning that Lori wouldn't be able to handle my job. She worries too much. Always has, always will."

"I know," was all I could think of to say, and the words drifted on the strained mood that hung between us. Desperate to change the subject, I asked, "Did you notice Carl Johnson was at the scene this morning?"

"Yeah. Don't let him spook you; he's harmless."

"He was hanging around my truck again. Every time I went out he stared, like he was memorizing my every move. It makes my skin crawl." Rubbing the gooseflesh on my arms, I realized that wasn't just a figure of speech.

"Typical patrolman. Seems you've forgotten that curiosity is a *good* thing. We *want* troopers who go the extra mile."

"But most troopers have better things to do than waste their time at a scene that's already crawling with local police and special ops teams. Plus, how do you explain all the crazy conspiracy theories he buys into? The guy could easily be in one of those far-right-wing militia groups."

"I can think of ten veteran troopers who are even more open about their *militant activities.*" He had sinisterly pronounced the last words with eyes wide open, then shot me a look that was a cross between a smirk and a grin. "Come on, fess up. Why are you so preoccupied with Johnson?"

"What's that supposed to mean?" I asked.

He narrowed his eyes. "It means, somehow he's managed to wiggle a burr under your saddle."

I thought for a moment, then decided it wouldn't hurt

to tell Nick the truth. "As a matter of fact, you're half right."

"Half?"

"I've heard my share of stories in the women's locker room, and I don't think they're just idle gossip. Supposedly he gets a kick out of stopping good-looking women on dark, deserted highways."

Nick managed to hold his tongue, although I could see it was hard. Finally, he said, "So, what you're saying is, Trooper Johnson harasses single women late at night while he's on patrol."

"That's right."

"And how *exactly* does he harass these women?" When I didn't answer fast enough, Nick urged, "Well? Does he expose himself? Make lewd remarks? Brush against their breasts? Grab their butts? Drag them into the bushes? All of the above?"

"Why don't you check his personnel file and tell me? I hear there have been several formal complaints, but nothing has ever been proven. The problem always boils down to his word against theirs."

"I've been here a long time, and I've never gotten wind of any kind of scandal involving him."

"The rumor mill also says that Lieutenant Colonel Jones is his uncle. We both know how quickly certain things are handled when the top dog gets involved."

Nick shrugged. "Every trooper has heard the crap about Jones. Like it or not, he put in his time to get where he is. And so far, he's been very supportive of our squad. Every time I've requested new equipment or personnel, he's come through. We both know Romeo wouldn't be here if he hadn't personally pushed through the funding."

"I know. . . . It's just I don't particularly care for the man. He comes across as arrogant."

"Probably because he *is* arrogant," Nick admitted, then

grinned. "Maybe while we're in Topeka you can pull Jones aside and ask him if Trooper Johnson's bloodline entitles him to special treatment."

"Or maybe I'll just keep my mouth shut and mind my own business."

"Ah, finally a good idea."

# three

1

The moment we walked into the conference room in Topeka, I realized the briefing Lieutenant Colonel Jones had organized was going to be a more elaborate affair than I had envisioned. Scattered on the large oak table were glossy eight-by-ten color photographs of the three devices we had disarmed, along with copies of the reports I had filed on each incident. Thanks to the miracle of digital technology, even a photo of the vest we had just defeated that morning was included in the presentation.

I recognized three of the men already seated as FBI agents, and ATF was represented by Frank Nichols, Simon Stanley, and their immediate supervisor, George Harper. The other members of our bomb squad, Jeff Jenkins and Marcus Allan, were having a lively conversation with a trooper I didn't recognize near the window. As usual, I was the sole representative of the female gender.

While Nick greeted everyone, I chose a seat, gave Romeo a command to stay at my side, then took a pad and pen out of my briefcase.

As so often seems to be the case when I'm around a trooper I don't already know, I overheard a few whispered remarks that implied my main job was to "service" Nick. I was glad that he hadn't heard, too, since he would've felt the need to intervene on my behalf. Instead, I walked over to the trooper and extended my hand. "Hi. I'm Jamie Stone."

I saw Jeff and Marcus exchange a knowing look as the trooper firmly returned my handshake. Running his free hand through his coarse red hair, he replied, "Sergeant Cartman. Nice to meet you."

The fact that he'd replied with his rank was a dead giveaway. Although he was in great shape, I was easily five inches taller. Unfortunately, some guys feel intimidated by my height and feel the need to dominate in any way they can. Smiling down at him, I said, "I was wondering if you'd indulge me for a moment, Sergeant."

"Certainly. What can I do for you?"

"I know this will sound strange, but as a woman trying to make her way in a man's world, I like to be certain my skills are equal to my peers'." Turning on the charm, I added, "It's so nice of you to offer to help."

Practically hopping into my trap, he said, "Just name it. I'm always glad to assist a fellow trooper."

"Great." I looked at my watch. Lowering my voice, I leaned close and whispered, "We've got a few minutes before the meeting. How about right here, right now?"

Cartman's eyes widened. "Excuse me?"

"You heard me. Let's go at it. I predict you'll last under twenty seconds."

Jeff and Marcus were visibly suffering. As Marcus bit

his lip, Jeff barely managed to say, "Go ahead, Cartman. Take her on."

I sat down and put my elbow on the table, opening and closing my fist.

Realizing he'd been had, Cartman shook his head. "No way. I'm not going to arm wrestle a woman."

Marcus chimed in, "We've both done it. Surely you aren't afraid you'll lose."

Tapping my watch, I added, "Time's almost up. Are you conceding defeat?"

Cartman's thoughts were easy to read. *If I lose, I'll never hear the end of it. If I win, I'll look like an ass.* Looking me right in the eye, he said, "Maybe some other time."

Standing, I shrugged. "This time it's your choice. But if I ever hear another remark about *servicing* my partner's needs, I won't choose such a genteel way of letting you know how I feel about your cocky attitude. Understand?"

He nodded, his pale cheeks turning bright red.

Feeling empowered and a bit smug, I took my seat.

Lieutenant Colonel Jones walked into the room as if he owned the place, which in a sense, he did. Romeo immediately began to fidget, looking repeatedly at me as he shifted back and forth. When I told him to settle, he whined, then lay down, but I knew he was still uneasy since his eyes kept darting up to meet mine.

Jones declared, "I know it's early, but since we're all here, we might as well get going. I called this briefing in order to ensure that our department is prepared to handle the serial bomber case with the highest degree of professionalism. As usual, our colleagues at the FBI and ATF have agreed to give us the full cooperation and support of their agencies."

I glanced sideways to confirm Nick's reaction to the insinuation that we might act in some way that was less than professional. As I expected, he was staring straight ahead, his jaw firmly set. I'd witnessed that look enough to be glad I wasn't on the receiving end of it.

Jones cleared his throat, then continued, "I'd like to start by having Lieutenant Terrell explain the progression of the devices, as well as the current evidence we have in this case."

Nick stood, then spent the next thirty minutes detailing everything we knew about the Vest Bomber's three strikes. When he finished, Jones opened the floor to questions or comments.

ATF Agent Simon Stanley stated, "The peculiar thing about this case is the *evolution* the bomber seems to be going through. It's as if he's enrolled in Bombing 101 and is using jewelry stores as homework assignments."

Frank Nichols joined in, "The choice of locations is peculiar as well. The first vest was in Hutchinson, the second in Salina. Possibly he picked smaller towns because they had a longer hazardous device response time. Neither of those vests had timers, yet the one this morning not only had a timer, it was set realistically."

Jones asked, "Realistically?"

Nichols nodded. "Too little time on the clock, and it would've proven to be a dud before the bomb squad arrived. Too much, and there's no performance pressure. I think our man knows enough about the inner workings of the emergency system, specifically the response time of the bomb squad, to plan his moves."

Glancing around the table, Jones asked, "Anyone else think this is an inside job?"

Nichols practically choked. "Hold on. I never meant to imply that the bomber was one of us or even someone in law enforcement for that matter. My point was that we're dealing with a person who either knows the system, or was lucky enough to make a damned good guess at Jasper's Jewelers."

Jones agreed. "Even so, we have to look at every possibility. Today's vest incorporated a military blasting cap, so it's safe to assume our bomber could have a military background." To one of the FBI agents, he asked, "Could you have your computer wizards do a statewide cross-reference of all firemen, ambulance, and police personnel for military service?"

"Will do," the agent replied.

Jeff, the youngest member of our bomb squad, nodded toward his partner, Marcus, as he stated, "That will probably turn up a long list. Both of us have a military background, and I know Sergeant Cartman does, too."

Marcus added, "I know at least ten KCPD officers on special ops teams who are enlisted in the Reserves or the National Guard."

I instantly thought of Carl Johnson, the trooper who had watched from a distance that morning, but I knew better than to voice a mere suspicion. Looking across the table, I made eye contact with Cartman. He returned my glare for a few seconds, then looked away.

Jones nodded, then said, "Still, I think we should run the check. Better to be safe than sorry. Turning his attention to me, he added, "I noticed that six weeks ago you recovered a spool of det cord on the shoulder of Interstate 35. Your report failed to explain how a highly controlled substance ends up in a ditch."

Without missing a beat, I replied, "There was no way to know with that particular spool. More than half of it had been used, and all the factory markings had been removed. But two years ago, we recovered a spool of det cord that had been reported missing by a construction company in Wichita. Their best guess was that the spool hadn't been properly secured for transport, and that it had bounced off the truck when it hit a pothcle "

"How tightly controlled is our inventory of ، ıch recovered substances? Do we know how many feet we have, or do we just keep track of it by the spool?"

"We only track spools," I replied. "Keeping an inch-by-inch count would be next to impossible, sort of like tracking how much is left on a reel of fishing line."

"Didn't the vest bombings start shortly after that spool was recovered?"

"Yes. But no det cord has ever been used by the Vest Bomber."

"How much would it take?"

"To do what, sir?" I asked.

"If det cord *was* used in a vest, how much would it take to kill a person?"

I shrugged. "Not much. One wrap around the torso would cut a human in half if it detonated."

Jones nodded. "I want to see it."

Puzzled, I asked, "The det cord we recovered?"

"That, and everything else. I spent the morning going over the bomb squad's expenditures for the last year. It seems we keep a fairly large stock of explosives on hand. What if this maniac got his hands on it?"

Nick suddenly pushed his chair back and stood. "Lieutenant Colonel Jones, our inventory is maintained with the utmost caution. What we don't have accounted for in the bomb truck or our personal vehicles is secured in the locker at the Training Center. Only ATF agents and my team have access to the locker, and it's extremely well protected."

As Nick talked, I glanced around the room. Jeff and Marcus were openly glaring at Jones, while every ATF and FBI agent seemed to be nervously looking out the window.

"Is it under video surveillance?" Jones asked.

Nick shook his head. "Sir, there isn't a hint of evidence that the Vest Bomber is running short of supplies. And quite frankly, I resent the implication that he could just waltz in and walk off with any explosives under my supervision."

"Calm down, Terrell. I wasn't implying a damn thing about your abilities or the control you have of your squad's supplies. My job is to make certain that we consider every angle of a case. Sometimes, that means looking at it from a distance. From where I sit, the Vest Bomber is having a grand old time playing with us, trying to see how good we are, how far he can push us. Very few people would have access to large quantities of the materials necessary to make these vests—specifically, plastic explosives and blasting caps. If the Vest Bomber is someone who's intimately familiar with our procedures, it isn't unreasonable to assume he might try to expand his arsenal at some point. Am I totally off base, Lieutenant Terrell?"

"No, sir."

Jones glared at Nick. "From this point on, I want to be involved in every step of this case. Understood?"

"Yes, sir," he replied.

"I'll be in touch with you early next week to set up a tour of your facility. Meanwhile, I'd like a word with you in my office." To the rest of us, Jones said, "Thank you for coming."

Only a few seconds after the two of them left the room, Marcus said, "Damn. What the hell's his problem?"

I snapped, "I don't know, but I have a feeling it's going to be a long drive back to KC."

"Anyone else think it would've been faster if we'd just lined up and bent over as soon as he walked in the room?" Simon Stanley remarked.

One of the FBI agents replied, "Would've had the same *end* result. . . ."

As everyone prepared to leave, they continued to crack jokes about Jones. Cartman was the first to go, and I instantly breathed easier. Since I had no idea how long Nick's private meeting with Jones would last, I took Romeo for a walk outside, then waited in the Suburban. After almost an hour, I was beginning to worry that we wouldn't make it back in time for Matt's birthday dinner, so I decided to check on Nick.

The moment I stepped into the foyer, I heard his laughter echo through the hall. Spotting him, I realized he was talking to a woman, a very pretty woman. Marching toward them, I stopped at his side, just as he said, "Then I'll see you tonight."

She grinned, flirting with every ounce of her womanhood as she spun around to stroll away. "I'll meet you there," she called over her shoulder as she headed the opposite direction.

I can't explain why I was mad, but I was. In fact, furious was more like it. "Where the hell have you been?" I asked, keeping my voice low.

"I made a date. Remember, I'm single now. It's allowed."

"With *her?* Who is she?"

"She's doing a study on the personality traits of individuals in high-stress jobs. Jones gave her permission to interview everyone on our squad. She showed me the questionnaire. It's actually a very interesting concept."

Even though we had stepped outside, I leaned close to whisper. "I can't believe you left me waiting while you flirted with some bimbo."

Nick laughed. "Bimbo? Alexa Dixon has a Ph.D. in psychology, and she teaches at Kansas Central University. I'd hardly classify her as a bimbo."

"She's had a boob job!"

"Good for her. But just out of curiosity, what makes you think so?"

I scoffed, "They're too high and firm for a woman her age. Gravity is pretty tough to escape, and those babies are as perky as they come."

Obviously enjoying every moment of our conversation, Nick joked, "Maybe she sleeps hanging from her ceiling."

"Like Batwoman? I suppose you intend to find out."

He stopped in his tracks to seriously ask, "What difference does it make to you?"

"Well for one thing, tonight is Matt's birthday party, and if I don't get out of here, I'm going to miss it. He'll be really disappointed that you're not coming."

"I wouldn't miss Matt's party for the world. I'm not meeting Bimbo Batwoman until ten."

"In Topeka?"

"No, she's from Kansas City, too."

I could feel the blood rush to my cheeks. "Oh . . . then I suppose everything will work out."

"Of course it will."

With a sigh, I said, "Nick, I just don't want you to get hurt. I know how hard it's been since Lori left. I just think you should be cautious, even though it's against your nature."

"Jamie, I'm forty-two. I was married twenty-two of those years—more than half of my life. I have no intention of falling head over heels in love again. Ever. What I would like now is to have some fun before I'm too damn old to remember what fun is. It's been a long time."

I touched his sleeve and gave him the *don't even think about it* motherly glare that I had perfected over the years. "Just take it slow. Be careful."

He flashed a killer grin. "I'm *always* careful."

# 2

For as long as I can remember, Matt has loved chips, salsa, and nachos. So it was only natural that we celebrate his birthday at his favorite Mexican restaurant, On the Border. The building is brick, the floors a flawed burnt orange tile that looked old even when it was brand-new. Antique fans whisper at the ends of long poles, dangling from high-beamed ceilings like miniature inverted windmills.

What makes the place special, the single thing that captured and has managed to keep Matt's attention for years, is the tortilla-making machine in the center of the main dining room. Cornmeal, flour, and spices go in one side, crispy fried tortilla chips come out the other. Since the tall sides are mostly glass, curious diners can watch the entire process, from mechanized grinding and rolling, through the deep fryer, until the sizzling chips roll out onto a mini–conveyor belt.

The four of us kept that machine busy for hours. Basket after basket of chips were inhaled as Nick entertained the boys with tales of our adventures at Redstone and Quantico. It dawned on me while we were struggling to simultaneously eat and laugh that most people would assume we were a typical American family. Okay, our average height was over six feet, so maybe not exactly typical, but we certainly seemed to fit the family angle.

Jesse and I have dark hair, while Nick and Matt are fair. The three men in my everyday life are all handsome: Matt and Nick in a rugged, outdoorsy way, while Jesse's face has more classic features—high cheekbones, large brown eyes, full lips. Jesse and Matt rarely spend more than a few days apart, and in many ways I feel he *is* a part of our family. The same can be said of Nick. Since

Lori left him last winter, he's slowly started to spend more time with us.

Swishing the remains of a frozen margarita in the bottom of my glass, I wondered what would happen when David stepped back into my life. How would his presence alter parties like these? I seriously doubted if Nick would ever befriend him, which troubled me more than I cared to admit.

Trying to distract myself, I glanced around the crowded restaurant. We seemed to be surrounded by happy couples. Most were eating quietly, a few were intimately touching, obviously in the early stages of dating. They seemed so comfortable, so *normal*. I had noticed a man dining alone in the far corner but hadn't given him much thought until that moment. Since he was openly staring at me, I reflexively nodded a silent greeting. He returned the gesture pleasantly enough, but something in his eyes sent a shiver down my spine. Looking back, I realize that my reaction was probably a combination of stress and lack of sleep, but for the rest of the evening, the man's presence was never far from my mind. My peripheral vision caught his every move, an unconscious defense mechanism that kept my nerves on edge.

At one point, Nick leaned close and whispered, "What's wrong?"

Lying, I replied, "Nothing. Why?"

"You almost jumped out of your skin when that waiter brushed against your chair."

"I'm fine. Just tired." Loud enough for the boys to hear, I announced, "Matt, you'll have to wait a few more minutes before I hand over your present." As he groaned, I pulled two envelopes from my purse. "But you can open these now."

"All right!" Matt exclaimed, ripping into them in record time. The cards were from each set of grandparents. Since they moved to California, we rarely see Matt's father's parents, but they never forget to remember him on special occasions. Sometimes I think seeing Matt is hard on them, because he looks so much like the son they lost twelve years ago. Even though it seems like a long time, there are days when I'm sure he'll come walking in, and I'll have him once again. My parents still live in Perry, Oklahoma, which is about a four-hour trip. Since my father suffers from advanced emphysema, he's on full-time oxygen and can no longer travel. We drive down to visit as often as we can, but I always wish there were a way to squeeze in a few more visits every year.

Matt held up two checks and grinned as I took a picture. Nick whipped an envelope out of his pocket and handed it to Matt. "Happy birthday. If you don't like this idea, I'm sure we can come up with something else that's both violent and entertaining."

Inside Nick's card was a gift certificate for three people to spend a day at Paintball Land. Matt jumped out of his chair and ran around the table to give Nick a hug. "This is an awesome present! Can I take Jesse?"

Nick grinned and slyly asked, "You mean you don't want to take your mother? I'm sure she'll be devastated if you go without her."

Matt's face fell as he turned toward me. "You don't want to go, do you, Mom?"

I laughed and shook my head. "Getting pummeled with paint is only fun if you have your best buddy at your side."

Jesse was obviously as happy as Matt, and they immediately began to plan the weekend. As they talked, a group of spirited waiters and waitresses came around the corner. I got the distinct impression that Matt wanted to crawl under the table when they handed him a balloon

bouquet and made him blow out the candle on a small
chocolate cake.

As soon as the applause from the other diners died
down, Matt glared at me and snapped, "Mom! You promised you wouldn't tell them!"

I stoically replied, "And I kept my promise. I had nothing to do with that public display of affection." Crossing
my heart, I added, "I swear!"

Jesse was fighting hard to keep from laughing as Matt
turned on Nick. "She put you up to it, didn't she? What
did she promise you? A home-cooked meal? Taking your
shift?"

Nick shrugged, suppressing a grin as he softly shook
his head. "I, too, am being falsely accused." He reached
for the cake, adding, "But since you obviously don't want
this . . ."

Matt snatched the plate, guarding it with both hands. "I
didn't say I didn't want the cake. I just hate being hu-
miliated in front of a bunch of strangers."

Jesse couldn't control himself a minute longer. Bursting
into laughter, he cried, "Your ears are *still* bright red!"

Eyeing his best friend, Matt moaned, "You didn't!"

Jesse confessed, "I did. But only because you salted my
water at my bar mitzvah. Now we're even."

"No, we're *not!*" Without attempting to hide a sly grin,
Matt added, "Now I'm *really* looking forward to going
paintballing this weekend."

The boys continued to quibble as they finished the
meal. I was relieved when they finally said they were
ready to go, partly because I was excited about giving
Matt his guitar, but more importantly, I wanted to be free
from the roaming eyes of the man in the corner.

I had transferred Matt's surprise to the back of my personal car, a charcoal gray Honda CRV, just minutes before we left home. Jesse was horsing around, rubbing one

of the balloons against his shirt, then holding it above his head to make his hair stand on end. He was doing a great job of keeping Matt distracted as I pulled out the guitar and declared, "Happy birthday!"

The expression of joy on Matt's face was priceless, a moment of happiness burned forever into my memory. Unlike most teens, Matt knows all too well the value of a dollar, and he knew that an expensive guitar wasn't in our budget. I had managed to truly surprise him, leaving him so stunned that he was totally speechless. Had it not been for the presence of Jesse and Nick, I'm sure he would've shed tears of joy.

Instead of speaking, he clamped his long arms around me, giving me a hug that pressed the guitar painfully against my torso and threatened to end one of my favorite pastimes: breathing. When he finally stepped back, he planted a kiss on my cheek and whispered, "I love you, Mom. Thanks." At the exact moment I reached out to hand the instrument to him, the balloon Jesse had been playing with suddenly popped. I jumped as though I'd been shot, releasing the guitar before Matt had it firmly in his grip.

If not for Matt's quick reaction, the guitar would have hit the pavement and probably been ruined. Lunging, he managed to get both arms under it before disaster struck. My heart still hadn't returned to normal when I backed out of the parking space, in spite of the lighthearted atmosphere.

The evening would have ended on a pleasant note, had I just kept my eyes on the road. But as I drove past the front of the restaurant, I noticed the man whose stare had rattled my nerves standing beneath the hunter green awning just outside the restaurant's front door. I knew he had been watching us the whole time. I knew, because he winked at me as I drove past.

# 3

When we left the restaurant that evening, Nick was completely energized, eager to go out and party. On the other hand, I was so tired that I wanted nothing more than to plop onto a soft bed. Yet I was certain that if I did exactly that, I still wouldn't be able to fall asleep. Every muscle in my body was screaming, aching from a long, hard day. I couldn't stop myself from wondering about the man at the restaurant. Although I desperately needed a good night's rest, I knew I'd have to unwind first.

After I changed into a robe, I softly knocked on Matt's door and walked in. Romeo hurried in front of me to jump onto the foot of the twin bed. After making three perfect circles, he nestled in for a nap. Matt was sitting on the floor, his new guitar across his lap. The television in the corner of his room was tuned to a music video channel, but the sound had been muted. "Jesse taking a shower?" I asked.

Matt nodded.

"Got a minute?"

"Sure." Stroking the neck of the guitar, he grinned and said, "Thanks again, Mom."

"Are you absolutely certain you like it? The salesman said that if you didn't, you could come by any time and exchange it. He said all guitars have a different feel and that you'd probably want to come pick out your own."

"No. It's perfect." He strummed a few chords of his favorite song.

I smiled and tapped at one of the balloons left floating near the ceiling. "What happened here?"

"Jesse and I were using them."

I sighed. "You know, sucking helium can't possibly be good for you."

He playfully scrunched his nose. "No, but it sure is fun."

With a motherly glower, I warned, "I know, but you've had enough fun for one day. What did you think about dinner?"

"It was great. Those stories you and Nick told about the FBI training academy were cool."

"Did you have a good birthday?" He nodded as I slumped onto the floor at his side and added, "I know you hate it, but you have to write thank-you notes to your grandparents, Nick, and Jesse."

"Couldn't I just E-mail them?"

"Nope. Old-fashioned, handwritten. First thing in the morning. Promise?"

Another nod, topped with a groan. Our eyes met as he replied, "Must've been a tough day. You look really wiped out."

"That's putting it mildly." I hated to worry Matt, but I knew the chances were good that he would hear about our latest call on the news or read about it in the morning paper. "The Vest Bomber kept me busy this morning, then we went to Topeka to brief the powers that be about the status of the investigation."

"Was it the same?"

I knew he meant the vest. At times like this, I regretted our agreement to always be honest. "No. More complicated. But it still wasn't an actual bomb."

He looked me straight in the eye as he predicted, "It will be next time."

"Unfortunately, I think you're right."

Leaning close, his shoulder touched mine. "You can handle it, Mom. You know your stuff."

"I'll do my best." I sighed, suddenly remembering the gifts from David and feeling instantly revitalized. "You know the package that came this morning?"

Matt nodded. "I was almost afraid to open the door.

It's June, and the guy was wearing a long black coat. Kinda freaked me out. What was it?"

"It was from David." I jumped up, glad the weight of the world had momentarily shifted to someone else's shoulders. "I'll be right back." Trotting downstairs, I retrieved the box and showed him the scarf. "It's gorgeous, isn't it?"

Matt held it, flipped it over to study the precise stitching, then took a long whiff of its unusual scent. "David has good taste," he declared with a grin.

"Wait till you see what else he sent!" Taking his hand in mine, I poured the diamond onto his palm.

Matt carefully raised the sparkling jewel, examining it as if he actually knew a high-quality diamond from a worthless piece of glass. "It's awesome," he declared.

I saw the gleam in his eye as he looked around his room, his gaze stopping on an old glass on his nightstand. Having seen that look a million times as he grew up, I knew exactly what Matt was thinking.

"Can I?" he asked with a sheepish grin.

"Sure. Just don't cut yourself."

Grabbing the glass, he dragged the cut edge of the diamond along the smooth surface. I think we were both equally amazed to see the thin trail the stone left as it easily glided along. Clearly excited, Matt announced, "I can't believe that actually worked! I always thought it was just an old wives' tale. Guess David's diamond is for real."

"I never doubted it for a minute," I professed, although in truth, it had crossed my mind that jewels bought in an open market might be like taking in a stray dog. Both could have spectacular traits without a pedigree, but there was always the risk that you might be unpleasantly surprised.

After handing me the diamond, Matt grabbed his guitar

and asked, "Mom, do you think you and David will get married someday?"

I shrugged. "It's possible. You like David, don't you?"

"Yeah, he's okay. But . . ."

"But what?"

He hesitated, as if on the verge of opening Pandora's box. "I want you to be happy, but I really don't want to move to Russia, or Hungary, or any of those other countries over there. I like Kansas."

I laughed. "We're not moving. Where did you get such a crazy idea?"

"I thought David really liked his job."

"He does, but it won't last forever."

"What if it does?"

I didn't want to admit that I'd been wondering the same thing, especially since reading his last letter. Using one of my grandmother's favorite put-offs, I replied, "We'll cross that bridge when we come to it."

"Okay. But I don't think David will ever be happy living in Kansas again. The last time I talked to him he sounded really, well, *different*."

"Different in what way?"

"I don't know, just not like a regular guy anymore."

Deep down, I knew he was probably right. David was experiencing new cultures on a daily basis while we worried about whether to go to McDonald's or Burger King for dinner. Curling my arm around Matt's shoulder, I asked, "When did you become such an expert on relationships?"

"I didn't. Nick mentioned it once. It was no big deal."

I stiffened. "What exactly did he mention?"

"That he didn't want to lose you. He says you're the best bomb tech he's ever had."

My anger was instantly defused, yet I couldn't help but

wonder if Nick was jealous of David or simply protecting his interest in the squad. Reaching into my pocket, I squeezed the tiny silk bag with one hand and took Matt's hand in the other.

# four

## 1

The sound of my beeper invaded my dreams and pulled me from sleep only to find Romeo's cold nose against my cheek. Pushing him aside, I rubbed my eyes and groaned. Still half asleep, I read the digital screen of my pager. Too tired to enunciate, I slogged out of bed as every cuss-word I had ever heard ran in circles around my brain. I looked at the clock long enough for three-thirty-five A.M. to sink in, then snatched the phone to dial the number on the display.

My voice was barely a croak. "Sergeant Stone."

"Sorry to wake you, but there was an explosion in a garage. As far as we know, there was one fatality. It's a mess."

Thankfully, my blood had started pumping, and my mind was rapidly clearing. "Address?" I jotted it on the pad I kept by my bed just for such occasions and ripped off the page. "Don't let anyone set foot inside. Have the fire department and an ambulance respond and hold at three hundred feet. Evacuate the houses within that boundary."

"Yes, ma'am."

I glanced at the clock again. "Sergeant Terrell's house is on the way. I'll swing by and pick him up. We'll be responding with the bomb truck, so ask the first-response officers to keep the access road clear. Remember, no one goes near that garage until it's been swept for bombs."

"Yes, ma'am."

As I began to dress, I dialed Nick's phone number. I actually stared at the receiver in disbelief when I got a busy signal. Assuming he was trying to call me, I hung up. After jotting a note for Matt, Romeo and I were on our way. From the description of the scene, I doubted if Romeo would get much of a workout. Once a bomb has detonated, the scent that Romeo is trained to find is dispersed throughout the area. Even so, there have been times when we've used him to check for other devices in the vicinity. The scum of the earth who build meth labs have been known to booby-trap practically every door and window in a house. To make the drugs that pollute our society, they crawl in and out the one window that is safe. Without Romeo, getting inside could be a nightmare.

Since I'm a died-in-the-wool morning person, I'm always surprised that there are people driving around at such an insufferable hour. Wondering why I still hadn't heard from Nick, I called him again. Busy. Next I tried his cell phone, but after four rings, his voice mail picked up.

Frustrated, I sped up, even though there was really no hurry. I knew from the description of the scene that the victim was beyond our help and that our primary job would be to find out how he or she ended up that way.

Whipping onto Nick's street, I slowed to a snail's pace, unable to believe my eyes. In the driveway beside his Suburban was a fire engine red Miata. As I parked behind it, my headlights illuminated a Kansas Central University faculty parking sticker on the lower corner of the back windshield. A wave of emotions rolled over me as I stormed up the sidewalk. I was about to see exactly how strong Nick's front door was by testing it with my boot when I caught a glimpse of light through the window. Feeling quite voyeuristic, I glanced inside. From the trail of clothes strewn on the floor it was more than obvious that Nick was happily preoccupied.

"Some first date!" I muttered, then slowly turned and walked back to my Suburban. To Romeo I seethed, "Your buddy, Nick, got a better offer. Looks like we're on our own this time."

Using every ounce of self-control, I forced the idea of Nick and the bimbo going at it out of my mind. Being distracted is the last thing a hazardous-device tech needs. I cranked up the radio, losing myself in the music until I pulled up next to the red-and-white bomb truck at the KSP Training Center and parked near its special enclosure. Since the bomb truck has a refrigerator, two air conditioners, a cell phone, several rechargeable flashlights, and numerous other pieces of equipment that require electricity, whenever the truck isn't in use, we keep it charging.

Still hitched to the truck was the total containment vessel. Unlocking the door, I climbed inside and deactivated the unit's alarm system. After running through a brief checklist, I stepped out to disconnect the power cord from the back of the truck, then called Romeo. Since Nick lives closer to the training center, under normal circumstances he would have driven the truck, and I would have responded directly to the scene in my Suburban. I was beginning to realize that there was nothing normal about that morning.

Although the bomb truck is equipped with emergency lights and sirens, techs rarely use them since traveling above the speed limit is not an option. With the TCV in tow, maneuvering the oversized vehicle is not the easiest thing I've ever done, even at normal speeds. As we drove, I noticed that Romeo seemed nervous, and I wondered if he realized that this was one of the few times I'd ever driven the bomb truck, much less worked a scene by myself. More likely, he sensed that I was unsettled, and he was reflecting my dark mood. That thought made my anger start to rise again, and I was glad when I could see the strobe lights of the emergency vehicles waiting at the site.

After parking the bomb truck in the street in front of the damaged house, I was greeted by the supervising sergeant. I thanked him for maintaining the perimeter and asked if he could position a few squad cars where their headlights would fully illuminate the area. With a pair of high-powered binoculars I retrieved from my jump bag, I scanned what was left of the garage as the cars moved into place. In a matter of moments, the blast site was well lit, and I had a good idea what I'd be up against. Rushing back to the truck, I exchanged the binoculars for a video camera.

Without entering the garage, I slowly panned the area, then began to zoom in on different sectors. Not only would the videotape become evidence, but as I worked I was looking for the cleanest path to take in. The upward force of the blast had collapsed the ceiling over the garage, spilling boxes, tools, and a wide assortment of junk from the attic onto the floor. With a small degree of irritation, I noticed a partial bloody footprint on the concrete floor. Since I strongly doubted that anyone had survived the blast, I had a pretty good idea whose track it might be.

The large amount of debris prevented me from using the preferred method to check for secondary devices: the robot. Equipped with a camera, it can crawl over things the size of a curb to give us an up close, impersonal look around. But in a case like this with so much debris on the floor, the robot wouldn't be able to maneuver enough to do much good. My only alternative was to check for apparent secondaries wearing the bomb suit.

Since it was already obvious to me from assessing the damage that we weren't dealing with an accidental explosion like a gas leak, I notified ATF, then tracked down the supervising sergeant to ask, "Where's the first-response officer?"

He pointed to a young man, probably fresh out of the police academy, sitting inside a squad car working on his written report. Approaching him, I introduced myself, then asked, "Did you enter the garage?"

After a sheepish nod, he fought to speak in a steady voice. "His mother was hysterical. She thought he might still be alive."

All the training in the universe can't prepare an officer for a real bombing site, or a fatal car wreck for that matter. Dealing with death is something we all have to learn, and when the victim is young, it's even harder. For some, coping seems to come relatively easy. Others have nightmares, their subconscious unable to keep the door closed on the gruesome images they've encountered. The grisliest scenes often bring out extremes in those of us who must work with life's worst tragedies: Some turn inward and hardly speak a word; others cope with humor. Both are natural defenses that people use to survive.

The scent of blood and gunpowder is something one can never forget. I remembered all too well the first blast victim

I had ever seen, and I knew from personal experience exactly how hard the macho big bad cop facade was to maintain when you're fighting to keep from tossing your cookies. "It's okay. Just tell me exactly what you did."

"I walked in. . . . Shined my flashlight on him lying there. Jesus. He was only fourteen. . . . Couldn't take his pulse 'cause his . . . 'cause both his hands were gone and his neck was . . . Well, you know, you saw him. . . . Then I came straight back out in the same steps I'd taken in."

I took a deep breath, thinking *ran out* was probably a more accurate description. "Did you step on anything?"

"Some stuff that had fallen from the attic."

I squatted so I could face him eye to eye as I sternly warned, "If you're ever on a nine-one-one Unknown Trouble call like this again, do *not* endanger your life by entering the scene of an explosion before it has been swept for secondaries. Understand? You could easily be lying there next to him."

He nodded.

More often than not, people who are building bombs have several on hand. The detonation of one device does not guarantee that they all have been destroyed. In fact, we frequently find unexploded devices hidden in strange places. Man's fascination with destruction seems to have no end.

I looked at my watch and pushed aside the tempting idea to send a squad car over to rouse Nick. I was pissed, but not enough to humiliate him in front of his peers or get him in trouble, even though trying to handle this site alone was going to be quite a challenge.

There are many good reasons why bomb techs work in pairs. One of the best is that it's impossible to put on the protective bomb suit alone. As far as I know, there isn't a hazardous device tech alive who relishes time in the suit. It's heavy, hot, and makes you feel as though you're about to be crushed alive. The drab green outer fabric covers layers of Kevlar, the same material used in bulletproof vests and ceramic woven plates. An assortment of buckles, straps, and Velcro flaps keep the pants and jacket nice and snug. Whoever dubbed the thing a suit must have had a sense of humor. With it on, a tech resembles an alien in an old black-and-white movie: stiff-limbed, slow-moving, a blob monster that a turtle with a limp could outpace in a long-distance race.

Still fuming, I climbed into the bomb truck to start the process by putting on a layer of hazmat blue paperlike biological protective gear. The video sweep had confirmed what I expected: The site was splattered with blood and would have to be treated as a biohazard area. Contracting AIDS and other deadly diseases is another risk we would all love to live without, but the prospects of that happening anytime soon seemed slim to none.

While I was assembling the supplies and equipment I expected to need on the street outside the truck, I saw Simon Stanley pull up. I was instantly relieved to see that Frank Nichols wasn't with him. He was definitely not an agent I'd want to cope with unless Nick was around to act as a buffer.

Simon's voice was gruff as he asked, "Where's Terrell?"

I lied, "He had to go get more X-ray film from headquarters. He'll be here in a few minutes. Are you working this one alone?"

He nodded.

"Could you do me a favor? Until Nick gets back, would you mind lending me a hand?"

With a tired shrug, he agreed, "Just tell me what you need."

"Thanks." Even though Simon had been an ATF agent for years and had worked dozens of bomb sites, it still took three times as long as normal to suit up, since I had to keep explaining every step of the process. The suit is actually composed of several pieces that overlap. First, I put on the leg portion by sliding my feet into the built-in boots, then tugging the suspenders over my shoulders. The lower leg of the suit breaks at a plate at the knee, overlapping the thigh panels to allow maneuverability. Simon zipped the legs up from behind as I closed the wide band of Velcro snugly around my waist. Since I was going into a biohazard area, I had Simon use duct tape to fasten oversized trash bags over the feet and lower legs of the suit. It's not the most professional look in the world, but it keeps the boots of the suit from being contaminated by blood from the scene.

Next, I put on the helmet and fastened the chin strap as Simon hefted the jacket so I could stuff my right arm inside the bulky material. As he wrapped it around my back, I twisted to find the left armhole and ease the heavy coat onto my shoulders. The back of the suit's jacket has thick ribs that will bend forward but not backward, to protect the tech's spine from snapping if they're hurled away from the impact of an explosion.

This is the point where I always begin to feel my heart rate climb. My shoulder muscles immediately start to twitch as if they know the worst is yet to come. "Next are the armor plates," I explained, and Simon slid the heavy panels into their appropriate pockets. Since I already had the helmet on, I couldn't see much of the suit, but I knew something wasn't right. After thinking for a moment, I added, "Fold up the neck guard." The flaps that enclose the base of the helmet keep shrapnel from hitting a tech's neck, an extremely vulnerable area due to the carotid artery and windpipe. "Is the air line secure?"

Simon answered, "Looks good to me."

"Power pack in place?"

"You're in good shape."

I had on everything except the face shield, which we always leave off until the last moment. Suddenly, I remembered that I had left the secure com headset on the counter in the bomb truck. The communication link inside the helmet was already in my pocket and set to be voice activated, but I didn't relish having to train Simon to do that, too. I quickly decided to go ahead with no one on site listening, even though if I needed help, my only choice would be to back out, use hand signals, or hope Simon could hear me through the amplified sound system in the suit. Through gritted teeth, I asked Simon to bring the paramedics and the fire department's incident commander to my location.

With a smile and a nod, I quickly introduced myself to the three men and said, "If there is a secondary explosion while I'm in there and I am incapacitated, you are to *only* walk in the exact path I followed prior to the blast, then drag me out along that same route. Even an inch variance could be hazardous. Everyone understand?"

They all solemnly nodded. Like being ten months pregnant with sextuplets, looking down at my feet was impossible. The suit has two T-handle fast-escape pulls: one hangs over the left shoulder and rests near the tech's heart, the other wraps around on the right side by the lower rib cage. I did my best with my limited mobility to touch them as I explained, "If I'm injured, you can get me out of this quickly by giving these a hard jerk. It isn't easy, but it does work, and the suit will fall away."

I was already starting to sweat, so I turned back to Simon and asked, "Could you help me with the face shield?"

"Sure thing."

The instant he snapped on the shield, I was thrown into the unnatural world very few people can completely understand. Like wearing a spacesuit, the helmet limits the tech's line of sight from about ten to two, if looking straight ahead is considered high noon. Breathing is always tough in the suit, made worse by the fact that the air system goes off-line at unpredictable intervals. Although you don't suffocate, it's like dealing with an intermittent case of hiccups: disconcerting and irritating at a time when not being focused could get you blown to smithereens.

When the suit's power shuts down, the helmet begins to fog, making each breath a struggle. Sometimes fooling around with the power pack helps, sometimes it doesn't. Having a partner nearby is a relief, since he or she can adjust the unit's wires or give it a good, hard rap. As I started to slowly turn toward the scene, I said a silent prayer that, for once, the power system would stay online.

Only the tips of my fingers protruded from the sleeves, so I reached down with my right hand and pushed the red button on my side. The button kicks in what we call the turbo air, which blows a stream of air through two vents on each side of the face shield. Turbo air keeps the shield from fogging, but its hissing noise makes me feel even more detached from the rest of the world.

Even with my limited visibility I could see the various emergency personnel inch slowly backward. Out of the corner of my eye, I caught a glimpse of Carl Johnson. Or at least, I thought it was Carl Johnson. The hair on the nape of my neck instantly crawled. When I instinctively whipped my head back to find him again, all I could see was the black inside of the helmet. To actually see the exact spot where I thought he had been, I had to shift my entire body to the side, which I did. By then, no one was there.

Turning back toward the scene, I inhaled a deep breath

of turbo air. A shiver slithered down my spine, even though I was already perspiring from the distinct blend of fear, dread, and determination being in the suit always gives me.

With trepidation, I took my first step into a real-life nightmare.

# 2

I've always thought of experience as life's little learning curve. Do something enough, and sooner or later the positive reinforcement will make you more at ease. Yet each time I put on the bomb suit, the same thing happens. My pulse races, my chest tightens. The adrenaline rush is so intense that the tips of my fingers tingle. I suspect it's similar to the feeling Houdini experienced whenever they wrapped him in chains and lowered him headfirst into a pool of cold, dark water. Like him, I knew the tricks of the trade, but I was also painfully aware that one wrong move could cost me my life.

Twenty minutes into the sweep I discovered what I thought was another device. Like everything that morning, it created a problem. The torso of the boy's body was lying atop what I suspected might be another pipe bomb, probably identical to the one he had apparently discharged before completing. There was no way to be sure without moving the body.

To add insult to injury, my face mask began to fog. I instantly knew that the air system was failing. Slowly reaching behind me, I tried to adjust the unit, and when that didn't work, I decided to give it a good solid whack. Moving to a clear area near where I'd been working, I rammed the wall with my helmet and shoulder where the power line runs. Still no air. I was about to try one more time when I heard, "Sorry, Jamie. I see the suit's light is out again. Be right with you."

Like a welcome breeze on a hot day, the sound of Nick's voice instantly calmed me. I opened my eyes but could still see only fog. Whenever the system goes off-line because of a short in the wires, the light over the protective shield on the helmet loses power as well. I struggled to breathe as I replied, "Air's off. . . . Path's clear to this point. . . . Watch your step. . . . Blood's very slippery. . . . Bring some rope. . . ."

"Hold on. I'll be right in."

I tried to relax, to use as little oxygen as possible. In a few moments I felt the reassuring grip of his hand on my shoulder as he said, "I'm here. Brace yourself."

After a few seconds of jiggling and tugging on wires, the suit came back on-line. I was enjoying the first breaths of fresh air as he asked, "What's the rope for?"

"Apparent pipe bomb under the victim's upper thigh. I'll tie the rope around his lower leg. We'll have to move him off of it by pulling from outside. It shouldn't be too hard. He doesn't look like he weighs much." I was doing my best to keep from imagining Matt lying there, blown to bits, and I was thankful to have Nick to keep me focused.

"Spot anything else?"

"Yes. The west workbench appears to have another pipe bomb, plus the supplies—powder, pipe, and end caps—to build a few more."

I had slowly turned to face him, glad the fog between me and the world was finally lifting. Even in full hazmat gear, Nick's eyes conveyed the depth of his guilt, and for an instant I actually felt sorry for him. To be sure our stories matched, I winked as I stated, "You certainly took your time. Have trouble finding more X-ray film back at headquarters?"

He cocked his head for an instant, then understood. Touching the headset, he nodded, then replied, "Sorry it took so long. I'll explain later."

"No need. I've got a pretty good idea of what the problem was."

There was a moment of hesitation before he said, "Then let's tie that rope so we can get you out of here. Are you sure you're up to it?"

To be honest, I could think of a million things I'd rather do, but I muttered, "Of course."

After handing me the rope, Nick backed away.

The bomb suit protects virtually all of a tech's body except the hands. When we move around, we pull our hands up into the sleeves, but doing intricate things, like tying a solid knot, requires manual dexterity. As I've mentioned, moving in the suit isn't exactly easy, and getting up and down is a challenge for even the most fit of us. With great effort, I bent one knee, then the other, to crouch beside the boy's mangled body. Thin surgical gloves were the only protection my hands had as I lifted his leg just above the ankle and forced the rope around his calf. After cinching the knot, I took a deep breath and started to stand.

To my surprise, Nick must have come back in to help me. I instantly pictured the all-male crowd outside watching, smugly thinking that I needed my partner's help to stand. I'm not sure why that made me so mad, but it did. I grumbled, "Thank you, but I can do it alone."

Still lifting, he said, "I know you can. But I'm going to help you anyway."

# 3

Had a nonprofessional witnessed the treatment of the corpse, they would surely have considered us truly horrible human beings. But the truth is, if the torso of a dead person—man, woman, or child—is lying on top of a bomb that could kill someone else, it has to be moved. Period. We mean no disrespect to the recently departed soul; it's our job to be certain no one else joins him any sooner than necessary.

Since I was still in the suit, I lumbered to the end of the driveway, while Nick and Simon stretched the rope tight that I had secured on his lower leg. They positioned themselves well beyond the outer side wall of the garage. The brickwork had withstood one explosion, so there was no reason to think it couldn't handle another. All other personnel had been cleared from the area, so I watched by myself as they counted to three, then jerked the rope as hard as possible. The corpse did precisely what we had hoped: it moved over about six inches, fully exposing what appeared to be another pipe bomb.

We had two confirmed secondary devices to render safe before any further work could be done at the scene. The most prudent way to deal with a suspected bomb, especially one that could have highly unstable homemade components, is to cause its detonation in the precise spot where it is found. For many years, the main tool used by hazardous device technicians to deal with such a device would have been a type of disrupter, like a water cannon that could be fired by the robot, if necessary. A water cannon shoots a precise, extremely forceful, narrow stream of water to disable the bomb. Our squad still has one, but we prefer to use the PAN disrupter whenever possible, since it has a wider range of firepower and offers more safety precautions.

As with so many of the tools of our trade, the PAN, which stands for percussion-actuated non-electric, was born out of tragedy. During a bomb training school, a tech was killed when one of the older model disrupters was accidentally discharged by static electricity caused by an unforeseen combination of dry winter weather and friction. In response to the need for a device that could be safely utilized in any weather, the FBI commissioned a lab to develop the PAN to eliminate the danger of such unexpected firings.

The weapon is stored in an oversized, rugged briefcase lined with foam that molds to each part. Once assembled, it resembles a souped-up shotgun sitting on a tripod. The barrel appears similar to that of a twelve-gauge shotgun, except that the bore (the inside of the barrel) is so highly polished that it looks like a mirror. Although the back end of the barrel is the size of a Kennedy half-dollar, it narrows to the width of a quarter in the front.

The PAN can shoot about twenty different types of ammunition with extreme power. We chose an AVON round, which is made of plaster of Paris mixed with fine shot like graphite powder. AVON rounds will destroy a target without damaging the surroundings. It does this by releasing all its energy on the target, then poofing into a harmless cloud of dust. AVON rounds don't ricochet, so there is no need to set up sandbags behind the target, a job every bomb tech used to dread.

Since I was in the suit, Nick loaded the PAN and handed it to me to carry back into the garage. Following procedure, the moment he put it in my hands he declared, "Go, on hot." His words verified that the non-electric firing tube had been connected, and the PAN was ready to be fired as soon as it was in place next to the target. The safety advantage lies in the fact that static electricity cannot cause an accidental discharge of the unit. Only special firing tools connected at each end of the non-electric tube will cause the PAN to fire.

As I moved toward the garage, Nick stayed near the bomb truck, uncoiling the tubing from a spool in my wake. Slightly larger than the diameter of a pencil lead, non-electric tubing is made from a hard plastic called shock tube. A bright yellow green, it's more flexible than a straw and extremely lightweight. The inside of the tube is finely coated with micrograins of explosive. When the PAN is in place and ready to be fired, the tubing is cut at a safe distance and ignited. The chain reaction of the explosive inside the tube travels at the speed of lightning to discharge the PAN.

In spite of all the safety precautions, we still treat the PAN as a deadly weapon. As I moved, I made certain it was never pointed at a person. Like trailing a thin rope, the non-el snaked along the ground in my tracks. When I was back inside the garage, I secured the PAN on its tripod, then pinpointed the pipe bomb in the red dot emitted by the laser sight.

Returning to Nick's side, he helped me take the face shield off so I could enjoy a few minutes of fresh air. As always, I took a deep breath and instantly felt better. Handing me the Scorpion igniter, he positioned himself to videotape the explosion, and on the count of three, I fired the PAN. Even after all these years, I still flinch at the cracking sound the disrupter makes. So much force is released so quickly that the weapon bucks high in the air from the recoil, a shiny metal gymnast doing a back flip for its finale.

As soon as the dust settled, Nick helped me put the face shield back on, and we repeated the entire procedure again on the second device. By the time we finished, I felt like I'd run an ultramarathon.

While Nick freed me from the bomb suit, Simon brought us up to date on the progress of the investigation that had been taking place while we worked. The boy's hysterical mother had settled down enough to tell the officers that her son had been quiet and withdrawn lately, but she hadn't given his actions much thought since she remembered her older son going through similar moody periods. Cash receipts were found in the victim's bedroom for the crude supplies he had purchased. Although no handwritten notes were found, the computer's log of sent E-mail revealed that he had recently told a friend that it would be cool to "blow up" things with pipe bombs, and that he'd learned "everything he needed to know" on the Internet.

Long before we returned to headquarters, I had decided that I was far too tired to work my normal shift. Being a single mother, I did all I could to make ends meet. When I work a bomb call, I can still report for my regular duty and collect overtime pay for the extra hours. I always try to stash my bonus pay in the savings account I've set aside for Matt's education, but last month, I used it to buy his birthday guitar. Even though I felt guilty about not working the rest of the day, I knew it was for the best.

By the time Nick and I were finally alone, it was almost noon. The tension was so thick in our small office that you could practically feel the air pulsing. I had no intention of bringing up the subject of Nick's late-night escapade. All I wanted was to finish my paperwork and go home to spend some time with Matt. I had just ejected the last diskette from the machine when Nick stood and closed the door.

"Thanks for covering for me," he muttered.

"You would've done the same for me."

A curt nod was his reply.

I suppressed a yawn. "Oh, yeah. I almost forgot. I was pretty freaked out right after I put on the suit. I would've sworn I saw Carl Johnson hanging back in the shadows."

"Really?"

"I'm not sure. By the time I turned so I could see out of the visor, whoever it was had disappeared."

Nick suddenly became defensive. "And if I'd have been there, I could've checked to see if it was really him. Nothing like having a derelict partner. I'm sure working with Stanley was a real treat, too."

"I didn't say that."

"But you were thinking it."

I stood, tossing the diskettes onto his desk. Infuriated, I warned, "Listen, we're both tired. Just back off and let this blow over. Okay, Nick?"

The cool tone of his voice matched the intensity of the emotions pulsing through me as he taunted, "No. Go ahead, get pissed. It'll do you good."

"What's that supposed to mean?" I fumed.

"It means that maybe if you got some, you wouldn't have such a stiff-lipped, bitchy attitude toward the world."

Absolutely furious, I growled, "Let me know when the head *on top of your shoulders* starts thinking for you again. I'm already fed up with the one *in your pants* calling the shots."

"And I'm fed up, too. You're so damn insecure you wouldn't even let me help you stand back up in the bomb suit. If you had fallen forward, you might've found out exactly how much protection that suit offers."

"You had no business inside that area without a suit on, and you know it. Besides, where were you when I slipped and practically did a spread eagle? Screwing your brains out, that's where!"

"What I do on my time off is none of your damn business! Last night happened. I'm not necessarily proud of it, but I'm not ashamed of it, either. I'm single now, Jamie. Get used to it. I finally have, and I like it."

I grabbed my clipboard and briefcase and motioned for Romeo to come as I added, "I'm out for the afternoon. Who knows? Maybe I'll get laid and come back all giggles and smiles."

I ignored his glare as I rushed out the door and pulled it quickly closed, forcing myself to walk to my Suburban as if nothing were wrong. I know it was my imagination, but every trooper I passed seemed to have a smirk on his face. At that moment, Romeo and Matt were the only two males I didn't suspect of being testosterone-laden assholes.

Determined to have a nice afternoon with Matt, I made it home in record time only to find another note on the kitchen counter.

*Mom—*
> *Waited all morning. I tried to call to be sure it was okay if I went to a movie with Jesse, but I got your voice mail. Hope you don't mind. Be home around 6:00. Don't worry about me for dinner.*

> *Love, Matt*

"Good," I said and meant it. With a sigh, I ruffled the fur on the back of Romeo's neck and tiredly remarked, "Come on boy, let's go take a nap."

# 4

I was amazed that just seconds after I closed my eyes I immediately fell into a deep, dreamless sleep, the kind where you wake up certain that a couple of minutes have passed only to find that you've been out for several hours.

Since the day we brought Romeo into our home four years ago, he's always felt it was his duty to double as a guard dog. True to nature, he faithfully started barking the minute Matt returned. I stretched and rolled off the couch, feeling more rested than I had in days.

Matt excitedly reported every detail of the latest Harrison Ford movie, one I was dying to see, right up to the final twist. I tried to listen, knowing full well I would never take the time to go see it by myself, but my mind kept wandering. Glancing at his long, lean body I noticed for the first time that his ankles and calves had grown thick and muscular like those of a man. By the time he was in the first grade, Matt had been taller than his peers, but up until that day, I'd always seen him as a child. I could hardly believe he would soon be grown and off on his own. The thought of how empty my life would be without him was hard to bear.

When he finished recounting the movie's complicated plot, I cast him a wide smile and ruffled his short, blond hair. "I'm glad you went. I really needed a nap."

"We had the best time! There were these two hot girls a couple of rows in front of us. They kept giggling and looking back, then we talked to them after the movie. Later, we all met at the food court and had wild, crazy sex during their discount orgy hour."

*Hot girls. Maybe he's spending too much time around Nick,* I thought and instantly felt guilty. Nick had never been anything less than wonderful to Matt, even if he hadn't used the best judgment on his date last night. I still couldn't believe he'd sleep with a stranger on the first date.

For a few seconds, the room fell silent. Then Matt asked, "Is something wrong?"

I shrugged. "Why do you ask?"

"I just told you that there was a discount orgy hour at the mall, and you didn't even bat an eye. Besides, you've got that *don't mess with me* look."

"I thought I always had that look. It's a trooper's trademark."

"Well, you're definitely not like most moms. I had to

kill a spider in the bathtub for Jesse's mother yesterday. It was just a daddy longlegs. You'd have thought it was a tarantula."

"Bombs and bugs are completely different. As long as you're under my roof, you're in charge of all bug removal." As he rolled his eyes, my mind flashed a mental image of a fifties mom clad in a housedress with an apron, happily baking every afternoon. "Okay, I'll admit I'm not Betty Crocker. I'm sorry if I embarrass you."

"You've been so busy lately. I thought we'd get to spend more time together this summer."

"I'm really sorry. I'll ask Nick if I can take a couple of days off next week. Besides, we both know that bomb calls always seem to come in spurts. Maybe this streak will end soon."

"A couple of my friends asked about the Vest Bomber. They think he's a real nutcase."

"I always knew you hung around with a bunch of smart guys. The problem with the Vest Bomber isn't that he's nuts, it's that he's very bright *and* nuts."

"Which means?"

"Think about it. The world is full of people who are a brick short of a full load. Nine times out of ten, they aren't the ones who end up hurting people. It's the highly intelligent ones, the ones who are capable of plotting complicated schemes yet have no moral soul, who usually harm society the most."

"Like Hitler?"

I nodded. "There are lots of others like him running around. People who think their way is the only right way and who'll go to any extreme to force their beliefs on others." The thought of Carl Johnson's tie to the militia popped to mind, but I didn't want to worry Matt any more than necessary. Pushing down that idea, I continued, "Take the bomb call this morning. We found evidence

that a boy your age was making pipe bombs from recipes
he found on the Internet. If he had stopped after building
the first two bombs, he might still be alive. But for some
reason he decided to build *one more*. It was a fatal mistake."

"Or divine intervention," Matt declared.

"Possibly, but he was just a kid. It's such a waste."

"Mom, *normal* kids don't build bombs for fun."

"True. But maybe every kid doesn't get a chance to
just be normal. We'll probably never know what made
him think he needed to do such things. Maybe it was a
cry for attention." I squeezed his hand. "You'll talk to me
if anything starts to bother you, right?"

"Of course. Don't worry. I'm not going to whack out
on you."

"Whack out?"

"You know, go bonkers. And if I do decide to crack
up, I promise you'll be the first to know."

I couldn't help but laugh and be thankful that we finally
had the chance to spend a quiet evening at home.

# five

## 1

By the time I returned to my office, two days had passed. I was dreading another confrontation with Nick, but one glance around the room told me he hadn't been in for a while either. Like most of us, Nick was a creature of habit. Every day before he left, he carefully cleaned off his desk, arranging his work in neat, orderly piles. Within five minutes of his arrival, his desk always looked like a miniature tornado had hit it. The moment I saw those wonderful stacks, I sighed, secretly hoping he had taken another day off since we weren't on call.

As usual, Romeo orbited his bed before plopping down for a nap. I could only imagine what it must be like to sleep all night, then on and off all day. Watching him snooze always makes me wonder if dogs are just very laid back, or bored out of their minds. For once I wasn't jealous, since I'd slept like a rock for two nights in a row.

I'd knocked off my morning run in record time, a sure sign that I was well rested. In fact, I was eager to get caught up on my work and put the trouble with Nick behind me once and for all.

The pile of papers in my in box had grown in the last few days, so I attacked it with a vengeance. After finishing most of the work, I decided to take a break and call the victims of the Vest Bomber. I left messages for the first two, and was told by the Jasper's Jewelers new store manager that I should contact Anne at home.

On the second ring there was a weak, "Hello."

"This is Sergeant Jamie Stone with the KSP Hazardous Device Unit. Is Anne home?" I asked.

The reply was a weak, "Yes. This is Anne."

"If you have a minute, I'd like to ask you a couple of questions."

There was a slight hesitation before Anne quietly replied, "Okay. Is everything all right?"

"Absolutely. I'm just doing some follow-up work on the robbery." It was almost eleven in the morning, but she sounded so tired that I added, "If you were asleep, I could call back later."

"No, no . . . now is fine."

Worried, I asked, "Would you prefer I come over and we discuss this in person?"

"No need. How may I help you?"

"I was wondering about the kidnapper's voice. Do you remember what he sounded like? Did he have an accent?"

Silence.

"Anne?"

"I . . . I'm sorry. I'm under a doctor's care and the medication keeps me pretty out of it. What was it that you needed to know?"

I asked again, and she mumbled something unintelligible. Drawing a deep breath, I was certain she wouldn't

be able to help in the state she was in, and even if she
did, the information she provided might not be reliable.
Trying not to sound disappointed, I cheerfully said, "I just
wanted to be sure you were doing all right, Anne. If you
think of anything else about the robbery, would you
please give me a call?"

"Sure."

"Then take care."

"Jamie?"

"Yes?"

She softly said, "Thank you again for all you did for
me. The doctor told me to try to think of good things
instead of dwelling on . . . well, what happened. I just
want you to know that I'll never forget the feeling I had
when I looked into your eyes. Clear, confident, certain
that everything was going to be okay. Bless you."

"I'm glad I was there to help, and you're more than
welcome. Have a good day." I hung up, warmed by her
words. Sometimes it's easy to forget why I chose this job,
then I get the chance to help someone like Anne.

All too soon, the feeling of pride faded into a nagging
worry. Considering how well everything had turned out,
I didn't like the idea that Anne was having such a hard
time coping. I knew that victims of violent crimes often
suffer long-term mental anguish, but I hadn't expected
Anne to fall into that category. I sincerely hoped that she
didn't have one of those doctors who thought sleeping
pills were the answer to life's problems.

Catching movement out of the corner of my eye, I realized Romeo had lifted his head and was looking toward
the door with his ears perked. A few seconds later, Nick
appeared, and Romeo softly chuffed to greet him.

As Nick slid into his chair, I couldn't help but notice
that his uniform was the only thing about him that looked
crisp and clean. Besides circles under his eyes, he badly

needed a shave. "You look exhausted," I commented. Trying to break the ice, I added, "How are things going with the professor?"

He cracked a tired smile. "Alexa *is* special. I can't believe I was lucky enough to find her."

"Just remember, you have to sleep sometime. Staying up all night and working all day is okay for college kids, but for us old fogies . . ."

"No kidding. Listen, I'm sorry I was so late the other day to the garage bombing. I'll try my best not to ever let it happen again."

"I know."

"Then stop looking at me like that."

I shook my head, wishing he had gotten some rest. "Like *what?*"

Rubbing his hand across his face, he grabbed a report and leaned back to read it as he muttered, "Never mind."

"If I look frustrated, it's because I am. I just got off the phone with Anne White. Apparently she isn't coping very well."

"It's only been a couple of days."

"Even so, it's a couple of days she should've been enjoying life, not walking around in a stupor because some lunatic scared the holy crap out of her. Nick, we've got to catch this bastard before he hurts anyone else."

He nodded. "It's almost been long enough since the first vest for the FBI lab to have some results. Maybe they'll shed some light on who we're dealing with."

"Mind if I send a friendly E-mail to give them a little nudge?"

"Not at all."

As I waited for the computer to access the network, I asked, "What did you do last night?"

Since I expected him to say, *None of your damn business,* I was surprised when he slyly grinned and replied,

"Alexa and I caught a movie, had dinner, then went dancing. I never actually made it back home because I went on a bomb call at two A.M."

I stiffened. "But we weren't on call."

He shrugged. "Jeff and Marcus rolled on a mailbox explosion. I decided to tag along."

"Anything interesting?"

He shook his head. "Typical teen prank. I should've gotten some rest instead."

"Why *did* you go?"

"Couldn't sleep. I kept thinking about what Lieutenant Colonel Jones said about the Vest Bomber having access to our supplies. Unfortunately, he may be right. When we went to his office the other day, he asked me to double-check our level of security while we're at crime scenes, preferably without anyone knowing."

"You've got to be kidding."

Nick shook his head. "Jeff and Marcus had no idea I was there. I parked a few blocks away and walked to the scene, being careful to keep out of sight. When they were both busy, I slipped into the bomb truck and started my stopwatch."

"How long were you there before they noticed?"

"Seven minutes. More than enough time to steal something."

"But we keep the drawers and cabinets locked. They'd have to be pried open. It would be noisy; someone would hear."

"Okay, so the thief pulls the door closed before he gets started. Jimmying the locks takes an extra two minutes. There would still be five minutes to spare."

"Except you're forgetting about one important factor."

"What's that?"

"I'd bet almost every police officer in the area knows who you are. If they saw you at a crime scene, or going into the bomb truck, they'd think you were supposed to be there."

"Possibly. Even so, I'm calling a squad meeting this afternoon. Until this situation has passed, we're going to have to lock the bomb truck every time it's out of our sight or post a guard at the door while we work."

I had to admit, it wasn't a bad idea.

Impatiently tapping my fingers on the keyboard while the site loaded, I said, "The network's really slow this morning. I think I'll run down and get a Diet Coke. Want anything?"

"Coffee. Black."

"High octane?"

"Of course. Thanks."

At the end of our hall is a break room, complete with a small refrigerator, pop machine, and two coffeepots. Naturally, the pot with decaf was full, and the one for regular coffee was empty. Sometimes the little things about working in a mostly male profession make me crazy. You'd think it would kill whoever drank the last cup to start brewing a new pot.

While I waited for a fresh pot to brew, I leaned against the wall and sipped my Diet Coke. I could hear the conversation of the troopers in the squad room across the hall as I waited. At first, what they were saying didn't even register. It wasn't until I heard my name that I tensed and moved closer to do some serious eavesdropping.

"... *working with a fine piece of ass like Stone.*"

"*You must be kidding. Highway duty is dangerous enough. Only a crazy bastard would apply for a slot on the bomb squad.*"

"*Must be why Carl Johnson is talking about it. He's about as crazy as they come. Heard he was turned down when he applied for the Drug Enforcement Team last winter.*"

*"Hey, either of you catch the Royals game last night?"*

The pot of coffee had long since finished, but I hung around to be sure their conversation didn't circle back to the bomb squad. After pouring Nick a cup, I returned to our office with an undeniable chip on my shoulder.

Handing the steaming drink to him, I sharply challenged, "Is there something you'd like to tell me?"

Nick merely shot me a *what the hell are you talking about?* look and took a sip of his coffee. In response to my silent glare, he rolled his eyes and snapped, "Is this about Alexa again?"

Reflecting his level of irritation, I declared, "No!"

"We're having a great time getting to know each other. Partying, really having *fun*. Why is that such a problem for you? Never mind, I already know. . . ."

I resented his implication that I had nothing to do but spend my nights home alone. It was easy to convince myself that I didn't give a damn what he did while he was off, as long as it didn't impact me later on the job. "It's your life," I cracked.

"Nice to know you care. So, if it isn't my sex life that's the problem, what is it?"

"Are you accepting applications for a new bomb tech?"

"No. What kind of question is that? You know there aren't any openings, and the budget is set in concrete. Why?"

"I just heard Carl Johnson was going to apply for a position on our squad."

"Then someone is pulling your leg. Besides, we both know a head case like Johnson wouldn't stand a chance."

I was thoroughly confused. More to myself than to Nick, I softly asked, "Why would he think there's going to be an opening?"

Nick replied, "He said that?"

"No! *He* didn't say anything. I just overheard a couple

of guys discussing him in the squad room."

"Then they don't know what they're talking about. There aren't any positions, and I doubt that there will be any in the next three years."

I slumped into my chair. "Unless an opening is *created*."

Nick shook his head. "Jamie. Our team is strong. No one is going to resign."

"Resignations weren't what I was thinking of," I admitted, biting my lower lip.

I watched as his face fell, then turned stone cold as he grasped my point. His voice carried every ounce of his outrage as he declared, "And, damn it, no tech under my command is going to *die,* either!"

# 2

Being a bomb tech is rarely a full-time job, so virtually all hazardous device technicians in the United States are assigned other duties within their law enforcement agencies. Since I don't drive a marked patrol car, I fill in wherever the KSP feels I'm needed. The next day, the operations commander had set up a spot drug check on Interstate 70, about halfway between Kansas City and Topeka. Shortly after the morning rush hour, we created a roadblock and began pulling over every tenth car, unless someone looked or acted particularly suspicious. Although most troopers consider such assignments to be mundane, I didn't. I had once worked a spot check that resulted in a fatal high-speed chase, so I took each inspection seriously.

Since I was working my regular shift, I was in full uniform: a French blue short-sleeve shirt with midnight blue slacks that had a lighter blue stripe along the outer

seams. The large brim of my campaign hat shielded my
face from the morning sun, but it was heavy and hot.
When I accidentally caught a glimpse of my reflection in
the tinted windows of a patrol car, I had to smile. Even
after ten years as a state trooper, I guess I'll always feel
like I'm masquerading as a Canadian Mountie whenever
I have to wear my hat.

Although Romeo is primarily trained to detect bombs,
he's been cross-trained to sniff for certain narcotics. Our
job was to thoroughly check each car. All troopers realize
that being stopped for even a few minutes is a major in-
convenience, so we try to work as fast as we can. Most
of the people we inspect have the decency to be polite, a
few mutter obscenities, some spout lectures on wasted tax
dollars. Funny how the latter type always seem to take
the longest to check.

It had been a slow morning. So far, Romeo hadn't
alerted even once. I was actually relieved to see Nick's
number appear on my pager and I quickly called to ask,
"What's up?"

"Jamie, I need you to meet me at the office when you
get a few minutes."

"Hold on." Although it wasn't technically necessary, I
asked the trooper in charge if I was free to go, then replied, "I'll be there in thirty minutes. What's going on?"

"We've got some interesting lab results back."

My heart started to beat faster. "On the Vest Bomber?"

"Yes, and Lieutenant Colonel Jones is on his way to
check out our squad. See you in thirty."

As I drove into town, I ran my fingers through my hair,
trying my best to get rid of my hat-head look. I made it
to headquarters with ten minutes to spare, so I gave Romeo a break and parked on the far north edge of the lot
near a landscaped knoll. To reward him for a morning of
hard work, I took off his leash and we played with a

Frisbee for a few minutes before heading inside.

Normally, I would have gone straight back to my office, but the receptionist waved for me to stop, so I detoured to her desk. At sixty-two, Bennie Calhoun had worked for the KSP for more than thirty years. Bennie was the heart of our headquarters, the one who made us feel as though we were all part of a family. She knew every single trooper by name, and she never failed to have a smile on her face and old-fashioned starlight peppermints on her desk.

I gave Romeo the command to sit, then knelt beside him to scratch behind his ears while Bennie finished transferring a phone call. As I stood to greet her, I caught a glimpse of a person on the outskirts of the parking lot. My fingers instinctively tightened on Romeo's leash as I watched the man stop at my Suburban, then glance warily in every direction to be certain no one was coming. Unfortunately, he had on sunglasses and a baseball cap, which made it impossible for me to identify him from a distance. To my amazement, he leaned against the passenger-side window, cupping his hands near his eyes to block the glare so he could see through the tinted glass.

"Romeo, stay!" I snapped, tossing the end of the leash to Bennie as I added, "I'll be right back!" Moments like those are why I'm glad I exercise regularly. As soon as I cleared the doors, I was moving at a brisk pace, in spite of the fact that the leather soles of my regulation shoes refused to give me much traction. The man looked up and broke into a full run across the grassy area.

I screamed, "Stop! Police!" but it was obvious he had no intention of being caught. As he fled, I realized that he was the same build as the lone diner who had spooked me at Matt's birthday party. I wouldn't have believed it was possible, but I actually picked up momentum as a fresh wave of anger fueled my legs and kept my arms pumping like a track star.

Wishing I had parked closer, I reached the grassy knoll just as he disappeared behind the five-story office building adjacent to our headquarters. By the time I rounded the building's corner, he was nowhere in sight. He could have gone inside, climbed into a car, or been beamed up by Scotty for all I knew. Catching my breath, I thought about searching the area, but I knew it was futile. Even if I found him, there wasn't a thing I could do. Peeking into a car isn't a crime, nor is running from a state trooper. Fleeing any armed officer definitely isn't smart, but if we arrested everyone who did something stupid, the streets would be pretty bare.

Bennie was anxiously waiting at the door with Romeo when I walked back in. Obviously concerned, she said, "My heavens. What was that all about? Should I have called someone to back you up?"

I shook my head as I struggled to catch my breath. "No. It wasn't anything important. Besides, by the time help could have arrived, it would've been too late." Pointing at my feet, which had already started to ache, I added, "These uniforms must've been designed by someone who never left their desk. Running shoes would be much better."

"Are you sure everything is okay now?" Bennie nervously asked.

I nodded and took Romeo's leash. Hoping to make her feel better, I explained, "I saw someone looking in my Suburban. Since it has thousands of dollars of bomb squad equipment, I try to keep a close eye on it. He didn't set off the car alarm, so I'm sure he didn't take anything."

Bennie seemed satisfied with my lame excuse, and with a grin, she crossed back to her desk to pick up a box.

Handing it to me, she declared, "This was delivered for you a few minutes ago."

The package was about the size of a box of saltine crackers. It was wrapped in shimmery red paper, the kind that reflects a rainbow of colors with even the slightest motion. An equally impressive pink ribbon was looped and professionally tied to create a huge bow in the center. One strand of the ribbon was fastened to the red paper with a clear sticker. In gold cursive letters the sticker read: Jasper's Jewelers. A small floral card stuck to the side of the bow said:

> *To: Jamie Stone and Nick Terrell*
> *With heartfelt gratitude*
> *from the entire Jasper family.*

Smiling so that Bennie wouldn't think anything might be wrong, I asked, "Did you know the person who delivered this?"

She shook her head. "No. He wasn't with UPS, FedEx, or the regular mail. I know almost all of them. I'll bet he works for the jewelry store."

I thought of the man in the parking lot, trying to fix the image in my mind to remember every detail. "Any idea what he was wearing?"

Closing her eyes, she concentrated. "Jeans, maybe? To tell you the truth, there are an awful lot of people who come through the lobby every day. Unless they're someone I know, I don't guess they register very well anymore."

"Do you know if he had dark hair? Light hair? Tall? Short? Sunglasses?"

Biting her upper lip, she shook her head. "Dark, I think. Definitely had on sunglasses. Average height, I think. But I really don't know for sure. I was on the phone when he handed it to me, and he just turned around and walked out."

"Thanks, Bennie," I said and headed back to my office. Halfway there, I sat the box on the floor, walked a few feet away, and gave Romeo the command, "Find it, boy!" After casting me an *are you kidding?* look, Romeo began sniffing the carpet along the walls. When he passed the box without hesitating, I said, "Good boy!" and gave him a hug and a treat.

Nick raised a brow as I gingerly set the box on the edge of his desk. "This just came for us. Bennie didn't recognize the man who dropped it at the front desk."

Standing, he leaned close to look at it, then back at me. "You know, the Vest Bomber could've stolen Jasper's Jewelers stickers while he was making off with the diamonds."

I nodded. "That thought did cross my mind."

With a shrug, he suggested, "There's no reason to take any chances."

"I agree with that, too, but I just ran it past Romeo's trusty nose, and he couldn't have cared less about it."

"Even so, we both know there are ways to mask the scent from even the best-trained dog."

While I trusted Romeo implicitly, Nick was right. Bombs can be tightly wrapped, then packed in aromatic substances to prevent the odor from being detected. Plus, every dog can have an off day, one when he's coming down with a cold or simply isn't in the mood to be bossed around. Thankfully, Romeo rarely had those days.

Since I had to go back to the Suburban, I moved it to an open space near the front door. In less than five minutes, Nick and I had determined that the box was indeed from Anne White's father. Tucked inside were two black velvet boxes, each with the Rolex trademark embossed on the top. Nick opened the larger of the two, while I snapped up the lid of the smaller. Each contained an elegant Rolex watch, in matching his and hers styles.

Nick whistled, saying, "Hot damn! I'll bet these cost a pretty penny. Too bad we can't keep them."

Admiring the one in my hand, I joked, "It *is* a shame. There are times when being honest just doesn't pay off."

In order to maintain impartiality and prevent the appearance that someone might be accepting an illegal payoff, virtually every law enforcement organization in the United States has a rule that forbids officers from accepting gifts from grateful citizens. Romeo's water bowl had been an exception, since, technically, it was a gift to him, not me.

Nick nudged me with his shoulder. "You did do a great job with Anne. Sometimes between the paperwork and the bureaucracy, it's easy to forget why we're here."

"I just wish we had some kind of lead to follow. It's so damn frustrating just sitting around waiting to see when he's going to strike next."

Nick declared, "We're going to catch him. No one is perfect. He will make a mistake, and when he does, we'll be there."

"You said you had some test results?"

He nodded and plucked several sheets of paper off his desk. "The FBI says that all the trace evidence on the first two vests came from either the victim or one of the response team. Our bomber is being very, very cautious."

I sighed. "That doesn't surprise me. Nothing does anymore. I just ran a footrace across the parking lot trying to catch a man I spotted looking into my Suburban." Nick stopped flipping through papers, instantly devoting his entire attention to me. His inquisitive stare encouraged me to continue. "I shouted for him to stop, then chased him around the building next door. By the time I got there, he was gone."

"Did you get a good look at him?"

"Yes and no."

When I didn't immediately volunteer more information, Nick urged, "Which means?"

"This time, I only got a good look at his back. But I think it's possible it was the same man I noticed at Matt's birthday party. Roughly five eleven to six one, dark hair, muscular, square shoulders."

Nick's eyes went wide. "What man at the party? Why didn't you say something? I was there, too. We could've easily had a chat with him."

I shrugged. "There was a guy sitting in the corner. He gave me the creeps. I didn't tell you because it was just a feeling. I always try to be objective, Nick. In this day and age, acting on impulse could get the KSP sued."

"Sometimes gut reactions save lives."

"And sometimes they're a bunch of bullshit. So far, I've X-rayed two perfectly harmless packages."

"I don't care if you X-ray every box you see within ten miles of here. Until we catch the Vest Bomber, we've got to be ready for him to change the rules of this game. He may not be a typical bomber, but I'll guarantee you this: He's having a damn good time, so he has no reason to stop."

I nodded, knowing he was right but wishing he weren't. "What's the plan for entertaining Lieutenant Colonel Jones?"

Nick glanced at his watch. "The squad is assembling at the Training Center in forty-five minutes. That gives us an hour to triple-check all our supplies and make sure everything is ready before Jones arrives."

I sighed. "Any idea how he plans to conduct the inspection?"

"Not a clue. He may want us to do some test blasts for him, or he may just want to make sure all the bells and whistles are in place. No matter what he asks, I'm certain we're all up to the task."

"Let's hope so." Even though I immediately looked down, Nick didn't miss the wide grin that I found impossible to suppress.

"What's so amusing?" he asked.

"Well, think about it. Do you suppose he's given any thought to what would happen if we *flunk* his inspection? What's he gonna do, shut us down? Maybe he wants to go one-on-one against the next vest himself."

Nick smiled, apparently amused by the mental image of Lieutenant Colonel Jones trying to defeat a device. The silence was broken when my phone rang. I answered, "Sergeant Stone."

"Hey, Mom."

"Hi. What's up?"

Matt took a long breath before replying, "Promise you won't overreact?"

I shivered, not from his question, but from the tone of his voice. "Did you burn the house down?"

"Of course not."

"Any*one* or any*thing* hurt?

"Nope."

"Then I promise not to overreact." At this, Nick openly started to eavesdrop.

"Okay. Well, you know how you told me that I should be extra careful right now because of the Vest Bomber?"

The skin on my scalp started to crawl, but I managed to sound calm as I agreed, "Yes."

"When I left to jog over to Jesse's house, I noticed a van parked down our street."

"Did it follow you?"

"Yes, but I took the shortcut by the Martins' house and came in his back door. I didn't think much about it until a few minutes ago. I was up in Jesse's room, and it drove halfway up the block, then stopped a few houses down *his* street. We got out his binoculars, and there was a guy just sitting inside it, looking around, like he was waiting to see if someone was going to show up."

"Why do you think it's the same van?"

"It had ABC Plumbing signs on the side."

"Magnetic or painted?"

"Definitely magnetic. One was crooked."

"What's the guy look like?"

"Hold on."

While I waited, I could hear Matt and Jesse talking excitedly in the background, then Matt returned to report, "Sorry. He was too far away, and then he left."

"Did you get a tag number?"

"No. And this is weird. He *backed* up the street, all the way to the stop sign."

My heart started to beat faster. "Do you think he spotted you?"

"No way! We were behind the miniblinds."

I felt a little relieved, but not much. "Are you two alone?"

"No. Jesse's mom is here."

"Okay. I need to talk to her." I heard Jesse yell for his mother to pick up the extension. While I waited, I pulled the phone book out and flipped to the business pages. There was no ABC Plumbing listed in the alphabetical section or in the Yellow Pages.

Marianne Coleman is about my age, yet I suspect she'll be running circles around me long after I'm old and gray. While her three kids were still in school, she went back to college to earn a degree in psychology. Besides working full time, she spent the last year systematically renovating their home. When Marianne was born, the doctor must have set her energy level on high and broken off the control button. "Hey, Jamie! What's up?" she answered.

"Hi, Marianne. Sorry to bother you."

"Anytime. I was just wallpapering the upstairs bathroom. I saw the news last night, and I know you have your hands full dealing with everything that's going on right now. As a matter of fact, I was planning to call you today to see if Matt wanted to stay here for a while."

I sighed. Only a true friend would extend such a generous offer. "Could he? Until we catch the Vest Bomber, things might be a little dicey at our house."

"He can stay here under one condition."

"Anything. Just name it."

"That you be extra careful."

"I will, and I'd appreciate it if you'd be a little more on guard than usual, too. At this point, the Vest Bomber's next target could be anyone. Matt's a little spooked, and frankly, that's a good thing. He needs to be on his toes. If he gives you any trouble, give me a call."

"You two are family, Jamie. He'll be fine."

One day last year, I had asked Jesse's parents to be Matt's guardians if something were to happen to me. Even though we had relatives he could have gone to live with, I always felt he'd be happier staying in the same neighborhood, the same school district, until he finished high school. Yes, my parents would have gladly taken him, but they lived on a farm in the middle of nowhere. I know that some people would argue that Kansas City deserved that distinction, but compared to Perry, Oklahoma, it's a thriving metropolis. Matt and I had discussed all the options, and after the Colemans agreed, I felt a true sense of peace.

"I really appreciate your help."

Marianne laughed. "Matt is a certified sweetheart, and he's welcome to stay with us as long as he likes."

"Great. I'll bring over a few of his things after work. Thank you so much. Please tell him I'll stop by later."

"Don't put yourself out. As far as I can tell, we have as many clothes here that are Matt's as we do Jesse's.

I smiled. "Even so, I'll bring by some of his things."

"See you then."

Hanging up, I rubbed away the goose bumps on my arms as Nick asked, "What was that all about?"

"My paranoia may be contagious. Matt thinks a van tried to follow him."

Leaning forward, Nick prompted, "And?"

"And he took a shortcut so he could lose the guy. He's pretty sure whoever it was doesn't know he's at Jesse's house."

"I think having him stay there for a few days is a good idea."

I bit my lower lip. "Maybe. But we can't run away forever."

## six

**1**

The next morning, I had just started to cool down from a brisk morning run when my pager sounded. The digital clock on my nightstand declared it was a few minutes shy of seven A.M., and I instinctively sensed that the bomb unit's activation would be another hand entry call. It was becoming painfully apparent that the Vest Bomber was either an early riser or a chronic insomniac. Romeo paced and whined as I dialed the phone and exchanged my shorts and jog bra for a bulletproof vest and uniform.

My stomach tightened as the dispatcher confirmed my suspicion. When the morning shift security guard had reported for duty at The Parlor, an exclusive, upscale store that catered to those who could afford to be pampered in every way, he had found the front doors unlocked and his colleague missing. After a quick search, he discovered the night guard in a small storage room outside the store's vault, unconscious and imprisoned in a tightly fitting vest bomb. She also informed me that Nick had answered his page and was already on his way.

While buttoning my shirt, I searched for a shoe that had somehow ended up under the bed, then rushed into the hall. I don't know why, but I stopped, suddenly struck by an overwhelming urge to tell Matthew good-bye. I hesitated at the top of the stairs, then remembered that he was staying with Jesse.

Romeo and I had barely pulled out of the driveway when the radio came to life. Unless someone is already utilizing it, we prefer to use tach one for conversations before we switch to the secure com. "Good morning, Nick," I said.

"What's your ETA?"

"I'd guess about twelve minutes."

He replied, "I'll be there in ten, so I'm up. Let's use secure com two."

"Once you're at the scene, I'll monitor in transit, plus I'll notify ATF right away."

"Good."

I scrolled down the numbers stored on my cell phone and punched the one for ATF. As soon as I gave them the information and hung up, I reached into the backseat and dug my secure com headgear out of my jump bag to save time later. After switching to the right channel, I adjusted it and said, "Nick, are you there?"

He shouted, "Son of a bitch!" so loudly that I winced.

"Nick? What's wrong?"

"Damn it, Jamie, I'm getting an engine light, and I can smell antifreeze. I'm going to have to pull over and put water in the radiator."

"You could have a squad car pick you up."

"That would take too long; besides, I'll need my hand

entry kit and the rest of my gear. If I keep adding water, I should still be there pretty soon."

"Okay. Did dispatch or the first-response officer give you any other details that I need to know up front?"

"The guard who found our subject took one look at the vest and decided he should call us from outside the building."

"Did he bother to see if the man was still alive before he hightailed it?"

"He thought he was, but he didn't take the time to check for a pulse."

"Did you already instruct the first-response officer to establish the perimeter at one hundred yards?"

"Yeah. And I've got fire and ambulance responding."

"Great," I said. The streets were just coming to life, and I easily wove through the sparse traffic doing at least twenty miles per hour over the posted speed limits. I knew exactly where The Parlor was located, even though it wasn't my type of store. I'd never set foot in it for the same reason I don't go look at the sparkling new houses they're building a mile from where I live. I've always figured it was better to be happy with what you have than to covet things you don't really need. My parents had both grown up poor, and they had taught me a valuable lesson in life. Except for the mortgage on my house, I only buy what I can pay for at that moment. It may sound extreme, but I've never floated the balance on a credit card, and I hope I never will.

As I pulled into the parking lot, Nick said, "Jamie, I'm stopping to fill my radiator with water. I'll duct tape where the hole appears to be, then with a little luck, I should be back on the road. I'm guessing I'll lose at least five minutes, but I'll get there as fast as I can. Sorry."

I could tell by the tone of his voice that he was feeling guilty. Apparently, the fact that I'd be up for the third time in a row disturbed him far more than it bothered me. "Nick, it's okay. We're a team."

"I know, but we're probably going to be up against another hand entry with a timer."

"You'll be there within a few minutes. In fact, you may only miss Romeo sweeping for secondaries."

"I hope so."

Turning the last corner, I pulled into the parking lot of The Parlor. It was a historic two-story red brick building that had been restored to its original glory. An elaborate wedding-themed window display caught my eye, and a fleeting thought of David crossed my mind before I said, "I'm at the scene. Let's switch to secure com two."

Since I expected the worst, I had shifted into what Matt fondly calls my "kick-ass mode." Rolling out of the truck, I called, "Romeo, come!" When he jumped down, I looped his leash over my wrist. In my rush, I left the driver's door ajar as I darted to the back of the truck and jerked open the rear door. Grabbing my hand entry kit with one hand, while tucking my X-ray equipment under my other arm, I rushed toward the patrolman and security guard waiting outside the building.

Practically sliding to a stop, I asked, "Where is he?"

The guard answered, "Just inside this door, you need to take a right. Go all the way past women's clothing until you see the jewelry department against the far wall. The door to the storage room is open. He's lying against the wall near the vault."

"What's his name?"

"Robert Shipley. But we all call him Bob."

"Do you know if Bob has any special medical problems?"

He shook his head.

"Okay. Both of you move back behind the perimeter and stay there." To the officer, I said, "If Bob is still unconscious, I may need to talk to a paramedic. Switch your radio to tach one. That way if there are any problems I can't handle alone, my partner can radio my request directly to you."

"Consider it done," he nervously replied.

Since the victim was such a long way from the entrance, I carried my equipment as I slowly started walking through the women's clothing department. I was painfully aware that a secondary could be hidden anywhere along the aisle, but I knew there wasn't time to sweep the entire area. Even though he was eager to be put into action, I kept Romeo at my side as I said, "Nick, I'm moving through the women's clothing section. As far as I can see, nothing has been disturbed. If there was a struggle, it must've happened somewhere else."

Unlike the stores I usually shopped in, The Parlor's aisles were wide, lined with plush carpet, and the clothes were displayed on spacious, decorative brass fixtures that could hardly be called racks. Each exquisite item hung from its satin-covered hanger a few inches away from the next item. The wasted space actually made my job easier, since I was watching for trip wires and anything that looked unusual or out of place as I walked. "I can see the jewelry counter ahead. So far, there's nothing out of the ordinary."

When we were near the door the guard had described, I placed my equipment on the floor and stepped to where I could look into the small room. For Nick's benefit, I said, "I can see the victim's feet, but the rest of his body is blocked by several boxes. The door to the safe is barely cracked open, an inch at the most, so I can't see inside." A little louder I called, "Bob, can you hear me?"

There was no reply.

Just in case he could hear my voice but was afraid or unable to answer, I stated, "This is Sergeant Jamie Stone with the Kansas State Patrol Hazardous Device Unit. Don't be alarmed. I'm coming in with my dog, Romeo, to search the room. He won't hurt you in any way." After moving my equipment inside, I softly said, "Find it, boy. Find it!"

Romeo worked around the perimeter of the room, stopping just beside the vest. As Romeo hesitantly sat, I got my first glimpse of Bob Shipley. Beneath the device, he was wearing the same khaki uniform as the security guard out front. Although it was hard to tell, I would have guessed he was in his late fifties. Besides his skin being a pasty white, he had several fresh bruises on his face and hands. To my surprise, his gun was still in its holster at his side. Either he never had the chance to draw it, or the Vest Bomber was making a statement.

"Romeo, come!" I commanded, then added, "Good boy!" and gave him a hug. Normally, I would've taken Romeo back outside, but it was too far and time was so precious, I walked him to the door and said, "Stay. Nick, Romeo alerted next to the vest. Bob was apparently involved in a confrontation. He is still unconscious and has visible bruises on his face. His knuckles are bleeding, and there are signs of a struggle in here."

Moving across the room, I described, "The subject is lying on his right side. It appears he was propped up against the wall, similar to how Anne White was left, then fell over when he lost consciousness. His mouth has been covered with silver duct tape, and his wrists and ankles are bound." I leaned forward and pressed my fingers against the flesh of his neck. "He has a pulse, but it's pretty weak. His skin is cold and clammy. Nick, without moving him, I can't tell if we're dealing with another clock."

"Is there any way to mirror it?"

"I'll try." I carried my hand entry kit to his side and

opened it to extract one of my mirrors. The one I chose had a telescoping metal rod, like an old professor's pointer. At the narrow end is a small, round mirror, similar to one that would be used by a dentist. Partially extending it, I knelt close to Bob, pressing my shoulder and face against the wall. Very slowly, I slid the mirror vertically along the border of the vest until I hit a hard, black plastic rim.

"Nick, it appears we have a timer in the lower center back like the last vest." As I edged the mirror horizontally along the plastic frame, the glowing numbers reflected back to me. "The clock is counting down at fourteen-fifty-four."

"I understand. I'll be there in less than five minutes."

Suddenly, Romeo barked—not a normal *woof*, but a *stop right in your tracks* yelp. It was so unlike him that it caught me completely off guard and I jumped, jerking the mirror out. In my ear I heard Nick mutter, "Damn. What was that?"

"Romeo must have caught a whiff of something." I ran to him, picked up his leash, and said, "Find it, boy. Find it!"

Romeo darted to the entrance of the vault. Since it was barely cracked open, he tried to force his way past the heavy door by pushing with his muzzle and scratching with his front paws. Before he could actually move it, I commanded, "Romeo, sit!" He did, but it was apparent he didn't like the idea one little bit. "Nick, Romeo is extremely curious about something inside the vault. Since the door is so thick, I can't see anything inside. I'm going to run a string for secondaries before opening it. You don't suppose our man's stepped up to a laser trigger, do you?"

"I don't think his technology would have advanced to that stage yet," Nick replied as I searched for any kind of string or wire that might generate an explosion if I opened the heavy door. Going back to my hand entry kit, I swapped the mirror for a flashlight and a weighted line. Similar to chalk lines that are available in any hardware store, my kit includes a long piece of string fastened to a weight. Luckily, I was tall enough to stand on my tiptoes to use the flashlight to check for wires along the top edge. Next, I forced the weighted end of the line over the top of the door. After feeding the string over about twenty-four inches, I began to slowly move it along the edge. If there had been a wire connected to a booby trap, the light-weight string would've snagged on it, hopefully without the force needed to trigger a device. When I was positive there were no trip wires attached, I said, "Nick, the string came through clean. I'm opening the door and taking Romeo inside, but this is really eating time on the vest clock."

"It's okay. You're still at twelve-twelve. Plenty of time left to defeat the device."

Stepping inside, I saw a petrified middle-aged woman strapped into a vest. Romeo bolted to her side, his butt hitting the ground as though a Buick had landed on it.

My already pounding heart picked up the pace. "Nick, we have *another* subject wired in a device inside the safe. Romeo hit *hard* next to her. Confirm." After years of working with Romeo, I can see the subtle difference between the way he indicates on particular odors. With the security guard, he hesitated, then sat, which made me think there was a reasonable possibility the vest was a fake like the others. This time, there was no doubt in my mind that he had pointed on the smell of some type of *real* explosive material.

"I understand. Two devices. Subject one is male, subject two is female. Hard hit on subject two."

The woman's eyes were pleading for help. Tears

streamed down her face, cascading over the jagged stripe of duct tape that ran from one cheek to the other. Her wrists and ankles were bound like the guard's, and her breathing was so shallow I was surprised she hadn't hyperventilated. Clad in a housecoat and slippers, she had obviously been kidnapped from her home. As soon as our eyes met, she began to point at her face without moving her arms. Muffled noises came from her mouth as she tried to speak.

In a calm voice I said, "My name is Jamie Stone, and this is my dog, Romeo." I gave him a hug to tell him what a good job he had done as I added, "We're here to get you out of this little predicament. I know it's hard, but take a deep breath and try to stay calm. I've got to step out for a second, but I'll be right back. I'll leave Romeo to keep you company. Everything is going to be all right."

Walking backward, I waited until I was outside of the vault to softly say, "Nick, she's pretty agitated. I'm going to mirror the back of her vest to see if it's on a timer like the other one. Meanwhile, what's protocol on which device should be worked on until you arrive?"

"Shit, Jamie. Normally I would have said women and children first, but it sounds like the security guard is in pretty bad shape. We'll have to give top priority to whichever clock has the least amount of time left. If they're in synch, then I suppose the security guard would go first, since he's apparently injured. I'll bring in all my gear when I arrive. And Jamie, wedge something between the vault door and the doorjamb so that it can't accidentally seal and lock, then keep the door almost closed to guard against sympathetic detonation."

I knew he was right. Most likely, being inside the vault would protect the other subject if the bomb on the guard exploded while I was working on it. The percussion force of one device can easily detonate another in the general vicinity. In this case, a sympathetic detonation would mean all of us could die. "Good point. Okay. I'll start working on subject one if the clocks are in synch. If not, whichever has the least time left will go first."

After propping a flat piece of cardboard against the doorjamb, I ducked into the safe with my extension mirror. Kneeling beside the woman, I said, "Please just stay calm. My partner is going to be here in a few minutes. For now, I'm just going to see what the back of this vest looks like. There's another man in a similar one just outside, but he's not doing very well. I may need to attend to him first."

Her eyes got even wider and she started shaking her head. Although she was frantically trying to speak to me, the tape muted every word, making her impossible to understand. "Is there something about the vest I need to know before I begin?"

Instantly, she bobbed her head in a short, intense beat.

"Then I'm going to have to get the tape off your mouth. I think fast would be best. I'll press down on your head to keep you from jerking when I rip it off."

Although she nodded, her eyebrows scrunched together and she closed her eyes to prepare for the pain. Her knuckles went white as she clenched her fists and gritted her teeth.

I could feel her trembling as I put my hand on her head and applied pressure on the abundance of coarse, bottle-blond hair that had been twisted into a bun. I pushed hard as I said, "On the count of three. One. Two. Three." The tape tore off in one swift motion. I hadn't realized I'd been holding my breath until I let out a loud sigh. "Sorry. I know that had to hurt. Are you okay?"

She nodded.

"What's your name?" I asked as I stuck the tape to a

metal shelf at my side. We keep all tape that we recover from a crime scene, since it is an excellent source of evidence. Besides the fact that fibers cling to it, the microscopic tears left on its edges can be matched to the original roll of tape it came from if it is ever found, thus allowing us to tie a suspected bomber to a particular incident.

It was obvious the woman's cheeks were still stinging as she carefully replied, "Delores . . . Delores Reese. I'm the . . . manager."

"What did you need to tell me, Delores?"

"Before he left, he said that if I move away from the wall, even a tiny bit, I'd be blown to kingdom come."

"You copy that, Nick?"

"I got it."

"Listen, Delores. We've beat this guy three times now. We're going to beat him again. But you'll have to be patient. What I'm going to do won't require you moving at all, so don't worry."

As I started to wedge the mirror behind her shoulder blades, she asked, "Are you sure? He said—"

"I'm *sure*." Inching the mirror lower, I realized this vest wasn't constructed like the others and began to move even more carefully. "Nick, subject two's vest has vertical *machine* stitching about every five inches all the way around it. The stitching appears to create three-and-a-half-inch-wide panels. I'm at the top of a rigid, black plastic box like the others. . . ." I didn't want Delores to panic, so I chose my words carefully. "Subject two's special feature is at fifteen-twenty-five. Talk to me, Nick."

"Okay. Shift all your attention to subject number one."

"Delores, you're doing great. Now, I really have to go help the security guard."

"You mean Mr. Shipley is still alive?"

"Yes, he is."

"Thank God! They told me he was dead and that if I didn't do everything they asked, I'd end up dead, too."

"Not if I can help it." Standing to leave, I added, "Remember, stay calm. We'll get you out of here. I'll leave Romeo in the vault to keep you company." Looking at him, I added, "Sit. Stay."

Nick said, "Jamie, I'm pulling into the lot."

"Great. It'll be much easier to get X-ray plates behind Bob's torso if you can help pull him forward," I said as I knelt down beside his body and started to set up the X-ray panels on each side. "Nick, could you bring in some Valium and water from one of the paramedics and tell them to be ready to roll?"

"Will do."

"I'm going to be shooting X rays from each side as I describe the device. Nick, time?"

"Subject one is at nine-forty-nine. Subject two is at fourteen-fifty-one."

I wouldn't have thought it was possible, but Bob's color had shifted to an even more ashen shade of gray. "Okay. Vest one is constructed of the same base material as the previous three. It appears almost identical to the one used on Anne White. The inner white layer is neatly whipstitched with bright orange thread. Our guy's getting to be quite a seamstress. Vest one has the same Y-shaped straps that go between subject one's legs and has double looped wires around the neck that disappear into the top. I'm shooting the first X ray. . . ."

As I slid the panel into the developer, I was interrupted by a screech from the vault, followed by a single, sharp bark. I stated, "Nick, subject two just screamed. I'm going back to see what the problem is."

Breathlessly dashing in, I asked, "What's wrong, Delores?"

Even more panicked than before, Delores frantically

gushed, "There's something craw—crawling on my head! Get it off! Please!"

I stepped closer, suppressing an involuntary cringe when I spotted eight furry legs high-stepping across her hair as though it were a golden nest of cotton candy. Although it resembled a tarantula in color and bushiness, it was barely the size of a quarter from tip to tip. I'll take bombs any day over spiders, snakes, and worst of all, wasps, but I was in no mood to waste time. I lied as I swatted it onto the carpet. "It's only a little bug."

She sighed and whimpered, "Sorry."

After grinding him beyond recognition under my shoe, I turned to leave. "Hang in there, Delores."

Charging out of the vault, I could hear the tools rattling in Nick's hand entry kit as he raced through the store. I set up the second panel and shot the X ray as he breathlessly rushed in. Cranking the first one through the developer, I shoved in the fresh one and said, "Welcome to the party."

"Wouldn't miss it."

Holding up the first X ray, we studied it together. "Looks awfully familiar," I said, as he handed me a bottle of water and the Valium. I asked, "Don't you think a pressure switch would've blown when he slid to one side?"

"Most likely. Plus, I don't see any indication of one on this panel."

"I agree."

Nick glanced at his watch. "This one's timer is at eight-twenty-one. Since it looks so similar to the last vest, why don't you go start on subject two while I work here?"

"But I defeated the last one. . . . Wouldn't it make more sense . . . ?"

"For you to handle subject one? No. This guy hasn't made two identical vests yet. Besides, you've already es-

tablished a good rapport with Delores. It's essential that
she stay as calm as possible."

I nodded. Without saying it, Nick had just implied that
I might jump to a conclusion about subject one's vest
based on what I had worked with on the Jasper's Jeweler
call. At another moment, my ego might have taken a
blow, but there wasn't time to quibble. I mumbled,
"Fine," and immediately began concentrating once again
on the tasks at hand.

After we looked at the second X ray together and decided where the blasting caps were hidden, I grabbed all
my gear and moved inside the vault, pulling the door almost closed behind me. Kneeling next to Delores, I said,
"Okay. Let's get you out of this fashion nightmare. If you
aren't allergic to any medication, the paramedics gave me
this to keep you calm."

"No, thank you."

"Are you sure? It's only a Valium."

"No. If it's my time to go, then I want to have my wits
about me."

Even though I thought it would be best for her to take
the Valium, I wasn't going to force the issue. Giving her
a confident smile, I replied, "It's *not* your time to go, or
mine, either. First thing I'm going to do is take some X
rays—one under each of your arms." As I slid the panel
in, I asked, "Did they strap this on you at your house?"

She nodded and replied, "Uh-huh."

"I know you're not planning to do a jig, but when I
count to three, I'll need you to hold your breath and stay
very, very still. Ready?"

Another nod.

"One . . . two . . . three . . ." Once the machine clicked
down, I moved to the other side as I asked, "How did you
get in here?"

"I went outside to get the morning paper, and a man

came out of the bushes. He put a hood over my head, then it felt like I was shoved into the back of a van. At least I think it was a van. I heard the side door slide before it slammed completely closed. I could tell I was lying on cheap carpet, and the ride was pretty rough."

"Very good observations, Delores. So there was only one man?"

"No. The one who jumped me kept yelling at the other guy."

"Did you get a look at either man?"

"The only one I saw was Bill Clinton. I mean, he had on one of those Halloween masks that look like famous people."

"When you got here, did they make you walk inside alone?"

She nodded again. "He told me if I even breathed funny that this thing would blow. He said it's wired for sound and that it has a remote camera. He said he could hear and see every move I made from in the van, and that Bob Shipley was dead because he'd been a 'wiseass fool.' I was supposed to shut off the video security system, take out the tape, open the vault, then sit down inside and wait."

*A new twist,* I thought as I shot the second X ray and touched my headset. "Delores, my partner, Nick Terrell, is just outside the vault working on Bob Shipley. He can hear us through this. Nick, do you see any indication of a listening device or camera on subject one?"

"Negative. What about on subject two?"

The instant she had mentioned it, I had begun looking carefully for anything that might be an antenna. Moving to the other side, I spotted a thin black wire running from the pit of her arm all the way to the bottom of the vest. Touching it, I discovered it was dangling, obviously not part of a circuit since one end hung free. "Affirmative.

There's a possible antenna emerging from the bottom of the left armhole."

"Then you're in the best position you could be. The thick walls of the vault should provide maximum protection against transient radio signals."

*Shit! Remote detonation capability.* Nick and I had already talked about the possibility that the Vest Bomber might step up to it. At any moment, if the bastard decided he had had enough fun tormenting us, he might be able to simply push a button. If any blasting caps were still in place, then we would be in deep trouble. In addition to being able to receive a transmission, there was a slight possibility that the antenna was connected to a switch that was held *open* by a radio signal. If so, and I cut the antenna, the switch would close. Again, big trouble. Since the latter might have been affected by the vault's walls, I decided the bomber probably wouldn't have taken such a chance. "Nick, I think it's safe to cut the antenna. Coming into the vault would've probably already risked at least a temporary loss of radio reception. Do you agree?"

"Affirmative. That's the same call I'd make."

"I'm severing the potential antenna as close to the vest as possible." To my relief, nothing happened when my wire cutters snipped easily through the wire. "That should minimize his ability to play any dirty tricks on us," I said, hoping that without an antenna, the thick walls of the vault would be more than enough to stop any signals.

As I waited for the X rays to develop, I began tearing off segments of tape and sticking them to my thigh. I asked, "Delores, did you shut off the video cameras like he asked?"

She nodded. "And he took the tape." Suddenly, her eyes widened. "You know, I only cut off the ones *inside* the store. The parking lot monitors are still on."

"Way to go, Delores! Talk to me, Nick."

"That may be the break we've been waiting for. I've exposed solid dark wires, no color-coding. Since there appear to be two blasting caps, one under each arm, I'm I-cutting the left side first. . . . Okay, I'm removing the brownish white substance and hopefully will expose the first cap soon. Talk to me, Jamie."

"My X rays are ready." The moment I peeled the covering off the images, I suppressed the urge to groan. "Nick, subject two has a series of metallic rods that run in the vertical pockets all the way around the vest. There are three places where the rods seem slightly darker, which I'm assuming from the size and shape of the shadowing are where the blasting caps are buried. We really need a chest view to be certain, since some of the rods appear stacked from the side view and I can't get much of a feel for where the wires run. There's also a shadow that circles around the vest, possibly a wrap of det cord. I'll still eliminate the blasting caps, which will neutralize the det cord. Delores, after you sat down in here, did anyone touch you again?"

She shook her head. "No, but he pointed a contraption that looked like a garage door opener at me and pushed a button. A red light flashed on the end. Then he sort of laughed, said something like, *'Adieu,'* then left."

"Talk to me, Nick."

"Subject one's clock is at three-oh-two. Subject two's is at . . . eight-oh-four. Jamie, can you get to any of the caps you've already located without moving her?"

"I don't think it would be wise. They appear to be on each side and near the front, but without a better idea of what we're up against, I wouldn't bet on it."

"Then try sliding a panel partially behind her on each side. That may give you enough of an angle to tell. And remember, those rods may be conductive."

"I know, but thanks for the reminder. You're up." I

made a mental note to use only plastic and wood tools once I was past the tough outer material. That way, if I accidentally touched the wrong thing, I wouldn't complete a circuit.

Nick declared, "I've just exposed a military cap on subject one. I'm going to cut it right . . . now. Cap number one is in a protector, and I'm moving to the other side. Talk to me, Jamie."

I shot two more X rays. Once they were developed, I looked carefully at the panels. "Okay. The new X rays confirm three potential caps. Although there does not appear to be a pressure switch, there is a small rectangular object on the lower left panel, approximately one inch by three inches by four inches. Since a wire runs from it to the left armhole, most likely it is some kind of transmitter. Judging from the positioning of the three caps, I think there's a good possibility that another cap is located above the clock in the back. Without X-raying it, there's no way to know. Nick?"

"Let's start by taking out the caps you've already pinpointed. When I finish here, I'll come look at the X rays, then we'll decide if we should lean her forward. I've just exposed the second military cap on subject one. I'm going to cut it right . . . now. Okay, both caps have been neutralized. Subject one's clock is at one-twenty-two. Subject two's is at . . . six-twenty-four. I'm going to use the last few seconds to trace the left wire back toward the clock."

"Got it. I'm going to I-cut the apparent cap in the front of subject two's vest first." Using a razor knife, I held my breath as I pinched the thick black material to hold it taut and began very carefully sawing through it. "Delores, you're doing great."

"Jamie?"

"Yes?"

"Would it bother you if I recited *The Lord's Prayer*?"
I shook my head. "Not at all."

# 2

"Nick. Time?"

"Subject one is cycling down at nineteen seconds."

With all my heart, I wished Nick would step inside the vault, just in case we had missed something, but I knew better than to ask. He was far too proud to leave his subject, even if doing so might save his own life. Though I desperately wanted to urge him to come help me, all I managed to say was, "No doubts, Nick?"

"No doubts, Jamie. Let's count subject one's timer down. Okay, ten, nine, eight, seven, six, five, four, three, two, one . . ."

After a couple of seconds, I released the breath I'd been holding. My heart was still pounding as I gushed, "Way to go, partner!"

"Hot damn! Now, I'm going to get Bob out of here. I've just snipped the wires around his neck, and I'm cutting the straps between his legs. I'm unsnapping the black fasteners from the bottom up. One . . . two . . . three . . . four. I've just got . . . to shift his body weight. . . ."

For what seemed like an eternity, I heard the sound of Nick struggling. It was easy for me to picture him trying to delicately remove the vest from an unconscious man, and Bob Shipley probably weighed almost two hundred pounds. I have to admit, I'm not sure I could've done it alone. I quickly offered, "Nick, I could come help."

Breathing heavily, he replied, "No need. The vest is . . . off. I'm putting . . . subject one . . . over my shoulder. . . . Jamie, I'm taking him . . . to the paramedics, then I'll . . . I'll be right back."

"Good job, Nick," I said, knowing that since my device had yet to be defeated, we couldn't risk bringing the paramedics inside the building. Concentrating on the problem at hand, I said, "Okay, I've fully exposed the first cap. The wires are multicolored, so it appears he has stepped up to color-coding. Along each side of the rod is about an inch of what appears to be the same brownish white substance that we've worked with before. I've located the cap. From the hot pink wires, it's a commercial one." Clearing the doughy substance from the cap's wires, I said, "Nick, I'm cutting the first cap. Could you bring in two more cap protectors?"

His breath was still labored as he answered, "Will do." I heard him sigh, then say, "Subject one is with the paramedics. Jamie, anything else we need besides cap protectors?"

"Grab a few more X-ray panels, just in case."

"Got it. You're at four-thirty-two. Jesus, it's a zoo out here. I requested the airspace to be restricted, yet there are helicopters just above the building. And four live news crews." At the top of his lungs, he screamed, "I want that perimeter moved back another fifty yards! Now!" Softly, he added, "That ought to keep them busy for a few minutes. Talk to me, Jamie."

"Good job, partner." I couldn't help but smile.

Delores must have noticed my response to Nick's words, since she eagerly asked, "Are you almost finished?"

"Just a few more minutes. You're doing great."

Grabbing a fresh razor knife, I began working again. "I've started the I-cut on the left side of the device. I'm peeling it open. . . . The material is now taped back." But this time, it wasn't the same brownish white substance that I exposed. I tensed, then pinched off a piece to sniff. Once I took a whiff of it, I tossed it away. Behind me,

Romeo let out a low whimper. "This pocket has a pure white compound, with the look and feel of bonafide commercial-grade C4." I started to work faster, digging out large clumps as quickly as possible until I could see the small, cylindrical tube. "Nick, this cap has been *taped* around the metal rod with what appears to be common black electrical tape."

I could tell Nick was running back inside as he breathlessly asked, "Can you remove enough of the C4 to expose the wires and cut them with the cap still taped in place?"

"I'll try." Scratching out chunks, I managed to clean away enough gunk to see that the Vest Bomber had been much more creative this time. Always mindful of worrying Delores, I kept my voice even as I said, "Nick, the cap's wires are coiled *very* tightly around the rod. I'm working through the wrap of electrical tape that's holding them snugly in place, but it's really going slow, and I won't be able to use a metal blade to cut through them."

I may have sounded calm, but deep down, the claws of panic were starting to scratch at my subconscious. Logically, I knew we were almost out of time, and I was certain that I was kneeling in a pile of real C4.

But what bothered me even more was a nagging suspicion that no matter what I did or how fast I did it, that this time, it wouldn't be enough.

**3**

Romeo must have sensed my apprehension. He had begun slowly inching closer to me, and he softly whined when Nick pulled open the vault door, rushed inside, and set down an armload of equipment. Without hesitation, Nick turned back and pulled the door as far closed as the piece of cardboard would allow. Neither of us had forgotten that the device might still be capable of being remotely detonated, and we would do anything we could to minimize that possibility.

"How can I help?" he gasped.

"Check the X rays and start on the other side. As you can see, I've got my hands full."

He glanced at the part of the vest I had exposed, then held the X rays up to the light as he said, "Delores, I'm Nick. I've got to tell you, I'm impressed with how you're handling all this. It's a pretty crazy predicament you're in, but we'll get you out of here."

"God always seems to work in mysterious ways."

"That he does," Nick replied as he stole a sideways glance at me.

Since the first plastic knife I had tried to use to cut the wires didn't work very well, I dug through my hand entry kit until I found a smaller, sharper version. While I kept working on removing the blasting cap on my side, Nick started cutting through the outer layer of the other side. After a few moments, he said, "Jamie, I agree with your initial opinion. Without a front-to-back picture, we might be in trouble."

"Time?" I asked, even though I really wasn't sure I wanted to know.

"Two-fifteen," he replied.

Delores shook her head and lightly said, "I can't believe it's that late already. Time really flies when you're strapped to a bomb."

"Amen," Nick said with a confident grin.

I realized that now that Delores could hear both sides of our conversation, Nick and I would have to be more careful with our choice of words. Then again, if we didn't hurry, none of us would probably be doing *any* talking, *ever* again. The second knife I tried worked much better, effectively slicing through the stiff wire. "Nick, I've got one wire cut, and I'm about to cut the second . . . Done."

"Can you get the cap off the rod now?"

"I'm working on it." Since there were several layers of electrical tape, I decided it might be faster to pull the cap out instead of trying to cut through more tape. After a few seconds of wiggling it back and forth, I finally felt it start to slip. Once I coaxed it slowly out, I said, "Nick, I've got this cap. What's your side look like?"

"Brownish white substance. No coiling of the wire. This one looks straightforward."

"All right!"

After stuffing the cap into a cap protector and pointing it toward the wall, I explained, "Delores, we need you to trust us a few seconds longer. We've got to shoot one last X ray of the vest to be sure we've done our job right. When I say go, I want you to inch slightly forward. I'll slide an X-ray panel between you and the wall, then just hold very still. Don't even breathe."

She looked up, nodded, then closed her eyes. To Nick, I asked, "Ready?"

He stopped what he was doing long enough to line up the X-ray machine.

At his nod, I said, "Okay, Delores, *go!*"

I stuffed the X-ray panel behind her, and Nick instantly pushed the button. My best guess was that we had about a minute and a half left on the clock, and an X ray would take just over a minute from start to finish. Nick went back to work on the other cap as I asked, "Delores, is there anything else you noticed about the man who did this?"

"He was tall. Probably at least six two."

"White? Black?"

She shook her head. "He was covered from head to toe. Besides the mask, he had on a set of brown coveralls and rubber gloves. Come to think of it, he even had some sort of plastic things over his shoes."

Nick leaned back on his heels and grabbed a cap protector. As soon as he stuffed what we hoped was the last blasting cap inside, the timer signaled the developing time was up. I peeled back the panel, and together we stared at it. It didn't surprise us to see another rod running straight down the middle of the back. At its base was the clock, which was surrounded by a nest of wires. It was impossible to tell if they were connected to the clock, but I strongly suspected at least one of the sets was, probably the one tied to the side with the coiled wire. We were mainly concerned that another blasting cap might be hidden near the clock, so we scrutinized the shot for any subtle shade differences that could indicate a short, cylindrical shadow. Although there didn't appear to be any, we both knew there wasn't time to cut through the vest's tough outer layer to remove the battery from the clock to add the next level of security.

At almost the same instant, Nick and I looked at each other and exchanged a tentative smile. In his eyes, I could see we shared the same degree of confidence. With a glance at his watch, he boasted, "See, no problem. Looks like we're clear with a whopping twelve seconds to spare."

# seven

**1**

Anticipation. As a certified control freak, it makes me crazy. Waiting for the timer on Delores's vest to tick down to zero was one of the hardest things I've ever done. The urge to run far, far away and never look back was practically overwhelming. Yet, I didn't. Nick and I stayed, not so much because it was our job, but because being a bomb tech is what we chose as our profession, knowing full well that there would be moments like these. No one forces us to risk our lives. We're proud of what we do, and we're pretty damn good at it.

Nervously biting my lower lip, I took a second to really look around the vault for the first time. Romeo was sitting in front of a floor-to-ceiling set of metallic shelves. Black velvet trays that probably had been emptied by the robber were scattered about the floor here and there. What little part of the carpet that wasn't covered with scattered

clumps of the different substances we had stripped out of
the vest was piled high with our assortment of equipment:
two hand entry kits, two X-ray units, three cap protectors,
a bottle of water, and a single Valium that was beginning
to look awfully tempting.

Delores was still seated against the far wall, seemingly
oblivious to the countdown at hand. The vest that she
wore looked substantially different than it had before Nick
and I attacked it less than fifteen minutes ago. Where the
three long I-cuts were taped back, the light seemed to play
on the shiny rods and the raw ends of the cut wires. With
a smile, I took Delores by the hand and noticed she was
no longer trembling. "In just a few seconds, we'll have
you out of this, then we'll clean up the mess we made."

She sighed. "I'll never be able to thank both of you
enough."

"This is what we do, but you're welcome," I replied.

For the benefit of the secure com recording, Nick very
softly announced, "We're cycling down at five . . . four . . .
three . . . two . . . one." The instant the timer hit one, the
clock in the back of the vest began to rhythmically squeal.
Delores tensed, and her eyes went wide as though she had
just been stabbed. Romeo chimed in, barking sharply as
though we couldn't hear the blasted thing ourselves. I admit, for the first couple of moments, I didn't breathe. Instead, I gritted my teeth and prayed that Matt would have
a good life.

When I realized we were all still in one piece, I called,
"Romeo, settle!" He did, but it didn't help much. Maybe
it was the confined space, or it could have been we were
all overly sensitized by then, but either way, that noise
*had* to stop. *Right then.*

About ten seconds into the irritating clamor, Nick stood
and said, "Enough! Let's shut that thing up!"

"Best idea I've heard all day," I called.

Nick held up the X ray that clearly showed the clock. Pointing just above it, he said, "If I cut here, we should be able to disconnect it."

I nodded and pushed my hand entry kit out of the way so that Delores could move her legs to one side. Although I wouldn't have believed it was possible, when she shifted away from the wall, the noise got even louder and more irritating.

Nick quickly made an I-cut, and I handed him strips of tape to hold back the material. When the top of the clock was exposed, he said, "Look at this mess. There must be twenty sets of wire in here." Shining his flashlight on the two wires that fed into the bottom of the clock, he added, "And this time, the factory shunts are gone. It was hot. You did a good job, Jamie."

"Can you make it stop?" I yelled.

He nodded, slipping the battery out with a grin that quickly faded. "What the hell?" he muttered, tugging out a tiny piece of paper that had been hidden behind the battery.

For two seconds, the vault plunged back into a welcome silence, and we all breathed a sigh of relief. Together, Nick and I read the simple block printing on the slip of paper:

## BOOM!

We exchanged a curious gaze, wondering what the Vest Bomber's message might mean. Our trance was shattered by an unmistakable sound echoing through the empty store. *Beep! Beep! Beep!* was the last thing we heard before all hell broke loose.

## 2

Everything happened so fast, I wasn't even sure it was real. Having detonated thousands of explosives in the last ten years, Nick and I instantly suspected that the distant *Beep! Beep! Beep!* we heard would be followed by a destructive sequence of events. As though he realized it, too, Romeo jumped up and started barking, warning us with Lassie-like fervor to take cover before the initial *crack!* of the explosion rolled our way.

I saw the panic in Nick's eyes as he deck-launched himself over Delores and me, effectively shielding us with his body and sending all three of us crashing hard to the floor. As the shock wave sliced through the vault, everything vibrated and rocked: the tools, the shelves, our teeth. In the confusion, I'm not sure exactly what fell from where, but I clearly remember the stale smell of dust, the taste of plaster, my ears ringing, and an overwhelming feeling of helplessness. I have no idea how long we stayed there, stunned and waiting for the explosion's rage to end, but there was one thing I was certain of: We were only alive because the vault had been strong enough to withstand the impact of the blast.

I felt Nick's lips move against my cheek, and I thought I heard him ask, "Are you all right?" but it was hard to truly grasp anything at that moment. I fought to regain my senses. "I think so. You okay?" I finally muttered and coughed, his weight heavy on my chest.

"Seems that way."

"Can't . . . breathe. Can you . . . move over a little?"

When he did, I took a deep breath and curled to one side. Reaching into the cloud of dust, I called, "Delores?"

Her hand found mine. In a shaky voice she replied, "I . . . think I'm okay."

"Are you in any pain?" I asked.

"Not really. Just sort of . . . dazed."

Nick replied, "Good. We were lucky to be in this vault. That was quite a blast."

Delores smiled at me as I commented, "Guess you were right. God decided it wasn't our time to go."

Softly shaking his head, Nick sighed. "No kidding."

Sitting up, I winced, certain I'd have a black and blue rib cage from Nick hurling me on top of my hand entry kit. If not for my bulletproof vest, I'm sure a few of my ribs would have been broken. The dust was beginning to settle, and as I looked at the debris surrounding us, I suddenly realized I couldn't see Romeo. Alarmed, I called, "Romeo? Where are you, boy?" The instant I stopped talking, I heard Romeo whimper. The lights flickered, then went out, making his soft whine even more disturbing.

Blackness completely engulfed the vault, and for Delores's sake, Nick explained, "That's just the firemen doing their job. They can't send in rescuers without eliminating the possibility of live electrical wires and gas leaks."

She replied, "It's okay. I'm not afraid," and I believed it. To this day, I've never met another person whose faith was as strong as hers.

While Nick was talking, I had been groping to find my hand entry kit. Fumbling through it, I felt the cylindrical shape I was searching for and snapped on my flashlight. In the dimly restored light I called, "Come on, Romeo, where are you?"

I followed the sound of muffled whines to a nearby spot where a solid metal shelf had fallen over. "Nick, help me lift this."

Propping the flashlight on its flat end so that it shone an artificial moon on the ceiling, we heaved the unwieldy frame about two feet off the floor. Nick held it up long enough for me to sweep Romeo into my arms, then low-ered it back into place.

"Where does it hurt, boy?" I asked, trying my best not to let his spine bend as I held him in my arms. Romeo stopped whimpering the moment he saw me, but he was shaking. I knew something was wrong, something more than just shock. My heart ached. Burying my face in the soft fur of his neck, I muttered, "It's okay, boy. We'll get you to a vet right away." A wave of tears rushed up from deep within, and I realized I had started shaking, too.

Nick picked up the flashlight and pointed it toward the only exit. The thrust of the blast wave had left the door to the vault standing wide open, but the amount of debris on the ground and dangling from the ceiling outside made it impossible to leave in a hurry. Looking at the devas-tation, I slumped to my knees and asked, "Subject one's vest?"

Nick knew exactly what I meant, and he replied, "I don't think so. The beeper seemed pretty far away, plus there was enough time to hear the detonation before the shock wave hit. If it had been the vest just outside, I don't think we would've had any warning at all, and I don't think the vault would've saved us."

"A secondary?"

He nodded. "Probably on the other side of the store, where Romeo wouldn't have gotten a whiff of it when you brought him in." Moving close to me, he shone the light on my face as he brushed some debris from my hair. "Jamie, are you sure you're all right?"

I took a deep breath and immediately felt my confi-dence climb. "Yeah. I'll be fine." Snuggling Romeo, I added, "I'm a little worried about my boyfriend, though."

"Fire and ambulance were standing by. They'll be in as fast as possible."

Neither one of us was wearing our secure com headsets

anymore, and Nick reached down and plucked them off the floor. Handing me mine, he winked and said, "Since we're stuck here for a few more minutes, why don't we make Delores more comfortable?"

I sighed, looking for a flat place to lay Romeo. As though he could read my mind, Nick cleared away a spot on the carpet, and I gently eased him down. I whispered, "Stay," even though I sensed Romeo had no intention of trying to move. Meanwhile, Nick had dug through his gear and found two more flashlights. Positioning them on the floor with the beams shining upward, the room was illuminated well enough to move around.

I discovered a tender knot on the top of my head as I tried to adjust the headset. Once I found a position that didn't hurt, I turned toward Nick and noticed he had a trickle of blood running down the back of his shirt. Pointing to the spot at the nape of his neck, I said, "You're bleeding."

Touching a place in the hair behind his ear, Nick shrugged it off and said, "Just a scratch." He must have caught the smell of natural gas at the same time I did, because he added, "Let's hope they get all the utilities shut off right away. Meanwhile, we'd better get busy."

"First, I'm going to switch over and call Matt to tell him we're okay." I reached down and flipped the setting on the transmitter to Telephone, but nothing happened. "My unit isn't working."

Nick tried his and shook his head. "Mine's out, too." Tossing aside the headsets, we went to work anyway. As we worked to set Delores free, I asked, "Nick, why did you move the perimeter back another fifty yards when you took Bob Shipley outside?"

"I had a bad feeling about this one."

A shiver crawled down my spine as I confessed, "Yeah. Me, too."

It only took a few minutes to cut the rest of the wires and straps. Each of us supported one of Delores's arms to help her stand. Even though she was a little shaky at first, she quickly found her balance and gave us each a bear hug. We could hear the shouts of approaching firemen as she said, "Would you mind if I ask you two a question?"

"Not at all," Nick replied.

"How could they possibly pay anyone enough to do something like this for a living?"

Nick and I simultaneously replied, "They don't."

# 3

I insisted that I be allowed to carry Romeo outside myself since I didn't want him to be more unnerved than he already was. In front of me, Delores was on a stretcher conveyed by two firemen. Nick was at my heels, his arms loaded with as much of our precious equipment as he could carry. Stepping into the bright sunlight, I flinched and squinted, trying not to stumble as I walked across the glass and rubble. Up until that moment, I had been too immersed in my own world to give the rest of the universe a second thought. If I had, I might have chosen to hide in the vault until the media madness had time to pass. Nick had been right. It was a zoo, and we were the special exhibit.

Behind the Do Not Cross line, the crowd roared as we walked outside. Cameras flashed and three helicopters jockeyed for position overhead. As they heartily cheered for us, I felt the blood rush to my cheeks. Stopping for an instant, I turned to anxiously whisper to Nick, "I've got to get word to Matt that we're okay!"

"No problem. I see lots of familiar faces. We'll borrow a cell phone."

Looking around, I realized that I recognized quite a few people, too. Not only fellow troopers but special agents from the FBI, ATF, and even Secret Service. And, of course, reporters from every television and radio station. Nudging him, I added, "I'll fix a brisket for Sunday dinner if you'll handle the pack of wolves alone."

Pretending to take a moment to consider, he winked and replied, "Throw in a French silk pie, and you've got a deal."

"Done." Turning, I moaned, "Oh, no." I had just spotted my Suburban. The windshield had splintered into a huge spider web, and all the windows on the side closest to the building had been blown inward.

"Shit," Nick muttered, eyeing his own vehicle's similar damage.

Like mine, most of his windows were shattered, but his Suburban had half a mannequin groom's torso hanging out one side. The wayward bride had landed about ten feet past his truck, but she'd lost her head. I thought how sad it was that a beautiful wedding gown had been destroyed in such a hideous way. "We need to take care of Romeo."

Nick grinned and pointed toward the crowd. "First problem solved. You can mark calling Matt or Jesse, for that matter, off of your to-do list. Matt just broke through the police line and is headed this way." Jesse had stayed behind the Do Not Cross line with his mother, where both were frantically waving their greetings.

One look at Matt filled my heart, then overwhelmed me with guilt. Rushing toward him, I cried, "Matt! I'm so sorry I couldn't get word to you! How did you get here so soon?"

"The explosion was on live television! I called headquarters, and they sent Trooper Allan to escort Jesse's mom, sirens and all. Are you guys all right? What's wrong with Romeo?"

A cameraman had broken through the line and was pressing for a close-up. Turning my back to him, I whispered my answer, "We're all okay. Romeo was trapped under a heavy set of shelves. I'm not sure what's wrong with him, so we need to get him to the vet right away."

Marcus Allan was wearing his bomb squad uniform. He is tall, with broad shoulders and a look of authority that demands respect, so he had no trouble pushing the cameraman behind the line where he belonged before he walked back to greet us. I met him halfway, smiling and saying, "Thanks for taking care of Matt and his friends."

"No problem. Apparently Jeff's been here since before the detonation, and the rest of the squad is on the way to help." Shaking Nick's hand, he half hugged him as he added, "Thank God you two are all right."

Nick said, "Thanks for coming. Romeo needs a lift to the vet, and I think we need to make sure he isn't harassed by the media."

Marcus replied, "My car is at the end of the block. I'll have him there in record time, and *nobody* will bother him."

I didn't want Romeo to be with strangers, so I turned to Matt and asked, "Would you mind going with Trooper Allan? I've got work to do, and I think Romeo would feel better with you nearby. Do you know how to get to the vet from here?"

Gently taking him into his arms, Matt smiled. "Sure, Mom. Don't worry. Romeo's tough."

I watched the crowd part for them as they joined Jesse and Marianne. Marianne touched her heart and blew me a kiss before she turned to follow Matt. The moment the crowd filled in the void from their departure, I felt as though the psychological armor that had been protecting me since the blast had finally collapsed. My shoulders felt so heavy, I wasn't sure I could keep breathing. It seemed as though there was too much to do, and all of it needed to be done right then. The noise of the crowd, coupled with the chatter of three news helicopters competing for position overhead, began to ring in my ears. I was so numb that I didn't know which way to turn. As if they could sense my weakness, two emergency medical techs descended on Nick and me, insisting we allow them to check for injuries.

We reluctantly followed them. While a tech was busy cleaning the cut on the back of Nick's head, he leaned close and said, "We sure know how to throw a party. Practically every ATF and FBI agent I know are already here. And our buddy, Lieutenant Colonel Jones, is over there doing an interview for Channel 2."

"Jones is here already? Last night he said he was headed back to Topeka. There's no way he could've gotten here so fast."

He shrugged. "Guess he changed his mind and stayed here last night."

I was taken aback by the sheer quantity of emergency personnel who had responded in what I perceived to be such a short time. Only later would I realize the extent of the media coverage, and that the blast had been seen on live television not only in Kansas City but all over the world via both CNN and Fox News. The powerful image of the mannequin bride and groom being catapulted through the wall of windows made for a favorite news clip.

As soon as the EMT allowed him to stand, Nick said, "I'll handle Lieutenant Colonel Jones while you check the damage to our Suburbans. Deal?"

"Deal." Sitting for those few minutes had allowed my

body to stiffen. With each step, I began to realize precisely how much strain I'd been under. I was suddenly aware that every part of me ached. Even so, with the media focused on my every move, I had no intention of acting anything less than perfect. I defied their readiness to equate weakness with my gender.

It wasn't long before Simon Stanley found me, with Frank Nichols on his heels. Like all the ATF agents on the scene, they were wearing official dark blue jackets with ATF in huge gold letters across the back. To my surprise, Frank acknowledged my presence with a curt nod and a slight turn of the corner of his mouth that almost qualified as a smile. Simon gave me a brisk handshake and said, "Stone, you look like you've been to hell and back. You and Terrell certainly made one hell of a mess. Which one of you cut the wrong wire?"

Deep down, I knew Simon was merely trying to lighten the mood in his usual glib manner, but by then, I didn't have an ounce of tolerance or patience left. Practically snapping at him, I challenged, "Do you honestly think we'd still be walking around if one of us were at the seat of the explosion?"

"As tough as you are, I wouldn't doubt it," Simon replied.

Frank had an odd look on his face, as though he were dying to say something. Challenging him, I said, "What is it, Frank?"

He matched my glare, then looked at my Suburban. "I overheard Lieutenant Colonel Jones a few minutes ago asking Jeff Jenkins if he had made himself clear at the Training Center last night."

"Clear about what?"

"Securing public access to all bomb squad equipment when there isn't a squad member around to guard it."

My heart sank. The driver's door to my Suburban was

standing wide open, exactly the way I had left it when I rushed inside. "Jesus."

Frank added, "Stone, he's a son of a bitch who doesn't have a clue what it's like to be the one under fire in the field. He's responsible for paperwork, not civilian lives. Ignore him. Just do your job. That's all anyone expects."

I was stunned. Although his words were supportive, there was something unnerving about the way he stared at me. It felt wrong, unnatural, as though the sun had just set in the east.

Simon wrapped an arm around my shoulder and declared, "He's right. You've got enough to worry about without adding a bunch of bureaucratic nonsense to the list."

With a sigh, I replied, "No shit," just as Nick signaled for me to join him. Kicking the door to my Suburban closed, I smiled. "Thanks, guys. On a day like this, a little encouragement goes a long way."

Glass crunched underfoot as I crossed the parking lot. Jeff Jenkins suddenly emerged from the crowd to intercept me. Jeff was the greenest member of our squad in both age and experience. At twenty-seven, he had been with the KSP over five years, but he'd only recently completed his first grueling training at Redstone. "Jamie! Dispatch just patched through a call for you."

Taking his radio, I said, "Sergeant Stone."

"Hey, Mom, it's Matt. I thought you'd want to know that the vet rushed Romeo in the minute we arrived. The X rays show his hip was badly bruised, but nothing's broken. He's going to be fine in a few days."

A rush of relief helped soothe my frazzled nerves. "Thanks. Give him a hug for me and take good care of him until I get home. I'll pick him up at Jesse's in a couple of hours. And Matt, be careful."

I handed the radio back to Jeff and started to walk off,

but he grabbed my arm, bringing me to an abrupt stop. After glancing each way to be certain he wouldn't be heard, he leaned close and whispered, "What was it like?"

Caught off guard by the intensity of his gaze, I tried to back away, but his grip tightened on my arm. "Jeff . . . what are you talking about?"

"Being at the seat of the explosion. Was there a white flash? What did it feel like when the wave of energy cut through you?"

Wrenching my arm free, I regained my personal space and replied, "Sorry to disappoint you, but there was nothing glamorous about it. It was like tripping and falling. One minute everything was fine, the next I was on the ground, stunned, fighting to regain my senses. Now, if you'll excuse me, Nick and Lieutenant Colonel Jones are waiting."

I walked away, slightly annoyed but too worried about leaving my Suburban unlocked to give Jeff much thought. Nick flashed a reassuring smile my way, then said, "Jamie, Lieutenant Colonel Jones has to get back to Topeka, but first he wants to hear your version of what happened. I'll be in a meeting on the northeast side of the building with the FBI and ATF agents to line up the postblast investigation team."

Nick left, and Jones turned his full attention to me. "Sergeant Stone, I want you to describe the devices. Specifically, what advancements in technology were employed that had not been used in the prior vests?"

I dropped my head, closing my eyes to think before I replied, "Subject one's vest was essentially the same as the last one. Subject two's vest was more intricate. It had what we think was either remote detonation capability or a radio transmitter, commercial blasting caps, what appeared to be genuine C4, a wrap of det cord, and tightly coiled wires taped to conductive rods. That's about it. Of course, as soon as the fire department clears the building for structural safety, we'll finish the render safe, and you can see the vests firsthand."

"I can't delay my return any longer. I just wanted to confirm Lieutenant Terrell's observations."

Although I couldn't understand what good it would do, I offered, "I can E-mail the reports and digital photos as soon as they're ready."

"I'd appreciate that. Nice work today, Sergeant."

"Thank you, sir." As I walked away, I kept expecting him to criticize me for leaving my vehicle unattended, but he never did.

When I finally tracked Nick down, he asked, "How did it go?"

"Okay. Strange," I sighed. "You know, when I was talking to him, I got the impression that he was making sure our stories matched."

Nick nodded. "You think *we're* suspects?"

"What I think doesn't matter, does it?"

"As a matter of fact, it does."

I motioned for him to move aside where we could talk in private. "Listen, I thought of something that's a little farfetched, but I still want to throw the idea out and see what you think."

"Let's hear it."

"Did anything about subject two's vest strike you as really unusual? Inconsistent with the other vests?"

Nick rubbed his forehead with one hand as he thought. Suddenly, he declared, "The det cord."

I nodded. "It doesn't fit, does it? With genuine C4 wired into commercial-grade blasting caps, a wrap of det cord would just be overkill."

"I agree. When we dissect the device, we'll have a better feel for it, but I think you might be onto something."

"Good. Then you won't think what I'm about to say is

crazy." I took a deep breath. "Could the Vest Bomber have gotten the idea for the det cord at the meeting in Topeka? Maybe he added it at the last minute as a statement. The timing is just too odd."

Again, Nick was silent for a few moments. "So we're back to suspecting an inside job?"

"Not necessarily. There are lots of ways to eavesdrop."

He hesitated. "You think someone bugged the meeting?"

I ran my hands through my hair. "Or overheard a phone conversation, or intercepted an E-mail. To tell you the truth, I'm suspicious of practically everyone—except you, of course."

"Thanks for the vote of confidence. Okay, on the assumption you might be right, we need to act discreetly. I'll see what I can find out without arousing any suspicions."

As I turned to leave, he stopped me and added, "Never question your instincts, Jamie. Training is important, but in pivotal moments, always lean toward what your gut tells you. Always."

# 4

My already hectic life became totally insane the next morning when we began the reconstruction phase of the postblast investigation. As is standard with every bombing, all emergency personnel were evacuated from The Parlor as soon as we were out of danger. The entire building was swept for more secondary devices, then the fire department personnel were allowed back inside. Jeff and Marcus assisted with the render safe, and by late afternoon, the site had been declared safe.

All of the exterior walls had survived intact, which

made our job infinitely easier, since there wasn't heavy debris to remove. The building was sectioned into grids, much like overlaying lines from a piece of graph paper atop the litter. All six bomb techs on our squad, plus about twenty-five ATF and FBI agents, were each assigned certain areas, and we began the tedious job of searching for the parts of the bomb. Depending on the size of the device and the level of destruction, the process can take days, weeks, sometimes months. Even so, by the time we piece the puzzle back together, we can routinely reconstruct up to 90 percent of the actual weapon. It's a very expensive process, but luckily, our government is dedicated to making certain the people behind such hostile acts are fully prosecuted.

In this case, it didn't take long to determine the seat of the explosion was exactly where Nick had guessed: in the sporting goods area on the opposite side of the store. The device itself was actually rather primitive: a wad of C4 with a detonator rigged to a common beeper, stuffed inside a black backpack that had been hanging on a wall with several others. When the bomber was ready for the place to blow, all he had to do was dial the phone number of the beeper. The electrical impulses generated by the signal traveled to the blasting cap. The rest is history.

The confirmation that he had advanced to remote detonation capability didn't escape me, and I could almost see the steel trap in Nick's mind snap closed around it. We had to assume the Vest Bomber was no longer in the learning stage of the game. He had passed the advanced test and was ready to escalate to the next level of terrorism.

It turned out we had been right about the two vests as well. The security guard's vest was a hoax, but Delores's vest was hot. The section with tightly coiled wires from the blasting cap had been surrounded with enough commercial-grade C4 to easily destroy everything inside the vault. Whoever we were dealing with ha ' access to both military and commercial explosives. That would make them slightly easier to find than the average needle in the haystack, but it still didn't shine a spotlight on where they might be obtaining the materials to build such powerful bombs.

No one on the investigative team thought that a check of people in the area who were licensed to handle explosives would do much good, but we tried it anyway. The general consensus was that the Vest Bomber was self-trained and a very fast learner. At the same time, we knew that neither military nor commercial C4 is easy to come by, although a black market does exist. Considering the amount of cash and jewels he had netted from his previous robberies, acquiring high-priced supplies wouldn't be a problem.

Searching through debris is backbreaking work, even when a tech is in good shape. The explosion had left my back looking like someone had beaten me with a baseball bat, then kicked me a few times just for good measure. I have to admit, there were times when I wondered if I could take it. The mere thought of putting on my bullet-proof vest made me shudder, and bending over occasionally brought tears to my eyes. I could tell by how carefully Nick moved that he had his share of aches and pains as well. We split a bottle of Advil, but neither of us uttered a single complaint—at least not in public.

Besides the reconstruction, there were meetings. Endless questions. The Parlor's bombing had been high profile, spotlighted on every newscast across the nation. Whenever the nation focuses on a criminal event, the FBI steps up its involvement. They contributed specially trained agents and high-tech equipment and, at least to me, an undeniable sense of impending doom.

For the most part, Nick worked closely on the reconstruction phase, while I reviewed tapes that might lead us
to the Vest Bomber. I watched the grainy black-and-white
security videotape of The Parlor's parking lot over and
over again. Luckily, the blast hadn't knocked out the taping equipment, and the battery backup had continued its
operation even after the fire department shut off the
power.

The video showed the Vest Bomber's arrival and departure in a new-model white van with darkly tinted windows and no license plates. But more importantly, only
one man was ever caught on tape. Unless his accomplice
was simply along for the ride, it was apparent the Vest
Bomber not only drove the van but handled his kidnapping victims completely alone. Since not a single victim
had ever heard more than one voice, all of us agreed that
the Vest Bomber was probably trying to throw us off his
trail by pretending to talk to someone else while the victims were present. A clever ploy if it turned out to be
true.

Working with an FBI specialist, I studied the crowds
that gathered at the site as well. Using equipment that
enhanced the grainy black-and-white footage into glossy
eight by ten pictures, four people stood out in The Parlor's
parking area. The first was a man on a motorcycle who
had arrived at the scene early, then left just moments before the blast. The second bore a striking resemblance to
Trooper Carl Johnson. That man arrived about five
minutes after the bomb exploded, stood behind the Do
Not Cross line for roughly three minutes, then left. The
last two were people I would have expected to be there,
although I couldn't explain how or why either had arrived
as quickly as they did. Lieutenant Colonel Jones and ATF
Agent Frank Nichols had both arrived at the scene less
than three minutes after the explosion. Jones had claimed

he was going back to Topeka at eight o'clock the previous night, and Nichols hadn't been one of the agents notified that morning by ATF dispatch.

I rewound the tape several times, studying the tall man's every move. After spending an hour staring at the still photos, it was clear that there was no way to tell if the man actually was Carl Johnson. He wasn't in uniform, and most of the time his face was obstructed from view by a light pole. The minute Nick, Delores, and I safely emerged from the building, he slipped back into the crowd and disappeared. Considering the number of law enforcement agents who had voluntarily arrived at the scene, his presence could easily be chalked up to either morbid curiosity or the desire to help. Either way, I decided that it was high time Nick and I had a chat with Trooper Johnson.

Even though I had promised I'd meet everyone for a drink after work, I ended up spending the evening sitting alone in a dark room at headquarters because I couldn't shake the feeling that I was missing something. Watching the videotapes, I developed a fascination with the man on the motorcycle. Although he didn't ever step off the cycle, it was obvious from his gangly legs that he was at least as tall as the man caught on the security tape. Besides the fact that he never took off his helmet, which was odd considering it was almost 80°F that morning, there was something about him that didn't seem quite right. Finally, it dawned on me to play the secure com audiotape in synch with the videotape.

My heart raced when I realized I had found evidence that could link the mystery man to the crime. Before I cut the antenna on Delores's vest, he had sat alertly astride the motorcycle, never moving an inch. Through the initial stages of the bomb call, his head had been tilted slightly to one side, as though he were intently listening to something. Within seconds after I snipped the antenna wire, motorcycle man's shoulders squared. He sat up straighter, suddenly more interested in what was going on around him. About a minute later, he reached into his back pocket, possibly to turn off a radio receiver. During the rest of the render safe, he began to fidget, rolling his wrist outward to glance at the face of his watch several times. At exactly two minutes before the secondary explosion, he cranked up his cycle and drove away. My theory was simple: When Delores's vest didn't blow on schedule, he left to dial the pager's number to detonate the secondary bomb.

Stretching to ease the knot between my shoulder blades, I yawned. I couldn't wait until morning, since I was eager to ask the FBI tech if he could blow up the frame large enough to read the numbers on motorcycle man's wristwatch. In my gut I was sure they not only wouldn't show the right time of day, but that the numbers in the frames would prove he was watching a chronometer counting *down* to a critical event: the timed explosion of the vest on Delores.

# 5

The next morning, I had just settled down at the kitchen table with my newspaper and a fresh cup of coffee when the phone rang. Pushing stiffly up, I grabbed the portable phone and half growled, "Hello," before easing myself back into my chair.

"Good morning," a spirited male voice replied.

Rubbing my eyes, I yawned and asked, "Nick, is that you?"

"In all my glory."

I groaned. "You don't usually sound so chipper before

noon. And believe me, I'd never have thought of you as glorious in any way, shape, or form."

He laughed. "I'm in such a good mood, I'll ignore the fact that you are obviously jealous of my newfound fame."

As usual, Nick made me smile. "Jealous? They called me, too. There isn't enough money in the Federal Reserve to convince me to appear on a live national news program, even via satellite. Although, Matt and Jesse tell me you were quite the heroic rogue. Very gallant."

"Youth recognizes great talent."

"Youth thinks that the MTV guy who puts dog crap on his microphone when he interviews people is cool, too. Don't let it go to your head. Why *are* you so charged?"

"I slept like a rock last night."

"I wish I had. I didn't get home until midnight, then I kept having nightmares. Creepy people hidden in the darkness, hissing and laughing while they watched us try to defuse a nuclear bomb."

"You should've had a beer with us after the show, blown off some steam."

Taking a long sip of coffee, I replied, "You'll be glad I didn't."

"Find something in the tapes?"

"Yes. We're going to need to contact the local television stations to be sure they've turned over any video footage of the other vest bombing incidents. I think our guy is like a pyromaniac. I'm pretty sure he gets off watching the fear and panic bred by his handiwork. And, Nick, is there any way we can sit down and have a talk with Carl Johnson soon? I can't be certain, but someone who looks an awful lot like him arrived at the scene about five minutes after the explosion, then left as soon as we came outside."

"I'll set it up, but I can't guarantee how soon it will

be. The powers that be might not like us inferring that one of our own could be behind this."

"Would they prefer picking up the pieces that are left of us if we don't catch the bastard soon?"

"No. We just need to be careful. We should sit down and make a tactful list of questions. Nothing emotional, nothing accusatory."

It was easy to see his point, so I quickly agreed. "Not a problem. Tact is my middle name."

"How's Romeo?"

Running my bare feet across my furry friend's neck, I replied, "Much better. He's still got a limp, but he seems pretty much back to normal. You haven't forgotten that you're coming here for Sunday dinner, have you?"

"Wouldn't miss it."

I took a deep breath, then added, "I was thinking. Would you like to bring Bimbo Batgirl along?"

"I believe her name is Bimbo Bat*woman,* and it's nice of you to ask. We're going out again tonight, so I'll see if she's free."

"Sounds like you've been spending a lot of time together."

"She's fascinating. We have long talks about everything from politics to the effect of technology on the future. My ex's idea of a deep conversation was what to have for dinner each night."

I didn't miss that he had referred to Lori as his *ex* for the first time. In fact, I thought it was a good sign, an overdue indication that he was finally moving on with his life. "Nick, I'm sorry if I wasn't very supportive earlier. Maybe I actually was jealous. It isn't easy trying to maintain a relationship with a guy halfway around the world, and it seems like you've found someone very special."

"It's okay. This has been one hell of a summer, hasn't it?"

"And it's not over yet."

Nick hesitated. When he spoke again, his voice was lower, more controlled, as he added, "Jamie, one more thing."

"Yes?"

"The chief of maintenance confirmed that my radiator was *intentionally* punctured, probably a couple of hours before the call at The Parlor. And it wasn't just my Suburban. The asshole screwed up Alexa's Miata while it was parked in my driveway, too."

Caught off guard, it took me a moment to understand what good it would do the Vest Bomber to only partially disable Nick's car. Finally it made sense, and I halfheartedly acknowledged, "To slow you down. And he made sure you couldn't just take a different car if you happened to notice an antifreeze leak under yours. Yet he didn't tamper with mine."

"Your Suburban would have been parked inside your locked garage. Mine was outside, on my driveway."

"True. Or maybe he didn't *want* to slow me down. Maybe his goal is to make me work alone."

"That's a possibility. Either way, from this point on, I don't want you getting into *any* vehicle without checking for a device or looking for any kind of tampering, even if it's been in the garage all night. That includes the bomb truck, since it wouldn't be impossible for someone to have access to where it's parked. Unlikely, but not impossible. Understand?"

"Got it. See you at headquarters."

"Will do."

For some reason, Nick's news didn't frighten me. Instead, I felt as though I had finally been pushed too far. I wanted nothing more than to catch the Vest Bomber and kick his ass, as my grandmother would have said, clear into next week.

# eight

1

Whenever I feel as though I'm losing control of my life, I resort to ritual. I clean. Everything in sight. The moment I stepped in my house that night, all I could see was dirt. Cobwebs that had imperceptibly graced the highest corners of the entryway for months suddenly caught my attention. Without even thinking about eating dinner, I attacked the place with a vengeance. No dust bunny was safe from the long arm of the law, which in this case was wielding the extension hose of a brand-new vacuum cleaner that claimed to have the sucking strength of an F5 tornado.

As I worked, I thought about David and agonized over Matt. Even though I tried to push all my professional worries to the back of my mind, the Vest Bomber's latest tricks kept creeping in to taunt me. In whichever room I was cleaning, Romeo would curl up near the air-conditioning vent and occasionally cast me an *are you having fun yet?* gaze.

I found myself toying with the idea of accepting David's offer for Matt and me to move to the East Coast. In my heart, I knew it was impossible to run away from my problems, yet for just a few moments, I craved an escape from the real-life crises that seemed to be knocking down my door. It was fun to imagine dropping everything to start a fresh, new life. Yet the moment I thought of leaving Nick to face the Vest Bomber alone, the fantasy vanished. Nick would never abandon me in a crisis, and I had no intention of bailing out on him.

After dragging the vacuum upstairs, I opened the door to Matt's room and felt another tug on my heart. I missed being able to talk to him, to eat with him, to simply have him nearby. Matt's bed was made, his desk neat. I missed him so much that it hurt.

My pager sounded, leaving me no time to wallow in self-pity. Reading the digital screen, I reached for the phone on Matt's desk. In a few seconds I had jotted the address onto a napkin and was rushing downstairs. There had been a house explosion with one confirmed fatality and another victim in critical condition.

Since Nick lived closer to the scene, I assumed he would be up. Romeo's slight limp made me pause for a moment, but I carefully lifted him into the Suburban just in case we needed his unique expertise. Most likely, he would simply rest at the scene.

As soon as I was on my way, I dialed Nick's cell phone. No answer. "Shit. Not again," I grumbled. Thinking his cell phone's battery might be dead, I tried tach one on the radio. "Lieutenant Terrell?"

Dead air. "Come on, Nick. This isn't funny," I muttered, then called ATF. Since the dispatcher told me Simon Stanley would be responding, I asked her to have him call my cell phone as soon as possible. Hanging up, I dialed Nick's number again. I left a voice message so he would know I was on my way to pick up the bomb truck at the Training Center before reporting to the scene.

Growing more frustrated by the second, I called dispatch. "Has Lieutenant Terrell answered his page?"

"No, ma'am," the operator replied.

"Keep trying every fifteen minutes. And thanks."

A few minutes later, my phone rang, and I was disappointed to see on the caller ID that it was Simon. "Sergeant Stone," I answered.

"You rang?" Simon asked.

"Yes. What's your ETA on the house bombing?"

"I'm close. Probably five minutes at the most."

"I'm on my way to pick up the bomb truck. Would you mind lending me a hand and making certain the perimeter is maintained at one hundred yards and the road stays clear?"

"Not a problem. Where's Terrell?"

"Temporarily out of contact. I think his pager must be broken. Thanks, Simon." I hung up and spent the next thirty minutes fighting my anger as I mentally prepared to enter another crime scene alone. I was relieved to see Simon heading my way as I parked the bomb truck and climbed out, wondering if I'd have to lock the door every time I stepped more than a few yards away from it.

"Terrell's Suburban is here, but I haven't seen him yet. Would he have gone inside?"

"No way. Not without the proper equipment," I declared.

Casting me a frustrated look, Simon added, "Any idea where he might be hiding?"

My heart skipped a beat and I swallowed hard to suppress the horrible thought that instantly jumped to mind. Leaning close to Simon, I whispered, "Last time the Vest

Bomber struck, he sabotaged Nick's Suburban to slow him down. You don't suppose it's possible that Nick arrived earlier than the Vest Bomber expected and . . ."

Simon softly shook his head as he protested, "And he nabbed him? Jamie, this isn't a jewelry store, so it would be way out of the Vest Bomber's profile for him to strike here. Besides, Nick is quite capable of taking care of himself. But just to be certain, I'll talk to the supervising sergeant and have everyone on duty watch for anything suspicious." His eyes sympathetically met mine. "Stop worrying. I'm sure he'll turn up any minute. Maybe he's evacuating houses on the other side of the block. Meanwhile, until he shows up, I'd be happy to fill his shoes as best I can."

"I'd really appreciate it. Pretty soon, you'll be an expert."

"Video and pictures first, right?" he asked.

I nodded. "Right."

"ATF uses the same kind of digital camera as your squad. I'll take the pictures while you shoot the videotape if that's okay."

Unbelievably impressed with his newfound attitude, I raised my eyebrows and asked, "Are you sure?"

"Absolutely. Just tell me what you want."

The knot in the pit of my stomach grew the entire time we worked. Since Nick's truck was here, he *had* to have gotten his page. And if he did, why didn't he call dispatch to report that he was responding? Surely his cell phone *and* his radio weren't out. Even if he had only been a couple of blocks away, he would've let them know he was reporting to the scene.

As soon as I finished the video sweep, I walked to Nick's truck and tugged on the door handle. It was locked, so I ran back to the bomb truck, grabbed a flashlight, then dug his spare set of keys out of my jump bag. We each have duplicates, for just such emergencies.

His clipboard was on the front passenger seat, and his cell phone and radio were still in their holders. The phone's digital display read "three missed calls." I knew they were all from me. The backseat held his usual equipment. Nothing seemed to be missing or even disturbed. I was beginning to feel relieved when I noticed his bullet-proof vest. A chill ran down my back. Nick would never have responded to a scene like this without putting on his vest. Never.

Simon stopped at my side and tried to encourage me. "I know you're getting more worried by the minute, but I'm sure he's okay."

I shook my head. "It's just so strange. Nick wouldn't do something like this. He knows it would put me in a bind, not to mention that it would scare the hell out of me. Would you do me a favor?"

He nodded.

"There's too much debris to send in the robot. I'm going to have to do a walk-through in the bomb suit. Would you man the secure com while I'm inside? I want to know the second any information on Nick turns up."

"You got it."

I cast him a stern glare. "If I tell you that the air has gone out, follow the exact path I used to get in. No heroics allowed."

"I'm not a rookie, Jamie."

"Sorry. This one has me really on edge."

Simon was far more adept at helping me into the suit this time. Before long, my heart was pounding as he fixed the helmet's shield into place and I was thrown into the claustrophobic world of the bomb suit once again. A few deep, calming breaths helped settle my nerves, but not nearly as much as usual. I missed Nick's supportive presence, but more importantly, I knew in my heart that something bad had happened. I remembered his advice on trusting my instincts all too well, but this time, I prayed my instincts were wrong.

Stepping inside the blast zone, I forced myself to think only as I'd been trained. I could immediately tell that the seat of the explosion was on the kitchen counter, and from the waist down I could see that it was a woman who had been killed. The explosion had thrown her against the oven, severely damaging her torso and blackening her face to the point where she was unrecognizable. Dental records would probably have to be used to identify the body, since both of the woman's hands were missing. I mentally noted to watch for them as I moved inch by inch across the cluttered floor, describing each step for Simon and the record.

The first-response officer had given me a rough sketch of where the second victim had been removed by the paramedics. I was almost to that point when the power to the suit blinked off. Even though I was thinking every cussword I had ever learned, I stiffly said, "Simon, stand by. The suit just shut down. I'm going to try to get it to come back on-line. Talk to me."

I waited to hear him reply, but he didn't say a word. "Simon, can you hear me?"

"Yes."

"When I say *talk to me,* it's okay for you to reply. You're just supposed to maintain radio silence when I'm working on something delicate."

"Got it," he snapped.

Moving closer to the wall, a beeping noise froze me in my tracks. The last time I heard a distant pager, it was quickly followed by a blast. Instinctively, I pulled my hands farther up into the bomb suit's protective sleeves and bent my arms. Every muscle in my body tensed as I tried to determine where the noise was coming from, which was practically impossible with the sound of my own ragged breathing echoing in my ears. The helmet was beginning to fog when I spotted the corner of what looked like a pager. It was buried under a pile of books that had fallen where a bookshelf collapsed about three feet from my left boot.

Simon's voice filled my head. "Jamie?"

"I'm okay. Still trying to get power." Looking around, I slammed my back and shoulder painfully against the wall, carefully avoiding the traces of blood and hair left when the second victim impacted the Sheetrock. The suit's light flickered, then the unit came fully on-line again. With a sigh, I declared, "The suit's back up. I'm stooping down to pick up a pager that's sounding."

Bending slowly, I stretched my hand outside the sleeve and wrapped my fingers around the small unit. Holding it in front of the helmet's shield, I read the digital display. As though a wrecking ball had swung across the room and struck me without warning, I staggered back against the wall. The pager was identical to my own, right down to the dispatcher's telephone number flashing on the small screen and the message typed below it. There was no doubt in my mind that I was holding *Nick's* pager. "Oh, God, no!" I muttered.

"Jamie, what's wrong?" Simon demanded.

Suddenly, I noticed the titles of the books scattered on the floor. Most were textbooks on psychology, the kind used in college courses. "Simon, whose house is this?"

"What?"

"Go ask one of the neighbors who owns this house! Now!"

It only took a few seconds for him to reply. "A KCU college professor named Alexa Dixon."

"Simon." I took a deep breath, unwilling to allow my

emotions to bleed into my voice. "Simon, call the hospital. Get an ID and status on the male victim."

"Why?"

"Damn it, just do it!" I raged, barely able to move. As I waited, I noticed once again the smear of blood on the wall near where I stood. Tears were threatening, but I knew I couldn't break down. I fought to stay focused because I had no choice.

A patch of dark material caught my eye, and I bent to pick it up. It was a heavy black mesh lined with white cloth. The lining had been sewn on with sloppy orange whipstitching. Scanning the length of debris that had blown up against the wall, I saw several more pieces of it, and my heart went absolutely cold—so cold that I was afraid I wouldn't ever be able to move again.

"Jamie," Simon's voice rang in my muddled mind.

I took another deep breath, already knowing what he would say. "Yes."

His voice was flat. Controlled. "It was Nick. He's in surgery. He's listed in critical condition."

Tears rolled down my cheeks, and my hand hit the face shield as I instinctively tried to wipe them away. After saying a silent prayer, I gathered my courage. It didn't take long for a horrified sense of injustice to pound down my heartache and give me a fresh surge of strength.

"Jamie, are you okay? Do you need me to come in?"

"Damn it, it's *him,* Simon."

"What? Who are you talking about?"

"The Vest Bomber did this. He came after Nick, and he killed Alexa."

"Who's Alexa?" he asked.

"Nick's new girlfriend!"

Dead air hung between us for several moments. I could tell Simon thought I was crazy as he asked, "Are you sure?"

"I'm sure. There are pieces of vest all over the place. We were right. He's targeting *us*."

More dead air.

I could hear the anger in his voice as Simon replied, "We'll catch him, Jamie. We'll do whatever it takes to bring him down."

"Damn right we will."

# 2

Even though I could have left to be with Nick, I knew he was in the intensive care unit and that there wasn't a damn thing I could do to help him at the hospital. Instead, I vowed to stay at the site until I found something that would lead to the person responsible for Alexa's death.

As usual, bad news travels fast. Word of Nick's injury quickly reached the other four bomb techs on our squad, Jeff, Marcus, Bill, and Larry. Although Marcus, Bill, and Larry each tried to comfort me before they started to work, it soon became apparent that Jeff was avoiding me. It was so obvious that I pulled him aside to ask if there was a problem we needed to discuss.

"No," he replied, his jaw firmly set. "I just want to catch the asshole who did this."

Since he was practically distraught, I assumed he was having trouble coping with Nick's injury and didn't press him. For the rest of the evening, we worked in dead silence.

Our first step was to establish that there were no secondary devices hidden in Alexa's house using the bomb suit and the robot. When we were finally certain that the area was safe, we entered in our biohazard gear and began to try to unravel exactly what had happened. Working harder and faster than I ever had in my entire life, I was fueled by an anger so deep it frightened me. I wanted to kill the Vest Bomber—slowly, painfully, with absolutely no regard for the law. Thoughts of vigilante justice kept me focused, made it easy for me to spend hour after hour digging for even the smallest shred of evidence.

I had just tagged and bagged another piece of vest when I turned to find Simon standing in the doorway, shaking his head. In his gloved hands were several pieces of color-coded wire. "Looks like you were right. It is the Vest Bomber's handiwork. This changes everything."

"I know. It was bad enough when we were just dealing with jewelry stores. Now it's personal."

Simon took a step toward me and softly exhaled as he tilted his head. "Are you sure you're all right? There are more than enough personnel to handle things here. No one is going to think you're wimping out if you go check on Nick. That's what partners are for. They care about each other."

I nodded. Since I wanted to talk to Nick as soon as humanly possible, I agreed. "I think I will go to the hospital now. That is, if you'll promise me something first."

He opened his arms and shrugged. "Anything. Just name it."

"Make sure everyone strictly follows procedure on this one. When we catch this guy, I don't want to see him get off on a technicality."

"I'll make sure the case is so airtight the bad guy won't even be able to breathe."

"Thanks for being here tonight, Simon."

"No problem. Now get your butt to the hospital. Your partner needs you."

With a curt nod, I did.

# nine

**1**

Since it was a little after two A.M. and the rest of the team still needed the equipment in the bomb truck, I took Nick's Suburban and dropped Romeo off at home. I grabbed a piece of cold pizza, put on a clean pair of jeans, and left for the hospital. Thanks to a freshly elevated level of paranoia, on my way I called in a request for a squad car to watch the Coleman house, just to be certain the Vest Bomber's next trick didn't involve getting to me through Matt.

When I arrived, I discovered that Nick was out of surgery to repair a compound fracture of his right forearm and was still being kept in the intensive care unit because of the severity of his concussion. Headquarters had already assigned a trooper to stand guard in the hall, and I quickly introduced myself before stepping inside. The night shift nurse was kind enough to explain that Nick also had several bruised ribs, a laceration on his left thigh, plus multiple scrapes and cuts from being hit with debris.

The small room where he slept was crammed with so many monitors that there was barely enough space to walk. Even though it was against the rules, the night shift nurse wedged a chair beside Nick's bed for me so that I could be there when he awoke.

For a long time, I just sat by his side, holding his hand and watching the rhythm of his heartbeat translated by a high-tech machine into a thin, green line. As is too often the case in times of trouble, I imagined the worst. I simply couldn't bear the thought of Nick dying, so I tried to think of how I could end the nightmare we were both living. Although no solution immediately hit me, I realized that even with a guard outside, Nick's life might still be in jeopardy. Being alone made him vulnerable, since anyone dressed as a hospital employee could gain access to him. Leaving for a few minutes, I rushed downstairs and returned with the jump bag out of Nick's Suburban.

Settling back at his side, I leaned my head on the edge of the mattress and watched the steady rise and fall of his chest. At some point I must have fallen asleep, because I awoke just after dawn with my hand still firmly clasping his. It took me a few seconds to realize where I was and that Nick's fingers had just squeezed mine.

Standing, I leaned so that my face was just a few inches above his. Even though his eyes were closed, I touched his forehead and whispered, "Talk to me, Nick. I need your help."

For a moment, he didn't move; then his eyelids fluttered.

I smiled as our eyes met. "You're going to be okay, but that hard head of yours took a pretty solid knock."

He managed a slight nod.

"Matt sends his love. He claims he's going to repeatedly whop your ass at some crazy video game while you're recuperating, and that once you're well, he'll give you some new bruises at Paintball Land."

This time Nick lightly shook his head and attempted a smile. His face was so swollen and battered that it was hard to look at him without longing to make the pain go away. Even so, I knew he would want to help if he could. Clasping his uninjured hand, I asked, "Think you can handle a few questions?"

Another nod, but I could already tell he wasn't up to much talking. There were so many things I wanted to ask, yet at the same time I didn't want to agitate or tire him. Watching him intently, I asked, "Do you think the Vest Bomber was targeting you?"

He closed his eyes as if in deep thought, and for a moment I thought he had lost consciousness again. Finally, he opened his eyes and barely shook his head. Very weakly, he said, "The package was addressed to Alexa. I may have been the indirect target. Is she . . ."

Squeezing his hand, I softly replied, "I'm really sorry, but Alexa didn't make it, Nick."

He shook his head and, with great emotion, choked out, "The bastard killed her to get to me."

In response to a sudden jump in Nick's blood pressure and pulse, the nurse came rushing in. After shooting me a warning glare, she announced, "I believe Mr. Terrell needs his rest. You'll have to continue this later."

"I'm sorry, but lives are at stake. I'll keep it short."

Glowering over her reading glasses, she warned, "You'd better."

My cheeks flushed and I was relieved when she abruptly turned and left. Clenching Nick's hand, I carefully leaned across the maze of tubes and wires to give him a good, solid hug. In his ear, I whispered, "How many people knew about you and Alexa?"

"Only you. I haven't told anyone else. Not a soul."

"Maybe he followed you."

I could almost see the flow of agonizing memories rushing through his mind. "Possible," he muttered. "Or my phone could've been tapped."

"How did it happen?"

He spoke slowly, almost methodically. "The package was on her porch when I picked her up. She was like a kid with a present, insisting she open it before we left for dinner. I was across the room, looking at a book. The second I saw what she was pulling out of the box, I screamed, '*No!*' But it was too late. I barely had time to block the blast wave with my arms. She never had a chance." He closed his eyes, then added, "Jesus. Poor Alexa."

"It wasn't your fault."

His eyes flew open, and his heart rate jumped again. "I should have known! We *both* should have known!"

The fact that he was probably right made my stomach roll and ripped at my heart. Unable to think of anything to say that wouldn't be a lie, I simply nodded. After waiting a few seconds to see if the nurse was going to go ballistic on me, I asked, "Did the package have a return address?"

He nodded, obviously fighting to remember details that were best left buried. "She said it was from a catalog that she bought stuff from all the time. It had Free Samples for our Valued Customer stamped on the outside."

"So whoever did this knew enough to make sure neither of you would suspect it was a bomb."

"There was another goddamned *vest* inside. It's like he wanted to be sure the last thing I thought before I died was that he had won."

"He's a sick, sadistic bastard." Wiping the beads of

sweat from his brow, I said, "That's enough for now. We can talk about the rest later."

Nick's voice was fragile yet eerily calm as he stated, "Look for a trigger that would've made contact when she had lifted half of the vest out of the box. My guess is it was probably on the lower back, about the same place as the clock on the last one. I want the shifts rotated between the other two teams, with our slot only on every fourth call. Pair up with Jeff. Everyone on the squad is solid, but I think the two of you will work best together. I don't want you responding alone. If there's an early-morning vest call, make it a goddamned threesome, but I'm warning you, Jamie, *do not* respond alone."

"There's plenty of time to figure all that out later. For now, I just want you to promise you'll get some rest."

Nick drew a long, ragged breath and closed his eyes again.

I chose my next words very carefully. "Up until now, the Vest Bomber has always had us perform in *his* court. Now he's coming to where *we* are. There's a guard in the hall, but just in case things get really *tight*, I brought your jump bag and put it in the drawer beside your bed. Your Sig's on top. If you get bored, you can scan the FBI blow-ups taken from the news footage of the Vest Bomber's crime scenes. They're right under your gun. But most importantly, you just rest and get well. I need you back at my side. Soon."

"Be careful," he whispered.

"I will."

Standing, I wiped a tear from the corner of his eye as he hoarsely urged, "No doubts, Jamie."

I smiled and shook my head. "No doubts."

Leaving him like that was one of the hardest things I've ever done. Nick is a strong, proud man, the type who would rather suffer silently than ask for help. But what bothered me at that moment was the nagging thought of the Vest Bomber somehow getting past the guard and creeping inside his room. If Nick were asleep, he'd be completely defenseless. After I explained to the trooper on duty how dangerous the situation might be, I took the elevator downstairs.

The elevator doors slid quietly open, and I started to step out just as Nick's ex-wife, Lori Terrell, began to step in. The moment her eyes met mine, she sighed and stopped. I could tell she had been crying. As the elevator went on without her, we exchanged a silent hug. Even though we had never become close friends, we had shared Nick's life for over ten years. During their divorce, I had carefully stayed in the middle, trying my best not to choose sides. Being the wife of someone who risks life and limb daily couldn't be easy, especially with a man like Nick, who seemed to go out of his way to find the most dangerous assignments.

Lori is barely five two, with soft brown eyes that reflect her every emotion. From the quick glance we had exchanged, I already knew she still cared deeply about Nick. Even though their divorce would soon be final, Lori wasn't the type who could just turn and walk away.

Pulling back, I confidently announced, "You can stop worrying. Nick is going to be fine."

She shook her head. "It's my fault. . . . I'm so sorry."

"Lori, this couldn't possibly be your fault. It was the Vest Bomber again. There's nothing you or anyone else could have done."

Guilt weighed heavy on her, and a fresh wave of tears started to roll down her cheeks. "Jamie, don't you see? First, The Parlor, now this? In all these years he's never even come close to being hurt. Now, he's . . . he's pre-occupied. He's not being careful. He just doesn't care anymore. It *is* my fault. I never should've left him."

Placing my hands on her shoulders, I looked her straight in the eye. "Lori, that's nonsense. I was at The Parlor when it blew, and Nick had done *everything* by the book. I promise you, he is *not* being careless. He would never risk anyone's life, and he *saved* two innocent people that day. Understand?"

She stiffly nodded, then confessed, "When I heard a woman had been killed, I was so afraid it was you."

I shook my head. "I'm very sorry you had to go through that." Although sooner or later I was sure she'd learn the truth about Alexa's intimate relationship with her ex-husband, I had no intention of telling her right then. Instead, I explained, "She was a friend of Nick's. A psychology professor at KCU."

Lori nodded and wiped away the tears. "I don't remember him ever mentioning her."

"They hadn't known each other very long. She was studying the personality traits of people in high-risk jobs."

As though it hadn't dawned on her that Nick would make new friends, she cocked her head to one side and said, "Oh. He'd be perfect for that." Almost as an afterthought, she asked, "Do you think seeing me would upset him?"

I smiled. "No matter what's happened lately, Nick still cares about you. He always will. Just do me a favor."

Sniffling, she replied, "Anything."

"No guilt trips. Nick is as professional as they come. Just be there for friendly support. Okay?"

"Okay." Another elevator arrived, and she stepped inside. Just before the doors closed, she smiled and said, "Thanks, Jamie. Give Matt a hug for me, and be careful!"

"I will!" I called, then turned to cross the foyer. As I headed for the exit, thoughts of Nick and Lori were quickly replaced by the job at hand. Every criminal makes mistakes; the trick is finding them. The Vest Bomber had somehow discovered the name of the catalog store where Alexa had shopped. He could've been watching her mail, talking to her friends, snooping around her house, or even breaking into her computer records if she shopped on-line. The possibilities were endless, but at least it was a place to start.

# 2

Maybe if I hadn't been so distracted, I would've looked outside and realized I was walking straight into an ambush before it was too late. The instant I stepped into the morning sunlight, first one microphone, then another was jabbed in front of my face. Seemingly endless questions were fired far too fast for me to answer, and my heart rate kicked into high stress mode.

*"You're Lieutenant Terrell's partner, Sergeant Jamie Stone, is that right?" "How is he? Is he expected to live?" "Was it the Vest Bomber again?" "Is he trying to kill Lieutenant Terrell?" "Do you think you'll be the next target?" "What was Lieutenant Terrell's relationship with Dr. Alexa Dixon?" "Was she killed instantly?" "Do you think the Vest Bomber will be upset that he murdered the wrong person?" "How will losing the head of the Hazardous Device squad impact your unit?"*

The last two questions made me so mad that I held up my hands and shouted, "Enough!"

When they were all quiet, I took a deep breath and gave them a brief statement. Projecting my voice with as much strength and confidence as I could muster, I announced, "I'm Sergeant Jamie Stone with the Kansas State Patrol Hazardous Device Unit. Our unit's commander, Lieutenant Nick Terrell, was injured last night by an explosion that is currently under investigation. He is resting well at this time, and we hope to have him back on duty as soon as possible. I'm afraid that's all the information available to the public at this time. Thank you."

Another barrage of questions stung as though they were pelting me with rocks, but I ignored them. Pushing past the tangle of cameras and cables, I practically ran to Nick's Suburban. After getting out of there as fast as I could, I pulled into an empty parking lot to calm down. Using my cell phone, I called to leave a message for Matt to be extra careful, plus I explained why a squad car would be lurking close by the Coleman house until the Vest Bomber was in custody. Knowing Matt would be safe gave me the energy to move on. My pulse was almost back to normal by the time I reached my office at head-quarters, although my nerves were still so tightly wired that I instinctively flinched at every unexpected noise. I wasn't surprised to see my own Suburban had been re-trieved from the Training Center and parked outside my office window where I'd be sure to notice it.

Typical of the concern troopers have for one another, not one person who saw me failed to ask about Nick and to offer their help in any way possible. Bennie stopped me at the front door to give me a hug and to reassure me that Nick was going to be just fine. In her words, he was as tough as a mule and twice as ornery, and he'd be back to kick us all into line in a matter of days.

Every kind word and act of thoughtfulness touched me, but it had an unexpected side effect as well. It restored my anger, making me want nothing more than to bring the person responsible for the bombings to justice.

**3**

I tried to work, but my mind refused to stay on track. After an hour, I realized it was pointless and decided I needed to go home and get some rest. I stopped to pick up Romeo so he could get some fresh air, then ran by Jesse's house to check on Matt. It was barely nine o'clock on Saturday morning, but Matt was already eating breakfast. He must have spotted me as I pulled into the circular drive, because he jerked open the front door when Romeo and I were barely halfway up the sidewalk, practically smothering me with a big hug. Without pulling away, he asked, "How's Nick?"

"Hanging in there. He'll be okay, but he has a concussion, and it's going to take awhile for his arm to heal. It was a really bad break. Is Jesse still asleep?"

As he nodded, I could see the worry and sadness in his eyes. With determination, he declared, "I want to go see Nick. Now. I know you're super busy, so I'll pay for a cab out of the money I've earned mowing lawns. Please."

My heart ached for him. "I'm sorry, Matt. He's still in the intensive care unit. No visitors allowed."

"That sucks," he dejectedly claimed.

"Did you get my message about being extra careful for awhile?"

"Yep. But I'm always careful." Whispering as if he didn't want anyone else to hear, he added, "My mother is ultraparanoid, you know."

"Funny, but true. More so now than ever. I want you and Jesse's family to go out of the way to make sure to stay safe. Ask them not to answer the door if it's a stranger, to keep the doors and windows locked all the time, and to use their burglar alarm whenever possible. For now, don't walk anywhere alone, especially to our house. I know it isn't very far, but if you think of something you need, leave it on my voice mail, and I'll bring it by as soon as I can. Okay?"

Pretending to be ecstatic, he whooped and declared, "All right! No more jogging?"

Against his wishes, for the last few months I'd been trying to get Matt to exercise regularly. Although I hadn't been cruel enough to force him to go on my predawn runs, I'd been adamant about him walking or jogging at least two miles every other day. When I saw the gleam in his eyes, I was glad that he could still find a positive angle in the midst of the mess our lives had become. With a smile, I replied, "Okay, you win. No running for a couple of days. But you should realize that the world won't come to an end if you still do a few sit-ups and push-ups."

He grinned, "It might."

I teased, "I promise, it won't." Since I knew that Matt had his eye on a girl he had met at school last spring, I added, "Besides, I thought you wanted a six-pack to impress someone special."

Cocking his head, he grinned. "Okay. I'll do the sit-ups. But I won't *enjoy* them."

"I just remembered; you were supposed to clean out the garage today."

His smile was so wide that he looked like the Grinch lustily spying Whoville from afar. "You mean I'm off the hook for that, too?"

"For now. We *will* reschedule it though."

"Maybe you'll forget."

I grinned. "Maybe. Then again, maybe not."

Romeo had plodded to my side and was sitting patiently near my feet. Bending one knee, I gave him a lavish, hair-ruffling hug and asked, "So, you big ball of fur, do you think you're ready to be back on hazardous duty?"

Matt stated, "Looks like he's still limping a little."

"He wasn't until he chased a cat halfway down the block before bringing the paper to me. Running on three legs didn't seem to slow him down much at all."

"That cat better watch out."

"Actually, Romeo may be the one in danger. If the cat

ever figures out what a softy he is, he may end up being at the other end of the chasing game. Let's just hope he's back to work soon. With Nick hurt, I'm going to need all the help I can get." I gave Matt another hug. "I'm heading home to take a nap. I'll probably go back to headquarters around noon. Do you have any big plans for the day?"

"Jesse wants me to go to the mall with him. His mom is forcing the family to buy back-to-school clothes early, and he thinks I'll help keep him sane while his sisters try on everything in the universe. You don't care if I go with them, do you? We'll be back by three, since Jesse has a guitar lesson this afternoon at four."

"Promise not to wander off by yourself?"

"I'm not a toddler, but if it'll make you feel better, I promise."

"Then watch out for the sinkholes," I warned with a grin. Kansas City's only mall is falling into a sinkhole because it was built over limestone.

"Always do."

I dug in my purse until I found my wallet. Handing him a twenty-dollar bill and his new credit card, I gave him my best motherly glare and declared, "Swear you won't lose this?"

"Of course not." Looking at the rectangular plastic card as if it had just dropped from heaven, he grinned, "Will they actually let me *pay* with this thing?"

"You just have to sign the back first and they'll send the bill to me. If you find some jeans you like, get them. Nothing outrageous. A sale would be nice. And make sure they're a little long. Last time I checked you were still growing like a weed."

I had just given my fourteen-year-old son permission to shop with a credit card. Half of me was proud, because I knew he was responsible enough to handle it. The other half longed to be one of those stay-home moms who

cooked, cleaned, and watched *Oprah* every afternoon. At
that point in my life, I could hardly imagine what a luxury
such a lifestyle would be. Then again, deep down I knew
I'd be bored to tears after two days. Maybe Simon was
right: Running through life with a ball of fire nipping at
my heels did seem to be my destiny.

As I headed for the door, Matt asked, "When will you
be off work again?"

Stopping to give him a bear hug, I replied, "I have
absolutely no idea. Just have fun, be careful, and always
remember that I love you."

"I love you, too, Mom. And *you* be careful, too."

# 4

I slept longer than I expected, finally crawling out of bed
when Romeo nudged me at one o'clock that afternoon.
After taking a quick shower, I called to check on Nick.
The nurse in ICU told me that he was resting comfortably
and was steadily improving. Relieved, I dressed, and Romeo and I headed to my office.

While I was working the scene at Alexa's house, every
time I thought of something that might lead us to the
bomber, I jotted it down. Unfortunately, after talking to
Nick, I realized that my approach had partially been from
the wrong angle. According to him, the Vest Bomber had
specifically targeted *Alexa*, not just him, as I had assumed.
Alexa's death made finding a motive even more critical.

Before, we had assumed that profit had been the primary motive, the vests merely a means to an end. But
now, it was safe to speculate that sick, twisted logic was
the bomber's main incentive, and that stealing the jewels
may have just been a way to finance his deviant habit.
Since there was no way he could have known when Alexa

would open the package, he obviously didn't care if he murdered Alexa, Nick, both of them, or anyone who happened to be in the room at the time.

Looking across at Nick's empty chair, I wondered why the bomber had decided to target Alexa instead of simply using a more straightforward attack. The answer was far too easy: to emotionally scar Nick; to make our personal lives hell. If so, that meant the bomber would have had to have been watching one or both of us night and day. I was almost certain Nick was telling the truth about keeping his affair with Alexa a closely guarded secret. Newly divorced people are funny that way—better to keep things quiet than risk having everyone know if another relationship fails.

Digging the list out of my pocket, I read the first task: *Confirm or eliminate Trooper Johnson as suspect.* Dialing the front desk, I asked Bennie to put me through to his extension. Since I got his voice mail, I tried the number she had given me for his pager. After ten minutes, it was obvious he wasn't going to return my call. Next, I contacted his supervisor, who informed me that Trooper Johnson was on a two-week vacation. Hanging up, I muttered, "Damn."

I was about to refer back to my list when my pager began beeping. Since only a phone number was displayed, when a man answered, I stated, "This is Sergeant Jamie Stone with the Kansas State Patrol. I'm responding to a page from this phone number."

"Jamie, it's Simon. I think we've finally got the break we've been waiting for in the Vest Bomber case!"

My heart started to race. "Really? What?"

"We recovered a partial print from the package's wrapping paper last night. IAFIS traced it back to a guy named Luke Layman. I'm wrapping up the federal search warrant right now. Since he's a suspected serial bomber, we'll need a bomb tech on board when we bust his sorry ass. I thought I'd give you first shot at the opportunity to nail the bastard."

IAFIS is the FBI's Integrated Automated Fingerprint Identification System. Ecstatic, I declared, "You bet. Just name the time and place."

He did, then added, "The tactical unit's assembling at five A.M. Be prompt. I've worked with these guys before, and they mean business."

"I'll be there. Thanks, Simon. I appreciate you including me on the team." Hanging up, I leaned down to ruffle the fur on Romeo's back as I declared, "Tomorrow morning we get to help nab the bad guy! Want to go catch a Frisbee to celebrate?"

His paws barely touched the ground as he scrambled to the door.

# ten

## 1

Sleep didn't come easy. Even though it was standard procedure to serve federal warrants at the crack of dawn to catch the criminal off guard, the waiting was hell. Unable to rest, I spent half the night playing FreeCell on my computer and surfing the Internet.

The designated place for the warrant team to assemble was the local police station closest to the suspect's house. By the time I arrived, the impressive team of ATF agents was ready and waiting in full tactical gear: body armor, helmets, goggles, and load-bearing vests. They had pulled out the big guns to serve the search warrant, the ATF's regional tactical unit that covered Kansas, Missouri, Nebraska, and Iowa. Besides Simon, Frank, and their boss, George Harper, a couple of other local agents were there to observe. Each man greeted me with a firm handshake, except Frank, who seemed to be back to his old, condescending self.

Judging from the restless energy that permeated the air, everyone shared my eagerness to put an end to the Vest Bomber's reign of terror. After a quick round of introductions, we went over the plans to enter the residence. When serving warrants, each team member must perform exactly as planned. Variances, even slight ones, can cost lives. Friendly fire is just as lethal as unfriendly fire.

Since Nick had made his position on my working alone more than clear, I had notified the rest of the squad to be on standby, then contacted Jeff. His intense questions on the day of The Parlor bombing still gave me an uneasy feeling, but I respected Nick's orders.

The predawn air was heavy with a thick morning dew, and the men were already sweating. A mixture of fresh cologne and nervous perspiration shadowed the gentle breeze. That unforgettable scent always brings back memories of training, first in Topeka, then at Redstone. As usual, one whiff knocked my level of anxiety up another notch.

Jeff, Romeo, and I were to wait at the curb near the Suburban, then sweep the house, car, and premises for hazardous devices after any occupants inside had been seized. When everyone agreed they were ready, the unit silently loaded into the jump-out vehicle, a special operations van. Together, they moved into position near the target house. Jeff, Romeo, and I followed in my Suburban, leaving the bomb truck and the ambulance at the police station, ready if needed.

Jeff tended to be quiet, but that morning he hadn't said a word since he first arrived. Trying to cut the tension, I asked, "Nervous?"

"No."

"Have any big plans for today?"

He shrugged, his face turned toward the suspect's house as he replied, "Bomb techs should never make plans. Too many unpredictable variables in our lives."

At first I thought he might be kidding, but as the silence between us grew, I realized he was serious. "Well, I make plans all the time, and more often than not, I'm there with bells on. Is this your first federal warrant?" I asked.

Since I only got a nod in reply, I gave up trying to be sociable and focused my attention on the house as well. The place had few distinguishing characteristics. Like the other homes in the typical middle-class neighborhood, it was a rectangular red brick house with white siding. The yard was neatly trimmed, and a porch light had been turned on to illuminate the weathered American flag flying on a wooden pole next to the front door. Judging from the way the flag was lit for respectful display, the man inside was patriotic, in spite of his apparently unseemly pastimes.

I knew from the suspect's profile that he had gained military expertise in the elite U.S. Army Delta Force in Operation Desert Storm. According to his medical records, he had been fighting a persistent battle with alcoholism and drug addiction since two years after he left the service. While on active duty, he had specialized in explosive ordnance detection (EOD) of chemical/biological warfare agents, which accounted for his access to military blasting caps and his detailed knowledge of explosives. Given his level of expertise, it made sense that the man we knew as the Vest Bomber hadn't simply woken up one morning with an overwhelming desire to build a few bombs.

In a matter of moments, the team was ready to strike. Jeff and I watched from a distance as the tactical squad crept into position. Technically, the lead agent is supposed to shout, "Federal agents! Open the door!" then wait long enough for the person inside to respond. In reality, that doesn't always happen.

I heard someone declare, "Federal agents!" at the exact moment the front door of the house was broken down with a single well-placed kick. The storm of heavily armored bodies crashed into the dark room, disappearing with calculated efficiency.

The next few moments passed quickly. From my position at the curb, I heard a muffled voice shout, "Freeze!" Next, flashes lit one window on the north end as the sound of multiple gunshots cut the air. Romeo barked and tried to pull free of his leash, but I held him firm. Within seconds, an ATF agent appeared at the front door and called, "Building is secure! Medic up!"

Jeff and I exchanged a nervous glance as he grabbed the radio. In a matter of minutes, the two paramedics arrived and scrambled inside with their gear. When another agent stepped outside to hold the door open for them, I asked, "Officer down?"

"No!" was the simple, sharp reply before they all disappeared inside again.

Relief rushed through my veins as I realized that no one on the warrant team had been injured. Ten minutes later, we learned that the suspect had been in bed when the first agent rushed into the room. In spite of the order not to move, he had reached for a gun on the nightstand. As would be expected, the team responded automatically, striking the man multiple times with lethal accuracy.

A few minutes after the ambulance crew emerged from the house alone, Simon walked slowly outside. He seemed disheartened, which I attributed to the period of lethargy that often comes after such an extreme adrenaline rush. I asked, "Is the suspect dead?"

Biting his lip, Simon nodded. "Damn it, Jamie, now we may never get answers."

# 2

Once Luke Layman's body was removed, it was our turn to go to work. First, Jeff and I did a thorough walk-through of the house with high-beam flashlights, making certain there were no obvious trip wires or booby traps. Next, I took Romeo through each room, allowing him to sniff every nook and cranny. As we systematically moved about the house without incident, I began to worry that Luke Layman might not have been the Vest Bomber after all.

With the interior sweep behind us, we focused on the old pickup truck parked in the attached garage. Again, Romeo didn't detect the scent of anything dangerous. Our last hope was a midsized storage shed that sat in the back corner of the yard. Built like a miniature barn, the building had double doors and was painted to match the house. When we were several yards from the structure, I said, "Romeo, sit."

He did, but he wasn't happy about it. In fact, I had the distinct feeling he would rather be headed in the opposite direction, toward the back of the house. Ignoring his jit-teriness, I pointed at the shed and urged, "Find it, boy! Find it!"

Even though we'd just been through the exact same process twice without luck, Romeo's enthusiasm didn't disappoint me. His tail was wagging as we approached the small building. Pulling against the leash, he led me around the structure twice, then gave me a curious look. As if I had forgotten how to do my part of the job, his big eyes seemed to ask, *Aren't you going to open the door?*

The seal between the two aluminum doors wasn't airtight, and there was a slight breeze, so I would've expected Romeo to be able to catch the scent of explosives from the outside. Since he had been acting with his normal degree of curiosity, I felt confident it was safe to use bolt cutters to remove the padlock and continue the search.

Inside were two lawn mowers, a Weed Eater, a chainsaw, shovels, brooms, and an assortment of small tools. Romeo walked in, stuck his head behind a burlap bag, sneezed, then backed out to stop at my side with his tail still wagging. Moving aside the dusty burlap, I saw a three-foot-high stack of old *Playboy* magazines. "I guess those even attract male *dogs*," I said as we stepped outside. Giving him a hug and a treat, I declared, "Good boy!"

Knowing every member of the team was going to be extremely disappointed that we had come up empty-handed, Romeo and I slowly headed back around the side of the house. The sun had just edged over the horizon, and we stepped in the line of footprints we had left in the wet grass a few minutes ago. We were in the middle of the backyard, about the same place we had been the last time Romeo had acted peculiar, when he once again started to fidget. Willing to try anything at that point, I said, "Okay, it's your call." Sweeping my arm in the general direction of the house, I challenged, "Find it, boy! Find it!"

Alternately sniffing the grass, then stopping to catch the scent on the breeze, Romeo made his way toward the back of the house where a twelve-by-twelve patio cover jutted out from the roof. About six feet from the patio door, Romeo's hindquarters hit the pea green artificial grass that covered the concrete slab, and he cast me a look that clearly said, *Here it is! Told you so! Told you so!*

I'm not sure why I didn't react faster, although I remember thinking that Romeo might be losing his touch. When I didn't respond as he expected, he inched slightly forward, tilted his head, then sat down again. Hard.

He had alerted next to a rusty old wrought-iron chair that was about six inches from the corner of the patio. With my flashlight, I squatted next to Romeo to check the area for trip lines, but saw nothing out of the ordinary. The chair had a mesh bottom and thin metal sides. It would be hard to hide a match on it, much less a bomb. Looking closely at the patio floor, I walked to the edge of the cheap indoor/outdoor carpet that concealed virtually all of the concrete slab. It didn't appear to be tacked down, but I gingerly ran my finger under the edge to be certain.

Romeo was still in his alert position, and he whined as if to say, *Be careful!* Not wanting to disturb any fingerprints, I hooked my foot around the leg of the chair to slightly move it so that the corner of the carpet was exposed. Using a small mirror on an extending rod that I had in my pocket, I eased the instrument under the corner of the damp green material. I couldn't help but smile when I saw what I was certain was the edge of a door to an old storm shelter.

After walking clear of the area, I hugged Romeo fiercely and gave him a handful of treats. Meaning every word, I declared, "You're the best, most talented dog in the entire world! Good boy!" Using my radio, I happily announced, "Jeff, Romeo just hit pay dirt. Have the fire department respond, then get out the ropes and pulleys. We've got work to do!"

**3**

After photographing the site as we had found it, Jeff and I began the painstaking process of entering the storm shelter. The indoor/outdoor carpet could have hidden a trip line or a light- or pressure-sensitive switch, forcing us to proceed with extreme caution. By attaching spring-loaded clamps rigged with cords to each corner, we could safely pull the carpet off of the cellar door. Once the clamps were securely fastened, we jerked them from a distance to peel back the damp, moldy rug.

Next, we set up a system of ropes and pulleys attached to the door's recessed handle. By running the ropes over tree limbs and around the corner of the house, we were able to snap the door open, using the brick walls as protection. If it had been rigged to blow, no one would've been close enough to be hurt.

Once the door was folded back flat on the concrete slab, we set up the Do Not Cross perimeter and headed back to the bomb truck. To be safe, we would wait at least thirty minutes before approaching the cellar again, in case there were light- or temperature-sensitive chemicals inside. Although it's hard to believe, crystallized dynamite can unpredictably detonate with a sudden temperature change of only three degrees. Patience is a bomb tech's best friend.

On the way to the truck, Jeff stated, "I'm up."

As I've mentioned before, none of us relish time in the bomb suit. I suspected Jeff was eager to be the one to handle the toughest part of the render safe not only because the case was important to our squad but also because he was a typical male trying to be chivalrous. Even so, this investigation was personal, compelling me to go in myself. I replied, "I know you want to do it, but if you don't mind, I'll go in. I've had a lot of firsthand experience with this guy's work."

He nodded, then quietly said, "Nick warned me that you'd want to handle it yourself. I don't want to be the bearer of bad news, but he specifically told me I'd be up."

I froze in my tracks. "He *what?* I'm the senior squad member at the site, so it's my call."

Jeff's eyes met mine. "It's nothing personal, Jamie. You're too close to this case. Think about it. He *targeted* the two of you. It's the right decision."

"But—"

"But nothing. I know how you feel, and I'd be mad as hell if I were you. In the end, it doesn't matter. We've got a job to do, and not an easy one at that. I'm up. You can call Nick to verify it if you'd like, but it won't change the facts."

I turned away, storming toward the bomb truck as I fought to come to grips with what I knew was good, solid logic. Unfortunately, logic doesn't always take into consideration the all-too-human need for revenge. I felt as though Nick had denied me the opportunity for closure. In my mind, I imagined the tongue-lashing I would've unleashed on him if he'd been at my side. Just *thinking* the string of cusswords made me feel a little better—not much, but enough.

Once the storm of emotions blew over, I knew that Nick's decision would stand no matter how long and hard I fought. Jeff was right. I had a job to do, and I would do it with the utmost professionalism and care. Anything less could cost one or both of our lives.

Jeff backed the bomb truck onto the grass along the side of the suspect's house while I briefed the fire and ambulance support personnel. Even though it was in the upper seventies outside, we cranked on the truck's air-conditioning units so that Jeff could be as comfortable as possible while we were layering the bomb suit onto him.

About halfway through the process, Simon stuck his head into the bomb truck. "You're not going to believe what Frank just found hidden in an air vent."

I could tell by the tone of his voice that it probably wasn't something I was going to like. Still working, I asked, "What?"

"A couple of diskettes with digital pictures of you and Nick, plus some personal effects Layman probably retrieved from your garbage. Apparently, this guy's been following you for quite some time."

My blood ran so cold, I could almost feel it sinking from my face into the tips of my fingers. "What *kind* of personal effects?"

"The usual. Preapproved credit card applications, notes, receipts. I'd guess he was looking for patterns, maybe thinking of copying your handwriting. Nothing earth-shattering, but enough to be considered seriously creepy."

A nervous laugh escaped as an involuntary shudder ran through me. "Thanks, Simon. Knowing someone has been digging around in my trash doesn't exactly give me a warm feeling, you know. Were there any pictures of Matt?"

Simon's expression verified the worst; then he added, "And I'm pretty sure the woman he photographed with Nick at a local nightclub was Alexa Dixon, but you'll have to ID her for the record."

I nodded, then asked, "How many pictures are there?"

"Hundreds. There are shots of the two of you working, shopping, even jogging. There are a couple taken at a restaurant that have you, Nick, Matt, and another kid Matt's age, plus some of the two boys shooting baskets in your driveway."

I must have paled even more, because Jeff shifted sideways to ask, "You okay?"

Grabbing the bomb suit's heavy jacket, I heaved it up so he could slip his arm inside. "I'm fine. Is the suspect's body still here?"

Simon looked at me as if I were crazy. "Why?"

"I just realized I need to see his face. That's the only way I'll know if it's the same guy who gave me the creeps at Matt's birthday party."

"The body's already been taken to the morgue, but I'll bet we can find a decent close-up shot of him on one of the digital diskettes."

"That'll do."

Simon shrugged. "I'll see what I can find."

About the time Jeff was ready to go, Simon returned carrying a video camera with a flip-out viewing screen. Shoving it under my nose, he asked, "Is this the guy?"

I took a deep breath, saying a silent prayer of thanks that the nightmare was finally over. "Yes. That's definitely him." I know I should have felt an overwhelming sense of relief. Instead, I was even more on edge, and an uneasy feeling settled in the pit of my stomach. Over the months, as Nick and I worked on the Vest Bomber case, he had proven to be a worthy adversary in every way. Not one scrap of trace evidence had been found, which is pretty incredible, considering the amount of his handiwork we had recovered. It was even more remarkable when his history with alcohol and drugs was taken into account.

Maybe I was just disappointed that the mountain we'd been climbing had suddenly crumbled into a molehill. All criminals make mistakes, and Luke Layman had not only made the biggest of all, he had paid the highest price for doing so. I shared Simon's irritation because I, too, knew that his death meant that we would never fully understand his motivation.

Other than the night at the restaurant and the day I chased him away from my Suburban, I couldn't ever recall having seen the man. I desperately wanted to know why he had fixated on Nick and me, and to a lesser degree, how he had assembled the supplies to execute such elaborate crimes. There were so many loose ends, so many questions I wanted to ask.

But the bastard had had the last laugh. He had taken the answers to his grave.

**4**

Over an hour after Romeo had first found the storm shelter, we were ready to begin the hardest part of the render safe. While Jeff maneuvered into position in the bomb suit, I took a handful of glow sticks and walked to the opening. Like the glow sticks that children use to be safe on Halloween, the ones we carry are thin cylindrical plastic tubes about the size and shape of magic markers. We use them because they're easy to transport and generate light without heat. When bent, a thin plastic barrier inside is broken, allowing the fluids at each end of the tube to intermix. The chemical reaction generates a greenish yellow glow that lasts for a couple of hours.

I activated five glow sticks and carefully tossed them into the dark room, one in each corner, the last in the center near the base of the steps. With a flashlight, I squatted next to the opening to describe the newly illuminated space. Jeff could hear my description over the secure com as I reported, "We've got a stairway that steeply descends into the center of what appears to be a rectangular underground area. The room is approximately twelve feet by eight feet, and the walls are concrete blocks. The floor appears to be a solid slab of concrete, although it is covered in places with dirt."

I pointed my flashlight a little higher and continued,

"The west side has a workbench with Peg-Board fastened to the wall. Hanging from the Peg-Board is a black vest similar to those utilized by the suspect we have been calling the Vest Bomber. There are five spools of colored wire, orange thread, and various tools on the Peg-Board as well. On the bench itself is a folded length of white cloth, a four-foot piece of what appears to be det cord, and a plastic container that holds a white substance that could be commercial-grade C4. In a shoe box on the bench is a package of sewing needles, a spool of fishing line, and a stack of pencil-sized rods that resemble those used in The Parlor bombing. Stacked along the south wall are two cases of vegetables, a case of bottled water, and a couple of blankets." Pressing my face against the porch's cool surface to get a better angle, I added, "On the ceiling is a light fixture, but it doesn't have a lightbulb screwed into place."

Very slowly, I shone my flashlight up each step, then across the room, following a precise grid pattern. "I see no indication of any trip wires or booby traps, but the back of the staircase is completely blocked from view." Walking to where Jeff was waiting, I adjusted the video camera we had positioned on a tripod and made sure the tape was rolling. Giving him a confident smile, I asked, "Are you ready?"

Handing me his face shield, he replied, "Let's rock and roll."

After snapping the shield onto the helmet, I verified that the suit's air was working and double-checked all the connections. Since I had already briefed the fire and ambulance crews, all I had to do was give the signal that it was time to begin. At the edge of the entrance, I turned on Jeff's three flashlights, one secured in a bracket on the top of his helmet, and two that we had duct-taped to the top of the bomb suit's sleeves. "Be careful."

"You bet."

As he took his first step into the storm shelter, I followed procedure and backed a safe distance away. Through the headset, I could hear the rhythm of his steady breathing. He sounded calm and collected as he began verbalizing each movement for the record. "Descending step two, three, four . . . Stopping to check the stairs below. They appear clear. Five, six, seven . . . Oh, *shit!* It dropped half an inch under my weight! Backing out! Backing ou—!"

My breath caught. Through my headset I had heard what Jeff had no doubt felt: the distinct *click* of a firing mechanism. Three seconds later, the earth trembled as my senses were suddenly overloaded by horrific sights and sounds. The shock wave knocked me back, while I watched Jeff fly up and out of the storm shelter on the leading edge of an enormous ball of flame. I will never forget the way the dull green bomb suit arched upward on the wave of the blast, as though it were a surfboard being tossed by a powerful ocean curl. Jeff landed over twenty feet away, with a *whomp!* so violent that I swear I felt the ground cringe beneath my feet.

Even as I took off running, I screamed at the fire crew to prepare for secondary explosions. As soon as the words came out of my mouth, two more blasts rumbled through the air. Clumps of burning debris rained across the backyard as I dove toward Jeff. The bomb suit was completely engulfed in flames, and Jeff wasn't moving at all. On the outside chance that he could hear me, I cried into my headset, "Hang on, Jeff! Hang on!"

There was no immediate answer, and my secure com flew into the air as I ripped the KSP polo shirt over my head. Using the knit material to beat out the flames on his chest, I jerked the fast-release T-handle on the suit's chest, then the other on the shoulder. I barely noticed the sting-

ing water hitting me from behind as I peeled the suit open
to expose Jeff's unconscious body. The suit had done its
job. There was no blood, no wounds from shrapnel. Three
firemen were at my side in an instant, and together we
dragged Jeff away from the sea of burning debris that had
landed all around him.

We stopped on the far side of the bomb truck, and the
paramedics took over. I stepped back to watch, automatically mumbling, "Thank you," when a well-meaning fire-
man handed me my secure com headset. Behind us, the
other firefighters were busy pumping water into what was
left of the storm shelter.

Simon appeared at my side and wrapped his arm around
my shoulder. "You okay?"

I nodded, too dazed to move or to care that I was standing there, soaking wet, in only my bulletproof vest. From
across the yard, I saw Frank Nichols glaring at me. Simon
must have sensed my uneasiness, because he gently
nudged my shoulder to get my attention. The moment our
eyes met, he declared, "Don't let this get to you. It wasn't
your fault. You followed procedure every step of the
way."

Shaking my head, I muttered, "I should've been up."

"Then you'd be lying there. The Vest Bomber did this,
just like he attacked Nick. Now he's dead. It's over."

I nodded, suppressing an involuntary shiver.

Simon reached down to lift my arm. Pointing at the
back side of it, he said, "You've got a pretty bad burn
there. Why don't you ride to the hospital with Jeff and
let Frank and me hold down the fort?"

Twisting my left arm so I could see the back of it, I
realized he was right. Oddly enough, until the moment I
actually saw the long, two-inch-wide streak of blistered
skin, it hadn't hurt at all. As if my brain finally realized
it had forgotten to flip on the correct pain sensors, the first

wave of agony slapped me hard enough to make me grit my teeth. Even so, I shook my head. "I'm not going anywhere until the rest of our squad arrives."

With a shrug, Simon replied, "No surprise there. At least have one of the paramedics treat it for you."

"They've got their hands full. I'll use the first aid kit in my truck after I call for reinforcements, then stop by the ER when I go to check on Nick."

"Okay. Just let me know if you need any help."

The paramedics had stabilized Jeff, but he was still unconscious. They were loading him onto the stretcher when I asked, "How is he?"

With a shrug, the man closest to me replied, "Severe head trauma. Too soon to tell."

I nodded and watched as they squeezed him into the ambulance. Just as they pulled away, I heard the whisper of approaching helicopters and noticed several news crews screeching to a halt on the street.

Arriving like a school of voracious piranha, the media began their latest feeding frenzy.

# eleven

## 1

As I've mentioned before, whenever I have to interface with reporters, my self-confidence refuses to come along for the ride. I'm suddenly certain that my nose is running, my teeth have spinach stuck in them (even though I hadn't had time to think about food all morning), and there is not a doubt in my mind that perspiration stains are growing exponentially every second that I'm on-camera. I try to form coherent sentences, but my mouth no longer seems to function properly.

In fact, to my horror, the cameras had been rolling for quite some time before I realized I was still only wearing a wet bulletproof vest and soot-stained slacks. A drowned rat would have looked more professional, although I did manage to answer a few direct questions with words that had more than one syllable.

I had just escaped into the bomb truck when my cell

phone rang. Since I recognized the Colemans' phone number on the caller ID, I answered, "Everything is okay, Matt."

"Mom! I just heard you on the news! Is the Vest Bomber really dead?"

For the first time in hours, I felt a rush of enthusiasm. "It certainly looks that way."

"There was a big bandage on your arm. Are you okay?"

"You bet."

"Jesse said you looked like Madonna in your Xena: Warrior Princess vest."

"Tell Jesse I'm flattered. I think . . ."

"After you left, they switched to a guy outside the hospital. He said Jeff has regained consciousness; that he's going to be okay, and Nick is, too." Excitedly, he added, "And they're doing a special tonight on *Dateline* about how the bomb suits are made that saved Jeff's life!"

With a yawn, I replied, "Really? They must work fast."

"Can I go home now? Please, Mom! I miss my guitar."

I grinned, digging a soft, old T-shirt I'd bought at Redstone out of the bottom of my jump bag. On the breast pocket was printed, *Hazardous Device Technician*. On the back it read, *If You See Me Running, Try to Keep Up.* Every time I see it, I smile. Tugging it carefully over my hurt arm, I replied, "I didn't think you were in that big a hurry to clean the garage."

He sighed. "I'm not. Jesse doesn't know it, but he's going to help me. In fact, he'll probably do most of it *for* me."

In the background, I could hear Jesse's vigorous protests, so I replied, "It doesn't sound like he's up for the task. Besides, it's *your* job, not his."

"He'll do it. He *owes* me. Among other things, he loaned my A&F hat to one of the kids his sister babysits, and told her it was my way of flirting because I was too shy to tell her I wanted to go out with her. She hasn't taken it off in two days! And she's only *twelve!*" Jesse was laughing hysterically as Matt added, "Plus, he keeps stealing my clothes, and he lost our bet on who could shoot the most baskets in a row. He's either going to help me clean out the garage, or I'll hide *his* guitar until he goes through withdrawal, which would probably be about ten seconds."

I couldn't help but laugh. Even though Matt was trying to sound mad, I knew he was just putting on a show. "Okay. You can go home. I'm going to the hospital to check on Jeff and Nick. Then I've got to go to a press conference. Lieutenant Colonel Jones called me a few minutes ago, and I didn't get the impression that my presence was optional."

"Lieutenant Colonel Jones called you? Awesome. Do you think you're gonna get a promotion?"

"A commendation, maybe. But don't let it go to your head. If I have any luck at all, my fifteen minutes of fame will be over before you finish cleaning out the garage. Speaking of which, I'll call you when I get a chance this afternoon, so be thinking of what you want me to bring home for dinner. I promised Nick we would come up to watch a movie with him tonight, but now we might just have to watch that *Dateline* special instead."

Matt sounded as happy and relieved as I felt. "All right! See you in a little while. Love you!"

"I love you, too!"

I hung up, tired but happier than I'd been in months.

# 2

By the time I left the emergency room, my arm was feeling much better. They had cleaned the burn, applied an ointment that greatly cut the nagging pain, plus given me a double dose of ibuprofen. After catching a glimpse of myself in the bathroom mirror, I washed smudges off my face and sprinkled water on my hair to try to coax the strands that had dried standing straight up back into place.

When I was finally halfway presentable, I found my way to the wing where Jeff Jenkins had been admitted. The nurse assured me that he would be fine, and since he was asleep, I decided to check on him again later.

Nick had been transferred to a private room. After softly tapping on the door, I glanced inside. Since he was alone and apparently asleep, I tiptoed across the linoleum to stand at the foot of his bed. As if he sensed my presence, his eyes slowly opened. Smiling, I said, "You must be doing better. I'm glad to see they gave you a place of your own."

The moment Nick spoke, I could tell he was much stronger than when I'd last seen him. "Me, too. ICU is enough to kill a guy. By the way, next time you go on national television, you might want to put on a shirt and comb your hair. Our squad does have standards, you know. Pretty soon all the special ops teams will think they can prance around out of uniform."

Fluffing my damp hair with my fingertips, I replied, "I always knew I could count on you for hair and makeup tips. Besides, my shirt gave its life in the line of duty. I know the budget is tight, but you'd better order me a new one. Better yet, make it two. That way I'll have a spare next time I need to put out a fire."

"I suppose I won't write you up this time. Just don't let it happen again."

I laughed. "Yes, sir! You really must be feeling better."

He managed a smile. "I feel like a bug who kissed a windshield at seventy miles per hour and can actually brag about it. So, how was it rigged?"

Pulling four Polaroids out of my back pocket, I handed them to him. "I had a feeling you'd be dying to know all the sordid details. The seat was directly below the stairs. The incendiary device was completely enclosed by the staircase's support beams and plywood. The pressure of Jeff's weight made contact with a striking device that ignited a blasting cap planted in a wad of military C4. The fire was fueled by a line of gas tanks that had been punctured so the vapors would react quickly. Apparently the Vest Bomber wanted to be sure that the moment anyone went into that storm shelter, the incriminating evidence would be destroyed."

Nick nodded. "Jeff still holding his own?"

"He seems to be doing pretty well. Guess he has a hard head, too."

A broad smile crossed his face. "Thank God he's okay. What's the suit look like?"

"A big lump of dull green charcoal."

"What about you? How's your arm?"

"Slightly toasted, but it'll be fine. I talked to Matt a few minutes ago. He can't wait to come see you tonight. There's a movie we think would cheer you up, plus *Dateline* put together a special on bomb suit technology."

Nick raised one brow. "Must be a movie with hot babes in skimpy bikinis. Tell Matt I'd like that a lot. And please bring some decent food. The stuff they call a meal here is a joke. And not a good one."

Since hunger is usually a sign of improvement, I smiled. For the first time, I really believed that Nick would be back at my side soon. "Everything go okay when Lori visited?" I asked.

He nodded. "I was pretty surprised she came at all."

Shaking my head, I said, "Of course, Lori came. The two of you were together for a long time. A stupid piece of paper isn't going to change that. She'll always care about you, and no matter how much you deny it, I know you care about her."

Reluctantly, Nick mumbled, "If you say so."

"Nick, I'm really very sorry about Alexa. I know how much she meant to you."

He nodded and sucked in a long, deep breath. "I still can't believe she's gone. I wish I'd never laid eyes on her."

"Life doesn't work that way."

"Think about it. If she hadn't started dating me, she'd still be alive."

"Maybe. Or maybe she'd have died some other way. Some people believe that if it's your time to go, then you'll go. At least she was happy the last days of her life."

Nick simply shrugged, but the look on his face was breaking my heart. I was certain he would've given his life without the slightest hesitation if it would have saved Alexa. The room fell into an awkward silence. Since Nick was preoccupied and staring at the ceiling, I pushed a chair next to his bed and sat down. Desperate to change the subject, I said, "It seems like years since we've talked, even though I know it's only been a few hours. Has the doctor given you any idea how long you'll be off work?"

"At least six weeks, maybe eight. He was yakking about rehab and physical therapy and a bunch of other nonsense." Yawning, he added, "Made me tired just thinking about it."

"Speaking of which, I'd better let you get your beauty sleep."

"Not so fast. I still have a few things I need to know. Any doubt that Luke Layman was the Vest Bomber?"

It was my turn to shrug. "We found raw materials similar to the first few vests. Same type wire, military caps, a black fishing vest, orange thread, aluminum rods . . ."

"But?"

"But it's like trying to force the wrong piece of a puzzle into place. I'll feel better when the autopsy report is in. If it shows he was clean and sober, then I'll buy it. But if his blood shows that he was still doing drugs and drinking, I just don't see how he could've pulled it off. At least, not alone."

"Have any of the jewels been recovered?"

"Simon never mentioned it. I caught a glimpse of Layman's checkbook lying on the desk. He'd made a deposit of $5,000.00 about a month ago, but he certainly wasn't living like a guy who had millions of dollars in diamonds stashed away."

"It's probably hidden somewhere. Hopefully, they'll find the answer when they go through his belongings."

"I hope so. Otherwise . . ."

As usual, Nick could read me like a book. "What?"

"I know the tapes of The Parlor's parking lot showed only one man, but what if someone else really *was* driving the van? What if he has an accomplice out there who has the jewels? What if it's his accomplice who has the up-close-and-personal knowledge of the inner workings of our department?"

Nick shook his head. "Layman would've had the knowledge to build the bombs, but I suppose someone else could've been the brains behind the brawn."

"Exactly."

"So, I can tell by that look in your eye that you have someone in mind."

I tried to lie. "Not a soul."

"That is such utter bullshit. Come on, tell me."

"Nick, I don't have a suspect, at least not in the way you mean."

"I believe we've already had the discussion about instinct. For once, ignore that overactive brain of yours. What's your gut telling you?"

"That's the problem. My gut suspects everybody, Nick."

"Jamie, this isn't on the record. Talk to me."

*Talk to me.* Three simple words. Yet what I felt was far from simple to explain. "Okay, but it's off the record. I'll claim you were hallucinating."

Nick smiled. "Deal."

I hesitated, then began. "First of all, there's Lieutenant Colonel Jones." Nick cocked his head, obviously hooked. "Don't you think it's odd that he's suddenly jumped into the middle of everything? He's never been a hands-on manager before, and now we're supposed to tell him every time we sneeze."

"It's a high-profile case. He doesn't want the KSP to look bad."

"Okay. You were there the night before The Parlor bombing. Didn't he say he needed to get back to Topeka before ten?"

Nick nodded.

"The tape of The Parlor's parking lot shows he arrived at the scene exactly thirty-five minutes after the initial call came in. Unless he stayed in Kansas City that night, it would've been impossible for him to make it that fast."

"Good point. Who else is on your hit list?"

I shrugged, not wanting to pick a fight. "Did you really tell Jeff that he'd be up when we served the warrant?"

Nick's face hardened. "What?"

"Jeff told me that you insisted he be up if we worked together."

Nick shook his head. "He called to ask if I had any advice for him. I told him that my partner and I share two very important characteristics. We're both stubborn and pigheaded, and that he should remember to treat you just like he'd treat his own partner, and he'd be fine."

"So he lied to me," I muttered, wondering if Nick really thought I was stubborn and pigheaded.

"Technically, it wasn't his call, since you were the senior member of the team, but I have a pretty good idea why he did it."

"Which is?"

"Think about it. There are six members of our squad, but two of us have suddenly become household names. Maybe he just wanted some time in the spotlight."

Remembering the odd way Jeff had acted after The Parlor bombing, I muttered, "Or maybe he just wanted to see what it felt like to be blown to kingdom come."

"What the hell's that supposed to mean?"

"Every tech knows the bomb suit's level of protection. Let's suppose you're the Vest Bomber's accomplice. What better way to throw everyone off your trail than to set up your partner to take the fall, then blow yourself sky high?"

Nick's expression had gone flat. "Jamie, you're really reaching."

I ran my hands through my hair. "I warned you. I'm just throwing out everything that's made me even slightly wary lately."

He took a deep breath. "So you honestly suspect Jeff could be involved in this?"

"Nick, I don't know what to think. He keeps to himself. No one on the squad really knows him yet. Besides, we're talking hypothetically right now, remember?"

Shaking his head, he said, "I hand-picked him—"

"You hand-picked *all* of us."

"True."

"Why did you assign me to work with Jeff?"

"You've got the most experience with the Vest Bomber, so I thought you'd be the logical one to help him through a hand entry if it came up. Anyone else?"

"Carl Johnson, of course."

"As a matter of fact, Trooper Johnson paid me a visit today."

Shocked, I cast him a sideways glare. "You're pulling my leg."

Nick smiled. "I have to admit, it rattled me when I saw him."

"Did he act—" I tried to think of a more professional description, but settled for "—creepy?"

"He definitely sees things from a different angle. I even asked him if he was currently connected with a militia group."

Wide-eyed, I exclaimed, "Really? That takes nerve."

With a sly grin, Nick replied, "When you have a big gun hidden under the sheet, it's easy to be cocky."

I bit my lip, resisting the urge to make a lewd comment. "You had your Sig under the sheet?"

"Hey! You had me totally spooked about him being the Vest Bomber. I'd been working on the FBI's pictures, so my jump bag was on the bed next to me. I just eased my Sig out when he wasn't watching and kept it by my side."

Nick must have seen the gleam in my eye, because he quickly continued, "Johnson claims he's not into the militia movement anymore. Says he only got involved with those people because he's always been fascinated by weapons and explosives. He told me all about the render safe this morning. Apparently Jeff flying out of that storm shelter in a ball of fire was quite a show."

An adrenaline rush made my fingers tingle. Trying to keep my voice even, I asked, "He was there?"

Nick shook his head. "Claims to have seen it on the news."

"The camera crews didn't arrive until *after* Jeff was in the ambulance. The only tape of that explosion is the one on the bomb squad's video camera, and it's locked up tight in the bomb truck." The idea that Johnson was still watching me, either in person or on television, made my heart pound. "Pardon my French, but what the hell was he doing up here bothering you?"

"He said he just wanted to introduce himself and tell me that he hopes I recover quickly. Seems for once the rumor mill got the story right. He's been keeping close tabs on our unit because he wants to join it someday."

"Did you explain the qualification process?"

Nick nodded. "He said he didn't care how long he had to wait, that he wasn't going anywhere."

"Now there's a scary thought. Are you sure you didn't feel threatened by him?"

"Why should I? Just because he's a little odd and spends his off-duty time listening to the scanner doesn't mean he's a killer. Besides, supposedly the Vest Bomber is dead. If that's true, then Carl Johnson is just another guy who needs to get a life. Trust me, there are millions of them out there." With a grin, he added, "And I can think of a few women who might fall into that category, too."

"Okay, you win. Even though he gives me the creeps, I'll back off Carl Johnson's case. Besides, I have enough on my hands trying to deal with Frank Nichols. I think in some twisted way that he actually blames me for what happened to Jeff this morning." Impersonating him, I added, "After all, women are inherently inferior."

"Don't let him get to you. In a few months, he'll be gone. I get the impression most of the ATF agents can't stand him either. With his attitude, I'm surprised someone hasn't slapped a sexual harassment lawsuit on him."

I replied, "They can't because he never touches anyone or verbally abuses them. He just exudes a subliminal message that is impossible to ignore, plus he's an expert at working around people he doesn't feel are in his league."

Smiling, Nick shrugged. "Either way, he's not worth worrying about. Speaking of which, I guess I wasted my time looking over those FBI photos this morning. I even thought I'd figured out what made our man on the motorcycle unique."

He had more than managed to pique my curiosity. "Well? Tell me!"

Pointing to the nightstand, he replied, "Mind getting them for me?"

I did as he asked, pulling the envelope out of his jump bag. Spreading several photos of the man on the motorcycle atop the sheets, he pointed at the tall, lean man's left wrist in each one. "See?"

Feeling as dumb as a brick, I studied the places he was pointing and shrugged. "Sorry, partner. Give me a break, it's been a really long day."

"How about a hint? You were right about his watch."

Looking even closer, I shook my head. "Did the blow to your head give you super-vision? I can barely make out the watch, much less the numbers."

Nick grinned and handed me a magnifying glass. "The watch face is on the *inside* of his wrist, plus look closely at this one frame."

He sorted through the stack and pulled out a different picture. It had less glare on the watch crystal than the others, but I was still missing his point.

"Look *behind* the hands at the face," he suggested.

Although it was partially blocked by the glare, there appeared to be a white line slanted from ten o'clock to four o'clock. At first glance, it seemed to be another glare, but under closer scrutiny its distinct form was obvious. I smiled, impressed that Nick had noticed. "Even after you've been kicked in the head, you are still damned good. Any idea what it means?"

"If that picture were in color, I'd bet the background is

red and that stripe is white. If so, it's a diving watch."

"As in scuba diving?"

He nodded. "It's not much, but I'd certainly want to know if we recovered a watch like that at Luke Layman's house."

"I'll get on it right away." I fought a yawn.

Nick asked, "You were too pumped about serving the warrant to sleep last night, weren't you?"

I nodded but couldn't suppress another yawn as I reluctantly admitted, "Guess I have been hitting it pretty hard."

"No shit. Why don't you go home and get some shut-eye? You look exhausted."

"Guilty as charged." As if my body had been waiting for permission to let down its guard, I was overwhelmed by the need for a long nap. Fighting the feeling, I said, "But I can't rest just yet. Lieutenant Colonel Jones called a press conference. Guess who's the main attraction."

Nick gave my hand a sympathetic squeeze. "Sorry. I know how much you love playing the media game. But you'll do fine. At least you'll have a shirt on this time, and you can always resort to technical mumbo jumbo whenever you feel cornered."

Standing, I glanced at my watch and replied, "Very funny. Come to think of it, I've got just enough time to run by the cleaners and pick up a uniform. I doubt if he'd want me showing up dressed like this."

"You could show up naked for all he cares. You caught the bad guy. The Kansas State Patrol is getting national kudos. He'll probably still be smiling in his sleep tonight."

"I'll be back with Matt in a few hours. If you think of anything you need besides food that'll clog your arteries, just call."

"I will. Promise you'll take care of yourself."

"Look who's talking!" I laughed as I leaned over and

gave him a long hug. I was surprised to feel his uninjured arm wrap around me, his fingers gently touch the hair at the nape of my neck. The stubble of his beard chafed my cheek as I slowly pulled away. I couldn't help but wonder if he had any idea how much he meant to me. Slowly standing, I moved across the room. "Take care," I called as I walked out the door.

I was only a few yards down the hall when I noticed a man in a dark gray suit walking toward me. He was carrying a basket wrapped in blue cellophane and tied at the top with a huge blue ribbon. I actually did a double take when I realized it was Simon Stanley. I'd never seen him in such a sharp outfit. Stopping, he seemed embarrassed. Nodding toward the gift, he muttered, "Trooper colors. It was Frank's idea, believe it or not. We all chipped in. I already left one for Jeff."

Through the clear wrapping I could see the basket contained a six-pack of beer, a *Playboy*, a box of Texas Fire Hot Chili Mix, several sticks of beef jerky, and a bag of pork rinds. Laughing, I joked, "If you're trying to kill him, that just might do it."

"He's been through hell, and we all miss him. There's no one at the crime scenes to tell us what lazy, worthless bastards we are."

With a sly grin, I said, "I'm sure your thoughtfulness will touch him deeply."

"Are you glad all the excitement is over?"

"I suppose. By the way, do you know if a diving watch was recovered at Luke Layman's house today?"

He thought for a second. "There was a watch on the nightstand. I didn't give it a second thought. Why?"

"The man on the motorcycle at The Parlor was wearing one. If Luke Layman had one in his possession, then it'll be another nail in his coffin." Stroking the smooth silk kerchief tucked into the breast pocket of his jacket, I added, "What's the occasion?"

He looked around, then leaned close to whisper, "A job interview. A corporate desk job, chief of security, no less. But the hours are great and its *triple* the pay."

Shocked, I said, "I'm surprised you're considering leaving ATF."

Simon shrugged. "A friend of mine convinced me to talk to these guys. It's a really good job, and we both know the hours and paperwork with ATF suck."

"I can't believe they didn't call you to do the press conference."

"They did. I told them I had an appointment I couldn't cancel, and they didn't push. I suppose you couldn't get out of it?"

I shook my head. "It never dawned on me to say no, although, right now, I certainly wish it had."

"You'll do fine. I'll try to catch your act if I get home in time."

"Good luck with the interview."

"Thanks, I'm going to need it."

Walking slowly to the elevator, I realized how anxious I was to put the press conference behind me. Having learned from my previous encounter, before I left the building I peeked around the corner to be certain I wasn't stepping into another unexpected media ambush. With a sigh, I was relieved that no one was waiting to pounce on me.

A slight cold front had kept the temperatures in the upper eighties, so I had parked the Suburban in the shade with the windows cracked. Romeo barked a warm greeting as I approached the car. Out of habit, I stopped a few yards away and crouched to check the undercarriage for bombs or leaking fluids. Stopping myself, I shook my head and smiled. "Romeo, life is going to be much easier now."

He barked again as I climbed inside and gave him a big hug. Picking up my cell phone, I dialed my home number. There was no answer, so I listened to the familiar recording on the machine and said, "Matthew Stone, I thought you were going to clean out the garage! Guess I can't blame you for enjoying such a gorgeous day. Listen, it's a little after four o'clock, and all I have left to do is make it through the press conference, then I'll be home. I should be there by six, so call and leave a voice message about dinner. We're going to see Nick at the hospital at seven. Love ya."

Hanging up, I felt an undeniable surge of fear, as though Matt were in grave danger. Calling again, I waited for the machine and left another message. "Hey, Matt. Call me as soon as you get this. Okay? It's no big deal, I just need to talk to you."

Even after I hung up the second time, I couldn't shake the nagging feeling that something was wrong. I knew it was irrational, I knew it was probably my maternal instinct reacting to the stress of the last few days, but with every passing minute, the knot in the pit of my stomach cinched a little tighter.

One thing kept running through my mind: *Where are the jewels?* The Vest Bomber had stolen over two million dollars in jewels alone. What had Luke Layman done with them? To my knowledge, no keys to safe-deposit boxes had been found at the scene. But logic told me he had to be the Vest Bomber. I was sure the watch would be a perfect match. Plus, even though we had never released details about the vests to the press, we had recovered orange thread, white lining, conductive rods . . . virtually everything needed to build a device.

As I drove, I tried to convince myself it was over. Case closed. But in my heart, I didn't believe it for a second.

# 3

The press conference was even more agonizing than I'd anticipated. Usually, such affairs are taped by representatives from each network, then they scurry off to edit the precise tidbits they choose to broadcast. This time the lieutenant colonel and I were in a television studio with a live satellite feed. We fielded questions by every local channel, plus from anchors all across the United States. At one point, Tom Brokaw asked the lieutenant colonel if any commendations would be given to the members of the bomb squad who had been injured by the Vest Bomber. To my surprise, he replied that Lieutenant Nick Terrell, Trooper Jeff Jenkins, and Sergeant Jamie Stone were to be awarded the highest honor in the state of Kansas—the Governor's Award—in recognition of our acts of extreme moral and physical courage in performing above and beyond the call of duty.

I was still reeling from the announcement when I was asked what I thought the most dangerous part of my job was. Without hesitation, I replied, "Hand entries. They require hazardous device technicians to lay their lives on the line. Unless a human life is at stake, we remotely work on virtually every suspicious device using robots and high-powered disruption techniques. But hand entries are one on one. Save one life, or lose two."

"Are you ever afraid?"

Without even thinking, I replied, "If I wasn't, I'd be dead. Fear heightens the senses, makes us more careful."

"I hear your dog, Romeo, was responsible for locating

the device that injured Trooper Jenkins. What does he think of having to work around bombs?"

One of Romeo's many tricks is that he's trained to bark when I give a hand signal. Obediently, at my silent command, he answered for himself with a sharp bark. Everyone in the room laughed, while I kept smiling, praying the torture would end soon.

Finally, the lights dimmed and the press conference ended. As I was leaving, Lieutenant Colonel Jones rushed to catch me. Although I had thought it was the studio lights that had kept Romeo on edge, when he snarled at Jones I realized I'd been wrong. Apologizing, I ordered Romeo to sit, then quickly said, "I'm sorry. He doesn't usually act this way."

Jones laughed. "Guess he knows I'm a cat lover. Never had a dog in my life, but my wife has always insisted we have a cat." He shook my hand and added, "I just wanted you to know that you're one of the finest troopers I've ever had the honor of working with."

"Thank you, sir." I instantly felt guilty that I had considered him a prime suspect. Even so, I was compelled to ask, "Would you mind clearing up something that's been bothering me, sir?"

"Not at all."

"How did you get to The Parlor bombing so quickly? Weren't you in Topeka?"

He smiled. "Since our meeting the other day, I've had dispatch notify me whenever the bomb squad is activated. I happened to have been at a special ops demonstration, so I had them fly me here in one of the helicopters. Very observant of you to notice. That's why you're so good at what you do."

"Thank you."

"I'm looking forward to the governor's presentation of your award. Of course, we'll schedule it after Lieutenant

Terrell and Trooper Jenkins are released from the hospital. Now, I'm ordering you to go home and get some rest. Understand?"

"Yes, sir." Relieved, I happily headed toward the parking garage. Being away from the scrutiny of the cameras lifted a weight from my shoulders, and I felt more relaxed than I had in weeks. I must have stretched a hundred times as I drove across town. My cell phone didn't show any missed calls, so I tried to call Matt again. Still no answer. I called Nick to see if he had watched any of the press conference. Since he hadn't seen the interview with Tom Brokaw, I gave him the good news about each of us being granted the Governor's Award. He sounded pleased but groggy, so I told him I'd see him later.

My son is a creature of light. He loves it, lives to bask in it. The moment I pulled into the driveway I should have known something was wrong, but I was far too happy to just be home where there were no microphones and no one trying to pry information out of me. The curtains were all closed, every shade drawn. Pushing the garage door opener, I watched the big door roll upward.

Matt's boom box was blaring, cartons that had been stacked in one corner had been moved to the center, and a big, black trash bag was stuffed to overflowing near the back door. Matt had obviously been hard at work, and I assumed the music had kept him from hearing my calls. Leaving the Suburban in the driveway, I helped Romeo down and said, "Find a tree, boy."

Normally, Romeo would've taken off, but that day he was in no mood to frolic. As I walked into the garage, he brushed against my leg and whined. Kneeling beside him, I noticed his tail was tucked between his legs and he was nervously shifting back and forth. I asked, "Did that press conference spook you, too?" Of course, he didn't answer, he only whined again and looked at me with those soft chocolate eyes as if he wished I could read his mind.

I switched off the stereo and opened the back door. The hair on the ridge of Romeo's back stood on end as he bared his teeth and growled. I stopped and snapped, "Quiet boy! Stay!" The kitchen table was overturned, three of the chairs were on their sides, and one was missing. My hand instinctively jerked the Sig Sauer from my holster, and my heart began to pound with such force I thought it might leap out of my chest. Scanning the disorderly room, I noticed the credit card I had given to Matt lying on the floor near the refrigerator, just below a long smear of blood that streaked down the shiny white door. More blood led in a trail out of the kitchen and into the living room.

"God, please don't take him from me," I whispered, praying with all my heart. Adrenaline was flowing as though the dam holding it back had succumbed to the unbearable weight of my terror. There was a roaring in my head, the unmistakable sound of panic awakening and soaring up my spine. I couldn't stop the rush of emotion, the overwhelming misery and fear of loss that slammed hard into my soul. That unanswerable question, *Why?*, crept in to torment me, as though someday the answer would suddenly strike like a bolt of lightning and I would finally understand why cruelty is so much a part of human nature.

But as I stood there, I didn't care why. With *No! No!* pounding in my head, the only thing I cared about was saving my son.

# twelve

## 1

Still frozen in the doorway to the garage, I held my gun in one hand while I reached down to wrap my other fist around Romeo's collar. A low growl was emanating from deep within his body, and I couldn't risk allowing him to rush into some kind of trap. Taking a few steps to the side, I grabbed an extra leash off one of the hooks in the laundry room and snapped it on.

As much as I wanted to find Matt, in my heart I knew that my theory about the jewels had been on target. We had been wrong about catching the Vest Bomber, and any move could cost one or both of our lives. Slowly inching forward, my eyes were drawn to the blood on the floor once again, which is probably the only reason I noticed a thin string of clear fishing line about an inch off the floor in the doorway leading from the kitchen to the living room. It had been carefully positioned where virtually anyone entering or leaving the room would step, and there was no question in my mind that it was a booby trap.

"Romeo, sit," I commanded, then leaned forward to see what the trip wire would have triggered. It was a primitive device that used a taut line on a mousetrap to discharge a shotgun shell seated in the hole of a brick. Not deadly, but nasty enough to badly mangle a person's leg.

Quickly moving back into the laundry room, I found a yardstick and ripped the shoestring out of one of Matt's tennis shoes. Tying the string on the end of the stick, I looped Romeo's leash around the doorknob and ordered, "Stay!" Even though I would have loved to use his skills, in a situation with booby traps, I couldn't afford to have him at my side.

Positioning the stick so that I could hold it in front of me to warn of any other trip wires, I slowly stepped away from Romeo. To describe him as agitated would be a vast understatement. I could almost feel the energy he was expending to stay seated when he knew there was work to be done. Even so, I had to find Matt as quickly as possible.

I made my way through the living room without incident before the shoestring snagged on another trip wire across the entrance to the den. Leaning forward, I confirmed that it was the exact same type of device. The moment I stepped over it and into the room, I spotted Matt and cringed.

Nothing could have prepared me for the horror of seeing my son's life hanging in the balance. One of the many rules of our profession is that bomb techs never work on friends and relatives. Although I hadn't ever given the rule much thought, in the blink of an eye, I understood why it existed. My hands were trembling, my heart racing. If anything happened to Matt, it would be my fault. My son's life was in my hands, and they were shaking so hard that I dropped the yardstick so I wouldn't have to watch it tremble.

He was in the corner, seated in the missing dining room chair. His head was covered in a black hood, and his hands had been fastened to the arms of the chair with so much duct tape that no skin showed. He was wearing one of the Vest Bomber's specialties, complete with wires tightly wound around his neck, over the top of the hood, and stretched across his upper thighs. When I saw the bomber's latest additions, my breath caught. I was no longer aware of the hammering of my heart, yet the pit of my stomach constricted so hard and fast it felt as though someone had just slugged me in the gut.

About three feet off the floor was a laser motion detector. The narrow red beam bounced in perfect alignment out one side of a black box, around two mirrors that were mounted atop photographer's tripods, then back into a small hole on the opposite side of the box. The chair was sitting dead center in the triangle formed by the beam, and it was close enough to prevent anyone from simply slipping under or over it to get to him. If there were a bomb inside the box, breaking the laser beam would probably detonate it. Yet there was no way to get close enough to work on the vest without breaching that thin red line.

As if that weren't bad enough, this time the vest's clock was in the front of the vest, located directly over the heart. And it was counting down at 15:02.

The black hood reminded me of something the Grim Reaper might have chosen, and I could see where blood had soaked through one side of it. Closing my eyes, I thought, *He needs you now more than ever. Pull yourself together!*

Taking a deep breath, I said, "Don't worry, honey. I'll get you out of this in no time at all. If you can hear me, answer softly or nod just a tiny bit."

I saw a slight movement, and sighed. At least he was conscious. "Okay. I've got to go get my equipment. I'll be right back. Hang in there."

I rushed out as fast as possible, careful not to step on the trip wires. Although I considered calling for backup, I knew that if I strictly followed department regulations, I would have to stand by and wait for someone else to help. By the time they arrived, there was a strong possibility it would be too late. Working on Matt by myself was one of the easiest decisions I've ever made. Losing my job for breaking the rules was a risk I was more than willing to take to save his life.

On my way out, I unhooked Romeo's leash and told him to come. Since all four windows were cracked open, I put him inside the car so that I wouldn't have to worry about him breaking free while I worked. Throwing open the rear door of the Suburban, I grabbed everything I could carry—my jump bag, my hand entry kit, and both pieces of the X-ray equipment—then raced back inside. Once I was in the den, I dropped it all into a pile on the floor. Switching my police radio to work as a phone, I dialed the hospital's number as I began to search for my laser pointer. By the time Nick answered, I had spread half of the items in my hand entry kit onto the carpet, and I had just found the small laser pointer. It was tightly wrapped in the palm of my hand when I heard him say, "Hello."

I swallowed hard at the sound of Nick's groggy voice, feeling a little more confident but still terrified. "Nick, wake up fast! Matthew is strapped in a vest. Don't give me any bullshit about not working on relatives, I know the damned rules. There's *no time,* and I really need your help. I've got to have my hands free, so get your secure com headset out of your jump bag. Switch over and call me back."

"Jesus, Jamie. Are you serious?"

My voice conveyed every bit of my fear as I snapped, "Do it, Nick! I need you!"

By the time I hung up, switched to the secure com, and put on the headset, he had called back. I could tell from the calm, cool tone of his voice that he was more than just wide awake, he was angry and eager to help. "Ready here. What are you up against?"

"First I have to defeat a triangular laser motion detector that encompasses the chair he's strapped into. It utilizes a series of mirrors to reflect the beam. Matt is sitting in a chair in the middle of the triangle. The beam originates on one side of the black box positioned at noon, it then loops via mirrors at four o'clock and eight o'clock back into a hole on the opposite side of the box. Each of the cube's sides is approximately a ten-inch square. I'm going to converge the beam of my laser so that it will replace the detector's beam, tape mine in place, then break the original beam. Talk to me, Nick."

"Good plan. Have you called for backup?"

Irritated, I seethed, "No time, *no time!* I'll be right to zero, and there won't be time to get another tech up to speed. There's a visible clock in the front of the vest that's cycling down at 14:15. I'm not going to waste a second trying to figure out if there's a bomb inside the black box until I defeat the vest, and I'm definitely not assuming the clock on his chest is the *actual* timing device, but it's all I've got to work with at this point."

I knew that the Vest Bomber liked to play games, so I fully expected the real timer to be hidden inside so that only he had a clue when it would blow. After all, why make things easy?

# 2

"Matt, the chair you're in is encompassed by a laser beam trigger. I'm going to tape a different laser in place that will fool the device so that I can get close to you. While I work on getting it just right, I'm going to describe the vest for Nick so that he can help me through the disarming process."

Looking around the room, I searched for something that was tall and stable enough for me to use to secure my laser pointer. I quickly unplugged a floor lamp and dragged it across the carpet until it was next to the bomber's black box. "Okay . . . like the others, the outer layer is a thick black mesh. The inside seems to be the same white lining with orange thread. There are four plastic fasteners in the front and a digital clock where the left breast pocket would be. A blue wire emerges from the area behind the visible clock, wraps around the outside of the black hood over Matt's head, then disappears into the top of the back side. A green wire emerges from the opposite side, wraps around the other direction, and runs into the back alongside the blue one. Nick?"

His voice sounded different, very strained as he answered, "I'm here. Color-coded wires from front to back."

"Right. The wires wrapping around the thighs are black and brown." I had bound enough duct tape tightly around the lamp's metal pole so that there was no chance the pointer would slide out of place. As long as no one kicked the lamp, my bluff should work. "I've got my laser beam in place, and I'm going to break the other beam . . . now." I didn't realize I'd been holding my breath until a few uneventful seconds passed after I had moved one of the tripods out of position. With a sigh, I continued, "Okay, the motion detector has been successfully defeated. Matt, I'm going to cut the hood off of your face. Nod if that's okay."

Although it was slight, I saw his chin move up and down again.

"I'm going to gently slide the wires to one side. . . ." Very carefully, I pushed each wire against his head while gently forcing it to the side to be certain I didn't disturb the connections. Once they were both clear of the hood, I continued, "Great. Now don't worry, I promise not to lop off any ears or a nose. You're doing great. Hang in there."

There are no words that can describe how I felt when the hood's black material fell away as I carefully slit it with a razor knife. It was Jesse sitting before me, not Matt!

Although his eyes reflected the depth of his terror and he had a deep gash along his left eyebrow, he didn't look as though he were seriously injured. I'm sure my voice conveyed every bit of my alarm as I exclaimed, "Jesse! Oh, my God! Everything is going to be okay!" Instantly, my shock turned to a heightened state of panic. *Where's Matt? Is he strapped into another vest somewhere else in the house?* Wanting answers, I looked at Jesse, and explained, "I'm really sorry, but I've got to rip the tape off your mouth. It'll only hurt for a few seconds; just don't jerk back. Okay?"

Another slight nod.

"On three. One, two, three . . ."

Jesse grimaced but quickly shook off the pain. His voice was hoarse from the tight wires still wrapped around his neck as he claimed, "He said if I moved it would blow me—"

I interrupted "—To kingdom come. Don't worry, I'll get you out of this contraption in one piece. I promise. Any idea where Matt is?"

Jesse was trembling, and I could tell he didn't want to answer the question. Even so, he reluctantly said, "He told me he was taking him. He said he was an insurance policy in case you managed to use another one of your nine lives to get out of this. Then he laughed and said you weren't a good enough bomb tech to defeat *this* vest, and that even if you did, you'd never be able to save Matt."

A flash of white-hot anger flowed through my veins. Touching his bound hands, I urged, "Jesse, I'm a damn good bomb tech, and we're both going to be just fine. Once I get you out of this, I'm going to find Matt, then teach that bastard—"

Nick's voice rang in my ear. "Concentrate, Jamie. There's time for that later."

I nodded and touched my headset. "Jesse, Nick can hear us, and he's going to help us get out of this difficult situation. Do you know who did this to you?"

"No, but I'm pretty sure Matt recognized him. Before he knocked him out, Matt asked him why he would want to hurt you, and the guy just laughed."

My mind was reeling, trying to get past the idea that my son had been hurt and kidnapped by a madman. "You're sure he recognized him?"

Jesse nodded and muttered, "Pretty sure."

"Copy that Nick?"

"I heard. Jamie, listen to me. In order for you to help Matt, you're going to have to save Jesse. I know it's hard, but you must focus completely on the job at hand. We'll save Matt. I swear. But right now, we're going to help Jesse. No doubts."

I nodded, certain he was right. "No doubts." I took a deep breath and asked, "How long have you been like this, Jesse?"

He thought for a moment. "We were cleaning the garage, so it was probably around four. Somehow he got inside the house while we were working out there. When Matt came in to check for messages, he must have attacked him. I came running in when I heard them shouting. I saw him hit Matt with the butt of his gun a couple of times, then put something over his mouth. I think he thought Matt would be alone, because he seemed really surprised to see me. I charged the guy, but he slammed me hard into the refrigerator." Jesse shook his head. "I actually saw stars. I always thought that was just something that happened in cartoons."

"So you got a good look at him?" I asked, while I set up the X-ray equipment and checked for anything that looked like an antenna. Since Jesse was seated in a chair with a high back, it would actually be easier to take X rays of the vest because I could use duct tape to hold panels in place along the back side.

"No, he had on a mask. Matt must have recognized his voice or something. When I came to, I was in this chair with this thing on, and he was still here. I could tell he was watching your press conference on television. I don't think he realized I could hear him, 'cause he said, 'The bitch cares more for that damned dog than she does anyone else in the world. Pretty soon he'll be dead, too.' "

If possible, my blood ran even colder when I understood the reason for the trip wires in the doorways. Even though they would severely injure a human, they had been specifically designed to kill Romeo. Anger rose as I realized the bastard had known where I was, when Matt would probably be home alone, and how long it would take me to get there after the press conference. But the important part of what Jesse had just told me was that the Vest Bomber was definitely someone I knew, someone close enough to understand the way I worked, the way I lived. "Nick, are you listening?"

"Heard every word."

"He's someone *very* close to us, and he's gone way beyond personal."

"I know."

As I strained to think of anyone who would want to make Nick or me suffer, Nick said, "Ask Jesse if the bomber pushed any buttons or flipped any switches before he left."

Although I was irritated, I did as he asked, and Jesse replied, "I could hear him moving around me, but I'm pretty sure he didn't touch this thing. I pretended to be unconscious, even though he was telling me that if I moved I'd die. I was hoping he'd say something that might help you guys catch him."

"That was an excellent idea, Jesse. Nick, I just shot two panels of the back, two of the front, and one on each side. As soon as they're developed, I'll start the I-cuts. Talk to me."

"What's left on the front timer?"

"Twelve-ten." It seemed to take hours for the first forty-five-second developing time to tick down, and I peeled open the X ray and held up the black-and-white image to study it. With the drapes closed, there was hardly any light in the room. Moving toward the wall switch, I said, "It's too dark in here to see the shadows clearly, I'm going to turn on the lights."

Nick's voice boomed in my ear, "Jamie, no! Don't flip *any* switches!"

I stopped the instant his words hit my ear. My hand was poised over the switch as I looked at the carpet by my feet. With a sigh of relief, I pulled my hand away and claimed, "Nick, you were right. There are traces of plaster powder on the floor directly under the switch. It's probably another booby trap. Thanks."

"Be careful near the window, too. He wants you working alone and as blind as possible."

After thoroughly checking for another device, I pulled the curtains safely open and peeled back the other X rays. Holding them all in the better light, I methodically scanned each one, then said, "We've got the same metallic rods running in vertical pockets all the way around the vest. There are four places where the rods seem slightly darker in two-inch strips, which, from the shape of the shadows, are where the blasting caps are buried. With less than ten minutes left on the clock, I'm going to expose them all, look for real C4, then worry about removing those caps first. After that, I'll try to trace the wires and disconnect the power supply. Nick, do you agree?"

"Yes, but watch those color-coded wires as you work. I doubt if he added them just to screw with your mind, although that's definitely a possibility."

Until then, I hadn't noticed the siren in the background on my headset whenever he talked. I asked, "Where are you, Nick?"

"I'm about five minutes out. I sort of borrowed a police car that was parked outside the emergency room. I'm sure the shit will hit the fan as soon as the officer realizes it's gone."

Shocked, I barely had time to mutter, "But—" before he cut in with, "But nothing. We're a team, so shut up, and concentrate on your work."

Even though I knew Nick was far too sick to be out of bed, the fact that he was on his way made me breathe a little easier. "When you get here, come in from the garage. Go straight through the kitchen and living room into the den. There are trip wires rigged to fire shotgun shells across the two interior doorways along that path, and stay clear of the floor lamp when you come into the room. Understand?"

"Got it."

As I picked up my razor knife and tore off pieces of

tape, Jesse asked, "Mrs. Stone? Is there any way this thing could be rigged to a beeper like the bomb that blew up The Parlor? Matt told me all about it."

I smiled and answered, "So he has actually been listening when I talk about my work."

"Every word. He brags about you all the time. He thinks you're really brave, and I do, too."

I felt the blood rush to my cheeks. "I'm not going to lie to you, Jesse. At this point, anything is possible. My best guess is that the Vest Bomber wouldn't rig this type of device with that kind of trigger. The vests are constructed so that he can get them on fast, terrorize his victim so he can take or do what he wants without them being a problem, then leave. Most likely the vest is built in one piece, then transported to where he wants to do his dirty work. The bomb in the backpack at The Parlor was probably harmless until the last minute. If I were the bomber, I wouldn't have connected the beeper until just before I left the building. Otherwise, I would be taking the chance, albeit a small one, that if someone dialed the wrong pager number, the bomb would blow early and possibly kill me, too. It's not a risk I would take, and from what little trace evidence he's left behind, the Vest Bomber is a reasonably intelligent guy."

Jesse nodded. "I think he's just plain crazy. Why would anyone want to hurt so many people?"

Taking a deep breath, I knelt beside him and said, "I honestly don't know, but we're here to stop him."

"Matt and I thought you'd caught him. That's why we came back here."

I touched his shoulder. "I have a feeling that's exactly what the Vest Bomber wanted all of us to believe."

Jesse's deep brown eyes softly pleaded as he asked, "If something bad happens, would you tell my family how much I loved them?"

*I'll be dead, too,* I thought, but I did my best to assure him by replying, "They already know, and you're going to be fine, but I'll make sure they get the message if needed. You're like a son to me, too, Jesse. And there's something you should know about bad guys."

"What?"

I smiled. "They never win."

"Thank God."

"Okay, I'm going to start in the front and work around counterclockwise. My first I-cut will be to uncover the cap directly beneath the clock, which has just passed eight-forty-two. Cutting now. Talk to me, Nick."

"He's a great kid. In your hurry, did you take off your ring and switch watches?"

Irritated at myself, I stopped and said, "Good call, partner." Laying down my razor knife, I unfastened my watch and tossed both it and my ring into the pile of stuff I'd taken out of my hand entry kit. To Jesse, I said, "Tough guy Nick says you're a great kid."

I could tell Jesse was close to tears as he managed a small nod. Even though he had grown to the height of a man, he was still a fourteen-year-old boy whose life had just been altered forever.

Concentrating on the job at hand, I pressed the edge of the razor through the rough black material. With all the practice I'd had lately, the first I-cut went smoothly. After I taped back the sides, I scraped out some of the brownish white substance and sniffed it before casting it aside. "Nick, the first cap is surrounded by the same type of material that was *not* an explosive in the last few vests. I'm leaving this cut and moving to the cap under Jesse's left underarm."

As fast as I could, I sliced open the next area and peeled back the sides. "I've made the second I-cut and have exposed what appears to be actual military C4. It's a greenish plank, a half an inch tall and an inch and a half wide, still in its original cellophane wrapping. I can even see where the lot number was cut off. Clock is at six-oh-five. Talk to me, Nick."

"Jamie, I'll be there in a few seconds. I think you should go ahead and tackle that blasting cap, and I'll start cutting on the other side as soon as I get there."

"Will do. Don't forget the booby traps on the way in." I began scraping away the explosive and found what I was pretty sure was the blasting cap. Holding up the X ray, I confirmed my guess by matching the shadow. "The cap wires are wound tightly around the metal rod again, but this time the cap isn't visible. It's completely wrapped in a few layers of something that looks like Teflon tape." From my hand entry kit, I grabbed a pointed, flat piece of wood that resembled a candy apple stick that had been whittled to a sharp edge on one end. Using it as a knife, I began sawing through the tape.

I could hear the siren of the squad car Nick had stolen coming down my street as I peeled away the sticky layers. Picking up the wire cutters, I said, "I've exposed enough of the cap to cut the wires, which are military-issue brown." I held my breath and added, "Cutting . . . now." With a sigh, I looked around for a cap protector. When I didn't see one, I hurled the cap toward the far wall.

Jesse stiffened, and his eyes went wide. "Mrs. Stone! Please be careful!"

Apparently all the warnings I'd given the boys about the dangers of blasting caps had sunk in. "It's okay, Jesse. Stable caps don't go off without a charge."

He nodded and grumbled, "Glad that wasn't an *unstable* one."

We could hear Nick screech to a halt in front of the house, and the squad car's flashing lights lit up the room in alternating tones of red, blue, and white. Winking at

Jesse, I announced, "Help has arrived! Remember the trip lines, Nick."

Picking up the X ray of the back of the vest, I confirmed where my next cut would be and started the incision. The moment Nick came into the room, I handed him the X ray of the front, right side and nodded to my hand entry kit. With a tense grin I said, "Welcome to the party. There's another razor knife in that pile over there. Be careful not to disturb the laser I've fooled."

To Jesse, Nick said, "Hey, buddy. Let's get you out of this damned thing. We've got some intense paintballing to do as soon as I can move my arm."

Jesse nodded, but he was definitely getting more worried by the minute. Unfortunately, he could clearly see the seconds ticking down on the clock on his chest, and the increasing urgency of the situation was eating away his composure. His face was completely covered in sweat, and his color was fading fast. To Nick, he remarked, "You don't look so good."

"Same to ya, big guy," Nick replied with a wink.

While I kept busy on my side, Nick studied the X ray, then immediately started to work on the other. I could tell he was in great pain whenever he tried to use his injured arm, but doing intricate cutting and taping work with one hand was out of the question.

Peeling back the material on each side of my I-cut, I uncovered more of the brownish white substance. "Another fake," I declared, and moved over next to Nick so I could work on the back part of the vest.

To avoid the laser I had taped in place, I had to turn sideways and squeeze between Nick and the wall. My arm was almost touching his, so I said, "Tell me when you get to a delicate area, and I'll stop."

"Not a problem. This one looks fake, too. Since there isn't time to remove all the caps, I'm going to start tracing the wires and see if I can disconnect the battery on the timer."

He shifted directly in front of Jesse, giving me more room to work. As he reviewed the X rays, I found another slab of authentic C4. "This one looks real, but it's white commercial grade, not military. Same tape on the cap, just like the other side."

"At least he's consistent. Where's your wire sensor?"

Even if we cut all the caps that were buried in real C4, the detonation of any blasting cap against Jesse's torso could kill him. Since we might not have time to cut out all the caps, our best bet was to remove any energy sources that could send a pulse of electricity to them. The pulse would be carried through a wire connected to either the visible clock or some other mechanical device. In order to ensure that we didn't cut a wire that could close a circuit that was currently held open, Nick was going to use a sensor to determine if any of the wires were already conducting a flow of electricity.

With a shrug, I replied, "I think it's in the very bottom of my hand entry kit."

Nick quickly found it and began to move the small electronic device over the wires. A long beep signaled a regular wire, while a series of short beeps indicated an energized, or live, wire. I had almost cut through the tape when he said, "Holy shit! Look at this, Jamie. The bastard went to the trouble to change the color of the wires under the arm."

I leaned over to look at the area where he was pointing. Although I hadn't noticed it when I was working on the blasting cap, I was amazed to see that the green wire had been carefully spliced with the blue one. Baffled, I said, "That couldn't have been easy. Why go to all that trouble? I haven't heard the sensor indicate anything we need to worry about yet."

"Has to be a mind game. He probably thought you'd notice it and freak. You're right. So far, not one of these is hot. Maybe he knows enough about explosives to mimic the tricks of the trade but isn't quite comfortable enough to set up a device with too many bells and whistles."

"I'm ready to cut this cap." I did, and hurled it across the room. It bounced once on the carpet and landed about six inches from the other one.

Jesse glared at me and said, "I *hate* it when you do that!"

I smiled. "Me, too, but doing things strictly by the book might not be our best bet right now."

Nick said, "I'm going to disconnect the two wires around his neck." He reached around and jerked both up at the same time.

Jesse took his first deep breath and sighed, "Thanks."

"No problem." Nick remarked, and moved the sensor to the wires cutting into the jeans on Jesse's upper thighs. As he worked he said, "Those damn rods are making this thing sing, but I'm still not picking up any live wires."

I leaned around and looked at the time. "We're at thirty seconds. We better eliminate the power source pronto, Nick."

He jerked loose the wires around Jesse's thighs and said, "The only thing showing up on the X ray is the visible clock. Let's cut around it, expose the timer, and get him out of here."

Noticing blood seeping through the bandage on Nick's arm, I said, "Move back, I can do it faster." He stepped away, and I began to cut. Nick shifted to where he was just inches behind me, his face next to mine. We could both see the inner workings of the clock as I exposed it. To my surprise, the wiring was basic, very straightforward, with only the one set of the military brown wires connected. As the clock passed fifteen seconds, I softly shook my head and my stomach tightened. "It can't be this easy."

Nick reached across, using the sensor to make certain the wires going into the clock weren't energized. "Jerk 'em, Jamie."

I did, then as the clock flashed four seconds, I dug behind the back of it and popped out the battery. The digital face fell dark, and for a few moments a hush filled the air. I'm sure I wasn't the only one who was afraid to breathe. Like the vest he had used on Delores at The Parlor, there was a tiny slip of paper inside the battery case. Although last time the word "BOOM!" had been printed on a computer, this time the writing was by hand in big block letters:

**COME ALONE TO SAVE YOUR SON OR HE DIES. I'M *ALWAYS* WATCHING.**

Nick and I exchanged a heartfelt look of dismay, and I bit my lip so hard that it started to bleed.

Jesse's voice brought us back to the moment when he meekly asked, "Is it over?"

"It's over," I stated, but felt absolutely no relief. I had learned the hard way not to trust the bastard behind these bombings, and his note emphasized the degree of his soulless brutality. Unsnapping the front plastic closures, I helped Jesse slide out of the device and said, "Can you walk?"

Nick and I each took hold of an arm as he stood. He was a bit shaky, but he nodded and said, "I'm okay. Really."

"Then I want you to carefully step over the trip lines in each doorway, then go out the garage. *Run* home. Take the shortcut. When you get there, lock the doors and set the alarm. And, Jesse, I mean *run* like your life depends on it. Don't stop for anyone or anything. Not even if you hear an explosion behind you, or a trooper tries to flag you down. Understand?"

A skeptical look of apprehension crossed his face. "Why? You said yourself that it was over."

"Jesse, it won't be over until we catch the *real* Vest Bomber. He has Matt, and it's someone we know, which means it may be another trooper. Please, go home. It's only a few blocks. Are your parents there?"

"Probably."

"Then have them take you to the emergency room to get that cut on your forehead checked. Tell them I'll call as soon as we're certain that Matt's safe."

Jesse firmly shook his head. "I don't want to leave you guys in here. You said yourself that he's insane. You should come, too. There could be another bomb upstairs—"

I hugged him. "Nick and I aren't going to hang around very long. I just need to put the caps into protectors, disconnect the trip wires, and make sure Nick gets back to the hospital where he belongs. We'll let the rest of our squad handle the render safe of the other explosives, especially that black box with the laser trigger. We'll be fine. I promise."

"You sure?"

I nodded. "Yes! Now go! It would help if you called nine-one-one when you get home and tell them there's a trooper down, in need of immediate medical assistance." Reacting to the look of horror on his face, I added, "I'm talking about Nick, silly. And Jesse, whatever you do, don't tell *anyone* besides your parents that the Vest Bomber has Matt. If the media gets wind that Matt has been kidnapped, I may not get the chance to help him. It's our secret. Promise?"

"I'd never do anything that might hurt Matt."

"I know. Now go!"

I walked him to the door and pointed at the clear fishing line to be certain that in his state of shock he wouldn't forget about it. The moment he was outside, I gave Nick a gentle hug and said, "Thanks for coming. I couldn't have done it without you."

He tossed me two cap protectors that he had dug out of my kit. His eyes revealed the depth of his sincerity as he replied, "I'd do anything to help you."

The simple statement was so powerful, it brought tears to my eyes. I nervously looked away.

Picking up the X rays, Nick walked to the window. He looked at each panel in the stronger light as I crossed to the other side of the room and placed the first blasting cap inside a protector. I had just picked up the second when I caught a glimpse of him out of the corner of my eye. In the fading sunlight, I watched the expression on his face instantly change from curious to rock hard.

"What is it?" I asked, rushing to him. He had laid the X rays on the floor beside the vest, so I picked up the one on top.

"I'm not sure." Grabbing the razor knife, he knelt beside the vest that was lying on the floor and began making a careful slit down the center of the back. Peeling away the inner white lining, he exposed two inch-thick slabs of commercial C4 and began digging out clumps of it.

As he worked, I scrutinized the X ray and saw what I was sure had caused him to double-check: an elongated, cylindrical shadow in perfect line with the rod. It was much longer than any blasting cap I'd ever been exposed to, so I asked, "Are you considering the long shadow beside the center rod? I assumed it was a couple of strips of det cord, thrown in for good measure."

He had scraped away enough C4 to expose a cylindrical

silver tube carefully taped to the rod. Tossing the razor knife, he grabbed my hand and exclaimed, "Jamie, it's a secondary! Get the hell out of here!"

With the X ray in one hand, I helped him up with the other and we bounded over the trip wires, running as fast as we could out the kitchen door. We were just past the edge of the garage when the force of the explosion propelled us into the air. After a short flight, we hit the ground hard and rolled a few feet before stopping in the grass. Somehow my right arm was pinned under Nick's torso, and the rest of my body was on top of his when we finally came to a rest. For several seconds we stayed perfectly still, as the shattered remains of the windows and furniture in my den rained down in bits and pieces on us.

When the last of the debris had fallen, I coughed and managed to ask, "You okay?"

"Think so, but I've definitely been better," he muttered. "Is my head still attached, or did it roll off?"

I barely shifted so I could see his face and replied, "It's still there." The percussion had numbed the back side of my body, and I wasn't sure if I was hurt or simply stunned. At first, I was afraid to even try to move.

After a few seconds, my senses returned enough for my analytical side to kick back in. "What the hell was that?" I asked, rolling off of Nick. To my surprise, the X ray was still in my left hand, crumpled but readable.

Nick groaned and clutched his injured arm as he slowly worked his way into a sitting position. Obviously fighting back waves of pain, he pointed at the shadow as he hoarsely answered, "I'm pretty sure it was a chemical pencil."

"A what?"

"I'll explain later. Let's make sure we're all in one piece."

I'll never forget the first glimpse of the destruction that surrounded us. "Oh, my God," I moaned, unable to look away.

There was a gaping hole where the den had been just a few moments ago. Most of the furniture that had been in the upstairs bedrooms was either in the front yard in pieces or where the den used to be. Every window had blown out, and part of the roof jutted out over raw beams. The thought that the kitchen and garage were probably in relatively good shape didn't offer much consolation. I'd seen hundreds of bombings, but they were someone else's things that had been destroyed. These were the few treasures I'd accumulated in my life: my photos, my son's keepsakes, our memories.

Nick's voice was soft as he offered, "Jamie. I'm really sorry."

Two squad cars and an unmarked police car all screeched to a halt in the street as the sound of more approaching sirens filled the air. A handful of men were rushing toward us. Even though my head was pounding, I was beginning to feel almost human again. Suddenly, the realization that my house was only the tip of the iceberg hit me hard. Bolting up, I said, "Nick, we've got to find Matt!"

"We will," he said as he shifted to one side and tried to push himself up. Giving him a hand, I could tell he was weak as he stood at my side. Romeo was barking fiercely inside my Suburban, and I looked over to see that he was jumping against the driver's side window and growling. "We're all right, boy!" My voice didn't calm him at all, so I shouted, "Romeo, sit!"

He half obeyed by lowering his haunches onto the driver's seat, but his paws still rested nervously on the window.

"Jesus. Are you two all right?" Simon asked, breathlessly stopping at my side.

Nick shook his head, noticing Simon's tailored suit. "What the hell are you doing here dressed for a funeral?"

Simon replied, "I was on my way home and heard the nine-one-one call."

"Damn, you're fast," Nick coughed. "Must be an ATF record."

Looking up at Simon, I realized that the 911 call meant that Jesse had made it safely home. I felt a little better knowing he was out of harm's way.

Simon asked, "What the hell happened here?"

"The Vest Bomber."

Eying Nick skeptically, he stated, "But that's impossible. He's dead."

Nick snapped, "Guess again. Luke Layman might have been his silent partner, but he definitely wasn't the brains behind the bombings."

Simon shot us an incredulous stare. "Anyone else inside?"

We both shook our heads. Nick explained, "We defeated a vest with about four seconds to spare, then discovered a secondary detonation mechanism."

"Guess you're lucky the Vest Bomber didn't get his timing quite right. How long did it take before the secondary blew?"

An ambulance rounded the corner as Nick closed his eyes and replied, "Maybe two minutes. Could've been three. We'll be able to tell from the secure com tape."

Looking at Nick, Simon slyly smiled and stated, "I suppose you asked permission to take that squad car from the hospital?"

Nick shrugged. "Well, not exactly . . . but the keys were in the ignition, and the door wasn't locked."

He grinned. "KCPD radio has been constant chatter

since you took off in it. I'll bet some heads are going to roll in the morning."

I turned away from the sickening sight of my house and watched a fire engine roll into place. Firefighters swiftly moved into action, and the fire chief rushed to our side. We quickly explained that even though the known blasting caps had been neutralized in cap protectors, there were still booby traps that might be extremely dangerous. He agreed to hold all personnel behind a 100-yard perimeter until the bomb squad responded.

Simon gave me a sympathetic look and said, "I know how you feel about publicity. I'll have some officers keep the media as far back as possible."

I halfheartedly muttered, "Thanks." A news helicopter seemed to appear out of nowhere, taking a position so low over my house that I thought it might try to land on what was left of the roof. Nick leaned close to say, "As if things weren't bad enough, this is going to turn into another three-ring circus."

Following the helicopter's powerful spotlight, I noticed the neck of Matt's new guitar protruding from one corner of the pile of rubble. Tears sprang to my eyes. Nick must have sensed that I might not be able to keep my emotions in check much longer, because he wrapped his good arm around me to shelter my pain from the prying eyes of the world.

Leading me to my Suburban, he practically shoved me into the passenger seat. The moment I sat down, Romeo jumped into my arms and barked.

"Where are the keys?" Nick brusquely asked.

I pulled them out of my pocket, too deep in shock to care what he had in mind. Since the squad car he had stolen was blocking the bottom of my driveway, he backed across my neighbor's lawn and tore out down the street.

"Where are we going?" I asked.

"Most of your gear is buried back there. We'll switch to my Suburban, then go out to the training center where we can think. Is my truck parked at headquarters?"

I nodded.

He grabbed my police radio and shoved it into my hand. "Okay, I want you to brief the rest of the squad on where the known booby traps were located. Be sure to tell them the upstairs will need to be swept in the bomb suit."

I nodded, thankful to have something to keep me from dwelling on Matt's situation. After thoroughly going over all the details with the other bomb techs, I put the radio in its holster and took a deep breath.

Nick said, "You'd better call your parents. I'd bet they're running this nationally as a breaking news story with live coverage."

I started to dial my parents' number on my cell phone, then stopped. "Nick, what am I going to tell them? My father's not well. He would probably have a heart attack worrying about Matt."

Nick thought for a moment. "No one knows about Matt except Jesse, and he promised not to tell anyone. Unless the Vest Bomber decides he wants more publicity, the news won't be covering Matt's kidnapping. Just tell your folks that everything is going to be okay and you'll call them as soon as you can to explain."

I nodded and finished dialing their number. "Mom?"

"Jamie! Your house! Are you all right?"

I could tell she had been crying. "Sorry I couldn't call sooner. Things are really hectic right now. I just wanted you to know that I'm okay."

"And Matt?"

"He . . . he wasn't at home when the bomb detonated." It was the most truthful lie I could come up with on short notice. I could hear the labored rattle of my father's breathing in the background as he asked my mother what had happened. In my heart I knew that there was nothing they could do to help. Besides, I was more than frightened enough for all of us.

"Do you want to come stay with us for a while?" she asked.

"It's sweet of you to offer. I honestly don't know what we're going to do right now. Listen, I've got to go. I just wanted to tell you not to worry. I've got everything under control. I'll call you tomorrow. Tell Dad I love him, and I love you, too. And please call the Stones for me. I'm sure they'll hear about it on the news, too."

"I'll call them as soon as I hang up. We love you, Jamie. Thanks for letting us know that you're okay. Bye."

"Bye." I hung up the phone and dropped it in my lap. Covering my face with my hands, I wondered if that would be the last time I ever heard their voices.

Nick interrupted my morbid thoughts by saying, "You did the right thing. They would've been up all night agonizing about something totally out of their control."

"I know." Clenching my fists, I cried, "Dammit, Nick! I *need* to know where Matt is!"

"This is part of his fun. Time is on his side, and he knows that every single minute that passes is like slow torture for you."

"Maybe I can do the same for him someday. Hanging him by his toenails over a vat of acid until the vapors eat off his flesh seems like an appropriate punishment."

Nick barely smiled. "Keep it up. Channel those thoughts of revenge to anger. It'll help you stay sharp tonight."

Beyond tired, there's a state where you function on pure adrenaline. Your nerves are taut, your mind a racing machine. The brain stops recognizing the aches and pains from muscles and bones that have been pushed too far for too long. Instead, it focuses on doing whatever it takes to survive. I knew I had reached that point, and I was sure Nick was there, too.

For the first time, I actually *looked* at Nick. The bandages on his arm were soaked with patches of blood, some dried to almost black, some so fresh the crimson patterns still seemed to be growing. I recognized the old shirt he had on as the one he kept at the bottom of his jump bag. It was the shirt from my first training session at Redstone, the one he had loaned me when a couple of the guys had hidden all my gear as a prank. His jeans were stained with blood and had snags and tears across the front. I was certain they were the pair he had been wearing on the night Alexa was killed. When I glanced down, I realized that Nick had left the hospital so quickly that he hadn't even put on shoes. He was obviously in pain, and I was overcome by the notion that I was abusing his loyalty and friendship.

With a sigh, I touched his cheek and said, "I appreciate your help more than anything in the world, but you really should be in the hospital."

He shook his head. "That's the first place that pack of wolves would look, and I have no intention of talking to anyone. According to the note, he's watching *all* the time. I doubt that's true, but if it is, I think we should make it a little more difficult for him to keep an eye on us."

"Even so . . . I'll find Matt alone. You can't go on like this. Please, Nick. I can't stand the thought of losing Matt *and* you."

"Jamie, listen to me. I am *not* going to be stuck in some goddamned hospital bed when Matt needs my help!" His eyes met mine as he confessed, "I've watched him grow up. I love him like a son. Please don't shut me out. Together, we can save him. I know it."

I nodded, fighting tears as I whispered, "I know it, too."

For a few moments, we drove in silence. Then I asked him again about the secondary device that had torn apart my home.

"It's a military device that looks a little like an ink pen. Chemical pencils are used by the military to time-delay a detonation without an electrical impulse. When you snap the button on one end, it breaches a vial of acid, which eats through and dissolves the barrier between two chemicals that are highly reactive. When the barrier breaks completely down and the chemicals make contact, enough of a flash is generated to act like a blasting cap. If I remember right, they're made in several different intervals of time; some go off in fifteen minutes, others can take hours to ignite."

More than just a little impressed, I asked, "How did you know what to look for?"

"The year before you joined the squad, a chemical pencil took out an entire bomb squad down in South America. They thought the device had been rendered safe, so they took it back to their office as evidence. The pencil detonated half an hour later. Seven bomb techs were killed. When their government asked for help dealing with the terrorists, our State Department sent out a bulletin."

Even steering with one arm, Nick expertly wove in and out of traffic. Romeo bounced against me when one tire sank into an unavoidable pothole as we pulled into the parking lot at headquarters. I hugged him hard and buried my face in the softness of his fur. As the car jerked, I suddenly realized that something thin and hard was poking my lower back. Shifting to one side, I reached down and pulled out a bright yellow computer diskette. A surge of panic wrapped icy fingers around my soul, stilling my breath while chilling my heart.

Boldly written in black marker on the diskette were the words: Matt's Good-bye.

# thirteen

## 1

Until the moment I saw that diskette, I would've sworn I knew the true meaning of fear. I didn't. What I had thought was fear before bore no relevance to the wave of absolute, total loss of control that splintered those first horrible minutes. I couldn't speak, I couldn't move, and I could actually feel my heart shift into a crushing beat so intense that I wondered if I might be having a heart attack. After what seemed like an eternity but was probably only a few seconds, Nick asked, "What's wrong?"

Still frozen in terror, I didn't answer.

"Jamie? What is it?"

His voice sounded far away, a distant echo calling my name from the fringe of a nightmare. I realized he had snatched the diskette from my hand, but I didn't react. I felt the cool touch of his fingers on my cheeks as he turned my face toward his. Those penetrating eyes searched mine, and I saw a glimmer of my own terror in their reflection. Through the tunnel of fear, I finally heard his voice demanding, "Listen to me, damn it! Jamie, Matt needs you! Come on! Everything is going to be all right, but we have to fight for him!"

Hearing Matt's name must have rattled my numb brain enough to knock me back into the world of the living. I meekly nodded.

Nick kept talking. "We have work to do. There is *no time* for you to feel sorry for yourself or to let your fear ride shotgun. Do you understand? More than ever in his life, Matt needs you *right now!* And that means the part of you who trained her butt off to become a great bomb tech. He needs that fearless woman who's always been there for him whenever it really counted."

I nodded, feeling a little stronger beneath the truth of his words. "I know. I'm okay. I can do this."

"Good." Holding up the diskette, he added, "First, we've got to see exactly what we're up against." He screeched to a halt in the space next to his Suburban. "I'll get my laptop while you move all the gear left in here into my truck. Take everything, Jamie. There's no telling what kind of booby traps and contraptions he'll throw between you and Matt."

Nick disappeared into headquarters as I unlocked his Suburban and ordered Romeo inside. Opening both rear hatches, I shifted ropes, pulleys, tool boxes, night-vision gear, water, and virtually everything else from my vehicle to his. When I was finished with the gear stored in the back end, I moved my radio, cell phone, and the contents of my glove box onto the floorboard behind his passenger seat.

Crawling into the driver's seat, I hugged Romeo as I wondered what was taking Nick so long. Finally, he emerged from the building. I could tell by the expression on his face that things had somehow gone from bad to worse. The moment he slid by my side, I sighed and asked, "You booted it up already, didn't you? You know what he's done, and considering the look on your face, it must be pretty damn bad."

He nodded, his expression stone cold. Looking at me, he declared, "It's nothing we can't handle, but you're going to have to use all your willpower from this moment on. When you look at this video, you have to see it as a bomb tech, not as Matt's mother. Otherwise, you're never going to get through this. And if *you* don't get through it, *Matt* doesn't, either."

"How am I supposed to do that? I *am* his mother! This is killing me. It's *my* fault he's there."

"Jamie, it is *not* your fault. You have no control over this maniac. Everyone thought the Vest Bomber had been caught. We were wrong; now we have to deal with it. I don't know how you're going to do it, but I know that when you see the images on that diskette, you *must* watch it from a purely professional point of view. He's made it perfectly clear that you're going to have to go in *alone*. We should have time to rig something so I can talk to you, but I don't think we can risk my tagging along. At least not in a way that might be seen."

"Where is Matt? Is he okay?"

"He's been better, and the video doesn't say where he's being held."

"How the hell does he expect me to go alone when I don't know where to go at all?" My hands were shaking as I took the laptop from Nick and sat it between us. Looking at him, I said, "Give me a minute or two after I see it the first time, then we'll watch it together as bomb techs. I promise."

Nick nodded and punched the keys that brought the digital video to life.

I gasped as the first image appeared on the screen, and my trembling fingers flew to my mouth. Biting my nails, I watched the nauseating forty-five-second digital movie play from start to finish. When the screen went black, I opened the door and crawled outside. Falling to my hands and knees, I sucked deep breaths of fresh air as I silently said a prayer for my son, then one for myself to have the strength to save him.

The sun was setting, painting the world in soft shades of orange and pink. According to the Vest Bomber's video, Matt would be dead by sunrise, and there wasn't a bomb tech in the world good enough to save him.

# 2

By the time I climbed behind the wheel of the Suburban, I had decided that there was no way I was going to let the Vest Bomber get away with torturing my son. I tried my best to keep all emotion from my voice as I said, "I'm ready. Let's go to the Training Center. From what little I saw, I'm going to need some serious rappelling gear, plus a shitload of tools off the bomb truck."

Nick nodded. "While you drive, I'll go frame by frame, and we'll discuss the steps you'll need to take."

I took a deep breath. "That's good. We'll need every minute. Bombers love to taunt their victims. If he had wanted to just kill Matt, he could've done it without going to all this trouble. There has to be some clue, some little detail that will tell us where he has him."

Nick nodded. "I agree. His ultimate goal is you. Matt is just the bait to get you in an environment he totally controls."

"How comforting."

"Sorry, but we both know it's true. You have to realize

that once you get Matt out of this, you're next. It might be right then, or it might be later. Considering how quickly he's been escalating his attacks, there's no way to tell."

"I have a gut feeling that one way or another, it'll end tonight."

"You're probably right. From this point on, keep your cell phone handy. He may get tired of waiting for you to figure out where he is and invite you personally."

"How would he get my number?"

"Matt knows it. Hopefully, he wouldn't feel the need to keep it a secret."

I nodded, grabbing my phone and tucking it into my pocket. "Before we get started, I think we've got a few things to consider about what happened back at my house. Like how the diskette got inside my car without either of us noticing."

Nick considered my question. "The windows were cracked. Anyone at the scene could've just dropped it in. At least we know your original theory is right. Whoever's doing this is at the crime scenes during the render safe and cleanup, watching you work."

"And Romeo was really agitated for a few minutes. That was probably when it happened."

Nick shook his head. "The son of a bitch was right in the palms of our hands."

I nodded. "We need to think about the timing, about who this could be. Jesse said they were attacked around four o'clock this afternoon. The Vest Bomber had time to deal with Jesse, booby trap my house, move Matt to another location and strap him into that contraption, shoot the video, then get back to the scene within a few minutes of when the secondary exploded at six-thirty."

Nick concluded, "Which means that Matt has to be within a thirty-minute radius of your house, probably closer. We can rule out two of the people we talked about this afternoon. Lieutenant Colonel Jones was on live television with you when the bomber was rigging Jesse's vest, and Jeff is still in the hospital."

"That leaves Simon, Trooper Johnson, and Agent Nichols," I said.

"Well, we spoke to Simon, of course, but did you notice either one of the others at your house?"

I closed my eyes and tried to remember every detail. "Nichols! I saw Frank Nichols talking to Simon across the street just as we pulled away."

Nick nodded. "Would Matt recognize him, even in a mask?"

"Probably, if he heard his voice. He's met both Frank and Simon several times."

"Jamie, if I'm right about that secondary on Jesse's vest being triggered by a chemical pencil, they're damned hard to come by. We could get immediate help from military intelligence."

I asked, "How can we verify that it's one of theirs?

"There's one that's never been activated in the evidence locker at the Training Center. Jeff confiscated it from the house of a Vietnam vet when his wife found a stash of all sorts of explosives after he died. It's been waiting for destruction for a few months." Reaching into his pocket, he pulled out the X ray of Jesse's vest. "If it matches this shadow, we have a good place to start."

"Thank God."

Nodding toward the laptop, he asked, "Are you ready?"

"As I'll ever be."

He started the video, then froze a close-up image of Matt dangling in the cruel apparatus. The lighting was poor but still good enough to tell that the device was quite sophisticated. I glanced over long enough for my stomach to knot, then concentrated on the road as Nick described the battle I'd be fighting. "It appears that he's suspended in an elevator shaft. The floor is about two feet below him, so I'd guess the Vest Bomber stood on the top of the elevator while he rigged the device."

Nick glanced my way, probably to be certain I was still in control. I said, "Go ahead. I'm all right."

He lightly touched my shoulder, then went on. "The device is mounted diagonally from two of the shaft's corners, hanging Matt halfway between the central cables and the concrete walls on one side. It looks like a combination of the vests we've been dealing with, coupled with a push-pull bomb strapped onto Matt's back. The push-pull is encased in a four-inch piece of PVC pipe, about a foot long. There's an arming hole evident at the center of the back. The string is still dangling from it."

Even though I'd never disarmed one in the field, I knew from my training at Redstone that a push-pull bomb is triggered by a certain degree of variance in the lines leading into each end of it. Since the bomber sets the amount of tolerance, only an X ray would determine how much the wires could be moved without the bomb detonating.

In this case, Matt's weight was suspended by thin wire cables that wrapped around compound hunting bows. The bows had been bolted onto two adjoining walls, and the cables were fully flexed, forming a perfect triangle of tension. I'd never seen such a rig, but I assumed that the combination of fulcrums and pulleys on the compound bows would decrease the pressure on the cables leading into the bomb. Cutting the cables, or Matt moving more than the tolerated amount, would detonate the explosive.

The arming hole Nick had mentioned is a typical component of many bombs. Since bombers don't want to risk their own lives, they include at least two switches when they build the bomb. The primary switch is the one they plan to actually use to detonate the device. In order to be able to safely move the bomb from the spot where they build it, they include an arming switch. Until the arming switch is closed, the device won't function as intended.

In many cases, tugging a string from the outside is all it takes to arm the bomb. Before arming the push-pull bomb on Matt's back, the Vest Bomber would've balanced his weight. Once he was satisfied that the positioning was perfect, he would've pulled the string on the arming switch, which would make the motion detector the last open switch.

Nick moved to a different frame of the video, then continued, "It looks like a length of cable exits the push-pull on each side. From there, each cable wraps through mounted compound bows on the side walls, then comes back to connect at the vest. Jamie, I think you're going to have to render safe the push-pull and assume that the vest might be operating on the same weight-bearing tension."

I glanced at him, certain I hadn't heard right. "Are you serious?"

He nodded. "Think about it. He knows that any tech who's been to Redstone can defeat a push-pull, but I think he's betting that you're going to want to get Matt out of there as soon as possible. We both know that Matt will be"—he touched my arm and looked me square in the eye—"in a certain degree of *discomfort* until we can get him out of this contraption."

I swallowed hard and nodded.

"So he thinks you'll render it safe, then immediately cut the cables to get him down and ease his pain and suffering. I'd bet that this vest isn't like the others. Those cables go *inside* the front buckles. It couldn't have been easy to rig so that Matt's weight still balanced perfectly. Why bother with such a complicated setup unless there's a reason to hide the suspension mechanism underneath?"

I nodded as I pulled into the Training Center and wound down the long road that led to the evidence locker. "A second inner push-pull trigger makes sense. But one thing doesn't."

"What?"

"Why would he give me this preview? Why allow me the time to study the device and gather everything I'll need to defeat it?"

"You said it yourself a few minutes ago. Bombers taunt their victims. The Unabomber would still be taunting people if his brother hadn't turned him in. He was very proud of his ability to terrorize people."

"It just doesn't sit right. There's no way he's going to let me waltz into wherever the hell he's hidden Matt and just go to work. He'll have a fail safe. I know it."

"Remote detonation capability?"

"Probably. That way, even if I defeat both switches, he can still blow it like he did the secondary at The Parlor." I took a deep breath. "You know he's going to be watching. He'll either be close enough to see the fireworks in person, or he'll have a video hookup."

"And, Jamie . . . don't forget. It's someone Matt recognized."

"Believe me, I know."

# 3

The evidence locker at the Training Center is in the building next to where we park the bomb truck. Although it is called a locker, it's actually a highly secure storage area. Explosives recovered by both our bomb squad and ATF are stored in the remote location, since the ATF's offices are on the seventh floor of a building downtown. ATF has its own locker there, but for obvious reasons, any explo-

sives must be kept at our facility, which is designed to
minimize the chance of accidental detonations. The interior is oak, with no metal of any kind allowed inside. Even
the lighting is generated by explosive-resistant bulbs that
create no sparks and consequently generate very little
light.

Only members of our bomb squad and ATF agents have
the peculiar keys needed to open the double magazine
locks on the outer door. The magazine locks resemble
enormous padlocks encased in bottomless steel boxes so
that they can't be removed with bolt cutters. To open the
lock, you have to reach up into the box and insert the key,
a process that isn't exactly easy in the confined space.

Explosives are stored inside the evidence locker until
they are destroyed. Although each time a person enters
they're supposed to sign in, we're on the honor system.
After we hurriedly signed the log, Nick double-checked
the case information we needed to find the chemical pencil. It took a few seconds for our eyes to adjust to the dim
light, then we located the appropriate cardboard box on
the oak shelf. Opening the sealed evidence envelope, Nick
tilted it toward me and shook his head. It was completely
empty.

Turning my way, Nick muttered, "It's all gone." Checking the evidence list on the outside of the envelope, he
added, "Two dozen military blasting caps, an assortment
of wires and switches, a chemical pencil . . . everything
we recovered from that nutcase's house is missing."
Glancing around the room, he seethed, "I wonder how
much more has been stolen."

"That explains the variety of caps and explosive materials the Vest Bomber has used." Trying to digest the
information, I leaned against the wall. "Getting into this
building would be next to impossible without inflicting
some kind of visible damage. That means the Vest

Bomber is either an ATF agent or he's on our squad."

After a meaningful glance, Nick sternly declared, "He's *not* on our squad."

I suggested, "Someone could've stolen one of the keys. Made a copy."

Nick shook his head. "Those keys are too funky to be copied, and if an honest agent or tech lost one, they would've reported it immediately. The Vest Bomber has to be ATF. And if it's Frank or Simon, it explains why the FBI labs never found a speck of trace evidence on a single vest. If there had been any, he could've removed it before shipping it off for testing. Even if he missed a hair or a fingerprint, the FBI lab would've attributed it to Frank's presence at the scene."

My heart sank. "Do you realize the type of government equipment an ATF agent would have access to? He'll be armed with the latest infrared and night-vision devices, maybe even thermal imaging. Jesus, Nick! Please tell me ATF doesn't have portable thermal imaging!"

Thermal imaging equipment senses heat. It can "see through" bushes, small trees, virtually anything that isn't extremely dense. If a person in a building leans against an outer wall long enough for the surface to heat up even two or three degrees, thermal imaging will show the slight variance from the outside. If the Vest Bomber had thermal imaging technology at his disposal, there would be no way Nick, or anyone else, could back me up without him finding out. Plus, even in complete darkness, he'd know exactly where I was.

Nick sighed. "As far as I know, only the special operations helicopters are equipped with thermal imaging. The Vest Bomber would have access to the same gear that we have, though. It's the state-of-the-art night-vision goggles that worry me. Unless we can discover where he is, there's no way I'll be able to sneak past him."

"Great." I sighed, then gulped a ragged breath.

Nick was quiet for a couple of seconds. "Do you know if Nichols has a diving watch that he wears turned to the inside of his wrist?"

I anxiously declared, "There's an easy way to find out. Let's go have a chat with him."

"Jamie, we can't go straight to Frank. What if we're wrong? Besides, if he knows we're onto him, he'll kill Matt and run. Remember, the Vest Bomber has millions of dollars of jewels stashed somewhere. We need to find out for certain who we're dealing with, then handle Matt's situation without tipping our hand. Besides, chances are good that right now the Vest Bomber is hanging close to Matt. When we find him, we'll find them both."

"Which brings us back to ground zero. If he's waiting with Matt, how does he expect me to know where he is?"

Nick sighed. "I still think he'll try to contact you, or he's left some clue that he expects you to find. We know Matt's in an elevator shaft somewhere near your house. Since he probably rigged the device after five, it may not be a vacant building, but he'd need to be confident that no one would use that particular elevator before morning. I'll drive while you think about the possibilities."

"Drive where?"

Nick shot me a glare. "The ATF offices downtown. This late, they'll be empty, and I'm not above breaking and entering."

"We won't have to. I know the head security guard. He'll let us in. Let's load up whatever gear we'll need from the bomb truck, then head there." I gave him a hug. "Thanks for being here, Nick."

"That's what partners are for."

# 4

Even though the security guard had opened the main door for us, I still felt like a lowly criminal as Nick and I stepped off the elevator on the seventh floor of the high-rise occupied by ATF. Very softly, I asked, "Any idea where we begin?"

"Why are you whispering? Who gives a damn if someone catches us up here?"

In my regular voice, I replied, "Good point. Since there aren't names on the doors, I suppose we'll just have to check each office. I'll go down this hall, you go that way. Holler if you find something."

Glancing at my watch, I was certain that every minute we wasted was sheer agony for Matt. About the time I turned the first doorknob and realized it was locked, I heard Nick shout, "Kick 'em in, Jamie. We don't have time for any bullshit."

Doing as he said, I stepped back and attacked the first door with a vengeance. Nick must've done the same, since the racket we generated reverberated through the silent corridors. It only took a matter of seconds to determine that I'd broken into the wrong office. Moving on, I kicked in the next door. As I flipped on the light, I realized it was Simon Stanley's office. I was about to take a look around when my cell phone rang. My hand was shaking as I took the phone out of my pocket and read the caller ID: *Kansas State Patrol*.

For a moment I considered not answering, but quickly decided that if Nick and I were wrong about Frank or Simon, the Vest Bomber might still be a fellow trooper. Taking a deep breath, I answered, "Sergeant Stone."

"Where the hell are you?"

I instantly recognized Lieutenant Colonel Jones's voice, and replied. "I'm at ATF headquarters, sir."

"Is Terrell with you?"

"Yes, sir."

"You both have some explaining to do."

I walked over and leaned against Simon's desk. "Yes, sir. We'll report back as soon as possible. I'm afraid neither of us can talk at the moment." I pushed the End Call button and started to leave. My phone rang again, but after confirming it was Jones on the caller ID, I let the automatic message system answer. I was turning to get Nick when some photos on Simon's credenza caught my eye.

The first was a distant shot of Stanley's ATF training class, the second a picture of him standing beside Frank Nichols, both wearing wetsuits. I stared at it for a few moments before the realization hit me. At the top of my lungs, I screamed, "Nick! I've found something! In here!"

The minute he stepped into the office, I pointed at the photo. "Look! Nichols isn't wearing a watch, but the face of *Simon's* diving watch is on the *inside* of his wrist."

Nick snatched the frame. "It's hard to tell, but it's the same size and shape as the one on The Parlor's tape. Let's tear this place apart. Maybe there's something here that'll tell us if we're right."

It didn't take long. At the bottom of Simon's in box, I found a file on a meth lab bust he had worked a few months before. It was in an old apartment building on the outskirts of town that had been condemned shortly after the arrests were made. When I flipped through the file, I discovered several items that I was sure didn't pertain to the investigation: a blueprint of the building, plus an odd collection of photos.

It was the stack of pictures that made me certain I was right. Among various shots of the utility room, I found a close-up view of the electrical panel with each breaker labeled. Then there were photos of the side entrance, and of the garage area in the basement. But more importantly, there were six shots of the elevator shaft, taken from various angles, including two that had been taken looking up through the car's trapdoor.

Nick and I had spread the photographs across Simon's desk and were studying them when my cell phone rang. My heart almost stopped. The caller ID read, "Unavailable." As I reached for my phone, Nick gently touched my hand. "Jamie, you can't let Simon know that you're onto him. Choose your words very carefully."

I nodded, then pushed the button to answer the phone. "Sergeant Stone."

"Jamie? Are you all right?"

Instantly recognizing the voice, I knew it wasn't the Vest Bomber. I softly shook my head so that Nick would understand and relax. "David? Is that you?"

"Yes! What the hell happened? You're all over the news again! Is Matt okay? I've been going crazy trying to find out if you two were all right."

"We're as well as can be expected." Another diversionary lie. I was getting good at them.

"CNN is reporting that the Vest Bomber blew up your house and then kidnapped both you and Matt."

"What? Why . . ." I thought of all of our friends and relatives who'd be worried sick.

". . . And they're saying the Vest Bomber killed a college professor and damn near killed Nick day before yesterday! Is that true?"

"Well, yes."

"Jesus, Jamie! Nick has a lot more experience than you do! What are you thinking staying there?"

Through gritted teeth, I asserted, "I'm thinking that it's up to people like Nick and me to stop this bastard before he hurts more innocent people."

"Is that what you want on your tombstone? '*Somebody* had to do it'?"

"I guess so."

David took a deep breath, then sighed. "I'm sorry. I know you've been through a lot and the last thing you need is another problem. It's just that when I called KSP headquarters, all they'd tell me is that you weren't available and that the best they could do was give you a message when you checked in. I *hate* living like this. I love you, and I don't want to lose you, but . . ."

"I'm sorry you had to go through all that, David, but I really can't talk right now. I've got some critical work to wrap up, then I'll explain everything. I promise."

"Don't tell me that after all that's happened you're still worried about work! Please, Jamie, quit that damn job before it gets you or Matt killed."

"David, things aren't that clear cut! I'll call you as soon as possible. For now, just trust me."

"I can be on the first plane to the States, probably be in Kansas City by late afternoon tomorrow. I'll help you financially. We'll do whatever it takes. I just want you safe!"

At that moment, I simply didn't have the energy or patience to deal with another emotional issue. Releasing more of my frustration than I should have, I asserted, "No! Do *not* come here! Stay where you are, David. I'll let you know if I need help, I swear. I'm sorry, but I really have to go now. Good-bye." I punched the End Call button, then stared at the phone.

Silence descended on Simon's office and hung in the air until Nick declared, "Time's up, Jamie. Shake it off. You can worry about David later. We've got to study these pictures and blueprints, then come up with a viable plan. Are you with me?"

Fueled by a mixture of fear, anger, and frustration, I declared, "One hundred percent. I'm in the perfect mood to kick Simon's ass. Let's get out of here and get to work."

# fourteen

## 1

"Where are you, Stone? I thought you *loved* your son."

Even though his words were altered by some sort of mechanical device, I still recognized a quality that made me certain it was Simon Stanley harassing me. I had no choice but to hold my temper. Taking a deep breath, my fingernails dug into the cell phone as I replied, "I love Matt more than you'll ever know. You forgot one little thing. I can't come to help him if I don't know where he is."

"I didn't forget. I thought you needed some time to think about the consequences of your actions. Besides, I wanted to be certain everything was ready for your arrival."

"How thoughtful. Where is he?"

"That depends. Where are you?"

Nick's face was next to mine, so he had heard every

word of the conversation. He immediately shook his head, meaning that I should lie. I quickly replied, "I'm at the Training Center. I didn't know where else to go. The media has converged on KSP headquarters, and we both know my house is a disaster area."

"Where's Terrell?"

I glanced at Nick, and he shrugged. We both knew that Simon had seen us leave my house together. "He's with me."

"I believe you were instructed to come *alone*. If I see Terrell, or anyone else for that matter, I'll blow Matt to kingdom come."

Through gritted teeth, I seethed, "I *will* come alone! Just tell me where you're holding him!"

"Let me talk to Terrell."

Since we were so close, all I had to do was tilt the phone in the opposite direction. Nick's voice was harsh as he simply stated, "Lieutenant Terrell."

"I thought for certain I'd taken you out of the picture."

I could practically feel the hatred pouring from Nick as he muttered, "Not quite."

"Alexa Dixon was a nice piece of ass. Too bad her ass ended up in so *many* pieces."

I softly squeezed Nick's hand, certain that he wanted nothing more than to scream a string of threatening obscenities. Instead, he calmly asked, "Why don't we just keep this man-to-man? Let's get the women and children out of the picture. If it's a fight you want, I'm up for the challenge. Even injured, I'd bet I can still kick your butt."

Simon sighed loud enough for us to hear him. "Terrell, you already lost your chance. What kind of tech doesn't check an unexpected package for a loved one?"

I saw Nick flinch, then mutter, "You bastard."

"It's Jamie's turn now. But I just wanted you to know that there's a bomb in your hospital room. I used enough

C4 to take out the entire wing, which I believe, happens to include your bomb squad buddy, Jeff Jenkins. I'll remotely detonate it if you get anywhere near this building or if you try to call it in. Understand?"

"Every word."

"Put Stone back on the line." The moment I tilted the phone back toward me, Simon said, "Matt sure is a big boy now. Six foot two. Exactly one hundred and fifty-five pounds. He presented more of a challenge than I expected, although I must admit I handled the situation well, don't you think?"

Trembling with anger, I wasn't sure I could stand his taunting. Since I already knew where Matt was, and Nick and I had devised a plan to rescue him, I was in no mood to tolerate Simon's endless taunting. *"Where is he?"* I cried.

Simon's reply was a hearty laugh.

Nick must have sensed that I couldn't handle much more, because he moved to where I could see him and silently mouthed, "Stay calm. His goal is to upset you."

Closing my eyes, I asked, "Why are you doing this? What do you want from me?"

"You'd never understand."

"I might. Try me."

"There are those that have, and those that never will. Those who want, those who refuse to give."

*"Have* what? *Give* what?" I demanded.

"Everything. And nothing."

He was right. I didn't understand. He was speaking in riddles. I cast a curious look at Nick, but he shrugged and shook his head. Shifting tactics, I asked, "Is there anything I can do to stop this? If you let Matt go right now, I'd take his place in a heartbeat. Unarmed. I swear. My life for his."

Simon laughed. "Nice try, but it's too late. You

should've thought about that a few years ago."

Again, I glanced at Nick. He didn't understand either. I lied, "Don't you see? I don't know *who* you are or *why* you've done this!"

"You will by sunrise. If you live that long."

I looked at my watch. "It's almost two o'clock in the morning. I thought you were going to let me try to save Matt. I saw the device you rigged. It'll take me hours to get him out of that elevator shaft. Come on. Quit stalling. You're as anxious as I am. Let's play ball."

For a few moments he didn't reply. Finally, he snapped, "Deal. Here's the first pitch. He's in a condemned, five-story brick apartment building approximately six miles due east of your house. I mean it, Jamie. Come alone. This is between the two of us. Matt's life is in your hands."

"I'll be there." Pressing the End Call button, I leaned against the seat and sighed. Nick and I were less than two blocks from the location he had just described, parked in the darkest shadows of an alley between two old office buildings. He wrapped his arm around my shoulder. "Good job. He thinks you're at the Training Center, so he'll expect it to take you at least twenty minutes to get back here. That gives us some time to see if we can pinpoint where he is while he's not on full alert."

"What about the bomb at the hospital? Now there are hundreds of lives at stake."

"Maybe, maybe not. He expected you to handle Jesse's vest alone. I think seeing me at your house rattled him quite a bit, made him scramble for a method to get me out of the way. The story about the hospital is probably just a diversion to help guarantee that I didn't come along on Matt's render safe."

"But what if it's not a diversion? What if there really *is* a bomb in your room? We can't take that chance."

Nick's cell phone rang. He listened, then replied, "Good work. Remember, only our squad can know what's going down. Absolutely *no* communication among our team that can be picked up on scanners or by any law enforcement agency. Our plans have just been altered. Each of you take out your designated targets as soon as possible, then discreetly meet at my room at the hospital. Pretend you're there to visit me and quietly check to see if the gift basket wrapped in blue cellophane is a potential bomb. If it's not, begin evacuation of the wing and sweep the entire floor for suspicious devices, especially Jeff's room. Romeo's with us, so you'll have to trust a visual search until we're through here. If you find anything, start the render safe, but *do not* allow anyone to call nine-one-one, and do your best to keep the news from spreading. If that means temporarily shutting down the hospital's non-emergency phone system, then do it. When we're ready for help, we'll contact you." He added, "Thanks," then hung up and looked at me. "The rest of the team is on board and in position. This will work, Jamie."

I sucked in a long, deep breath of muggy night air. Glancing at the stars, I murmured, "God, I hope so."

# 2

I was in full assault gear: a load-bearing vest, a backpack that held the X-ray equipment and plenty of film, a belt that contained seven pouches stuffed with as many hand entry tools as I could fit inside, glow sticks, various types of tape, and several minitorches. Nick had used duct tape to securely fasten a flashlight onto each of my forearms. The tightly wrapped adhesive rubbed against my burn, making my arm hurt like hell every time I moved. I didn't

care. I just wanted to get Matt out of Simon's control as
soon as possible.

Crisscrossed over each of my shoulders were lengths
of rope coiled into large loops. Because of the strenuous
nature of the task before me and the fact that I'd need
both my hands free to rappel, there was a good chance
my communications link would get dislodged. To try to
prevent that from happening, Nick had used clear tape on
my ear and neck to affix a small high-tech earpiece and
microphone in place. Since the thin, skin-tone wire ran
from my ear down my neck and into the secure com unit
in my pocket, we hoped that Simon wouldn't be able to
see it.

Knowing I'd be able to talk to Nick while I worked
helped boost my seesawing confidence. Unlike other police channels that Simon would have complete access to,
there would be no way for him to eavesdrop on our conversations using the secure com.

Nick had broken into the office building next to the
alley where we were parked and was making his way to
the roof. Since I was wearing over sixty-five pounds of
gear, I sat down on the Suburban's running board and
stroked Romeo while I waited. We couldn't afford for
Simon to realize that I had lied about my location, so I
had to wait at least five more minutes before making my
grand entrance. Through my earpiece, I heard Nick's
voice. "Jamie, for the record, I'm going to state the nature
and cause of this operation."

I listened as he described the note we had found in
Jesse's vest, the diskette, our unlawful entry and search
of the ATF's main offices, and how and why we planned
to handle Matt's rescue using bomb squad personnel and
equipment in ways that were both unauthorized and illegal. In a way, I felt as though he were dictating our letters
of resignation, since I was certain neither of us would ever

be allowed on a police force again, much less on a bomb squad.

After he identified the suspect as ATF Agent Simon Stanley, I asked, "Where are you now?"

"In an office on the top floor. I'm cutting a hole in the lid of a cardboard box the size of the lens on my night-vision scope. That way, if he scans the rooftops, he'll see a square brown object instead of the outline of a person. From this distance, I doubt if he'd be able to make out much more than shapes without a powerful zoom lens, but we don't want to take any unnecessary chances. I'm moving onto the roof now."

I could hear the sound of his body scraping along the gritty surface as he continued, "I'm nearing the edge, staying behind the box and keeping low so that if he's watching, he won't detect any movement. . . . Okay, I'm in position. I've got my night-vision gear focused through the hole in the box. . . . I can clearly see inside the building that he's in. There are no lights on. . . ."

Dangling from a cord around my neck was an ITT night-vision scope similar to the one Nick was using. His had a sixteen-power zoom lens, while mine showed only a standard view like you would see through an ordinary camera. Utilizing fourth-generation electronics, both enable the user to see clearly in the darkness, as though it is high noon on the brightest day of the year. In fact, the technology was so advanced when it was issued to our squad that the U.S. government required us to sign declarations stating that we wouldn't allow the gear to fall into the hands of any foreign government. While Nick would employ his high-power lens to spy on Simon, I planned to use my gear to look for trip lines and booby traps as I made my way through the dark building.

"Jamie, I've spotted our man. It's definitely Simon Stanley. He's on the second floor, southwest corner. He's wearing full camouflage tactical gear and has a holster and a gun on each shoulder. It looks like he's set up a sort of command post there. I can see a laptop that has a dark image on the screen, but I'm too far away to tell exactly what it's showing. My guess is that it's a video feed to the elevator shaft as we expected, although it could be a link to a perimeter camera. On the table is a canvas jump bag, and I'm pretty sure there's a police scanner beside the laptop. He's pacing . . . just looked at his watch. Talk to me, Jamie."

"Do you see any cameras on the outside of the building?"

"No. But they could be mounted inside. I think you should go in where we originally planned. From his current position, you'll be on the opposite side of where he's waiting, plus it's closest to the stairwell you'll need to access the elevator."

Standing, I gave Romeo a big hug and whispered, "Everything's going to be okay." Climbing behind the wheel, I gathered my courage and declared, "Nick, I'm ready to roll."

"I'll let you know the minute he's on the move. Once I lose him, I'll swing wide and try to access a roof on the opposite side to see if I can spot any of his other surprises."

"Just don't let him see you, and don't set off any burglar alarms."

"Stealth is my middle name."

As I started the engine, I said, "Okay, I'm on my way." Even though I felt compelled to rush, I drove without my headlights, purposely creeping up and down the streets as if I weren't certain where I was going. I circled the block twice, then bumped up on the curb and deliberately parked so close to the dilapidated red brick building that the passenger side mirror scraped noisily along the wall before it slammed with a *snap* against the window. Taking a deep breath, I said, "I'm in position. I'll leave the Suburban running with Romeo inside in case either of us needs to get out of here in a hurry."

"Slow and steady, Jamie. You have to be in one piece to help Matt."

"Got it." Opening the driver's door, I ordered, "Romeo, stay!" Grabbing a blanket from the backseat, I climbed out of the Suburban, then tossed it onto the car's roof. Opening the rear door, I slid out an oversized plastic box that Nick and I had emptied at the Training Center. After closing the rear door, I set the box on top of the car, then stepped onto the running board below the driver's door. Steadying myself by putting my hands onto the car's roof, I used the upward momentum of a gentle push against the seat combined with the strength of my arm muscles to crawl on top of the Suburban. Lying on my stomach, I softly closed the driver's door to make certain Romeo didn't try to come along, then stood and looked up at the building. As planned, I was just a few inches below a second-story window.

Thankfully, the window's glass had been broken long ago, and I was tall enough to easily toss a glow stick through a gaping hole. From my belt, I pulled out a telescoping rod with a mirror on the end and moved the plastic box directly beneath the windowsill. Balancing on top of the box, I positioned the mirror so that I could see the reflection of the room. Carefully, I studied the area for any signs of danger. Since the room appeared to be safe, I used my billy club to knock out the rest of the glass. The clamor echoed in the empty room and was quickly replaced by a stillness that made me shiver.

As though it were a horse's back, I tossed the blanket over the sill to keep from getting cut, then jumped slightly so that I was high enough to hoist myself through the window. With all the gear I was carrying, rolling inside was a struggle. Finally, my feet were planted solidly on the floor. Crossing through the eerie green light, I stooped to pick up the glow stick. My voice was tense as I declared, "Nick, I'm in. So far, so good."

"Simon already knows you're there. He's intently watching the laptop, occasionally switching screens, but still holding in his command post."

"There's no door between this room and the main hallway. I'm going to mirror the hall, then proceed down it to the stairwell."

"Good. You're on the same floor that he is, opposite end. That'll take you even farther away from him. Don't forget to use the line we rigged."

Exchanging the mirror for a different telescoping rod from my belt, I extended it and unfurled a string that, when held at arm's length, barely dragged the floor. "Got it. Moving into the hallway now." Without the benefit of moonlight, the hall was much darker than the other room. I gently tossed the glow stick as far as I could to give me a better idea of what I'd be up against. Using my night-vision scope, I spent a few seconds examining the ceiling, then the floor. Even though I hadn't seen anything unusual, I crouched low and only took a step after the string showed that the path was clear.

At the end of the hall, I sighed and stood upright. "The stairwell door is closed. Opening it . . . now." Again, I bent low, covering my head and face with my free arm as I turned the doorknob and flung the door back. After a few seconds, I rolled the glow stick inside, then checked with the mirror. Moving into the stairwell, my first attempt to toss the glow stick up to the third-floor landing missed, and it tumbled down to the first floor. Snapping another, I took better aim and heaved it harder. It dropped onto the third-floor landing and rolled against the door.

Although freeing Matthew safely from the device was my primary concern, I knew it would only be half the battle. If I succeeded in rescuing him from the elevator shaft, we'd still have to escape from Simon, who was as heavily armed and as dangerous as any criminal I'd ever encountered. Pulling up my night-vision scope, I was painfully aware of what had happened to Jeff on the staircase in the storm cellar. I looked for any height or texture variance on each step going up, then turned my attention to the stairs leading down. My voice was barely a whisper as I warned, "Nick, I've spotted a trip line on the stairs between the first and second floors. Looks like you were right."

It had been Nick's idea to come in through the second-floor window. His theory was that Simon would devote most of his antipersonnel effort to the garage entrance and first floor, where he would have expected me to enter. I heard Nick say, "Good. But I've been wrong before, so keep exercising every precaution."

"I will. I'm on my way to the third floor. . . . Okay, he must've expected me to come through this door at some point. It's rigged on the inside to blow when pushed open from the hallway." Using the night-vision scope, I followed the trip line. "The line is attached to the firing pin of a grenade strapped at eye level in the corner." I dug through my pouch and found a pair of scissors. "Cutting the line now. Nick, should I leave the grenade in place?"

"No. I'd move it so that he can't use it against you later."

After carefully peeling back the tape, the grenade rolled into my hand. Personally handling such devices was against everything I'd ever been taught, and doing so almost made me nauseous. "I've got it. I'm going to tape it on the inner part of the handrail. Can you tell if he's watching me?"

"I don't think so. He's getting really antsy. I don't think he expected you to move this slowly."

"The grenade is in place."

"Jamie. I'd bet that's the floor closest to where Matt is, the one he thinks you'll be leaving from once you get him out of the device. As we discussed, he probably expected you to come in low and get at him through the elevator's trapdoor, not from the top."

"Then should I just go to the fourth floor and pry open the elevator doors?"

"Hold on, I'm checking the blueprint. . . . No, you'd be vulnerable from two different directions. I'd still access the elevator from the utility area on the fifth floor. That way you can use the rebar anchors already embedded along the side of the shaft as planned."

"Got it." I repeated every step until I was standing on the landing of the fifth-floor stairwell. "Nick, I'm ready to enter the hallway. Moving now."

The moment I stepped out of the stairwell, I heard Nick warn, "Jamie, maintain radio silence! Simon just jumped. He must finally have you in sight. Don't reply, just carefully work toward that utility room. Remember, you're not supposed to know exactly where you're going, so look a little lost."

*That shouldn't be hard,* I thought. With the string extended to check the way, I inched along the hallway using the night-vision scope. For Simon's sake, I pretended to look into each room. When I spotted the surveillance camera inside the doorway of the utility room, I did my best to ignore it, although I made certain that the side of my head with the secure com wire was never completely turned in that direction.

At the entrance to the utility room, I found another trip wire. Following the string to its source, I discovered a primitive contraption like those that Simon had set at my house. Stepping over it, I knelt on all fours, my face only a foot from the weapon.

Since it was a crude device that used a mousetrap to fire a shotgun shell, I dug through my supplies until I found a stack of cotton squares, the kind women use to take off makeup. I always have them in my jump bag to slip between contact points in order to keep switches from closing. After carefully inserting three of the soft squares where they would absorb the shock of the trigger, I used a telescoping pole to trip the line. The mousetrap snapped against the cotton as expected, but the shotgun shell didn't fire. Nick must've heard the noise, because he said, "If you're okay, hum something for me."

For some reason that I'll never understand, the first tune that popped into my head was "We Are the Champions" by Queen. As I hummed a few bars, I looked around the utility room using the night-vision scope. Since we had carefully studied the pictures of it in Simon's office, I had a good idea how to proceed, but didn't want to tip my hand too quickly.

Moving to the far east wall, I found the thick plate that covered the service hatch to the elevator shaft. It was a metal grate, hinged on one side and screwed shut on the other. From the rust caked on the tops of the screws, I was certain that Simon had not used this entrance when he was working on Matt's device. Digging through my side pouch, I found a miniscrewdriver and within a few moments, removed all the screws.

The plate creaked so loudly when I folded it back that I cringed, certain something horrid would happen. When nothing did, I exhaled and put my screwdriver back in the pouch. As I expected, the elevator shaft was completely devoid of light.

My hand was trembling as I raised my night-vision scope to my eye. From the video, I had a pretty good idea

of what I was about to see. Even so, the emotional intensity that slapped me was staggering. I let the night-vision
scope fall against my chest as I slumped to my knees.

I knew Simon was watching. Probably smiling, proud
of his work.

Turning toward the camera, I shook my head and
pledged, "It's over. This ends tonight."

# fifteen

## 1

After several deep breaths, I stood, willing myself to move on. Nick's voice was gentle in my ear as he urged, "Step by step, Jamie. You should be able to speak softly to me as long as your back is to the camera. Simon will assume you're talking to Matt. Is there anything different in the shaft than what we expected?"

Since I was afraid Simon might have planted listening devices so he could eavesdrop, I started talking so softly that I wasn't sure Nick would be able to understand. "The elevator has been lowered since the video was shot. Matt's completely suspended in midair, almost level with the doors to the third floor. The elevator car looks like it's in the basement. I'll have to do the render safe while suspended from the top by the ropes, then figure out how to get Matt out of here. Oh, and I almost forgot, Simon has rigged locks on the *inside* of the elevator doors that lead back into the building. Talk to me, Nick."

He was silent for a few seconds, probably trying to think of something encouraging to say. Finally, he replied, "Still not impossible. Is there any kind of line attached from Matt down to that elevator car?"

Shrugging both lengths of rope over my head and off of my shoulders, I said, "Not that's visible with the night-vision gear."

"I could sneak into the garage and access the elevator. If I raised it to the floor just below Matt, you'd have a survivable drop if needed."

I thought for a moment, then glanced at my watch. Simon could easily have rigged a device that would be triggered by any motion, plus if he saw Nick, he might be able to remotely detonate Matt's vest. "It's too early. I don't think we should risk it yet."

I switched on the flashlights strapped to each of my sleeves, then leaned slightly into the shaft to declare, "Matthew, just stay very still. I'll have you out of there in a couple of minutes. I'm dropping a few glow sticks down the shaft so that I can see a little better. Don't worry when you hear them hit the floor."

After falling almost fifty feet, the plastic tubes made a hollow thud as they landed on the roof of the elevator. Although I could see a little better without the night-vision gear, their green glow was so far down the shaft that it did little to illuminate the middle part where Matt was hanging.

"I'm securing a rope so that I can rappel down to you." Carefully blocking Simon's view as I worked, I fixed the rigging as Nick and I had planned. I began by pounding an anchor into the floor, then one inside the shaft just above the entrance. To anyone unfamiliar with the setup, the rope would appear to be fastened securely to the floor of the utility room, then held steady by the anchor just inside the top of the service hatch.

In reality, after I'd performed those tasks, I leaned over to carefully feed the rope through a three-inch arch of rebar about a foot below the hatch's opening. The rebar had been embedded in the shaft's concrete wall when the building was constructed for use in maintaining the system's cables. By using a pretied knot and threading the rope through the arch, the bulk of my weight would be borne a foot down from the service hatch opening, along the north wall.

There were a few inches of slack between the first line and the safety knot, so that if Simon decided it might be fun to watch me fall, I'd be warned when he cut the deceptive line in the utility room. In order for him to successfully stop my attempt to save Matt, he would have to lean far enough into the shaft for me to have a clear shot at him.

Nick and I had discussed at length whether that old piece of rebar would hold my weight. I hoped I didn't have to find out.

# 2

Although rappeling isn't a skill required for certification as a hazardous device technician, it is highly recommended that it be mastered. Within a few weeks after I completed my first training at Redstone, Nick had insisted I take the course offered by our special operations team. From the moment I put on the gear, I hated it. In fact, I can't think of a single thing I like about rappeling, except maybe the feeling of being safely back on solid ground when it's over. Yes, I passed the course, but not with flying colors.

I was already wearing a harness that fastened around my chest to form a fabric seat, so I was ready to go as soon as I used a carabiner to clip myself to the rope. To Nick, I muttered, "Damn, it's been a long time since I did this. You should implement a new rule requiring refresher rappeling courses. Talk to me."

"You're the last person I thought would ever request more rappeling. Just keep a loose grip on the rope and go easy. Remember to bend your knees to absorb the shock as you contact the wall, and get a good push-off. Be sure to stop a few feet *above* Matt. With all the gear you're carrying, going slowly down will be much easier than trying to climb back up."

Crawling over the edge, I declared, "Here goes." At first, I slid far too fast, banging so hard against the wall that I thought I would surely plummet all the way to the bottom. The flashlights on my wrists made wild, psyche-delic patterns of light on the dank walls as I swung hap-hazardly on the rope, trying to get a grip on myself. Remembering the same feeling from the training course, I twisted until my feet found the wall, then adjusted my weight, and tried again.

I had barely begun to feel a little more comfortable when my foot crashed into something as I bounced off the six-inch ledge below the fourth floor's metal doors. I felt, then heard, the *crack* as I lost my balance, slamming my full weight painfully against the object. Catching a glimpse in one of the bouncing beams from my flash-lights, I realized it was another camera, one that was now broken and swinging on the end of an electric cord that ran up and through the gap at the base of the doors. A breath after it happened, Nick declared, "Jamie, Simon is on the move! He jumped up and bolted out of his command center."

"That's because I just pissed him off."

"How?"

"Accidentally took out a surveillance camera inside the shelf of the fourth-floor elevator doors. What do you think he'll do?"

After a moment, Nick replied, "Find another way to watch you sweat."

"That's what I was afraid of."

"Jamie, you can't worry about him now. Stay focused on Matt, and I'll see if I can find out what Simon is up to. It's almost three-thirty. In six minutes, it won't matter if he knows I'm here or not."

I took a deep breath, praying Nick's plan would work. "True. Be careful."

"No doubts."

I grimaced at my first up-close look at the horrific device that held Matthew's life in its balance, wondering if *any* bomb tech in the world could defeat it. Although I replied, "No doubts," deep down I had more doubts than I dared to admit, even to myself.

# 3

Matt's head was still beneath the black hood, so I softly called, "I'm only a few feet above you. You're doing great. I'm going to slowly ease down so that I'm level with you."

Since even nudging one of the lines could kill us both, I maneuvered into position like a tree frog, keeping my knees bent and hugging the wall as I inched along. At the heart of a push-pull bomb is a piece of conductive material poised precisely between two contact points. Movement of the lines leading into the device pulls the contacts closer to the conductor. If they touch, the circuit closes. In that instant, enough power flows through the circuit to fire the blasting cap, which sets off the explosive material. Defeating this bomb would be unbelievably hard, since I couldn't afford to accidentally touch either the bows, the cables, or even Matthew.

Once I was level with him, I tied off the rope just above the front of my harness so that I could begin to work without using my arms for support. It was painfully obvious why Simon had lowered the elevator. Making me do such delicate work while dangling from a rope greatly reduced my odds of success.

Before I turned to face Matt, I pulled a two-ounce container of breeching paste from my belt. Bomb techs use breeching paste to quickly stick explosives to flat surfaces. Although the texture is similar in some respects to Vaseline, the adhesive is about ten times as thick. Once something is stuck on with it, it usually stays for quite awhile. After snapping several glow sticks to life, I used a glob on each one to secure them along the inner wall.

Cast in the greenish glow, the device seemed even more threatening. My first up-close look at the bomb in that eerie light only multiplied my worries. The fully flexed compound bows seemed downright evil up close, and I wondered if that was exactly why Simon had chosen them. Concentrating to keep the urge to panic at bay, I quickly followed the path of one side of the cable that supported Matt's weight. Simon had intricately zigzagged the line, looping from grommets on the vest back and forth through the bow's taut string. The pattern accomplished two things: It more evenly distributed Matt's weight, and it made my job infinitely harder.

Scanning the vest, I noticed that it bore little resemblance to the others. Although it was black, the material was much heavier, and there were no wires running around the neck. Instead of wires, this vest had an entire flap that passed between Matt's legs, which was essential since it supported most of his weight. It appeared to be sewn onto the lower back, then again at the midsection of the front. Using the flashlights on my forearms, I searched for anything that might be an antenna but found nothing obvious.

I saw no visible clock, and unless he had changed the vest since taking the video, I wouldn't find one on the back, either. Simon was getting good at the game. This time, the *lack* of the timer was one of the things that bothered me the most.

Unzipping the pouch on my left side, I took out a pair of scissors and gently pushed myself close to Matt. Knowing I needed to keep the mood as light as possible to prevent him from panicking, I kept all traces of fear out of my voice as I said, "I'm going to cut the hood off of your face. Nod just a tiny bit if you understand."

His head slightly moved. "Great! Don't jerk when you feel my touch. I promise not to lop off anything very important." Like a blind person would touch the face of a new acquaintance, I gently ran my fingers across the thin, black material, making certain there were no wires hidden beneath the material. Using the scissors, I cut first one side, then the other. Lifting the hood up and off, I let it float to the bottom of the shaft as my eyes met his.

I doubt if any mother in the world was as happy to see her son's face as I was at that moment. Even though duct tape covered his mouth, I could see a glimmer of hope in his swollen eyes. I desperately wanted to hold him, to reassure him that we would be okay, but I couldn't do either. The best I could do was to let him see my confidence as I explained, "The tape on your mouth is next. I can't risk tearing it off fast, since it might jar you too much. I'm sorry, sweetie. It's going to sting like crazy for a few seconds."

He gave me an encouraging mini-nod, then closed his eyes. As I ripped it a quarter inch at a time, I noticed his fists were clenched in such tight balls that his knuckles were white and shaking. Even so, he was doing a great job of handling such a horrid situation, and I felt a surge of pride well up from deep inside. Finally, the tape was off.

Matt opened his mouth wide, stretching the burn from the skin around his lips. With a lopsided half smile, he said, "Hi, Mom."

"Hi, handsome. Are you hurt?"

"Not too bad. Did you help Jesse? The Vest Bomber told me that he blew him up in our den."

"Jesse is fine, but I'll admit that the den will need a few repairs."

Visibly relieved, Matt sighed. "Thank God."

I touched his cheek. "We're sort of in a tight spot here."

"No kidding." Worry creased his brow again. "Mom, I can't feel my legs at all. They're still there, aren't they?"

I pretended to look, then declared, "Yep. Still there and still long. How did you end up like this?"

"When I went into the kitchen to answer the phone, he jumped me from behind. I was trying to fight him, but he put a smelly rag over my face. Next thing I knew, I was in the back of a van strapped into this vest. He told me he'd blow me to kingdom come if I didn't do exactly as he said."

"How did you get in here?"

"He put me in the elevator, then stopped it between floors. He made me crawl up a ladder so I was standing on top of the car. After that, he put the hood on and just ordered me around."

"Do you know how he rigged this device?" As we

talked, I used an extension mirror to get a close-up look at the bomb on his back.

"Sorry, Mom. I couldn't see anything."

"After you were up here, did he ever open the vest and connect anything else inside?"

"I don't think so. It felt like he just hooked wires on with clamps from my shoulders down to my hips."

"Matt, it's really important that you be sure, since the original wires emerge from *inside* the vest. Once you were suspended, did you feel him tug on anything? I need to know if he ever tripped a switch *inside* the vest after you were in this position."

He closed his eyes. "No. I'm sure he didn't. He kept cussing about how heavy I was. I heard him climb back down the ladder into the elevator, then he moved the car just a little bit lower. Man, that was a scary feeling. The floor just fell out from under me."

"And once it fell, did he come back up and pull any strings or wires?"

Matt hesitated. "I'm pretty sure he didn't come all the way back up from inside the elevator. It felt like he might have tugged on a string from down below. I don't know how much later it was, but the elevator started moving again. I could tell it stopped a lot farther down."

"Did you ever see his face before he put the hood on you?"

"No. He always had on a mask. But I know that voice. I can't remember his name, but I'm sure it's that ATF agent you introduced me to at the mall." I saw his eyes dart to the network of compound bows and wires, drinking in every detail of the contraption that, literally, sustained his life. "What *is* this thing?" he asked, growing more apprehensive by the minute.

Without missing a beat, I lightly answered, "A push-pull bomb. But don't worry. Nick and I are going to get you out of here as fast as we can."

His eyes searched the dark shaft. "Nick's here?"

I touched my earphone. "In spirit. He can hear us both, and I can talk to him."

Matt seemed to relax a bit. "Hey, Nick. Mind hurrying up and getting me out of this?"

Nick's breath was so labored that I was sure he was running when he answered, "Tell him I'm still gonna kick his ass at paintballing as soon as my arm heals."

I did, then added, "And I'll have to kick *your* ass first if you don't do exactly what I say. Seriously, Matt. There is absolutely no room for error. If I say freeze, don't even breathe. Understand?"

"Yes. That's pretty much what that asshole ATF agent who did this to me warned. He said if I sneezed, I'd die. Ever notice that when someone tells you that you can't sneeze, that's when your nose starts to itch the most?"

"I'll bet. Listen, I'm going to hug the wall for a second while I get out the X-ray equipment." With a smile, I added, "Don't run off. Okay?"

"Not a problem, Mom."

With my face pressed against the damp concrete, I pushed off one shoulder strap, then the other as I said, "Nick, I don't think we have to worry about an internal-pressure-sensitive switch anymore. Do you agree?"

"Yes and no. I think the chances are slim, but you'll need to trace the string to the arming hole in the push-pull on his back to make sure it only activated the one device after Simon had everything in balance."

"I'll double-check. When I mirrored it a few seconds ago, it looked like a single piece of fishing line. Once he cut it, it sprang back and coiled just outside the arming hole."

I felt like a contortionist trying to get out of a straitjacket as I twisted and turned, working to slide the pack off my back, then around to where I could hold it. Finally, it was firmly in my hand, and I used another carabiner to snap the top handle onto my rappeling harness. The extra weight made me tend to list forward, but it wasn't anything I couldn't handle. Unzipping the pack, I pulled out a panel of X-ray film that Nick and I had specially prepared with a length of adjustable rope taped from one corner to the other.

"Matt, I'm going to need your help to do this. I'm about to slip this over your head and align it so that I can get a good, clear picture of the device on your back. I'll have to reach very carefully above and behind you to get the panel into the perfect position. Okay?"

"I'll help if there's any way I can," he offered.

"In just a second . . ." Trying to lean close enough to manipulate the panel into precisely the right place with the weight of the backpack keeping me off balance was next to impossible. After almost knocking the cables twice, I said, "This isn't working. I'm going to have to put the X-ray equipment on the small shelf below the third-floor doors. It's only six inches wide, so I'll take each piece out and hope that I don't lose anything. Be right back, son."

Easing over to the wall, I unloaded every piece of equipment as though it were made of the finest porcelain, fully aware that losing even one item could keep me from defeating the bomb. With a sigh, I announced, "Okay, let's try this again."

Pushing back toward Matt, I stopped so close that our cheeks barely touched. Holding my breath, I maneuvered the X-ray panel around the wires and adjusted the length of the rope until it dangled just outside of the large piece of PVC pipe that held the explosives. Exhaling, I pulled back slightly and said, "I know this is weird, but I need you to bite firmly on this rope to hold it in position while I shoot the X rays. Think you can handle it?"

"Sure."

I carefully placed the rope in his mouth, keeping tension on it as I asked, "Got it?"

He winked.

Moving back, I set the power level on the X-ray machine and lined it up. For Nick's sake, I said, "The first panel is in place. Matt, when I count to three, you'll need to hold your breath. Ready?"

Matt winked again.

Lifting one knee, I steadied the heavy machine and said, "One, two, three . . ." It seemed to click forever, growing exponentially heavier with each second. Sliding it back onto the shelf when it was done, I leaned toward Matt and took the rope from his mouth. Reversing the process, I pulled the X ray over his head.

Cranking the film through the developer was much harder than I'd expected. First I tried to do it freehand, then gave up and sat the developer on the shelf so that I'd have some leverage. Since my hands were full, Nick counted down the developing time for me. When it was finally ready, I peeled back the covering and felt my heart sink. Even in the dim light, my first glance at the device told me how sensitive it was. If Matt's weight shifted more than an inch in either direction, it would blow. Not wanting to worry Matt, I said, "Okay, now that we know exactly what we're dealing with, we can get you out of this contraption. Nick?"

Nick replied, "Jamie, I've been watching the building from the north. I caught a brief glimpse of him on the fourth floor. He checked the street, then disappeared again. Looks like he's carrying some of his equipment with him."

"Do you think he'll go back to his command post?"

"I doubt it. There's a good possibility he has more than one place set up."

"Can you see Romeo? Is he doing okay?"

After a second, Nick replied, "Nervous, but staying put. Tell me what you're up against."

"The X ray shows we've got about an inch tolerance on each side of the switch. I'm going to immobilize the cables leading into the bomb next. Nick, are you sure you're well enough to execute the rest of the plan once I get this thing off of Matt?" I asked.

"You bet. I'll be there."

Matt interrupted by softly asking, "Mom?"

I could tell he was suddenly much more serious. "Yes?"

"No matter what happens, I love you. And tell Nick that I love him, too."

Tears jumped to my eyes, and I had to blink hard to fight them back. Touching his cheek, I said, "I love you, too, but we'll have plenty of time to discuss that later."

In my ear, I heard Nick confess, "Tell him that I love him like a son, and that I hope after all these years he's learned one thing from me."

"What's that?" I asked.

"Never give up."

# 4

*"Having fun?"*

At first, hanging as I was in the middle of an echo chamber, I couldn't tell whether Simon was above or below us. From a distance, I probably looked as if I were giving Matt a bear hug, but in reality I was holding a mirror in one hand while I made certain the fishing line that led into the arming hole hadn't been connected to anything else. Yes, I was wrapped around him, but it took all my concentration to keep from touching any part of his body.

Matt whispered, "Aren't you going to answer him?"

I softly replied, "He wants to distract me. Piss me off. Just ignore him."

"Jamie! You're doing it all wrong." I could tell the words definitely were floating down from the service hatch on the fifth floor as he added, "One hundred and fifty-five pounds balanced precisely. There's no way you're going to counterbalance it like they taught you at Redstone. Standard plastic forceps will snap in a heartbeat under that kind of pressure. Matt's predicament is terminal. Why don't you give up now and try to save yourself?"

In answer to the look of horror that filled Matt's eyes, I calmly confided, "Typical profile of a psycho bomber. Very proud of his work. Wants to watch. Loves to see his victims agonize over his creations. Don't believe a word he says. If he hadn't built this thing with enough tolerance, it would've blown when he closed the arming switch."

"Jamie Stone. If you don't answer, I'll remotely detonate the damn bomb right now! I mean it!"

Matt cringed, which completely incensed me. I shouted, "Believe it or not, I'm a little busy! What do you want?"

"To warn you."

Sarcasm dripped from my voice as I shouted, "Really, of what? That there's a bomb down here?"

"No. That I know you didn't come alone. I'll deal with you in a few minutes. Right now, I've got to make sure Terrell doesn't interfere." His cold, sick laugh crept down the walls like a plague of spiders. My skin was still crawling as he added, "Guess I'll get to dance on your partner's grave sooner than I expected."

Very softly, I urged, "Nick?"

"I heard. He must've spotted me on a camera we haven't located. Don't worry about me. I can take care of myself."

Ripping off long lengths of duct tape, I loosely stuck them along the front of Matt's vest as I declared, "I'll try to hurry."

His voice confirmed the depth of his conviction as he harshly ordered, "No! Do *not* hurry! We both know that each step has to be methodical, calculated. Take your time. I'm heavily armed, and I have on full tactical assault gear. Plus, I've brought along a few tricks that should catch him off guard."

"I couldn't see him, but it sounded like he was in the utility room on the fifth floor."

"I came in on the second floor, then went down to the first, so I have some time before he finds me. I've been slowly taking out his arsenal of surprises. If you need it, the stairwell is clear to the first floor now. Next I'm going to make sure the third-floor elevator landing is safe, in case you want to leave in a hurry."

"Good. I'm almost ready to lock the first cable in place."

I took a deep breath. In order to get Matt down without triggering the bomb, I would have to firmly secure the cables leading into the device. As Simon obviously knew, under normal circumstances I would've kept the lines taut by using plastic forceps that lock into place when closed. In this case, there was too much weight on the cables leading into each side of the PVC pipe to trust such delicate instruments. Thanks to Simon's video footage, Nick and I had included several heavy-duty needle-nose vise grips in my assortment of tools.

The trick to disarming a push-pull is to clamp an instrument on each side of the bomb where the cable enters the device. Once the clamps are in place, the tech firmly secures them to the pipe with enough duct tape to be certain they won't move. The ultimate goal is simple. When the cable is cut, the tension inside the bomb must stay exactly the same as it was when the lines were intact. The vise grips fool the bomb's trigger mechanism, hopefully long enough for the victim to escape. In this case, if either vise grip were to allow the line to slip more than an inch, both Matt and I would die.

If I could've worked from the other side, clamping the vise grips onto the cables would've been relatively easy. Dangling as I was, with Matt's torso and the network of cables between me and the bomb, it was practically impossible. After a few minutes of struggling, I had properly positioned the vise grip and was trying to adjust it to the tightest setting possible, when my foot slipped off the wall. I managed to swing back without knocking any cables, but the vise grip I'd been working with plummeted down the narrow shaft and clanked against the top of the elevator.

In the wake of the clamor, Matt quietly asked, "How many of those things did you bring?"

"Three."

"Three more?"

I shook my head. "Two more. Exactly what I need. Guess I'd better be a little more careful from now on."

Sweat glistened on his brow. "Yep."

Bracing myself in a more stable position, I started again. I had clamped the left side in place and was securing it with duct tape when I heard Nick softly say, "Jamie?"

"Go ahead."

"Don't do any sensitive work for twenty seconds. Starting now."

As I counted in my head, I told Matt, "Don't jump. There's probably going to be a small explosion."

At precisely the time I silently chanted *twenty one-thousandths,* we heard a low rumble, and the building seemed to shudder from the bottom to the top. Dust rained down on us, but nothing significant. "Everything's okay here. Nick?"

"I'm good. Simon's command post is history. Now he's really gonna be pissed."

"Oh, joy. Think any of the neighbors will call nine-one-one?"

"Let's hope not. If Simon feels cornered, he'll probably just blow the whole building. I didn't use a very big charge. Since this area is mostly industrial, maybe the night watchmen and janitors will all write if off to a sonic boom."

"I'm beginning work on the second vise grip." Because I'm right-handed, I expected to have even more trouble than before. To my surprise, attaching the second grip went a little easier than the first. Before long, I had locked and taped both grips solidly into place. With a triumphant sigh, I declared, "Nick, the push-pull has been defeated."

"Hot damn! Let's neutralize that vest and get the hell out of here!"

"My thoughts exactly."

Taking out my knife, I began cutting Matt's hands free from the duct tape that bound them.

"Why didn't you do that sooner?" he asked, rubbing and flexing the life back into his wrists.

"Because if you had reflexively moved your arms, your weight might've shifted enough to trigger the bomb. Now that the push-pull isn't as big a factor in the equation, we don't have to be so careful."

He smiled. "Let's be careful anyway. It's still a bomb, isn't it?"

"Afraid so."

Although part of the wiring on the vest had been clear

on the first X ray, I needed to check the entire thing before attempting to get Matt out of it. The process went much faster because Matt held the panels in place under his arms and on each side of his back as I shot the X rays.

After I took the third X ray, he asked, "Isn't a lot of radiation bad for people?"

"You've just been exposed to about three visits to the dentist."

"Good. Then I can skip my checkup next week. I hate the taste of that fluoride."

"I don't think so. . . ."

I had cranked two of the three X rays through the developer when Simon's voice rang from above. "Terrell sends his love!"

Without warning, my rope dropped about three inches. The portable developer crashed loudly onto the elevator car below at the same moment my heart practically leaped out of my chest. "Shit!" I muttered, struggling to find my balance again.

In response, Nick anxiously asked, "What happened?"

"He just cut the first stage of the rappeling line. The developer fell. Hopefully the two X rays I've already processed will be good enough to give me an idea of how to render the vest safe. Where are you?"

"Fourth floor. I'll head up to the utility room and make sure he doesn't cut the main support line."

"Don't lean into the shaft. We'll be ready to fire a few shots at him from this way if he tries to cut the next section." Unsnapping the leather on my gun's holster, I asked, "Matt, how steady are your arms?"

"They're okay. Why?"

I pointed to the top of the elevator shaft. Luckily, Simon had left my glow sticks on the utility room floor, so the opening emitted a soft green light. "You have a much better angle than I do. Think you could fire my gun at that service hatch if necessary?"

He nodded. "Sure."

"From this moment on, your job is to watch that hole. If Simon leans in and tries to cut my rope, fire at him. It doesn't matter if you hit him, just blanket the area so that he thinks twice about trying again." I turned my Sig so that the handle slipped into his hand. "It's ready to fire. And remember, it's got a lot more kick than your paintball gun. Hold onto it firmly, and don't worry if the shock jolts you backward. The slack will be taken up by the compound bows, and I promise the push-pull won't detonate." At least, I hoped it wouldn't.

I had barely finished my sentence when Matt screamed, "Mom!" At the moment I glanced up, Matt began firing at the silhouette leaning into the elevator shaft. I'm not sure whether it was the force of the weapon, or the reaction to his arms pumping up and down, but his entire body pivoted so that he was practically lying flat. Lunging, I grabbed his legs to try to stabilize him, suddenly all too aware of how thin the cables were that held him in place.

My ears kept ringing long after the firing had stopped. Like any well-balanced object, Matt swayed back and forth for a few seconds after he was upright. I was both relieved and amazed that the sudden rocking hadn't detonated the push-pull. "Nick?"

There was no answer.

"Nick, we're okay. Talk to me."

The sound from above mixed with Nick's voice in my headphone to create an odd sort of stereo as I overheard the fight taking place in the utility room. There were several crashes, then I heard Simon warn, "Nice try, Terrell. If you move again, I'm going to blow them to hell."

Breathlessly, Nick seethed, "Go ahead. Give it your

best shot. Punch the Send button on that cell phone. Let's get this over with."

Simon laughed. "After all these years, you finally realized what a *bitch* she is!"

Nick scoffed, "Hardly. I realized what a *bastard* you are."

"Fine. Now their death is on *your* hands, not mine."

I held my breath and grabbed Matt's hands. When nothing happened, I sighed.

"What the hell? There's no way Stone could've stopped that bomb from detonating!" Simon screamed.

Nick's voice was cold. "She didn't. The rest of my squad took out every cell tower in a ten-mile radius of here. That pager detonation isn't going to happen."

More scuffling was followed by several shots. Several low *thumps* made me shudder, because I was sure they were the sound of bullets striking home.

# sixteen

## 1

"Nick? Talk to me, Nick!"

After what seemed like an eternity, I could barely hear him answer, "I'm . . . okay."

"Where's Simon?"

"Got away."

"How badly are you hurt?"

"Vest took . . . a couple of hits . . . chest and . . . back. Probably just . . . bruised ribs."

"Can you walk?"

"Don't have . . . much choice. He'll . . . be back soon."

I heard him groan and mutter a broken string of obscenities as he tried to stand. "Nick, I left the extra rope on the floor by the service hatch. I need you to secure it, then throw it down. Are you well enough to do that?"

His breathing was so strained that I was certain he

wasn't telling me the truth about his injuries. "No . . . problem. What's the plan?"

"There are way too many wires and probable blasting caps in this vest to try to neutralize it in this situation. I'm going to see if we can squeeze Matt through the neck hole. If he grabs a rope and pulls himself up and out, I won't have to worry about using a torch to cut the cables. Plus, if the vest stays attached to the original cabling, the push-pull will remain as stationary as possible."

"Good . . . plan. Tying off . . . now."

The rope slithered down the wall. Reaching for it, I lifted myself onto it and purposely bounced around. I needed to be certain that it could sustain the burden of Matt's weight before I risked letting him pull himself up with it. "Perfect, Nick. Thanks. Now get the hell out of that utility room. You're a sitting duck in there."

"Will do. I think it's . . . safe to call . . . backup now. We knocked out . . . cell phone triggers . . . he can't re-motely detonate. Might as well . . . make this a party."

He had barely finished speaking when more shots rang out. I counted five, then lost track.

"Nick? Nick!"

Silence echoed around us. Matt's eyes had filled with tears, and he was shaking so hard I was certain he was going to drop the gun at any moment. "Is Nick okay?" Matt asked.

I took the gun from his hand and shoved it back into my holster. "Let's hope so. I need to get you out of this so I can help him. First, I'm going to hold open the neck of the vest. I want you to thread your right hand down into the armhole so that it's against your body on the inside of the vest. Next, work it slowly across your stomach, then bring it up past your chest and out the opening for the neck. Got it?"

He nodded.

I sensed our time was running out. "Do it!"

When one of his arms was sticking out of the top, I reached around and grabbed the rope Nick had just dropped. "You're doing great. Hold onto this rope with your free hand, and repeat the same process with your other arm."

Floundering, he gasped, "It's too small. I don't think I can!"

"It's going to be tight, but you *have* to."

Matt took a deep breath, then began pushing and squirming until half his arm protruded from the vest's neck hole. "It's no use, Mom. It's stuck!"

Biting my lower lip, I looked at the X ray one more time. I knew exactly how big a risk I was taking as I reached over and unlatched the vest's top closure. As I stretched it wide open, Matt's arm slid out. I exhaled the breath I'd been holding, then declared, "Great! Are you strong enough to hold onto the rope and pull yourself up?"

"I think so."

"Then let's do it. Remember, as little sideways movement as possible. On three. One . . . two . . . three . . ." As he hoisted his weight off the vest, I put as much downward pressure on it as I could. Writhing like a butterfly trying to escape its cocoon, Matt edged slowly upward until he was completely clear of the horrendous device.

I was gradually easing back the tension, keeping my eyes on the compound bows as they slowly began to straighten. Although I had clamped the vise grips firmly, I didn't want to test their strength again with another sudden jerk. By the time most of the tension on the cables had been successfully alleviated, I began to think that we had a good chance of escaping alive. My hopes were immediately dashed when I heard a low rumbling noise from below and felt the entire shaft begin to tremble.

The elevator car was rising toward us.

# 2

Absolutely furious, I screamed, "That's it! I've had it with your games, Simon!"

Reaching into the center pouch on my belt, I took out a 1¼ × 1¼ × 1¼ cube of C4 already wired to a fuse igniter with a three-second delay. Manufactured to produce a highly directional blast with no shrapnel, such devices are commonly called door charges. Nick and I had each packed several, in case we had to deal with locked doors as we worked through the buildings.

Using a glob of breeching paste, I slapped the cube hard onto the bolt that secured the elevator doors, then unscrewed the end of the fuse igniter. With a clean jerk to the cord, I began the three-second detonation process of the charge. Shouting to be heard over the din of the approaching car, I urged, "Matthew, push as far away as you can, then try to protect your ears. And hold onto that rope with all your might!"

Pivoting and shifting away from the door, I raised my shoulders while lowering my head to protect my own ears. Just as the blast's impact rushed upward, the pressure backlash coaxed Matt and me dangerously close to the elevator's moving cables.

Opening my eyes, I saw that Matt was okay. As expected, the door charge hadn't thrown any shrapnel our way. Relieved, I looked over my shoulder to see that the doors to the third floor were fully open.

"Mom! Jump!" Matt shrieked. "The elevator's coming!"

One glance told me that he was right; there were only a few seconds until impact. "Go ahead," I shouted. Since Matt was only holding onto his rope, he had no trouble swinging over and letting go. He safely landed a few inches inside the foyer. Unfortunately, I had securely tied my rope into place, plus it was attached below the knot to my rappeling harness. Before I could jump, I would have to free myself.

With my right arm, I lifted all my weight off the rope, then struggled with my left hand to push open the carabiners that held the rope in place. Although I was concentrating on the job at hand, from my peripheral vision I knew the elevator was only a few feet below me, climbing fast. At the last moment, I realized there was no way I could separate myself from the rope in time. Instead, I grabbed the razor-sharp knife from my utility belt and severed the rope. After falling three feet onto the roof of the elevator car, I planted my feet and dove through the small opening onto the landing.

Rolling near Matthew, I scrambled to my feet and shoved him toward the exit, as I yelled, "Run! When the elevator crushes that vest, it's going to blow!" We made it about ten steps before the shock wave swept us off our feet and hurled us against the far wall. Stunned by the impact, I was vaguely aware of the debris that peppered our legs and backs. For a few seconds, we both just lay there, facedown on the floor. Lifting my head, I glanced each way, and realized that most of the building was still intact. Simon must have been smart enough to know that if he used a charge potent enough to blow the entire building, his own chances of survival would be minimal.

Matt groaned at my side, reminding me that we weren't out of trouble yet. Rocking onto all fours, I fought a flash of dizziness, then ordered, "Come on. We've got to get out of here!"

"But . . ."

I harshly shouted, "Matt, unless your legs are broken, get up! Now!"

Dazed, he stood and leaned against the wall. A large cut on his forehead had already covered half of his face with blood. Moving beside him, I slipped my shoulder beneath his arm to sustain part of his weight, and together we staggered down the hall to the stairwell. I knew that Nick had already cleared the booby traps, so we moved as quickly as possible down the flight. At the landing, Matt turned to keep going down, but I stopped him. "No. You're going out this way."

I could tell he thought I was nuts. "Look, Mom. This is the *second floor,* not the *first.*"

Nodding toward the hallway, I replied, "I know. Move it."

As we scrambled, Matt began to regain his footing, needing less and less of my support. By the time we reached the room I had initially entered through, he was running on his own. Crossing to the window, I looked down to be sure the Suburban was still where I'd left it, then ordered, "Jump onto the roof, then the ground. The car is running. Just climb behind the wheel, shove it into drive, and get the hell out of here. Call headquarters on my police radio. We need police, fire, *and* ambulance."

Matt's eyes were huge. "You want me to *drive?*"

"Yes! And be sure Romeo doesn't bail out when you open the door. Now go!"

"Aren't you coming?"

"Not yet. I've got to go help Nick."

Matt firmly shook his head. "No way! I'm fine. I'm staying. We'll help Nick together."

"Bullshit! Nick might be bleeding to death. The best

way you can help him is by calling nine-one-one. Tell them there's a trooper down." I wrapped Matt in my arms and held him close as I begged, "Please, Matt! I want you safely out of here! I promise I'll be careful."

Our eyes met for an instant. He silently begged. I sternly refused.

"Okay," he muttered, brushing a kiss across my cheek before he bounded out the window. I stayed long enough to watch him lay rubber as he careened off the curb and down the street, the gray plastic box noisily hitting the pavement and shattering in his wake.

Turning back to the hallway with a sigh, I remarked, "Thank you, God."

Drawing my gun, I reloaded it. Holding it ready, I moved toward the stairwell. "Nick, if you can hear me, hang on. I'm coming."

# 3

Although I couldn't smell any smoke, the blast in the elevator shaft had caused enough damage to generate a thick cloud of dust that tightened my chest and made my eyes burn. The leaden air, coupled with the darkness, made searching for booby traps even more difficult. Since I'd already cleared the path from the stairwell to the fifth floor, I stuck to it, hoping that Simon had been too preoccupied to set new devices while I'd been busy freeing Matt.

I was in the stairwell, making my way between the fourth and fifth floors, when I felt my hand slide along something cool and slimy on the handrail. Pointing my flashlight at the substance, I realized it was blood. Moving the beam up and down the staircase, I traced the path of dark smears. The trail was between the two floors, but there was no way to determine which direction the person had been traveling. Either Simon or Nick was badly wounded, and they had recently been this way.

The choice was tough, but I decided to continue toward the fifth-floor utility room. Since that was Nick's last location when I'd heard his voice on the secure com, it was the most logical place to begin my search. Unless his unit had been knocked out, he wouldn't have moved without letting me know.

The damage was much more severe on the fifth floor. Debris hung from the ceiling and littered virtually every inch of the floor. Live electrical wires dangled here and there, popping and snapping in unnerving harmony. The dust that had been heavy on the other floors was even thicker, so dense that I had to put my upper arm across my mouth and breathe through my shirtsleeve. I tried looking through the night-vision gear, but it was futile. In a situation where every sense needed to be as sharp as possible, I was down to only two: touch and hearing.

On the outside chance that Nick's secure com had failed, I thought about calling out to him, but I was afraid of revealing my location to Simon. Part of me wanted to believe that he had fled, that all I needed to do was find Nick. Another part, the part that truly understood the depth of Simon's insanity, knew that he would never leave as long as I was still alive. For some sick reason, extinguishing my life had become his mortal goal.

Each step I took crunched loudly underfoot, as if the haunted building wanted Simon to know exactly where to find me. Staying low, I kept my right side tightly pressed against the wall as I inched along. I was about ten yards from the utility room when I bumped into something stiff. It turned out to be a shoe.

Sucking in a deep breath, I pushed aside enough debris to see that it was Nick, almost completely covered by a layer of ceiling tiles and insulation. I immediately cleared enough debris to tell that he was lying on his back, sprawled as though he'd been hurled backward by some kind of impact. His injured left arm was crooked above his head, while his right hand was at his side. Although his body was completely relaxed, I noticed that his index finger was still threaded through the trigger guard of his Sig.

With a trembling hand, I knelt at Nick's side to check for a pulse. Thankfully, I felt a strong beat beneath my fingertips. Bending so that my cheek was beside his mouth, I was equally relieved to feel the steady flow of his warm breath.

Encouraged, I moved aside more clutter until I found his police radio. After sliding it off of his belt, I pushed the Emergency button on the top to activate the signal that would lead to our exact location. Switching it to tach one, I declared, "Trooper down! I need full hazardous device and medical support immediately! The building has survived a series of explosions without major structural damage, but it should still be considered extremely unsafe due to multiple booby traps. Lieutenant Terrell is unconscious on the north end of the fifth floor. Over."

"Already on our way, Jamie. Matt called it in a little while ago. We'll be there in less than two minutes."

I dropped the radio beside Nick's motionless body. Two minutes. Hardly more than a few breaths on a normal night. But that night was anything but normal.

# 4

Carefully pushing aside the rest of the debris, I began gently checking Nick for wounds. Running my hand along the floor on the opposite side of him, I pulled back my arm, expecting to see my fingers covered with blood. Instead, they were chalky white with plaster powder. Since I had no idea what had caused him to lose consciousness, I didn't want to risk injuring his spine by moving him.

Leaning my face close to his, I gently touched his cheek and said, "Come on, Nick. Talk to me."

"I'll talk to you, bitch."

Simon's voice barely reached my ears before the sharp report of gunfire charged the air. My senses instantly overloaded as I was smacked by the impact of a bullet striking my shoulder like a white-hot arrow. Reeling, I instinctively reached for the wound with my left hand as I tried to pull my Sig out of its holster with my right hand. I knew he was somewhere behind me, lurking between Nick and the stairwell.

"Don't even think about it, Stone. Toss both those weapons over here right now, or you're dead."

Without turning, I said, "It's over, Simon. I know you're the Vest Bomber. Just give up. In a matter of seconds, this place will be swarming with police."

"I said, toss them *now!*"

Pretending to be hurt worse than I actually was, I groaned and weakly slid my gun toward him. Leaning close to Nick, I used my left hand to slowly remove his weapon from his limp hand, then slid it toward Simon as well. At the same time that I was turning over our guns, I was secretly slipping my right hand into the open pocket of my utility belt. Because of their unique cube shape, it didn't take long for me to wrap my fingers around another door charge like the one I had used to open the doors to the elevator shaft. Clasping it in the palm of my hand, I eased it to my side where Simon wouldn't be able to see what I was doing.

The lower right half of Simon's shirt was drenched in blood, and a long, dark pattern was spreading down his pant leg. He was hurt badly enough that he didn't try to pick up the guns. Instead, he just kicked them well out of my reach as he taunted, "Ironic, isn't it? You'll both be dead, and I'll be the hero, the one who finally ended the Vest Bomber's spree of violence."

"You . . . a hero? You really . . . are nuts." I spoke as though every breath were a struggle, trying to buy enough time to unscrew the cap on the fuse igniter without Simon noticing.

"Am I? I'll say that during one of the explosions, Terrell and I ran into each other. He thought I was the Vest Bomber and wounded me. I tried to go for help but lost consciousness. Unfortunately, the Vest Bomber later found Terrell and finished him off."

I groaned, then weakly coughed, trying my best to convince Simon that I was on my last leg. "What about . . . me? How are you . . . going to explain . . . *my* untimely death?" My thumb and index finger slowly rotated the cap half a turn every few seconds.

"Thanks to that meth lab raid a few weeks ago, I've got a great throwaway .44 Mag. I already used it a few times on Terrell. The Vest Bomber's been trying to finish the two of you off for months, so selling that story won't be hard at all. He filled you full of holes, then disappeared. Never to be seen again. In a couple of months, I'll discreetly retire, unable to overcome the trauma of this night. After all, I'm worth millions now. I can go anywhere, do anything."

I had no intention of pointing out that Matthew was alive and would tell the world the truth. Trying to stall, I asked, "What about . . . Luke Layman? How did you . . . frame him?"

"Luke wanted to make a few bucks, so I had him do

some surveillance work for me. Planting the explosives in his cellar and making sure the digital photo disks were there was simple. Have to admit, you had me worried for a while. I was afraid Romeo was going to saunter right past all my hard work. I even warned Layman that the neighborhood had reported several robberies lately. It's a real shame he had that gun right on his nightstand when the team busted the warrant—"

"Why? Why did you do this?"

What would've normally been a laugh came out as a weary chuckle. "See . . . that's exactly the problem. You killed her, and you don't even remember."

"Simon, I have no idea what you're talking about."

"My daughter. The two of you killed my daughter, Pamela."

*Oh my God. Pamela Stanley.* Four years ago. Nick and I were working a routine drug check. Three teenagers in a black Corvette. Romeo alerted the moment the driver rolled the window down. I signaled Nick. We barely had time to hit the deck when the teen in the backseat opened fire. They sped off. We pursued. Twenty miles later, the high-speed chase ended when they crossed the center line of the interstate and hit a semi head-on. They all died instantly. *It wasn't until later that we learned it was a cap gun.*

I groaned even louder, bending lower as if the pain were overwhelming. "One of the kids who died in the Corvette?"

"Damn right. I transferred here the next year. The longer I watched the two of you, the more I knew I had to put an end to this."

It had taken months for me to get over the guilt. Nick kept reminding me that in such a high-stress situation, we had no way of knowing it was only a prank. The review board agreed with him.

"Simon, we thought they fired on us and fled. We followed at a reasonable distance. They were going over a hundred miles per hour when they crossed the center line."

"My daughter was fifteen. Fifteen! *She* wasn't driving. *She* didn't fire on you."

"I'm sorry . . ." The cap was finally off the igniter. I faked a cough and leaned close to Nick to be sure Simon didn't hear the muffled *pop* as I pulled the cord. From that instant, I had exactly three seconds before the C4 would detonate. Even the slightest miscalculation would mean both Nick and I would die, right then, right there.

Simon was still rambling about Pamela, but I didn't hear another word. Every ounce of my being was concentrating on my silent chant, *one one-thousandth, two one-thousandth* . . .

A breath after two seconds had passed, I turned toward Simon and hurled the door charge straight at him. As soon as it was out of my hand, I threw my body over Nick's. Through the haze, I caught a brief glimpse of Simon raising his gun, but he was half a second too late. I closed my eyes and covered my ears as the C4 rocked our world.

Since door charges are specifically designed to create a blast without shrapnel, I knew that if it had detonated too far from him, there was a slim possibility that Simon might just be momentarily stunned, which would mean he'd still be armed and dangerous. Then again, if the explosion had been extremely close to his head and neck, there was a good chance it had been lethal. Either way, I wasn't in the mood to take any chances.

Standing as quickly as I could, I took two steps and almost blacked out. I knew my shoulder was bleeding, and using my right arm had become almost impossible. I don't know how long I leaned against the wall fighting to regain my senses, but as soon as the world came back into focus, I staggered toward the new cloud of dust where Simon had just been.

The blast had tossed him about ten feet backward, where a wall had abruptly stopped his flight. I approached his motionless body very cautiously, even though I was almost certain that he was unconscious, maybe dead. The thought of checking for a pulse crossed my mind, but to be honest, I didn't care if he were dead or alive—I just wanted to be sure that he wouldn't try to hurt anyone again.

Kneeling at Simon's side, I bound his wrists and hands together with so much duct tape that the ends of his arms came together to form a silver stump. As an afterthought, I duct-taped his feet together, too. Even with him immobilized, when I stood, I couldn't make myself turn away, couldn't take my eyes off his evil form. Yes, it may have been completely irrational, but in my heart I believed that if Simon could find a way, he'd gladly blow up the entire city just to finish us off.

Stepping away, I found my Sig and took careful aim at the center of Simon's head. Slowly stumbling backward over debris, I finally slumped to the floor at Nick's side. Using one knee for support, I steadied my weapon and confirmed my target as I declared, "No doubts, Nick. The bastard is *not* going to win."

When the tactical team finally arrived, I was crouched at my partner's side, trembling from head to toe. Simon Stanley was still in my sights.

# seventeen

## 1

As far as I'm concerned, the easiest meal in the world to cook is a brisket. Although I would never admit such a thing to Nick, all you need is a roasting pan, a warm oven, a bottle of good barbeque sauce, and lots of patience. To be certain Nick didn't discover my secret recipe, I had insisted that he take Matt to a movie while I slaved over the Sunday dinner I had promised to make for him. Watching two squirrels frolic in his backyard, I slowly inhaled the rich aroma that filled his kitchen.

I sighed, catching a glimpse of a small blue tuft of cellophane peeking out from under the lid of the garbage can in the backyard. I knew it was the gift basket Simon Stanley had given to Nick in the hospital, and I had to smile when I thought of all the trouble it had caused. An X ray had revealed it was harmless.

Beside the remains of the basket was the wrapping paper from Matt's special gift. All of the troopers at our headquarters had chipped in to buy him a new guitar, exactly like the one that had been destroyed in the blast. Nothing could have touched me more. Sometimes it takes a tragedy for us to realize how special the people are that we take for granted on a daily basis.

When we were released from the hospital, Nick had tried to convince us to stay with him until we found another house of our own, but I resisted. I was afraid the people at headquarters would start to gossip, especially since we would both be on medical leave for at least another five weeks. For a few days we stayed in a hotel, until I discovered that my homeowner's insurance didn't cover the cost of renting another place to live while the repairs on my house were under way. Forced to reconsider my options, the harsh financial reality made the decision to move in with Jesse's family much easier, not to mention Matt's overly enthusiastic response to the idea.

I must admit, it had seemed very odd living in another family's home. It made me feel like a scrawny puppy being taken in on a cold night: I welcomed the warm bed but still felt uneasy. After the first few days, Matt and I began to adjust and to heal. Slowly we came to realize that we would never move back to our old house, even after it was repaired. We didn't talk about it much, but I knew that I wouldn't feel safe there again, and I was pretty sure Matt felt the same. In a few weeks, we would start looking for a new place, but, for a little while, the generosity of Jesse's family had given us the luxury of taking our time.

My right arm had been in a sling since the confrontation with Simon, so I was getting good at doing things with only one hand. I'd been lucky and unlucky at the same time. I was lucky because the bullet that struck my shoulder had passed all the way through, damaging only muscles and tendons on its way. I was unlucky because if it had been an eighth of an inch closer to my spine, my load-bearing vest might have stopped it completely. Even so, if I did as I was told, the doctors thought I'd be back to work on schedule. I'd been warned it might take a couple of months of physical therapy to regain full use of my right shoulder and arm, but considering everything Simon had put us through, that seemed like a very small price to pay.

Nick had a slightly longer road of rehabilitation ahead. Besides the arm injured in the bombing that killed Alexa, Simon had shot him six times. Thanks to his load-bearing vest, not one bullet had broken his flesh. They did, however, crack three ribs, and the high-impact blows had severely aggravated his concussion. He'd been unconscious for two days, the longest forty-eight hours of my life. I still give him grief about it, claiming he did it just to buy sympathy. He always grins and winks, reminding me that we still have our jobs, and the highest honors awarded by the Kansas State Patrol for bravery in the line of duty.

For the first time I could remember since childhood, I had spent my mornings sleeping late, my evenings curled up with a good book, while Matt, Jesse, and his sisters played video games and watched more than their share of televised sports and violence. Being alive at all was good, made better by the support of loving friends and family.

At that precise moment in my life, my biggest problem seemed to be how to get an eighteen-pound, steaming hot brisket out of Nick's oven with only one good arm. Looking at Romeo curled in the corner of the room, I asked, "Promise you won't tell?"

He raised one eyebrow as if to say, *You've got to be kidding*, but didn't move off the fluffy new sheepskin bed Matt had bought for him a couple of days ago.

"I'm taking that as a yes," I declared and gingerly slid my arm out of the sling. "Remember, this is our little secret, handsome." Knowing I'd have to be extremely careful, I eased on the protective mitts, then pulled open the oven door. The wave of hot air curled around me and I leaned back until it wasn't quite so overwhelming. Wrapping my hands around the handles on each end of the roasting pan, I got down on one knee so I wouldn't have to strain my back as much. Gritting my teeth, I took a deep breath to prepare for the pain.

A split second before I would have lifted the heavy pan, Nick's voice boomed from the doorway behind me. "Don't even *think* about it."

I was so startled that I lost my balance and toppled into a heap on the kitchen floor. As he and Matt cracked up laughing, I glared at Romeo and asked, "What kind of guard dog doesn't warn his master about unwelcome intruders?"

This time Romeo climbed to his feet, shook from head to toe, then plopped down with his face to the wall as though I were rudely interrupting his afternoon nap.

Nick helped me up as I called to my four-legged pal, "Traitor! I guess a dog really is *man's* best friend, not *woman's*." Turning to face Nick and Matt, I added, "Is this house soundproof? How did you two sneak up on me like that?"

Matt grinned, "We knew you'd try to do too much if we left you alone, so we parked down the street and snuck in the side door. We've been watching you for almost twenty minutes. Nick was right. Women can't be trusted."

I shot Nick a dirty look, which he promptly passed on to Matt.

"Is that the kind of thing you're teaching him?" I asked.

Nick's face lit up with a cocky smile as he challenged, "If you're smart, you'll give up now. There's no way you're going to win an argument about trust just seconds after we catch you red-handed doing exactly what you've been ordered not to do." With a wink, he added, "Trust has to be earned."

I couldn't help but grin, knowing full well that trying to undo whatever twisted ideas Nick was teaching Matt might be next to impossible. "Okay, you win round one, but I've still got a lot of fight left in me. Now, would one of you please put the brisket on the counter before the oven heats up the kitchen to two hundred degrees?"

Matt puffed out his chest and smiled. "I believe I'm the only one here who isn't still on the injured list."

I threatened, "You will be if you start treating women like playthings."

Nick laughed. *"Playthings?* Is that the best you could do?"

I shrugged and asked, "It's obvious you didn't go to the movies, so where have you two been?"

Matt enthusiastically answered, "Headquarters."

Casting Nick a *have you totally lost your mind?* look, I calmly said, "Really?"

"Mom, it was so cool! Nick let me see the photos of the bombs and booby traps at our place, plus pictures of all the stuff they recovered from Simon Stanley's house."

"Such as?" I asked.

"Disguises, tons of guns, and more types of explosives than you could imagine."

Nick chimed in, "Apparently Simon had been helping himself to items from the evidence lockers for a long time. He had accumulated quite an arsenal. And the scary part is that there could be more hidden with the jewels."

"He still hasn't said where they are?"

"Nope. I doubt if he ever will. Believe it or not, he's still claiming he's innocent. He's sticking to his sick version of what happened that day, still blaming the mysterious disappearing Vest Bomber for everything."

"His trial is going to be a royal pain in the ass. A media atrocity."

"No kidding. They're going to dig up all the dirt on the high-speed chase again, even though the review board cleared us ages ago."

Shaking my head, I sighed. "He could have stopped any time, and he probably would never have been caught."

"Greed and insanity don't make good company. By the way, Lieutenant Colonel Jones sends his regards. He was at headquarters for a meeting."

"I'm glad I wasn't there. Romeo keeps acting like he wants to rip his leg off."

"Come to think of it, I noticed his aftershave was pretty strong. I'll bet you a hundred bucks he uses Aqua Velva."

"No way I'm taking a sucker bet like that."

Nick opened the door to the refrigerator. "Holy cow. Would you look at that!"

Proud of my creation, I remarked, "I always suspected a French silk pie was the answer to all man's problems."

Taking a step back, Nick reached into his pocket and pulled out a shimmering scarlet silk bag that I instantly recognized as the one holding the diamond David had sent to me. Dangling it in my face, Nick grinned and said, "Matt told me you'd probably like to have this back."

As he placed it in my hand, I couldn't take my eyes off of it. "Where did you find it?" I asked.

"It was recovered from the debris in your house during the investigation. Apparently they thought it was something the Vest Bomber had stolen. When Matt reminded me that David Darnaby had sent it to you, I withdrew it from the evidence locker." He was quiet for a few seconds, then added, "I know it's special to you."

"I almost thought I'd lost a lot of things special to me. But you never realize just *how* special they are, until you think they're gone, do you?" I took his hand. "Come on and help me set the table."

# author's note

Although the characters and story in *Render Safe* are fictional, the danger faced on a daily basis by hazardous device technicians around the world is all too real. The technology, science, and procedures I have described in this book are based on fact. Like all works of fiction, my goal is to entertain, fascinate, and hopefully inspire the imagination of the reader. For the safety of those who routinely risk their lives to protect the innocent, I have slightly altered certain forensic elements to prevent the technology I've described from ever being used to endanger the life of a bomb technician.

We live in a world with too few heroes, where the quiet protectors of our freedom, well-being, and liberty are often ignored or even scorned. I hope that after reading this book, each of you will come to the same conclusion that I did while researching and writing it: Every man and woman who dedicates his or her life to working on hazardous devices is, without a doubt, a hero.

Next time your local police department holds an open

house, please stop by and shake the hands of a few *real life* heroes. Let them know that their work is appreciated, and that their dedication and sacrifice really does makes a difference.